The Depths of Ruin

The Eternal Dream, Book Three

Lane Trompeter

To my father, who fanned the flames when they were but an ember.

To my wife, who turned those flames into a bonfire.

To my child, whose mind burns brightly already.
I can't wait to see the light you cast on the world.

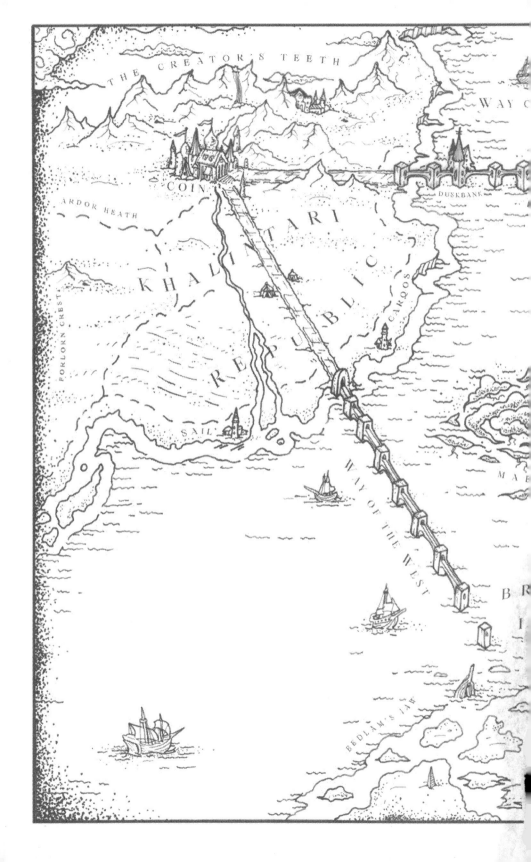

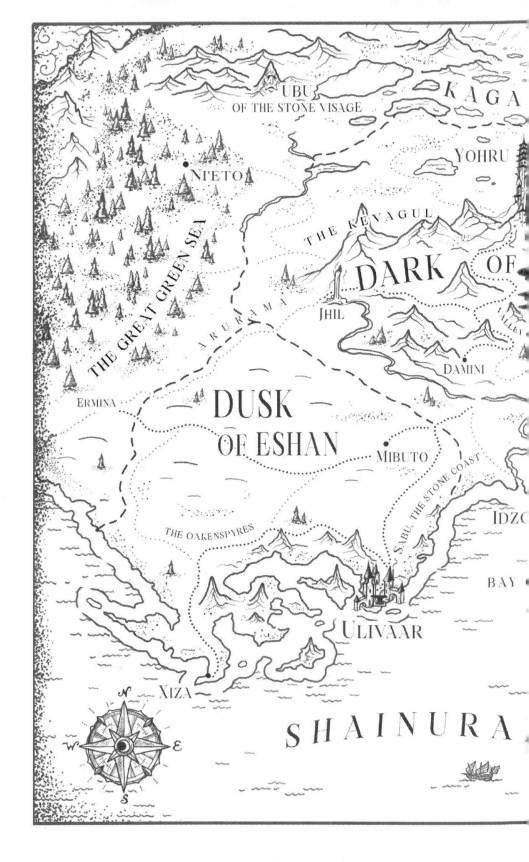

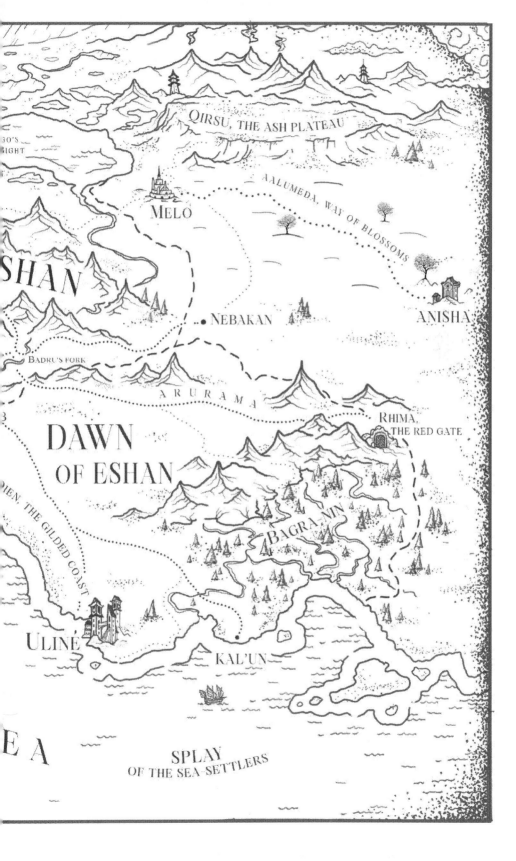

Shaper Manifest

Revision XXVII : Mourningtide - First of Autumn
Year 5222, Council Reckoning

Master of Water (azure) Helikos, Sovereign King of the Sea Kingdom. — Aged 153

Master of Beasts (crimson) Kronos, Lord General of the Sea Kingdom. — Aged 121

Master of Wind (white) Altos, the Vengeance of the Council Shapers. — Aged 197

Master of Stone (gray) Itolas, the Mason. — Aged 97

Master of Light (yellow) whereabouts unknown. Western Khalintars? *bandits* — Aged 27

Master of Shadow (black) Kettle, "Mother" of the Family. — Aged —

Master of Time (——) The Eternal, Once Queen of Isa. — Aged ?

Master of Thought (silver) Khalintari scribe... House Batir? — Aged 22

Master of Lightning (sky) whereabouts unknown. — Aged 18

Master of Forces (bronze) whereabouts unknown. Gast? — Aged —

Master of Garth (emerald) Iliana, Princess of the Sea Kingdom — Aged 18

Master of Fire (sungold) whereabouts unknown — Aged 18

Master of Tones (violet) whereabouts unknown. — Aged —

Master of Roots (umber) whereabouts unknown. — Aged 1 season

Master of Metal (ochre) whereabouts unknown. — Aged 18

Dramatis Personae

The Family

Kettle – Mother of the Family
Timo – Lieutenant of the Family (deceased)
Corna – Lieutenant of the Family
Ezil – Khalintari 'triplet' of the Family
Koli – Khalintari 'triplet' of the Family
Inia – Khalintari 'triplet' of the Family
Hom – Brother of the Family
Yelden – Brother of the Family
Kit – Son of the Family
Elan – Son of the Family
Tera – Daughter of the Family

The Kingdom of the Sea

Helikos – Emperor and Master of Water
Kranos – Lord General and Master of Beasts
Iliana – Queen of the Khalintars and Master of Earth
Torlas Graevo – Duke of Aelanar (deceased)
Hoiran Paloran – Duke of Paloran (deceased)
Birnen Relwen – Duke of Hespir
Markis Calladan – former Count of Firdana (deceased)
Nariah Calladan – former Countess of Firdana
Poline – Soldier of the Tide and personal guard to Iliana
Jon Gordyn – Master of the Imperial Bank
Aurelion Kraft – A'kai'ano'ri Tempered, associate of Jon Gordyn
Reknor – The Historian
Jace of the Simply – Ward of the Historian

The Khalintari Republic

Eledar Cortola – Minister of Finance
Mila Nabih – Minister of Sails
Idris Qadir – Minister of Faith
Munir Rahim – Minister of Shields
Anis Saderin – Minister of Rams
Tahana Zhayet – Minister of Bulls
Lana Syed – Minister of Spears
Yamina Jazhri – Minister of Swords
Wahed Jalaal – Minister of Steeds
Bastian Batir – Master of Thought
Lavilion Batir – Brother of Bastian

The Seers

Min'dei – Seer (deceased)
Talan – Seer (current)
Te'ial – former captain of the *Mason's Fall*
Sanar – Commander of the Umbral Guard
Lentana Tenkal – former slave of Eledar Cortola

The Ensouled

Jynn Dioran – once-Ensouled of Thought
Asimir – Ensouled of Thought
Yatan Tecarim – Ensouled of Voices

Prologue
The Coup
The Seventh Day of Winter
In the year 5204, Council Reckoning

The quill tip glides across the page with such grace that the letters seem to possess an identity of their own, as if, rather than being created, they're being discovered. Their meaning is simple: a recipe for a creamy soup involving potatoes and cheese, but their construction is art exquisite. The tattered yellow parchment lying next to the fresh paper contains the same words written in the same script, or nearly so. The letters are slightly more refined, the hand more confident, but the peculiar curls sprouting organically from certain words could only belong to one will.

Belden, the Master of Earth, licks his finger in an unconscious gesture and flattens the recipe with care. Little of his age is evident in the steadiness of his hands, but the rumpled, fraying parchment speaks well enough to the three centuries resting on his shoulders.

He jumps as a knock sounds at his front door. Blinking blearily at the flickering stub of a candle to his left, he frowns. It is a strange hour for visitors. The echoes of the knock don't have time to fade before the door, unlatched even in these trying times, swings open. Levering himself to his feet, he calls on a trickle of power. The faint outline of a symbol briefly flickers into being low on his ankle, and just as soon disappears.

"Never good news," he mutters to himself, bustling towards his visitor at the front of the house. "Never good news when he comes calling."

Contrary to his words, Belden smiles when he sees

Helikos, Master of Water, standing in his foyer. Dressed in a traveling cloak of the deepest midnight blue, his noble bearing and powerful frame are worthy of any hero of old. The Sealord smiles in return, clasping his oldest friend to his chest. If Belden feels tension in the embrace, it can be attributed to the strangeness of the time and the difficulty of presiding over such turmoil in the Council of Shapers. Never in Belden's three centuries have there been so many deaths on the Council, and never in living memory, some five thousand years, has the Vengeance been called on so many times for his official duty.

And Telias, of all people… yes. If anyone has a right to carry tension, it is the Master of the Council.

"What news, Helikos?" Belden says finally, stepping back and clapping him on the shoulder.

"Nothing good," Helikos answers, his grin fading. "There has been little good of late."

"Too true, too true."

A moment of tense silence settles between them. The air is smothering and thick inside the home of the Master of Earth. A stranger might think it odd, more perception than reality, but they would be wrong. The air moves strangely in Belden's domain. Though sounds are muffled in the dense atmosphere, a distant whistle infiltrates the silence between them.

"A kettle?" Helikos gestures towards a darkened room. "Is there water to spare?"

"A kettle?" Belden asks quizzically, then jumps in surprise. "Ah yes! I had forgotten. Caught up, you know, transcribing some of Mam's old recipes. Still the best, I say, still the best. I'd hold Mam's cooking up against any of your fancy chefs, you'd better believe it. In three hundred years, I've never found anything to match it!"

Belden crosses his arms proudly as Helikos regards him with half of a lopsided smile.

"The kettle?" Helikos asks after a moment.

2

"Oh, right." Belden bustles off towards the kitchen in short, choppy steps. "I put it on an hour ago. If it hasn't boiled off, there may be enough for a cup."

The Sealord softens as Belden hustles away, his eyes melancholy. When he follows, his footsteps drag on the rustic wood like some invisible burden weighs heavily upon him. His shoulders remain straight and proud, but only by an effort of will. As much as he has dreaded this night, he knows the facade is necessary for a few minutes yet. He sits in his customary chair, well-worn and comfortable, his eyes lost to the black horizon. A few twinkling lights, the Stars of Donir, glimmer in the cold dark, but they do not reach the gloom settling on his soul.

Moonrise, she told him. *Moonrise, and not a moment later.*

Steaming cup in hand, Belden meets him in the study, the same study where they've argued countless times, passionately debating the nature of the world and the creatures inhabiting it. A thousand times, he'd tasted Belden's tea, a thousand times he'd laughed as the diminutive man pointed a stubby finger his way and swung it about like a rapier deftly handled. Those decades had been happy, carefree, a time of indulgence and discovery. That all changed eighty-seven years ago.

Belden had never noticed the difference, as far as Helikos could tell. The sadness that lingered beneath their arguments, the visits that grew more and more infrequent. He couldn't bear spending time with the Master of Earth, not after he learned what must be done. Creator knows, he would rather it be anyone else.

"So," Belden says, settling back into his favorite armchair and regarding the Sealord over steepled fingers. "I assume there's a reason for you to barge in here so late?"

"There is," Helikos agrees, but doesn't continue.

"Well?" Belden shifts, crossing his arms and narrowing his eyes. "Whatever it is, it can't be good, not with you looking like you've swallowed a toad. Come on, out with it. You know I hate suspense."

3

"Do you remember the myths of the Eternal?" Helikos looks down at his hands, killing the urge to squeeze them into fists. "The histories, I mean?"

"Sure. They teach every Shaper the same thing until we can't forget it."

"You remember how I got a bit… passionate, about it?"

"Hah!" Belden says, slapping his leg. "You were damn near obsessed when you were younger. All those trips, that crazy nonsense about the Maelstrom… of course I remember. And what did you find? Nothing!"

Don't make him suspicious. Don't let him access his power. If he does, you will cause untold suffering.

"That isn't entirely accurate." The Sealord can't bring himself to look at his oldest friend. "I found her."

"Nonsense," Belden returns immediately.

"But I did." Helikos finally brings his head up, locking eyes with the Shaper at last. Belden flinches back as if struck, his face slackening in surprise. He mutely shakes his head, though whether in denial or acceptance, it is impossible to say. "She still lives, down below the waves of the sea. She… spoke to me."

"Five thousand years," Belden breathes, closing his eyes. "Impossible."

"I wish you were right. The burden she laid upon me…"

"Burden? What burden?"

"Something is coming," Helikos says, finally allowing his hands to clench into fists. "A threat the likes of which the world will only know once. Chances are, we will fail, and life will end. Forever. She told me… she told me that I am the only hope."

Belden regards his friend in silence, his shock fading before skepticism, then pity.

"Helikos, listen to yourself," he says, in the same pedantic tone he once used when Helikos was a child, more than a century ago. "You speak madness."

"I wish you were right," the Sealord whispers again, tears

4

brimming in his eyes.

"Come, let's to bed," Belden says, standing and offering his hand. "You're under a lot of stress. A good night's sleep will do you well, and we can talk about this in the morning."

Helikos stares past the proffered hand, unmoving. The jagged edge of the horizon grows distinct, silver light just limning the edge of the city to the east. Now that the moment is upon him, any hesitation falls away, any reservations dissipate. Though he will mourn his mentor in the decades to come, he won't regret this moment. He believes his actions will echo through eternity as the savior of all life.

The Eternal chose her words, and her man, well.

He reaches out and accepts Belden's hand, pulling him close and calling on the power coursing through his veins. Blood, warm and pulsing with life, erupts from a tiny cut on his palm and shoots forth, too fast to follow. In the short space between them, it shifts, hardening and freezing into a narrow spike of crimson ice. Plunging through the socket of Belden's eye, the ice punches into his brain and kills him instantly.

As his body slumps to the earth and his heart beats its last, emerald power pulses into the night. The earth trembles, the stone walls shaking dust down onto the Sealord's head. Then... silence.

Helikos sighs, relief and sorrow and exhaustion melding into one aching exhalation. The sigh drives him to his knees. He clenches his fists and pushes them into his eyes. There will be no explosion, no cataclysm marking the end of the longest-living Master of the Council. Belden didn't suspect a thing; no matter how strangely the Sealord was acting, he could never doubt his own surrogate son.

Eyes closed, Helikos does not see as Belden's body begins to glow. The barest hint of light shimmers into being and disappears into the earth. On and on, the power, separated from the will that held it in check, flows down through stones cut by

5

man, down through centuries of detritus and human waste, and finally reaches the beating heart of the earth far below. The dormant soil, buried beneath untold tons of rock, *shifts*, then lurches upwards towards its fallen master's light.

The earth's groan is imperceptible at first. Helikos feels it in his skin, a tingling vibration that spreads swiftly to his bones. He snaps upright as the first sound of fracturing stone drowns beneath the growing roar of tortured earth. Already, the stones jump beneath his feet. He rips open the door and sprints away from the house, hardly knowing where his desperate strides will take him, just hoping it is far enough. He flashes past a dozen streets, the windows of the houses lit and cheery in the Winter night, the sounds of song and laughter fading as the earth opens its shattered maw to scream in anguish. Its broken, deafening roar fills the world with titanic sorrow.

If there are screams, the scream of the earth encompasses them all.

Silence falls eventually, or relative silence. The clattering fall of rubble will be heard for days yet. Donir falls silent with it. The people of the proud city dare not look out their windows, dare not speak lest this nightmare be made real.

***

In a house to the south and east, nestled near the mighty walls, a woman clenches her eyes closed, dark hair plastered to her head. A handmaiden squeezes her hand, in support and fear.

It should not be me, kneeling here, the maid thinks to herself, her eyes darting between the laboring woman and the dozen soldiers standing at sinister attention throughout the room. *Where is her husband? He would not stand for this. He would make sure that she was safe and comfortable. He would not allow anyone, even the Healing Hand, anywhere near his wife.*

A cry of pain and determination.

A flicker of light. Emerald light.

As a newborn wail pierces the night, Kranos, the Master of

Beasts, gathers the baby into his arms and turns to leave. A whimper pulls him up short. He glances back. The woman lying on the sheets, the lines of her beauty evident even through her exhaustion and pain, lifts her hand in silent plea. He had almost forgotten. She will be a problem, if left alive. Helikos cares for her too much... as does their enemy.

With a gesture, he signals a soldier near.

"We have what we came for. She is a traitor, equal to her husband. Execute her."

"As you command, General," the soldier responds, pounding a clenched fist to his chest.

"Nadine," Kranos says, turning heavy eyes on the mother of the child in his arms. "Don't worry. Your daughter will be well-looked after."

"He will kill you for this," she whispers in a broken voice, eyes yet blazing with life. "You know he will."

"He will try," Kranos agrees, a sinister grin spreading across his face. "It's a pity that you chose him over Helikos. You could have been a queen. Instead, you will die, as will the brat yet waiting in your belly."

The fire leaves her eyes as her hands snap to her stomach, to a sensation of movement and growing pain.

"No, Kranos, please..."

After he steps into the street, the door closes behind the Master of Beasts with a quiet thud. He is several blocks away before her shouts, begging him for mercy, fade away. He pauses after a few more steps, his power pulsing life into the feeble baby in his arms. He turns back to watch as flames rise into the night, illuminating a smile wrought only of madness.

Chapter 1
Kettle
Midspring
In the year 5223, Council Reckoning

"Again?" I groan, letting my head sag back against the wagon's sturdy bench.

"Again." Aurelion's voice is muffled from the undercarriage, but intelligible. And clearly resigned.

"We *are* carrying quite a bit of weight," Nolan calls from the other side. "Especially for a… road… like this."

Squinting up at the cloudless sapphire sky, Nolan's comment drags a humorless and bitter laugh from deep in my belly. 'Road' is a far more generous term than I would ever give to the half-overgrown ruts of earth that wind their way eastward to the horizon. If it weren't the *only* path continuing east, we would never have left the relative security of the gravel road that marked the edge of whatever passes for civilization this far from the center of the world. We haven't known a decent road since we crossed the Empire border half a season ago, but I never thought it would get this bad.

"People live out here, right?" Aurelion mutters.

"Undoubtedly," Nolan says, clambering onto the wagon and settling next to me onto the bench. "Hence, the road."

"Not just a few random farmers." Aurelion rolls out from under the wagon and stands, his head level with my face. "Towns. Cities. *People.*"

"If we travel far enough, I'm sure we'll encounter other civilizations. Church records speak of others, though more in the vague 'here there be savages' kind of way than providing any real detail. At the very least, we will eventually make it to the western edge of the Khalintari Republic."

"You mean the Empire of the Sea," I growl, sitting up finally and turning a glare on the horizon. "It would be my luck to steal the wealth of a man who now owns the entire world."

"The Ways, mighty they may be, are not the world," Nolan assures me, gently patting my shoulder.

"The People have to get their silk from *somewhere*," I say, sighing as I tread over the same argument again. "And it is from the east. Not the Khalintars. *Someone* has to be making it."

Aurelion regards me with a disgruntled expression. Dust covers his face, and I absently reach out to wipe it away. Lightning quick, he snatches my hand and presses it to his cheek, his smile wide and genuine. Of course, I can't help but smile back. Fools that we are.

"What is life without a little adventure?" he asks finally, letting my hand drop.

"I could do with a little more adventure and a little less broken wagon."

"Ah, but that's the fun of it. It's all about the journey, Kettle my dear, not the destination," he says with such a twinkle in his eyes that I want to punch him. "Enjoy what precious moments we have."

"Nolan?" I say, not taking my eyes off Aurelion's.

"Yes?"

"Do you remember the prayers for the damned?"

"Kettle…" he begins, but I cut him off.

"Are cliches heresy? I think cliches are heresy. I'll tie him up, you get your robes, and we'll have ourselves a nice little bonfire."

Aurelion bursts into laughter, and even Nolan offers a polite chuckle. A soft sound from the wagon bed quiets them both. The younger children often lie for naps in the late morning, and today is no different. Tera raises her head and blinks at me,

9

and I put a finger across my lips. She lazily drops her head back down onto her crossed arms, her blonde curls swaying.

They haven't complained, but I know the journey is wearing on the children. We've taken turns leading them on 'expeditions' away from the wagon, providing them what respite we can from the endless, jostling monotony. Ezil, Koli, and Inia have been teaching them all sorts of acrobatic maneuvers like handstands and cartwheels, and Hom and Yelden have taken the older ones aside to begin teaching them swordplay. And Corna... let's just say, I'd rather she *stop* teaching them how to lie. That is one skill children can learn well enough without a teacher offering them a master class. Shaking my head, I turn my eyes back to the horizon.

We knew that stealing the Sealord's treasury meant we would have a reward on our heads the size of, well, a kingdom. That meant not only leaving, but disappearing so wholly as to shake off any soldiers or bounty hunters searching for us. Even if the Way of the North hadn't been blocked by the entire Khalintari military, it would have been the first place anyone would have looked for us, and there aren't exactly many places to hide on a featureless expanse of stone thousands of miles long. Staying wasn't an option, since we were relatively well-known, and our descriptions were no doubt circulated to every authority in the Kingdom. That left us two choices: head south and take our chances in the Isles, or head east, and look for the edge of the map.

It is time to come home.

The Seer's words, cast forth into the winds of time. A man's entire life, uprooted and destroyed simply to deliver a message. A whole branch of the future followed so closely that the messenger knew where to be and when to be before I was even born.

And what had I done the second I heard the message?

The opposite.

My eyes, as they often have, are turned southwards, not eastwards, imagining a land of jungle and ocean, of soaring spires and wooden streets, of silk and security. It is time to come home. How is it possible that Isa could ever be my home again? After what I did, knowing what they wanted to do to me, *would* do to me, if given the chance? I finger the scar on my cheek, the enduring reminder of that horrific night. No, there is no home to the south. I've made my choices. Hopefully, they are what the Seer foresaw, and I am doing what she meant me to do. That's the problem with prophecy, of course; it's impossible to know. Sighing, I wrench my gaze to the east, where a thin line of dark figures have appeared.

"There they are," I say, standing and shading my eyes. "Finally."

Distance is hard to judge in the vast plain, but I'm certain that they are some minutes out yet. I glance back to the west. Aside from the slant of shadow cast by the sun, there isn't a discernible difference. Creator, but it's been a journey. Every time I've let any of my family out of my sight, fear has perched on my shoulder and whispered nightmares.

"They've got someone with them," I say in warning. Aurelion turns and shades his eyes against the sunlight, but they're still too far from his vantage. "They look like they're walking free, though."

The figures eventually resolve into the party I sent out half a day ago to find civilization farther along the path. Corna leads them, followed closely by the three Khalintari sisters and a man, his rough clothing marking him as rustic. His dark hair is bound under a wide-brimmed hat, but a few escaped strands glisten black in the sunlight. We've definitely left the Empire behind.

"Ho, the camp!" Corna shouts brightly, the twist of her lips making mockery of the traditional greeting. The bright acid green of her irises stands out even from a distance. Though we've all grown accustomed to Corna's new appearance, I'm surprised to

11

see a stranger following along in her wake. "Or, ho, the wagon, I guess."

"Welcome back," I call flatly. "It took you long enough."

"No, Kettle, damn it," she says with a frown. "You have to say it back."

"No."

"Yes."

"Absolutely not."

"Ho, the party," Aurelion calls weakly, his hand raised in a lame salute.

"There we go!" Corna says, expression returning to happiness like quicksilver. "Someone's got the spirit."

"Did it break again?" Ezil asks, striding past Corna and offering the wagon with flat stare. "We thought you'd be closer."

"Yes," I say, giving the wagon a scowl of my own. "The axle splintered. Again."

"Well, Mr. Inara here might be able to help with that," Corna says, gesturing to the stranger just walking up to our stranded wagon. "He says he's got some expertise."

I jump down and stroll over, eyeing the man closely for the first time. His rough hands and the crow's feet around his eyes speak to a life of labor, but he doesn't look to be much past his thirtieth Winter. Dark of eye and hair, his expression is carefully neutral as he appraises me from under the brim of his hat. A hint of nervous energy creeps into his posture as his eyes dance between me, Aurelion, Nolan, and the rest.

"Well met," I say, forcing a friendly expression onto my face.

"As you say," he answers dubiously, his voice surprisingly deep and faintly accented in a way I've never heard. He doesn't relax.

"You have nothing to fear from us," I say softly, catching his eyes. "You can be at ease."

"There are only two types of people who come from the

west," he says gruffly. "Merchants, and those with nothing to lose." He glances around briefly, his eyes taking in our party. "It is the wrong time of year for merchants."

"We are…" I trail off, frowning. Well, damn. I guess we don't particularly have anything to lose.

"Yes," he says, nodding through a frown. "There are other rumors lately, of shadows in the night, of demons stalking the darkness. But I do not think you are demons."

"Mother?" a high voice calls from the wagon. I step back so that I can keep my eye on the stranger and the wagon both. Elan stands at the opening, his chin resting on the high seat. "Who is that?"

"A friendly man who's offered to help us." I give Inara a more genuine smile. "Right?"

His face eases at the sight of the children appearing in the back of the wagon. Their heads pop up like the thin doglike creatures we've seen occasionally inhabiting the plains.

"Yes. I will help you."

***

Hona Inara turns out to be quite helpful and knowledgeable about wagons, pointing out several things we've done wrong in the course of our journey, from the weight distribution to the way our two sturdy horses are harnessed. He also turns a confused glare on the wagon several times as he adjusts the cargo and doesn't see the return he hopes for. Of course, he could never predict that a fortune in gold and starsilver rests between the thick floorboards. He just has to work without that particular variable.

"It is remarkable you've made it this far," he says after an hour's work, sweat glistening on his brow. "This wagon is meant for paved roads, not tracks like this."

"We've had some trouble," Aurelion says honestly. "But we've managed."

"It's been a bloody nightmare," Corna groans. Memories of

every able body lifting together to shift the colossal weight, groaning timbers and feet sliding in mud… ugh. Along with my… troubles… calling to shadow, it has been a trial. "You're the first friendly face we've seen in forever."

"I have to admit," Hona says, turning to take us all in. "When four foreign and beautiful women appeared at my door, I wasn't sure whether I was dreaming or if the Creator had decided to take me in my sleep."

"Are you sure you aren't dreaming?" Corna asks. "Especially with my pretty eyes?"

"Yes," he says, shaking his head. "I am not so creative, even in my dreams. Your group is… strange."

"You have no idea," Corna says wryly. "Did I tell you, Kettle? He didn't even blink when he saw my eyes."

"Her people I have seen. And yours." Hona points at Corna, then me, and finally gestures towards Nolan. "And the Creationists are known to us. But, the rest…"

"We may come from many mothers, but this is one family," I say, spreading my hands and smiling.

"So I see."

He ducks down sharply, his expression turning fearful. I slide down against the wagon next to him, the others all slipping into the tall grass or dropping into defensive postures. Nolan looks nonplussed as he glances in the direction Hona was watching, then back at us.

"What is it?" I whisper, resisting the urge to look over the edge of the wagon and silhouette myself.

"Bandits," Hona mutters. "Or demons."

"This far out?" I whisper, more to myself than him.

"It's just Hom, Yelden, and Sario back with dinner," Nolan says, shrugging.

"And Kit?" I say quickly, a tremor of fear thrumming through my heart.

"No… ah, there he is. He was hidden by the others."

14

"Ho, the camp!" Yelden calls out cheerfully, a brace of rabbits slung over his shoulder.

"Ho, the party!" Corna shouts, jumping up and waving excitedly.

"Many mothers," I say, shaking my head as Hona looks on. "One dysfunctional family."

***

Hona walks in silence as he leads us back to his home. The wagon creaks ominously over the rough terrain for several hours of the same mindless journey. But, as the sun touches the horizon, Hona turns us down a secondary trail, and the twin ruts of the wagon path become flat and even. The unending sea of grass gives way to lush fields and manicured paths winding between trees dripping in hanging moss. Though he doesn't look to be a man of means, his land stretches to the horizon, well-cared for and lush. A few youths wave as we trundle past, each the spitting image of Hona himself: dark eyes and hair, tanned skin and strong shoulders. After we pass, they call to one another in a melodic language I can't understand.

A large, well-established residence comes into view ahead, easily the size of a manor in Firdana. The longer we ride forward, the more impressed I become. The same space in the Empire would make a man fabulously wealthy, and most likely nobility. The architecture is simple and straightforward, straight lines and sharp angles. Even so, it feels foreign, exotic, indescribably off.

"Hona," Corna says finally, her eyes scanning the horizon. "Is this all yours?"

"Yes," he says with a proud smile. "It was a hard decision to choose to live out here, but I have no regrets."

"By out here, you mean in the middle of nowhere?"

"It must feel that way, having come from the west," he says, glancing back at the setting sun. "It is a long journey through uninhabited lands. We may be outside the border, but not so far that I would call this 'nowhere.'"

"Border?" I break in, my heartbeat quickening. "Is there a kingdom nearby?"

"The Dusk of Eshan," Hona answers, brow furrowing. "You are strange travelers, to make this journey with no knowledge of your destination."

"Would you enlighten us?" Aurelion asks.

"I am a simple man, and I left those lands long ago, but I will tell you what I know. Over dinner."

Hona directs us to leave the wagon outside as a young man of about fifteen Winters appears to care for our horses. The children clamber down and stare around at the manicured grounds in wonder. Close to the house, a vibrant green lawn spreads into an indulgent waste of perfectly good land. The picture his home paints is more idyllic peace than utilitarian farm, and my children seem almost stunned by their new environs. At Hona's encouragement, though, they break into play, running freely across the grass. A pair of red-haired girls, Rin and Lesi, disappear around the corner of the house. I start to step after them in concern, but Hona gently catches my arm.

"They are safe here. My daughters will make sure they do not find trouble," he says, nodding towards a pair of girls on the cusp of womanhood, laughing at the children's exuberant explosion of energy. "After the sun has fully set, they will bring your children in to eat."

"I don't know why I trust you," I say, holding his eyes. "But I do. Please, for your sake and mine, don't give me cause to regret it."

He doesn't bother to respond aside from a quiet nod, turning and leading the adults towards the manor. The interior of Hona's home is full of quiet, rustic beauty. The hardwood floor is polished to a rich golden sheen. Greenery rests on every available surface, even hanging from the ceiling in dangling vines. Some are herbs used in cooking and common medicines, but there are many more I've never seen before.

A female voice calls in the lilting language of these lands, the flow of words like a stream of thick honeyed wine. Hona responds in kind, and a woman with brown skin and rich black hair appears at the door, still removing a pair of delicate leather gloves from her hands. Her expression as she takes us in conveys both welcome and suspicion.

"Good evening, travelers," she says finally, her accent thicker than her husband's and more beautiful for it. From the way Hona stands deferentially at her right hand, it isn't hard to tell who is truly in charge here. "What brings you to our humble home?"

"I could never describe such a beautiful home as humble," I answer, bowing my head in respect. She seems used to the compliment, but, from her expression, it is not unwelcome. "As for us, we seek a new beginning, far away from the tyranny of the lands to the west. We do not expect to find it on your land, but your husband was generous enough to offer us his help for tonight."

"He is ever generous, my husband," she says wryly. "You look like bandits. How did you convince him you are not?"

"I think it was our children, who stayed outside in order to play."

"Children are as good a lure as any." She shoots her husband a glare. "Idiot."

"You have nothing to fear from us," Aurelion says, stepping forward. "We can pay for your hospitality, if that would smooth over your concerns."

"Your money is no good here," she says, frowning.

"We have other goods then, things you may…"

The woman makes a sound of annoyance deep in her throat.

"I will have my sons draw up hot water for a bath. You will take turns, unless…" She makes a face. "Unless you prize economy over decency."

17

She turns abruptly and disappears into the back of the house. Hona looks after her with a fond smile before turning to us.

"You have an hour or so," he says warmly. "She will delay the meal to give you time to wash up."

"Hona, what just happened?" Corna asks slowly.

"You offended my wife by offering to pay for lodging," he answers with a gruff laugh. "Which was the right thing to do. She is a hard woman, but only because she must be. Living out here, we often entertain people of questionable quality."

"And we, somehow, put her at ease?" Hom asks in confusion.

"It is an instinct, really, something we've developed over years. Myn was never going to turn you away after I offered you hospitality. That would be dishonorable." A pair of young men appear at the door, saying something to Hona in their language. "Ah, your baths are ready. Please, wash away the grit of the road."

Corna glances between the two youths and Hona, her brow furrowing.

"Hona, how many children do you have?"

"I am blessed with seven sons and five daughters," Hona answers happily.

As we follow the sons towards the back of the house, Corna leans in close to me.

"He has more children than we do?" she whispers incredulously. "And he's *happy* about it?"

＊＊＊

After a hot bath and a change into fresh clothing, I feel better than I have in any of the endless days of hard travel. It's more than just being clean. A quiet hope has kindled in my chest. The great rolling plains, wild and untamed, had stretched from horizon to horizon for so long that I had begun to fear that we would eventually come to the end of the wagon trail, stranded in the wilderness. All of the fabulous wealth hidden in our wagon would be useless if there were nowhere to spend it. Instead, we've come upon a farm seemingly built from dream and fancy, where a welcoming family offers hospitality to strangers, even dangerous vagabonds like us. If they are in any way representative of their people, we may finally have found a land we can call home.

The dinner table is a raucous celebration of life and happiness. The children have their own table in the next room, their laughter loud even muted by distance. Kit had, at first, been reluctant to join the children, but he was mollified when Hona's older sons went without complaint. Both familiar and foreign, the food fills us in a way road-cooked rabbit could never manage. From spiced lamb and white rice to a strange purple vegetable I've never seen, the food is delicious and hearty.

"Thank you again for your hospitality," I say as the meal winds down. "We have not felt so welcomed in a very long time."

"And we expect payment," Myn says sharply.

"But..." Aurelion begins, perplexed, but Hona waves his hand.

"News," he says simply. "Stories. We live far from your homeland, and would hear how the world turns."

We each look at Corna, who offers the pretense of an uncomfortable scowl at the attention. She can't fake it long before launching into the news with the same flair and passion of a bard with an epic tale. The Inara couple listen attentively, asking pointed questions that belie their claims of ignorance.

It makes sense, of course. Any travelers that come from the west would encounter their farmstead before any other. Serving as a welcome respite from the road heading either direction, they represent a crossroads of news and gossip. Still, even they seem shocked to learn of the Empire's formation.

"We are speaking more from rumor than firsthand knowledge, but..." Corna trails off.

"Go on, girl," Myn says, waving her hand impatiently.

"There are seeds of truth even in the wildest lies."

"They say that the Sealord called forth the entire ocean. That he swept aside the Khalintari forces like the Creator reborn. I would have disregarded it as an impossible exaggeration, but we've heard the tale so often it must be true."

Myn sits back in her chair, her eyes drifting to her husband. The look they share transcends words, an unspoken conversation passing between them.

"From how you speak, you do not enjoy this knowledge," Myn says finally. "You hail from the Kingdom of the Sea, yes? Shouldn't you be rejoicing?"

"We are loyal only to each other," I cut in firmly. "No king could claim our allegiance. Especially not the tyrant they call the Sealord."

"What of your lands?" Aurelion asks, steering the conversation away before it can touch on the deadly secret hidden in our wagon. "I admit that I'm entirely ignorant of your people. You mentioned a nearby kingdom, the… Dusk, was it?"

"The Dusk of Eshan," Myn says, nodding sharply. "Westernmost of the Three Faces of Eshan."

"Night, in your tongue," Hona says. "Dusk, Dawn, and Dark: the Three Faces, the three kingdoms of Night."

"Are they allied in some way?" Aurelion asks.

"More by myth and legend than any real alliance," Myn says, scoffing. "The kings of Dusk and Dawn behave more like belligerent children than dignified monarchs. Always bickering, or currying favor with the Amanu."

"The Moonlord, in your tongue," Hona says absently, filling in details that his wife has no patience for. "A ruler, of sorts, but only in name."

"Yes, only in name," Myn sneers. "Eshan may have two kings, but there is only one true power. The current Amanu carries more weight than he should, and speaks as if he is the Eshani himself. It does not help matters that he is Blessed."

20

"Blessed?" I ask.

"As your sea king is Blessed, so is the Amanu," she says, tossing her hair over her shoulder. "Young, foolish, and far too powerful to be either."

"The Moonlord is supposed to be a placeholder," Hona breaks in helpfully. "We await the return of the Eshani. Of course, we have been waiting for generations beyond counting, but still the Amanu should know his authority is not supreme."

"In case this Eshani comes back?" Corna asks, struggling to keep the skepticism out of her voice. She leans forward, her brown ringlets swaying in the candlelight. "And how would you know if she did?"

"Legend and myth," Myn growls. "No more real than my husband's shadow demons stalking the night. You can hear the story from any passing idiot with an instrument, but I won't have it repeated here. If the Eshani were going to return, she would have done so already. Now, her name is thrown about like a religious cudgel, ignoring the faith it once represented."

Myn stands abruptly, gathering plates and disappearing deeper into the house. An awkward silence descends on the group. Hona stares after his wife. Finally, he rouses himself, turning to us with a smile.

"That passion is what drew me to her," he says. "Her rudeness comes from deep-rooted anger."

"We would never call her rude for *that*," Corna says graciously.

"It *was* rude, but I make no apology for her. Her father was a man who believed strongly in the legend of the Eshani. He passed on that belief to her, but his faith led him to ruin. It is not my story to tell. Myn does not like to be reminded of her faith, shaken or otherwise." Hona stands with a sigh, stretching his arms over his head to audible cracks. A muffled crash sounds in the other room, followed by sudden silence as the children, all twenty of them, pause to listen. Hona chuckles. "We should look after the children before they bring the house down around our ears. I'm sure you have many questions. We will speak again in the morning before you depart."

***

"Something about this is off," I whisper to Aurelion, sliding a blanket up to Rin's chin and brushing the curls off her forehead. The little girl sighs sleepily and leans into the touch. Despite my words, my heart swells to bursting at the sight of her, safe and tucked into soft wool blankets. Aurelion glances up from where he's just finished the same operation for Elan, his expression largely hidden in the dim shadows.

"Kettle," he says softly, taking my hand and leading me towards the door. His touch, devoid of hesitation, does something entirely different to my heart. I half-expect him to tell me I'm being paranoid, that I need to relax, but he doesn't. "What could be off?"

"I… I don't know," I say honestly. "These people, their generosity, what if it's just a front? Taking in weary travelers, setting them at ease…"

"And then using their twelve children to murder guests in their sleep?"

"Kraft," I growl as we pass into the sitting room adjoining the children's rooms. "I'm not being paranoid. Don't make fun of me."

The room is pastoral luxury made real, a mess of leather chairs and wooden beams, the dim embers of a fire casting a red warmth over the scene.

A flicker of panic, of fear and pain, claws its way from deep within the confines of my soul. Darkness lit with crimson light… the horrific echo of snapping bone, the blinding, mind-rending pain… an ache forms in my hand, and I glance down. My fingers have clenched around Aurelion's so tightly that my knuckles are white, the stub of my missing finger pulsing painfully. Dragging in a shaky breath, I force my fingers to release and drive the memory down as deeply as I can.

"I wouldn't dare," he says innocently, ignoring my moment of panic. Creator bless him. "I mean, you've got a point. They accepted us, despite reservations that we would do the same thing to them. It stands to reason that the only way they might feel secure is if they have some sinister plan of their own."

"Aurelion..."

"Especially since they forced their own children out of their beds so that ours could sleep in comfort. You know, because bloodstains are easier to clean out of sheets and mattresses than off this beautiful floor."

Twisting my hand out of his, I slump down onto a leather armchair and rub the empty space my middle finger once occupied.

"So you think I'm crazy?" I ask, scowling at the floor.

"I think that you've been on edge for far too long." He kneels in front of the chair, gently lifting my chin until I meet his eyes. "When was the last time you weren't worried about someone else? When was the last time you relaxed?"

"I relax all the time." I pause, frowning. "Well, what do you define as 'relaxing?'"

"Not worrying over whether your friends or your children will live or die from day to day. Let's start with that."

"Oh, then... never?" I say, some of my tension dissolving in the steadiness of his eyes.

"So. Relax. Your family is safe. No one knows who we are this far from the Ways. We have a chance at a new beginning, a fresh start. I know that your instincts are telling you to run, that anything so obviously safe and peaceful must be a trap." Aurelion looks around, taking in the wood worn smooth by countless feet, the chairs worn comfortable by a larger family than ours. "In this case, though, I think that we can trust Hona and Myn. I may not be a perfect judge of character," he smiles mischievously, his hands coming to rest on my knees. "But there haven't been any

23

signs of falsehood from them, subtle or otherwise."

"There wouldn't be," I protest weakly.

He just gives me a wordless stare. The aura of safety and ease contained within the Inara family estate is a hard temptation to resist. We are so far from civilization that no one could possibly find us. Having spent the better part of two decades running from theft to theft, ceaselessly worrying for the family I created, fighting to save my sister from the most powerful people in the world... any thought of relaxation feels foreign.

But he's right. What do we have to worry about? Wealthy beyond reckoning, our only enemies half a world away... I've earned the chance to relax, the chance to *breathe...*

My shoulders rise an inch, releasing a burden I didn't know I was carrying. Filling my lungs with air, a mighty sigh escapes my lips, and I ease into the comfort of the leather chair's embrace. Aurelion laughs at the sight, rich and pure.

"What?" I say, fighting an embarrassed smile.

"I didn't imagine that you relaxing would be so..." he struggles for the words, waving his hands helplessly.

"Apparent?"

"Adorable," he says, grinning.

He stares at me in silence, his smile finally fading after a minute, though the twinkle doesn't leave his eyes. The warmth of the room seems to grow from the pit of my stomach. My chest feels tighter the longer his gaze lingers. Finally, he blinks, glancing around and sighing.

"Have a good night, Kettle," he says softly, standing and turning to go. "Sleep well."

"Wait." The word leaves my lips before I can think, but I fight through the nerves. "Don't go."

"Okay," he says simply, turning back.

"But, we... we do..."

"What?"

Get a grip, woman.

"Sorry. Nothing," I find myself saying, even though they are not the words I want to say.

"No, no," he says, kneeling in front of me again and taking my hands in his. A spark crackles in the fireplace, and the brief flare of light ignites his bronze eyes like molten metal. I have to remind myself to breathe. "What were you going to say?"

"That is so not fair," I whisper.

"What isn't?"

"Nothing," I say again, clearing my throat. "I was going to say…"

"Yes?"

"That, perhaps, since we're safe and everything…" Though I trail off again, he doesn't push. He waits patiently, like the decent man he is. It doesn't make saying the next words any easier. "Well. I don't want *you* to go. But perhaps *we* could go."

"Where would we go?" he asks slowly, carefully.

"Somewhere away from the house, away from the children and the others. Not far, of course. But away. Just… just the two of us. To talk. About… the two of us."

Just throw me in the Depths now. My words are stumbling over each other like drunkards staggering out of a tavern at dawn. We've danced around each other the whole season, stealing a glance, briefly clasping hands, but never moving forward. The kiss we shared on the streets of Donir feels a thousand years gone, yet the tension it created stretches between us, taut and electric. The journey has offered little room for time alone; lost in the middle of a wild sea of grass, traveling with eight children and nearly as many adults, constantly looking over our shoulders for signs of pursuit, always wondering if we made the right decision…

It is only here, a relieved ease stealing through my chest, that the flames that kiss ignited grow bright once again.

And, Creator help me, I just ruined it all by acting like a stuttering adolescent too afraid of her own shadow to speak. Inwardly, I groan, the terrible pun not lost in my shame. Whatever

25

relief I might have been feeling is long gone now, and—

"That sounds wonderful," he says, standing and lifting me to my feet.

"Really?"

"Kettle," he says, squeezing my hands gently. "I've been waiting for... this. For you. Wherever you lead, I will follow."

***

The night is alive with the whirring of insects and the calls of birds, far louder and more numerous than in the Kingdom. It feels more like the Isles, places where day and night are differing worlds, where the fall of the sun brings new sounds and extraordinary sights. It is a reminder that we have no idea where we are or what we will face in the days to come. The somber thought can't pierce the haze of nervous joy hovering over my mind, not with Aurelion's hand still firmly in mine. The stars are numerous beyond counting, the crescent moon casting just enough light to enhance their beauty rather than eclipse it.

When the house is a glimmer in the dark, we come upon an orchard filled with flowers of white, the trees patiently waiting for the right time to bear fruit. As we wander through the ordered rows, Aurelion slips his arm around my waist and draws me close. The feel of him, warm, strong, and unshakeable, unweaves even more of the tension I've been carrying. Leaning into him, I let him lead me towards a gap in the trees, a soft bed of grass springing up in their absence. Sliding apart, we drop to our knees, facing each other in the darkness.

His face is unreadable in the night, but I can feel the intensity of his regard. As he slowly leans forward, his powerful hand coming up to gently cup my cheek, a careless thought drifts through my mind.

I guess we won't be talking after all.

***

Waking up is so gentle that I don't even open my eyes. My eyelids glow red from the morning sun, and a strong arm drapes over my ribs, his hand trailing on the ground. His breath comes even and slow, mind yet wandering through the unfathomable pathways of dreams. The softness of his skin surprised me last night, and still does. To become an A'kai'ano'ri, and Tempered as well, requires extraordinary physical and mental training. Yet the calluses on his hands are hardly noticeable. A breeze rattles through the trees, and its coolness trails along my skin. Slowly so as not to wake him, I push backward until our bodies press together again. He sleepily curls his arm and pulls me even closer.

Well, then. It might not have been what I expected to come out of last night, but I'll take this feeling as long as I can keep it.

The sound of distant voices brings a frown to my face, a reminder that this moment can't last very long. We should be getting up, getting dressed, and preparing to continue our journey east, but I can't make myself move. Not yet.

An angry shout shatters the morning's peace, and my eyes snap open. Aurelion stiffens, but I'm already gone, snatching up the twisted straps of my traditional Isles leathers. My shadow drifts uncertainly for a second, surprised at the sudden movement, but then darts into my clothes as I force the supple leather over one leg, then the other. Another shout echoes across the fields, and I mutter a curse. I don't recognize the voice, though it barks with authority and expectation. The words would be hard to distinguish at this range, but I'm fairly sure it speaks the language of this new land. Aurelion jumps up at the second shout, throwing on his clothes.

"You're such an idiot," I snap, dragging at tangled straps, trying to force them over my shoulder. "And now you've made me one."

"What?" he asks, freezing in place.

"We aren't safe!" I practically shout, though I try to keep my voice quiet so as not to alert the enemy of our location. "We're never safe. Only *I* can keep us safe, and I let you convince me… by the Depths, I'm a fool."

"But—"

"Shut up," I growl, heaving at the twisted strap until the leather stretches, finally popping over my shoulder. "You've said and done enough."

"Kettle…"

But I'm gone, calling on my shadow to speed my steps.

The extraordinary effort of our escape from Donir burned new shapes and pathways into my body, hollowing out the space within. Like a child in woman's clothing, my body feels like it no longer *fits*. Kit's strange power, whatever energy he gave me, is the cause. My shadow and I were once so in sync that I struggled to discern where my body stopped and it began. Now, I have to concentrate, to focus solely on the shadow to hear its voice.

My need cuts through the fog between us, and the darkness lunges forward against my clothing, turning each stride into a bounding leap covering half a dozen paces. The twisted leather cuts into my skin. I don't care. The shriek of metal on metal erupts ahead. I push myself harder. Passing through the orchard in a few lengthened strides, I put on a burst of speed over the open lawn. The Inara household blocks any view of the danger. As the corner approaches, I steel myself to face whatever may appear. Whoever they are, they *will not* harm my family.

Calling forth twin blades of shadow, my dead sprint carries me faster than my legs could normally move, even after the shadow has left my clothes. Normally, I would slow down to consider the best approach, but the sound of ringing steel echoes again. I don't have time. Lunging around the corner, I slide to a halt, blades of darkness at the ready.

Easily twenty strong, a squad of soldiers in unfamiliar colors, brilliant scarlet with silver accents, stand in a menacing circle around the front of the Inara home. Hona is on the ground, a thin trickle of blood dripping from his brow and a dazed look in his eyes. Yelden stands in the doorway, his sword at the ready, the soldier across from him holding a flexible spear with a leaf-shaped blade that catches the morning light. Hom holds back Myn, who is actively trying to push past him like she's going to charge the ring of steel herself.

The soldiers turn as I appear. Like an invisible wave, expressions of shock and fear and something else wash across their faces. I can't lose the initiative. I tense to charge… and the man closest to me drops his spear, falling to his knees and pressing his forehead to the ground. A second follows suit. The clatter of weaponry falling to the gravel path fills the morning in a chorus of dull thuds and faint scrapes. Before I can react, the rest of the soldiers have joined their fellows, pressing their foreheads to the ground in surrender… or reverence. They whisper and murmur to one another, but I can only pick out a single common word.

Eshani.

Chapter 2
Jace
The Seventy-First Day of Spring
In the year 5223, Council Reckoning

The Kinlen Forest, silent but for the crunch of our feet breaking through untrodden snow, stands sentinel to our struggle. Most of us travel in single file, following the trail Bota's broad form powers through the snow. The furrow he plows helps the rest of us along, but bone-numbing cold and aching weariness are inextricably married to our souls. The sound of Bota's passage ceases. Curiosity drags my gaze up. His head sways from side to side, seeking the path forward again.

Exhaustion pushes my eyes back down, settling briefly on Juliet's back. Her shoulders, once thrown back with pride, are slumped so far that she looks like a withered crone. A fitful flicker of crimson light occasionally burns as the sleeve of her coat shifts aside. Bota may be leading the way, but Juliet is the only reason we've made it as far as we have. Whenever our strength fades, she is there with a ready hand, sending warmth and life into our weary muscles. As if she has the energy to spare. As if she isn't making the same exhausting trek as the rest of us.

Alice is a step behind, her hair hiding under the hood of her thick coat. Her pixie face is barely visible, her face stoic and exhausted. Her weak smile lifts a corner of her mouth, but I can't give anything in return. Of Locke, there is no sign. His powerful legs allow leaps of such grace and strength that he avoids much of the snow, dancing from rock to rock and branch to branch, ranging far and wide while we stagger on. He spends much of the time scouting ahead, looking for the correct path, or at least, the path we hope is correct.

Stick to the golden and avoid the silver. How easy it seemed, back in the warmth of the sewers. Alice once lived at the base of the mountains, and she knew what we were looking for. Leaves, green on the surface but gold beneath. All we had to do was follow the path, right?

Of course, we left in the middle of Winter, just before the first true snowstorm of the season. No leaves. No gold, no green, no silver. Nothing but endless white.

So we waited. Not only for the leaves to return, but for the rest of the Enclave to appear. Alice led us to an area of the woods she remembered to be free of habitation, a third of the way up the mountain. That we stumbled on a cabin, abandoned and secure, felt more like destiny than luck. With a roof over our heads and plentiful game far from civilization, we passed the Winter in relative comfort.

In all those long days, we looked west back the way we came, not east, hoping for any sign of Da or Iren. They were a pair on that day in Donir when chaos reigned. Da would never leave Iren behind, not if he drew breath. We held out hope for them even as Winter turned to Spring. Da is weirdly capable, but Iren, soft, matronly Iren, would struggle to find her way up the slopes.

They never appeared, even as Locke and I both felt a growing sense of urgency to head west. There was no sign of pursuit, no indication that anyone cared where we went or who we were. Even so, as the snows melted, my uneasiness grew. When I moved into the trees, they no longer felt empty of life. It felt like something lurked, just out of sight, haunting the shadows and dogging my steps. The second green began to appear on the branches, we set out, packs near to bursting with provisions.

Alice was able to find the path without difficulty. Unique to the Kinlen Forest, two kinds of trees, known as the raithar and uithur twins, grow near one another. Their leaves appear identical from afar, but the underside of the raithar shines gold, while the uithur glimmers silver. For a while, we moved with confidence, pushing through the lingering snow and following the golden leaves of the raithar. The path was winding, but clear, tracking through shallow valleys across ridges, always leading higher and higher into the mountains.

Winter, as it turns out, was reluctant to release its grip on the higher slopes. The snow thickened the higher we got, and soon the twin trees dwindled until there was little left but pine and scraggly undergrowth. So we pressed on, hoping we continued in the right direction. And hoping the new 'gold' and 'silver' were not leading us astray.

Turning back, my eyes rest on the same sight they've stared at for days on end: a thick, rumpled layer of snow coating the ground.

"Anything?" Juliet asks, her voice loud in the stillness.

Bota thrums, his posture uncertain.

"Creator, not again," I groan, sliding the near-empty pack from my shoulders and throwing it into the snow. "That's the third time today."

"He's doing his best," Juliet says reproachfully, her blue eyes flicking back to me for an instant. Her hands move as she waits for me to speak, weaving a trio of twigs, freshly cut and supple, into a pointed shape. When she sees me looking, she glances at the strange mess of branches and her fingers pause. It isn't the first she's made, though they all end up looking the same. "Just keeping my fingers busy."

"I know he's doing his best," I sigh after a minute, only remaining standing with an extraordinary effort.

"Spread out, everyone," she calls, her face solemn. "You, too, Jace."

"I know," I mutter again, staggering forward and to the right, my steps instantly sinking deeply into the untouched snow away from Bota's path.

32

Eyes shifting over the deceptively smooth surface, I look for divots and shadows among the pristine white. Hidden from sight, stones mark the path forward, or at least we hope they do, their edges glinting golden in the sunlight from one angle, silver the other. Locke had made the connection, darting ahead and finding other, similar stones, following the golden sheen. For twenty days, we've been following the path like skiers at slalom, always sticking to the gold and avoiding the silver. The track has led us predominantly east, though it feels like we've begun to turn south the longer we've marched. As we push onward, the snow drifts grow higher, the rocks more hidden.

And we're slowing. The food reserves we brought are dwindling, and none of us have an ounce of woodlore. Alice was taken from the woods while still young, and her father was a smith for the woodsmen, not a man of the forest himself. The closest thing to a hunting weapon we have is a few knives weighted for throwing. The coats we donned at the base of the mountains seemed heavy and stifling at first. Now, as we climb higher, they've become the only thing keeping frostbite at bay.

A likely lump looms out of the snow, and I plow forward, legs too weary to step over the drifts. Kneeling to brush away the top layer, I find only dull gray stone. Stifling a curse, I push myself to my feet. My legs feel like anchors weighing me to the earth. The saber on my belt drags at my left hip. I resist, for the hundredth time, the urge to throw it into the snow and leave its cumbersome weight behind. Something tells me I'll be glad for it before this journey is over.

A thrum echoes from my left, the sound of Bota's joy heralding the discovery of another marker.

"This way!" Juliet calls happily, beckoning me over. The little twig sculpture she's been weaving has disappeared, probably into her pack. "Alice found it."

"Great," I mutter, lurching into motion once again.

***

33

"We're being followed."

"Good evening to you, too," I groan, pushing up from my bedroll onto one elbow. I can't see Locke, as the blackness of night is total under the dense canopy of pine. His silent arrival probably should have been a surprise, but, instinctually or otherwise, I knew he was there. "Couldn't you have, I don't know, checked if I was awake?"

"What do you want, a soft good morning and a love song?"

"Damn right I would."

"You weren't asleep anyway, and we both know it," Locke says with a smile in his voice. He's right, of course. Even though I can hardly move a muscle, nagging anxiety keeps my mind racing. We'll run out of food before long, and we have no idea how far we still have to go. My heart tells me the distance is great.

"So. Followed. Are you sure?" I ask.

"I wasn't for a long time. Whoever is on our tail knows the forest better than we ever will. I haven't caught so much as a glimpse of them or a track they've made. But I just had a feeling, you know? Like there is no way Kranos would let us go so easily. What our pursuer didn't count on is how quickly I can move. I went back more than a day's travel along our trail before I found any sign."

"So that's why we haven't been finding as many markers lately," I say, sighing. "You've been behind us rather than ahead."

"You've managed. Slowly."

"What sign did you find?"

"A campsite nestled in a dense copse of trees. A tiny fire well-hidden and mostly out. I think it's an individual, maybe two. Somehow, he's not leaving any tracks behind, even in the snow." My eyes have adjusted to the darkness, at least some, so I can see the concern on his face. "It doesn't feel natural. I don't care who you are or how lightly you walk. Even Alice breaks through the top layer of ice, and she's roughly the weight of a large toddler."

"Maybe... maybe he has some gear we don't? Special

shoes or something?"

"Maybe," Locke echoes, not sounding convinced. "There's more. The campsite wasn't just well-hidden. The branches were curved around it."

"So he bent some branches…"

"Curved," he cuts in. "Not bent. Like the trees grew that way. Like they were helping him hide."

The chill that races across my skin has nothing to do with the cold. Any thought of sleep dissipates before an intangible pressure. Someone watches, invisible. It seems like it's more than just my imagination, like a presence farther down the mountain… looms. The feeling only adds to my spinning thoughts. With an enemy before me, sword in hand, fear lends a helping hand, forcing me to be sharp and focused. This ominous dread, though…

"We can't keep going," I whisper, a realization dawning.

"Your thoughts echo mine," Locke agrees softly. "If we join the Vengeance's rebellion, we'll lead the enemy right where they want to go."

"We have to deal with him ourselves," I say, but the declaration comes out more like a question.

Locke huffs a laugh.

"In three days of searching, I haven't seen a single sign but for the camp. And even then, I got out quick. I had a feeling like I was being watched, and that isn't a feeling I'm going to ignore. He knows that we know, so I bet he'll be even more careful."

"In the open, though…"

"Sure," Locke agrees. "Between me, you, and Bota, we can probably handle whoever it is."

"Of course we can," I say, trying desperately not to sound like I'm convincing myself. "So, what can we do to force his hand?"

***

Sending Bota, Juliet, and Alice ahead, Locke and I set up

in ambush. For anyone tracking us, the wide path Bota forges through the snow may as well be a flaming beacon in the darkness, so we move a dozen paces into the trees to conceal our presence.

We watch the trail. From dawn to swiftly closing dusk, only shifting to keep blood flowing to our extremities, we watch. Even if boredom is all we have to show for it. The forest remains still and featureless. The sun, partially obscured by high gray clouds, crawls across the sky and falls swiftly towards the horizon. There is no sign of anyone but ourselves. If it weren't for the nervous tension crackling through my bones, the day would have been peaceful, my legs finally given the chance to rest with nothing but the patter of lightly falling snow as company.

A rustle whispers from a scraggly bush a dozen paces in front of me. Resisting the urge to move, I let my eyes slowly drift towards the sound. Most animals, humans included, are drawn to motion, and any movement I make now will disturb the light dusting of snow on my coat from the long hours spent motionless. The bush shifts again. Keeping my breathing slow, I try to calm my racing heart. Maybe we didn't waste our time after all...

A flash of silver flickers through the fading sunset. Bursting from my hiding place, I try to sprint forward, but my stiff muscles and the thick snow force me into a lumbering flounder instead. Locke glides into view from my left, his legs flexing backwards and exploding forwards. Despite traveling more than twice the distance, he reaches the bush and bursts through before I'm halfway there.

A few seconds later, I struggle through the clinging branches. Locke crouches in front of a gout of bright red blood staining the white snow. A rabbit, its expression frozen in permanent surprise, lies dead in the snow. Locke slides his knife swiftly out of the carcass before lifting it by its hind legs.

"Well, there goes any hope for an ambush," Locke says sourly.

"They weren't coming anyway," I answer, strangely certain of the words.

"Probably not. Do you think we were made? And what do you mean, they?"

My eyes are unfocused, my thoughts far away. They aren't coming. I know I'm right. They aren't close enough to see us, not with the naked eye, but I can... feel them, almost, waiting out of sight. The brush of their awareness tingles on my skin, as if they have some invisible way of seeing without their eyes, and, apparently, I can sense their regard. They know we're waiting, and they know we know...

Creator, my head hurts.

"Let's go," I say finally, dragging my eyes back to the track sloping upwards. "We need another plan."

Night falls as I set out on Bota's trail. Locke, his ranging strides wasted in my ponderous pace, disappears into the gloom. Almost immediately, the darkness presses closer, the high clouds obscuring even the dim light of the stars. An occasional sliver of moon sets the frozen slopes glimmering like a field of sapphire crystal, but even those dim bursts of light fade as the night wears on. Soon, I'm stumbling along in total darkness, hardly able to see my hand in front of my face. If it weren't for the wide and obvious trail, I'd be lost in a heartbeat.

The day of rest did my legs some good, but weariness creeps again into my bones before long. It must be nearing midnight, but I can't see the stars well enough to tell. No sounds disrupt the stillness of the night, none but those I bring with me: my breathing, labored in the growing altitude, and the soft crunch of boots in trampled snow, loud as breaking glass in a night so placid it borders on the unnatural.

That feeling is only aided by a creeping sense of dread that continues to grow.

Locke must be well and truly gone, for as my weary steps drive onward, the twin presences behind me grow closer. At first,

37

it's little more than the feeling of being watched, but then the awareness shifts, focused not so much on me as the world around. It's absurd, it's impossible, but it feels more and more like there are eyes in the trees, in the snow, drifting on the air…

In the corner of my eye, a flicker of movement in the darkness sends me rolling to the side. My heart racing, I resist the urge to draw my saber. It's just the wind. Just a tree branch moving in the wind, a wind that I can't *feel*, but *know*, even with the darkness so complete I can hardly tell if I'm—

Something is crawling on my shoulder. Twisting aside, I slam my hands against the creature, crunching through… snow. Nothing but snow that my coat picked up as I rolled away from—

I sense more than see something hurtling towards my head. Stumbling backwards, I plant my back to a tree as an icicle, large enough to cause me serious harm, slams into the snow. This time, I do draw my blade, a desperate calm washing over my mind. The icicles hanging high in the trees fall occasionally, sure, but rarely without wind to shake them, and never so large. Something else is happening here, something having to do with the awareness—

I try to lurch forwards, but I can't move, the collar of my coat digging into my throat. The tree ripples behind me, a crack rippling open like the maw of a giant beast. The wood pinches my shoulder blade even through the thick fabric, the jagged timber jaws extending to crunch, to rend, and finally to swallow. Reversing the saber, I stab backwards over my shoulder, but the point of the blade sticks dully into the living wood without any apparent effect. The mouth opens again, drawing me in, closing on my left shoulder and squeezing until the bones creak in protest.

Eternal's broken tomb, I need to do something, now, while I still have an arm free. Steadying my breathing, I set the edge of the blade along my own chest. As the wooden maw opens again, I slice down and away, the sharp edge of the saber cutting through thick cloth and fur and lightly scouring my chest. Ignoring the pain, I throw myself forward and rip free of the coat just as the tree's jaws slam closed.

The momentum sends me stumbling into the snow. Holding desperately to the saber, I set my hands to rise, but before I can begin the motion, the snow writhes beneath me. Pain erupts all over my body as jagged needles of ice burst from the ground and slash into my skin. I throw myself away. The thin spikes cut wider furrows as they leave my flesh. Staggering to my feet, I blink desperately as a trickle of blood flows into my eye, obscuring what little vision I have in the darkness.

This must be a nightmare. The trees rattle and shift in the darkness, sentient and filled with malice. The snow and ice grasp at my thick boots, burrowing towards my vulnerable skin. Warm blood flows down my chest and legs. Fear worms its way into the recesses of my heart. How can you fight trees and snow? How do you cut wood and ice?

How can I win against something that does not bleed?

A shard of ice slices through my shoulder as I dodge the grasping branches of a tree above. I block the next chunk of ice by instinct more than conscious thought, but a branch loops over my ankle and drops me tumbling to the snow and its sharp embrace. I try to twist aside and take the damage in profile, but... a grunt of pain explodes from my lungs as a dozen new cuts open across my side. A sudden weariness, deeper than any I've ever felt, flows into my limbs.

Creator, I'm tired. It would be far nicer to surrender, to relax, to sleep...

As the fight leaves me, as peace descends...

The world explodes into light.

The entire forest burns. Fire in extraordinary hues extends in all directions as far as I can see. A myriad of ambers and greens illuminate the trees and the earth, over which blue fire swirls in the snow and ice. The air itself shimmers in swirling white, and, as my hand lifts in wonder, fire crackles even beneath my skin, crimson and pure. There is no heat, no warmth; in the distant corner of my mind untethered from the brilliant fire, I can still feel the cold of the snow and the pain of my wounds. Even so... I have no doubt the flames are real.

A sharp pain in my stomach demands my attention. Ice has wormed its way deeper, digging into my skin. The ice itself is alive with the blue fire filling the snow, but the color is off. Distantly, I can hear my own desperate screams of panic as the blue fire plunges deeper, but my conscious mind latches on to the mystery instinctively. The sapphire flame is impure, interlaced with hues of something silver, metallic.

A path of the aberrant light wends away in the distance back down the slope. Another stream of tainted light, steel mixed with umber, twists through the air from the animated trees. At the end of those streams, twin silhouettes of gold and crimson flame stand out against the rest of the shimmering forest. Crimson... like me.

Standing swiftly, ignoring the gibbering voice sobbing for me to lie down, to let the pain and fear end, I explode forward through the snow. Retracing my path, intuition guides my feet to dimples in the blue fire where my passage already packed the snow hard. As I move, the metallic streams twist and retract. The steel-blue light sharpens ahead and to my left. The intent is clear as moonlight, and I deflect the hurtling shard of ice without conscious thought. My sword burns the bright ochre of the desert at noon. The deep brown of a bush ahead becomes infected by the metallic intent, and I dance aside as the branches grasp for my legs.

Sidestepping a final attack of grasping snow, I am there.

And they fall.

The light of their life, silver and gold and red, pours from their bodies in drifting waves of flame. As they breathe their last, the light ripples in the air and then explodes in all directions. I flinch, but the flames wash over and through me harmlessly. The blood leaking from my wounds freezes, and the forest writhes in pain and agitation. After the twin explosions, there is silence. The bodies, draped across the ground like forgotten garments, go dark, the fires of their lives fled from the shell they once occupied.

In a tapestry of fire, the twin shadows lying still on the ground are the sole scar of darkness.

Sorrow crashes into me, the sight of their black silhouettes speaking to a part of me beyond conscious thought. What once was fire has been extinguished. What once burned bright now lies dark. A weight drags me to my knees, and the brilliant fire of life fades from view. Again I am in the forest, knees pressed to rumpled snow, dark blood pooling from the cooling corpses of my foes. The perfect, unfathomable beauty of the flame is but a memory, a swiftly fading dream.

Though my blood may have frozen with the man's—the Shaper's—death, warm tears run unchecked down my cheeks.

I hardly hear Locke's approach, his shouts of alarm. I barely feel his careful hands, their examination of my wounds. I am cold, far too cold to stir myself. He disappears. Alone again. With the empty holes in the tapestry. The empty holes *I cut* into the tapestry.

A gentle hand brushes through my hair, coaxing my eyes to open. Perfect sapphire eyes appear before mine. Her hand rests on my cheek.

When did morning dawn?

Her hand imparts warmth, the only warmth I can feel. Like day rising to banish night, the light of her touch spreads through my body, driving away the cold. As the last vestiges of numbness recede, my mouth opens of its own accord.

"I killed them," I whisper.

"I know," she answers softly.

"They'll never..." I can't continue. How do you find the words for a world of fire? How can you speak sorrow into being?

41

But her eyes stare into mine, hold and encompass mine, with an understanding beyond the scope of words.

"I know," she says again.

***

By the time I awaken again, night has fallen. The deep thrum of Bota's snore vibrates through my chest, and the soft sigh I've come to associate with Alice's gentle breathing whispers across my senses. A figure hovers in the darkness, close to my head.

"Juliet?"

"You're awake," she says, weariness slowing every syllable to a crawl.

"How long has it been?"

"Just a day."

Bracing for pain, I force myself upright. My body responds easily, any harm the fight wrought on my body healed by Juliet's power.

"You really are a miracle, you know that?" I say, smiling.

"Sure," she says dreamily. "Miracle, sure…"

Trailing off, Juliet topples over and slumps to the snow. Shaking my head, I move her legs to the side and tuck her arm under her head. I head out of the impromptu camp the others set up around me, ignoring the tempting call of a fire's embers casting warmth into the air. Another call of nature is far more urgent. As I'm finishing up, there's movement in the corner of my eye. With a strangled yell, I try to draw my sword and hold my pants up both, succeeding at neither. The snicker that emerges from the shadow sets my eyes rolling as I cinch up my breeches.

"Damn you, Locke," I mutter, trying to slow my racing heart. "You just about killed me."

"You'd be surprised, how many people I've killed doing just that." He steps forward into the dim starlight, his expression set and serious. "We need to talk."

"About the fact that two Shapers tried to murder me in the

middle of a Creator-forsaken forest, or about how that Master of Water most definitely was *not* the Sealord?"

"Both," he says heavily. "It appears your girlfriend isn't the only person Kranos has... gifted."

"Her name's Juliet," I say, more sharply than intended.

"So?"

"So use it," I mutter, hoping he can't see the burn of my cheeks in the dark. "But yeah. So he's giving the power to people. But who? I don't think they were soldiers; they didn't even try to avoid my blade."

"They might have. You've never seen yourself fight," Locke says, shrugging. "But still, say you're right. I saw the aftereffects. The icicles at unnatural angles, the snow mounded in strange places, the trees bent literally out of shape. It can't be easy, breaking the laws of nature. You may have just reached them before they could stop, I don't know, focusing?"

"Maybe," I say, remembering the metallic light suffusing the fire. The world's fire? We'll go with that. When I got close, the stream seemed to come from their heads, their minds. Thought? Intent? "Regardless, this is intelligence that the Vengeance will need."

"If we ever find him," Locke growls, turning to the endless forest. "We haven't been making very good time, but I'd wager we're closing in on three hundred miles into this Creator-forsaken forest. How do you rebel against a kingdom if you aren't anywhere near the damn kingdom?"

"Provided we're even following the right trail," I say, the anger in his words settling on my heart. "What if we've just been walking along following a random collection of stones into the middle of nowhere?"

"Hey," Locke says, lifting a finger and stabbing it towards my chest. "We're following *your* man's directions, remember? If we're lost and doomed to die in this blasted forest, it's on you."

"I know," I say, trying to ignore the fear clawing at my

belly.

"They say the Vengeance can fly," Locke says conversationally, pulling a piece of dried meat from his pack and chewing on it absently. "I guess, if I could fly, and the most powerful man in the world wanted me dead, I'd probably live in the middle of nowhere, too."

"Turn in. I'll take the rest of the night," I say, glancing up at the stars. "I've slept long enough."

***

The sun's early rays can't pierce the thick canopy of branches, but dawn comes nonetheless. The slowly brightening light illuminates the strangeness surrounding our little camp. For a dozen paces around, the trees have warped like the wood was made liquid, then frozen again before it could finish falling. Unable to survive the trauma brought on by the change, the needles of the pines are already browning in all directions.

Even stranger, the only snow within sight is freshly fallen; the rest turned to solid ice. Abnormal shapes peek out of the undulating waves, though there is enough familiarity that I feel like I should be able to recognize them. Feet sliding on the slick surface, I manage to reach the strange shape and immediately regret the choice. Formed entirely from ice, a face lunges upwards, countenance locked into a permanent scream of pain and sorrow. But for the color, the visage is so believable it feels like tears should be cascading from the impossible blue-white eyes.

Alice whimpers in her sleep, and I barely restrain the startled jump that tries to seize my limbs. Her hair has wriggled out of the hood of her coat, jerking this way and that like a cornered animal. Glancing back at the screaming face, I can guess what nightmare disturbs Alice's slumber.

Twin streaks of frozen blood lead me to the bodies of my foes, dragged away and placed unceremoniously under a nearby bush. Steeling my heart, I step close to examine them. The melody of sorrow's song is distant, the raw emotion from their deaths fading with time. They were my enemies. They sought to kill me, to kill me and leave my body buried in the snow. Even if I may mourn the loss of life from the world, their death no longer feels so tragic.

From their appearance, they were, in fact, soldiers. Even stiffened in death, the proud posture and honed musculature of warriors is evident. The first is a woman, slight in stature, but strong. Even studying her face, I don't think I could pick her out in a crowd. The blandness of her features tickles something in the back of my mind. Locke once spoke of how some soldiers were recruited as much for their ability to blend in and be forgotten as for their competence.

Turning to the man, I flinch. His limbs are contorted into a grim rictus of death. The woman was arranged to rest peacefully, her hands clasped on her chest. Clearly, his body refused to lose the shape it took upon death. And his face... well. Its agony is a perfect match for the unnerving sculpture frozen in ice across the clearing.

The dim thought to bury them drifts through my mind, and I glance around for a likely place. The frozen wasteland stretches out of sight. I bend down and brush aside the snow dusting the surface. Thick ice stretches more than a foot, pure and pristine. The earth is just visible through the wavy crystal. My breath leaves in a sigh. Breaking through to bury them would be a trial I'm not sure we could survive, considering the state we're in.

Locke stands fluidly at the edge of the clearing and lifts his arms in a stretch that defies human limits. He catches my horrified gaze and grins, whipping his arms forward and back past where any normal human would break.

"Let's get them up," I call, shuffling back towards the camp. "We may as well press on."

Bota stirs at my call, while Locke glides over to gently shake Alice awake. She starts, but relaxes as she catches sight of him, her rigid hair falling back into her hood. She gathers herself and stands, stretching stiff muscles. Juliet remains slumped where she fell last night, the blanket I threw over her undisturbed. Sliding to a stop, I kneel at her side and gently rub her back. She doesn't respond to my touch, so I jostle her a bit more firmly. Her body rolls limply to the side. Her face, pale as the snow, rests vacant in the growing morning.

"Juliet."

Her name evokes no response.

"Juliet. Juliet!"

I'm shaking her, a terrified sob building in my chest. Her head flops about, uncontrolled, unresponsive, even when it cracks against the ice. The others are shouting, their hands pulling at mine, but I can't let her go. She used too much, gave too much of herself to save… me.

Creator, not this. Anything but this. Not her. Not the woman who gives herself to save others, who lost everything and chose, even still, to heal. Not this lost girl who I've just managed to find. Take me. Take everything from me. Not her. If the world knows anything of justice, she can't die here.

If he hears, the Creator chooses not to break his silence.

Squeezing her limp body to my chest, I grit out sobs, each pulse black agony like a blade rests buried in my heart.

Not her.

Not now.

"Jace, stop." Locke's voice comes from miles away. "You have to let her go."

"No."

The word rips from my throat like molten iron. Her lifeless face, cold and still, ignites the world. The glimmering white of the frozen air floats past in enigmatic swirls, and the brilliant blue of the uncaring ice below burns sullen and slow. My arms are a circle of crimson fire enveloping a dim silhouette. Dim… but not dark. The flame in her chest flickers fitfully, like a star twinkling in the night sky. The scarlet fire of her body is nearly out, the silver flame of her thoughts almost gone. As they fade even further, something else begins to shine through.

New light, golden light, glows from deep within her chest. A sphere of shining perfection, its warmth palpable even though I know this fire does not burn. For a moment, it hovers, as if reluctant to move from the home it's always known, but finally it floats away from the darkened silhouette lying in my lap. The golden light drifts towards the sky, diffusing, losing shape, fading...

There is nothing I can do. What life existed in Juliet's body has left it. My hands lift anyway, fingers outstretched towards the fading light.

Stay.

Please.

The light pauses, smudged golden paint untidily spread across the frozen Winter sky. Unexpected hope rises in my chest. It... she... is listening.

Come back.

Don't leave.

She wants to, by the Creator I can *feel* it, but she can't. Her body cannot sustain her anymore, the light of her very being only able to be contained for so long. She needs help, needs something more. If only *I* could give...

At the thought, ice spreads through my chest like frozen lightning. Golden light flows up my outstretched hand, pouring from my heart. Like Juliet's, yet somehow intrinsically different. My light reaches hers. A miniature sun illuminates the clearing. The whites and blues and browns of the surrounding forest brighten in turn, Juliet's light bathing them in glory. Slowly, but with certain intention, the golden orb falls back to her body.

Twin fires, crimson and silver, reignite deep within her. Gold continues to flow unabated from me to her, pouring in a steady stream. As the colors of her body grow stronger, my own chest grows colder.

I am giving too much. My breathing slows, my heartbeat lengthens.

I want to stop, but I—

***

"Creator, you're warm," a woman's voice murmurs, lips pressed against my hair.

As my eyes flicker open, my first thought is that no time has passed. The light isn't materially different, and the hard ice pressed to my back is certainly familiar. Based on the arms wrapped around my shoulders, though, it seems that Juliet and I have switched places. And yeah, she's right. Sweat soaks my skin. The heat of her arms is almost oppressive. I don't try to pull away, though. Creator knows it's a relief after the days of ice and snow.

"Back at you," I whisper, relaxing into her embrace.

My ear presses to her chest. The strong beat of her heart is the music to which the world turns. For a few moments of blissful silence, we relax, the cold a distant memory, the fear a fading specter. Whatever happened to me, whatever *is* happening to me, at least her heart still beats.

"Is anyone going to tell me what in the Eternal's cursed name just happened?" Locke asks, shattering the peace of the moment.

"I wish I could tell you," I answer, stifling a groan. Extricating myself from Juliet's arms is one of the hardest things I've ever done, but I manage.

"How long have you known?" he asks, his tone flat.

"Known what?"

"That you're a Shaper."

My mouth opens to disagree, but the words die in my chest. I haven't had time to process the extraordinary events of the past two days. Fighting the Shapers, seeing their will wrought in flames, flames which do *not* terrify me for once, was one thing. But now... seeing Juliet's life fading, the golden light for which I can find no name… maybe there is truth to Locke's words. But what I've done doesn't align with any element I've ever heard of.

"I'm not really sure that I am," I say slowly.

"That symbol of power says otherwise," Locke says, scowling.

"What? What symbol?"

"You held up your hand, and it appeared on your palm. A symbol glowing gold."

Holding up my left hand, the hand that rose unbidden to plead to the light, I can't see anything special about it. Long-worn calluses earned through countless hours of swordplay mar the skin of my palm. There is nothing to read in their myriad lines, crossing like tributaries to a mighty river. A symbol of power? Here? The longer I stare, the more impossible it seems.

"What power is gold?" Locke asks, voicing the question before I can. The others glance about, but they all shake their heads in turn. "Well, what did you do?"

"I… I'm not sure. I saw everything, not like this, but set on fire. Not normal fire, not burning, but… in colors, strange colors, beautiful colors. The ice and snow are blue, the air is white, our bodies the brightest red…"

"I felt you," Juliet says, her hand fluttering over her heart. "Your will, your… fear. Your…"

"Your light is beautiful beyond words," I say, only realizing how intimate that sounded after the words leave my mouth.

"Thank you, I guess?" she says, ducking her head to hide an embarrassed smile.

Locke glances around, his expression skeptical, but a look of wonder steals over Juliet's face. A few steps away, Alice grins with the delight of a child offered a favorite story, her hair dancing in an unseen wind. Bota's face is split by a broad smile that lends him a boyish joy in contrast to his massive stature. He scampers over to me, clapping a massive hand on my back and knocking the wind straight out of me.

49

"Your Blessing graces us all," he rumbles, ignoring my choking gasps.

"Right," Locke says, shaking his head. "A Shaper, and a Blade. What next? Son of a king?"

"Not guilty on that count. My mother worked at the Simply."

"That isn't reassuring, for some reason" Locke grunts. "We need to keep moving as soon as we can. We've bought ourselves some time, but we need to find the Vengeance sooner rather than later."

Recovering what remains of my furs from the monstrous tree which is again just a tree, I wrap the tattered coat about my shoulders and huddle as close to the fire as I dare. As it is still mid-morning, we eat a lean breakfast from our dwindling rations and set out again, slipping and sliding across the unnatural contours of snow made ice. After ten bruising, frustrating minutes, we make it out of the affected area and return to the endless expanse of white snow and dark trees. Locke sticks with us this time, his lithe form constantly in sight as he dances about our flanks. The encounter with the Shapers must have spooked him into caution. Indomitable as he is, the thought is sobering.

Juliet takes up her customary place in front of me in silence. Close brush with death aside, her steps come strong and sure, and the glow of crimson peeks from underneath her coat as we walk. Still helping Bota, still giving her own life to keep us strong. I open my mouth to tell her to stop, but I hold in the words. It's easy to picture the incredulous, offended look she would shoot me, the insistence that she's fine, she's just doing her part. My soul shakes in fear that she will march herself right into the grave, and that, this time, I won't be able to save her.

As we walk, I try to shift my sight, to see the light of the world. It's remarkable, really, how quickly I've lost my long-held fear of fire. Well, mostly. I can't imagine I'll be sleeping next to the campfire any time soon, but the memory of the brilliant hues of flame that make up the world sets my heart soaring. Despite my best efforts, though, the world remains cold and dark. What use is a power that only comes in desperation? What if I need it, and it won't come?

The sun hasn't reached its zenith when my legs grow heavy. When I glance up, Juliet has opened up a lead, keeping the pace despite giving her strength to others. Gritting my teeth, I try to force my weary legs to respond, but they only slow. The cold bites deeply through my coat, each gust of wind cutting daggers into my skin. My limbs start to tremble, from exhaustion and cold. Juliet glances back and frowns, slowing, but I wave her on.

"I'll be fine," I croak, or try to, coughing as the words compete with my desperate breathing.

Ignoring my protest, she staggers back down the trail. A wave of fresh energy washes through my shaking limbs. The warmth does little to cheer my spirit, but plenty to illuminate just how tired I really am. Juliet's power can't offset the empty pit yawning in the center of my chest. The arm she throws around my shoulders is the only thing that keeps me from sinking to the ground.

"We need to rest," Juliet shouts, her voice carrying in Locke's direction.

"We don't have time," he calls impatiently, loping towards us. "Even if the Empire wasn't sending Eternal-damned Shapers after us, we need food."

"I know that," she snaps. I can't see her face, but her glare brings him up short, his hands raised. "Jace can barely stand."

"I'm fine," I say, trying to speak through the chattering in my teeth. From the change in Locke's face, I don't quite manage it. "Maybe…"

"Sit, man," Locke says. Stepping forward, he lends me the strength of his arm and, together, they lower me to the ground. My legs thank me, but the cold seeps even deeper into my bones. "Take a minute. Whatever you did for Juliet probably took a lot out of you." He sighs. "I don't know how much longer we can survive this damn forest."

"Then what are you doing out here?" a strange man calls from somewhere hidden nearby.

Locke disappears in a puff of shifting snow, and Bota rolls to his feet, a rumbling growl building in his chest. Juliet hardly reacts, her concern only for me.

"Help me stand," I whisper. "And give me the strength to speak, if you can spare it."

Another wave of warmth and life thrums through my body as I take her offered hand. A few seconds have passed, but tension permeates the air thick enough to swim in. From this stranger's perspective, I can't blame him if he's hostile. Any travelers would be concerning this far from civilization, and some of us barely look human. Gathering my strength, I take a deep breath of the icy air.

"We are seeking the Vengeance's rebellion," I call as firmly as I can. "Though we aren't sure we're on the right path."

"There are no paths out here," the man says, still invisible in the trees. "What could you hope to find?"

"We stuck to the gold and avoided the silver as best we could, though the snow makes it difficult."

Between one blink and the next, the empty air next to a towering pine is filled by the figure of a tall man, lean despite the thick furs wrapping his body. A bow rests in his hands undrawn, the arrow pointed towards the ground, and a sword decorates his hip. His features are sharp enough to cut, a mop of his sandy blonde hair cutting across his forehead. Though he speaks to me, his eyes don't leave the growling bear that is Bota, leaning on his knuckles to my left.

"Be calm, Bota," I say gently. "I believe we've found what we came for."

"Few have made the journey of late," he says, eyes flicking about. "And none quite so… unusual."

"Yet here we are, bearing tidings the Vengeance needs to hear."

"We'll determine that," a woman says, appearing next to the stranger. I'm struck immediately by the brilliance of her emerald eyes, bright and sharp even from a distance. Her fiery hair curls in a thick braid down her shoulder. "Your ally in the trees isn't making you any friends, either."

"Locke," I start to call, but he appears on his own, a cold look on his face. If they notice his strange loping gait, they don't comment. When he reaches my side, I open my hands. "The news is grim in the west. The Master of Beasts uses his holy power to break the bodies of others in twisted experiments. In Donir, the people rebel against the Sealord's rule, though only because the Wave is otherwise occupied. The Kingdom of the Sea is at war with the Khalintari Republic, and that is the least of it."

"Your news is out of date," the woman says, shaking her head. "The *Kingdom* is no more. All hail the Emperor Helikos the Sealord, conqueror of the Khalintars and ruler of the Empire of the Sea."

Chapter 3
Iliana

The Sixty-Seventh Day of Summer
In the year 5223, Council Reckoning

The wind sings a tale of shimmering heat to my drifting gaze. The eastern horizon, impossibly far away across the flat expanse of desert, has just begun to lighten. Soon, the sun will climb and set the sands aflame, an innumerable sea of glittering diamonds, but for now, the chill of night still holds sway. From the highest balcony of the House of the Republic, the pure white buildings of Coin glow starlight blue straight to the shadow of the mighty wall. A city of straight lines and clean harmony, the Jewel of the West is quiet. Though I've found that Coin rarely sleeps, even her people respect the silence before dawn.

The frigid night air has worked its way into my skin, but I hardly notice. A servant, kind in spite of tyranny, placed a blanket over my shoulders at some point in the night, but it fell to the marble a few hours ago, right next to the pillow she silently offered for my comfort. There is no need. My body has endured far worse. No physical need drives me here.

I come for the gift of stillness.

The luxury of silence.

The grace of emptiness.

For here, before the world reawakens, I can be nothing.

The soft scuff of leather on stone alerts me to the approach of a servant. Not just any servant. My personal servant, practically my shadow, chosen from among a thousand possibilities. The Lord General picked her out himself, no doubt for her blind obedience and sterling reputation. Once a slave to the Minister of

Finance himself, she has been considerate and thoughtful, especially for someone no doubt reporting my every move to Kranos.

"Your Eminence, I—"

"Peace, Lentana," I say dully. "The world can wait for dawn."

"Very well, your Eminence."

The eastern sky brightens slowly and all at once, lancers of brilliant orange sallying forth to make war on the darkness of night. Despite the beauty of the burning panorama spread across the horizon, the peace of the night slips through my fingers like sand through a sieve. With a sigh, I force my stiff limbs to move. Though I would sit here, unblinking, until the sun tore the sight from my eyes, duty drags me from my rest as surely as the sunrise.

"The Lord General requests your presence at the throne," Lentana says, falling into step just off my elbow as we pass through the sumptuous apartments that the Minister of Finance abdicated for my use.

On the upper edge of the eastern wing of the House of the Republic, my rooms are a practical sea of opulence in gold and royal blue. Like a dress tailored for someone else, the apartment doesn't fit me. Lentana *does* seem to fit, though; tall, strong, and graceful, her bronze skin and bright smile more befitting a pirate queen than a mere servant. Clad in a dress of pristine white cotton, she wears the servant's attire like it's the height of fashion.

An echo of disquiet whispers in my thoughts. The woman's place at my elbow is somehow right and yet so very *wrong*, knowing who *should be there.*

Pressure builds in my chest, like a titanic boulder held at bay by a single trembling, struggling length of thin wood, splintering... green eyes...

Pain erupts in my mind, and I gasp. The eyes fade.

"Get me dressed," I say aloud, voice cold, inwardly

demanding that tiny sliver of self-control to hold.

Standing before a mirror, I barely recognize the woman staring back at me. Her eyes are cold and severe, face locked in a careful stoic mask. A pair of meek slaves join Lentana as she bustles around, removing my thin silk nightgown and replacing it with a sapphire dress of Empire make. It has to be strange for the slaves to work with corsets and thick skirts, but, under Lentana's direction, they work with quiet confidence. A part of me wonders about the fashion in Coin, and whether the people think me strange in the thick dress of colder climes. But my choice is deliberate. I am not one of them. As they finish up, Lentana steps back to admire her handiwork, her lips spreading into a satisfied smile.

"We have to hurry now, your Eminence. The Lord General wishes to open court early today."

"Of course," I say softly. "I live to serve."

"But you are the queen, your Eminence," she says carefully, refusing to meet my eyes in the mirror. "Why do you bow to a mere general?"

"Silence, girl," I say, not bothering to look at her. "You speak of things you can't understand."

"The servants whisper, your Eminence. About you. About how the Creator-chosen Master of Earth, our queen, stoops to serve another."

"What has gotten into you today?" I turn abruptly, studying the woman as she averts her eyes and ducks her head.

"I apologize, your Eminence," she says meekly.

"I will not tolerate treasonous comments from my servants. My loyalty is to the Empire, queen or no."

"How can it be treason for a queen to rule her land as she sees fit?" Lentana asks, glancing up quickly.

Her delivery is flawless, presented as little more than innocent curiosity, but her eyes betray her, flashing with something else, something deeper. I open my mouth to chastise her, but her question sticks in my brain.

Am I a queen in name only? Should I not assume the mantle of sovereignty, step forward to shoulder the responsibility of my rule? Why do I listen so blindly? Why have I always listened… pain lances through my brain, growing to overwhelm my thoughts. Sickening, thought-shattering pain, yet somehow familiar. It is a pain I've felt before, but, Creator help me, I can't place it. Shaking my head, I try to hold back involuntary tears.

"Know your place," I snap, spinning on my heel and striding through the halls. Lentana's quick steps echo mine as she catches up. Brilliant green eyes drift like mist before me, gone even as I think to remember.

Gritting my teeth, I hurry down the stairs and towards the throne.

***

The grand hall from which the Ministers once ruled is poorly shaped for a throne room. A flattened circle crafted for nine equals, each Minister had a place of importance in the ringed gallery looming over the inlaid marble pillars. Shifting that focal point to a single chair, however grand, makes the entire room feel off. The twin rows of the Tide standing at silent attention also do not belong. My shining throne of glass, formed from the very sands of the desert, is an unwelcome departure from the unbroken expanse of rich burgundy and pearl marble. I formed it to fit the contours of my back perfectly, but no chair has ever felt less comfortable.

Shifting my weight, I glance at the empty spot where the Lord General normally looms. Odd, for a man pressing to start the court proceedings early to then disappear just as abruptly. Normally, I would never start without him, but I don't want to sit here any longer than I have to, and the line of petitioners is short this morning. If I get through them all, I have more than enough excuse to end the charade. My eyes slide to the balding man standing in his typical place to my right, ill-fitting turquoise armor marking him as a Tide. Or at least, a facsimile of one.

For there is no way that this man has passed the rigorous standards of the Tide. Slovenly in appearance and build, Captain Silken stands near the throne only through Uncle's direct command. Uncle introduced him with implications of the Deep, but he's not one that was under my command in Donir. He is supposed to be an aide and counselor, yet I don't trust him at all.

He meets my gaze as the thought crosses my mind, his bland face shifting into a knowing smile. His eyes are cold and dead.

Shivering, my eyes flick to Lentana's back where she stands at quiet attention ahead. I need her now, impertinent questions or no. Most of the supplicants speak fluent Donirian, and Uncle normally fills in the gaps with his extraordinary ability to pick up language. Without him, though, she will have to translate if there is a language barrier. Can I trust her? Shifting uneasily and facing down the curving hall towards the entrance, I reluctantly raise my hand for the Tide to open the doors.

Luckily, the first petitioner speaks capable Donirian, as do the second and the third. Their concerns are comfortingly familiar, from accusations of swindling to claims of unfair market practices. Merchants the world over are the same: loudly declaring their own innocence while blatantly flouting the very rules they demand their competitors follow. I long ago learned that the more I allow angry merchants to speak, the deeper the hole they dig themselves with their words. The Khalintari are no different. They leave as equally dissatisfied as their Donirian counterparts once did.

The fourth supplicant, a small, bent old woman with covered gray hair and withered features, creeps uncertainly through the doors, looking at the assembled ranks of the Tide and hesitating. The sight of her awakens something in me I haven't felt in more than a season. I want to step forward and help her into a chair, offer her the dignity she's earned after a long life.

She reminds me of Yrena.

Creator. I haven't thought that name in… how long? What happened to her? A torrent of memories cascade through my mind, a hundred hours spent with her comb in my hair, her strong hands tugging on my clothes, her gentle fingers running across my cheek. A rush of bittersweet sorrow fills my heart before a desperate terror surges to overwhelm it. Pain, same as before, begins to pulse at my temples. Still I force myself to continue down this train of thought.

Yrena practically raised me; Eternal damn it, she was like the grandmother I could never have. And I forgot her. Somehow, the woman who looked after me and showed me unquestioned love has disappeared from my memories. When did I see her last? Was it… the headache rises with such force it feels like my skull will split in two. Struggling not to cry out at the pain, I force my eyes open.

Something is wrong with me.

The look on my face must be terrifying, for the old woman at the doors is wild at the eyes, like a colt on the verge of flight. Forcing a smile, I beckon her forward. She reluctantly obeys, her slow, choppy steps the only sound in the cavernous room. She totters to a halt a dozen paces away, clasping her hands before her chest and bowing her head. At my encouraging nod, she opens her mouth and speaks a stream of unintelligible Khalintari. I wait patiently, my smile growing more natural as the old woman shakes her fist in indignation. When she's finished, I shift my attention to Lentana.

"This is Matron Nahira of the West Gate Orphanage, your Eminence," she says dutifully. "She begs your royal pardon, but she doesn't know where else to go. Two nights ago, a group of armed soldiers came and took her charges. They did not wear any symbols, but she thinks they were pale, like you. She hesitated to come because she was afraid of them. She thinks, had she not been out seeking medicine for one of her children, that she would not have survived the night."

"This sounds like a load of lies to me," Silken says, picking at the skin of his face. "Some rebel trying to spread dissent."

"Tell her…" I trail off, unsure how to proceed. Silken's dead eyes are on me. I push through my doubt. "Ask her if she saw where they were headed."

"She says, your Eminence, that they crossed through the Plaza of Stars, but she lost sight of them near the House of the Republic."

"Def'nitely lies." Silken folds his arms, leaving his hand close to the dagger belted at his side. "Would you like me to silence her, my queen?"

"I'll hear her out and judge for myself," I say firmly.

Part of me agrees with Silken in doubting the woman's account. Of all the clandestine military operations the Lord General might arrange, stealing parentless children in the night doesn't seem likely. It's not that I think she's lying; her sincerity shines through, even though I can't understand her. No, this smacks of something else. After a moment of silence, the old woman speaks again.

"She says that her story is not unique," Lentana translates, concern growing on her face. "She went to a home for invalids and the mentally disturbed that her friend runs, and no one answered the door. She knew where the secret key was in case one of the patients managed to lock the door, and, Creator forgive her, she says, she went inside. Nothing was missing, nothing was out of place, but everyone was gone. Others in the community, too, have stopped responding to letters."

"Oh, come now," Silken blusters, his fingers wrapping around the hilt of his weapon.

"Tell her," I say firmly, ignoring the man for now. My thoughts feel slow, like I'm pushing through a wall. I grit my teeth and focus to force the words out. "That her queen did not order any such action, and that I will do my very best to discover who may have. I will try to find where her children have gone. She has my word."

The matron purses her lips and gives me a sharp nod, her hands once again clasped at her chest. Silken eyes her with such hostility that she quails when she looks in his direction. She glances at me hesitantly, as if wondering if she has been dismissed, then turns to leave. Lentana turns a questioning look towards me, and I nod slightly. My servant bows slightly and hurries after the old woman, taking her arm and helping her to the door, whispering all the while.

"You look worried," I say as she returns to her station.

"Of course I'm worried," she says distractedly, losing some of the formality she's maintained over the days she's spent in my service. "People without a voice to speak for them are disappearing in my city."

"Lies, you Khalintari bitch, and nothing else," Silken says evenly. "I don't know why the Lord General picked you, but a few words from me and you'll disappear." He grins lewdly, his eyes dragging across Lentana's fit form. "But maybe we can have some fun first."

"At least try to act like a professional in my court," I snap, glaring at Silken. "Lentana is my servant, and I'll not have your disgusting predilections aired in my presence."

"She's jus' a dirty sandworm, your highness," he says, clearing his throat like he's preparing to spit. At my glare, he reluctantly swallows whatever grossness he's dredged up. "I'm loyal to the throne."

"Then loyally see yourself out."

His face freezes, eyes calculating. Finally he nods slowly, moving towards the door.

"See you later, sandworm," he calls over his shoulder. "I hope we get to work *closely* together."

"Lay a finger on her and I'll cut it off," I growl.

He doesn't respond other than to give an errant wave. The

urge to put a glass dagger in the base of his skull nearly overwhelms me. It's hard to be disobedient when you're dead and buried.

"Don't be afraid of him," I say, turning back to my servant.

"Men like that do not scare me," she says, her eyes flashing dangerously.

"I'll do my best to get to the bottom of this. I would never give an order to harm children, nor would I allow anyone under my rule to do so."

Lentana opens her mouth to answer and then stiffens, her eyes towards the door. Eledar Cortola, the old Minister of Finance, has appeared in the hall. A man aging with grace, the gray spreading from Cortola's temples only highlights the perfection of his elegantly coifed black hair. Cortola was the sole representative of the Ministers to remain at his post. Though stripped of his title, his dedication allowed him to remain near the seat of power. For all that, the man is less trustworthy than an adder and twice as deadly.

The other Ministers, those that survived the war, fled Coin with whatever wealth they could scrape together. Some of them are rumored to be causing trouble in distant parts of the continent, but most have merely fled the shame of their incompetence. The *Habuni Elwit*, or Fool's Agreement, as the people are calling it, exposed their entire military force to the unchecked power of the Sealord. Committing even their defensive Shield, the Ministers laid the Republic bare to our armies, so completely that there wasn't even a fight when we came to finish the conquest.

In retrospect, their incompetence probably saved the lives of thousands of their citizens. War rarely remains exclusively between soldiers.

In a stark contrast to my last petitioner, Cortola moves forward in measured strides. When he reaches the appropriate distance, he presents himself formally with a perfect genuflection.

As he opens his mouth to speak, though, his eyes dart to Lentana. He's far too capable a politician for most to notice, but, when he sees her, he hesitates for the briefest instant.

"Your Eminence, I come with unpleasant news," he says in a voice like warm butter. "I had hoped to address both you and the Lord General, but he does not seem to be in attendance."

"Convenient, that you should bring dark tidings the first time he is absent," I say sharply.

"I assure you, your Eminence, it is nothing of the—"

"Eledar, I have a question," I say, cutting him off. "Why do your people call me 'eminence?'"

"It is the term of respect given to the great Khals of old."

"I see. So I am granted the same title as the tyrants you overthrew centuries ago. Perhaps you hope to repeat the exploits of your forebears," I say, smiling. He opens his mouth to protest, but wisely holds his tongue when I raise a finger. "Don't worry, Eledar. I like it. I *should* be a reminder of the Khals, who held sway over these lands much longer than your petty Republic."

"My lady…"

"Don't stop now," I say, enjoying the feeling of watching him squirm. He doesn't literally squirm, of course. His posture remains perfect. But his eyes tell a different story. "Say it."

"Your Eminence," he says, pausing, but I merely raise my eyebrows in polite curiosity. "I have news you may not like to hear."

"What is your relationship to my servant?" I deflect again. Lentana remains as stiff as a wooden board.

"She is my slave, your Eminence," he says, swallowing his news and flicking narrow eyes to Lentana. "By right, her contract is still active. She is my property."

"Your property?" I say, the cold anger in my chest suddenly heating.

"Yes, as is our way. I bought this girl's service for thirty years, and she fled the terms of her contract less than a decade into her commitment." The former Minister has many slaves, a household full of them. I'm sure that he has no idea what half of their names are. Seeing the way he eyes Lentana, though, my stomach twists in disgust. She can't be much older than twenty. If his... attention... began when she was bought... he continues to speak. "It would be a great boon to me if you were to return her to me. She is here illegally, after all."

Even standing still, Lentana has always held herself with the grace and confidence of a queen. Cortola's words rob her of that natural dignity. Her hands, drawn behind her back, clench into white-knuckled fists. Her dress can't hide the tremble in her knees. Yet her chin does not waver, and her shoulders do not bow.

"Lentana, is this true?"

"Yes, your Eminence," she says in a voice devoid of hope. By the Creator, she actually thinks I'm going to give her up. "Every word."

"And do you think it just that you return to his service?"

"Your Eminence, I—"

"I did not ask you a question, Eledar," I say with dangerous civility. "Please allow Lentana to speak."

"It would not be just, your Eminence," Lentana says, turning to meet my eyes.

"Why not?"

"I was kidnapped from the streets of Sail and falsely sold into slavery," she says, voice raw with emotion. "I started out working in the Minister's household, in the kitchens. As I grew older, he started to notice me, and my duties changed. He kept me close. He made me..."

"How old were you?" I ask kindly.

"I was thirteen, the first time he forced me to attend him."

"And is this why you fled his service?"

"No," she says, frowning. "Another... servant, I guess you would say, was left to die on the streets of Halfway. I worked for days to save his life, and the Minister was gone before he was well enough to continue."

"You wretched bitch," Cortola snarls. "You should have let him die—"

His words cease abruptly as a blade of glass appears at his throat. A bead of bright red blood rolls down the razor edge.

"Interrupt this conversation again and you won't have time to regret it," I say pleasantly. "So his ownership of you isn't just. What would justice look like?"

Cortola's face changes as he finally realizes how precarious his position is. His eyes dart between Lentana and me, horror dawning on his face when he recognizes that his former slave may well decide his fate. A slave he abused. Lentana does not answer immediately; something that lends greater weight to her words when she finally speaks.

"There can be no justice in this," she says slowly. "I have lived what feels like an entire life in the years since I've seen this man. He is no more a part of my life than the parents who left me in an alley as a child."

"I assume you would at least like to continue in your current duties, free from the slave mark he would clamp around your ankle?"

"Very much, your Eminence," she says, bowing her head.

"Eledar, thank you for the gift of this slave's contract," I say, allowing the glass dagger to float back to my waiting hand. "It was very generous of you, and I accept gladly. Unless you have something else to say on the matter?"

"No, your Eminence," he says, the picture of respect but for his burning eyes.

"To the ill tidings you bring, then. What other disappointment do you offer?"

"The last three caravans from the Ram have not arrived, nor has the latest from the Bull. Last reports mark them crossing the Vein at Alzir, but they disappeared somewhere between the there and the Way of the West."

"What goods did these caravans contain?"

"Food, your Eminence. The latest yield from the far west, many wagons full of necessary crops and livestock that would serve the people of Coin. Though three caravans are not significant in and of themselves, if these disappearances become a trend, my people and your soldiers both will soon feel their lack. And, with how fast you're draining our treasury, we'll notice sooner rather than later."

"What do you believe is causing these... disappearances?" I ask, ignoring the last. Something happened back in Donir, and Uncle won't give me the details. It is a well-kept secret that most of the wealth of Coin is flowing west and out of the Khalintars. It undercuts my rule and my authority, but I have no say in the decision. "Bandits?"

"Perhaps," he says, though he shakes his head even as he says the word. "But I think it may be more than that. There are rumors of an organization, some fools seeking the return of Khals to this land. Their leader apparently calls himself the Khal of Nothing, or some absurdity like it."

"You come to me with rumors?"

"Information on these people is incredibly hard to find." He smooths his hair behind his head. A nervous habit. "You know as well as I that my people do not have the military might to oppose your rule, but some fools would rather die to destroy than live to build."

"Our," I say, my mind far away.

"What?"

"Our people. I am your queen."

"Of course, your Eminence."

"I'm going to make you an offer, Eledar," I say, holding his eyes. "The military forces of the Steed remain loyal to Coin, do they not?"

"Save for those who deserted before you arrived, yes."

"I want you to prove their, and your, loyalty to me. Take the Steed stationed in Coin and root out the rebel forces. Personally."

He doesn't bother to argue. Though, by the look on his face, the effort to remain silent is taking years off his life.

"If you fail, I will use the Tide," I say, meaning every word. "And I will show no mercy. The rebels, or instigators, or this Khal of Nothing, will have sympathizers, friends, family... if the Tide must bring their might to bear, all of those connected—*our people, Eledar*—will suffer for your failure."

"As you say, your Eminence," he says, bowing his head and spinning on his heel to leave.

I can feel Lentana's regard, but I take a moment before I meet her eyes. Whatever gratitude she might feel for her freedom doesn't show on her face. Instead there is fear, for her people and of me. Putting aside the concern of a simple servant, I lift my face towards the open doors and raise a hand for the next supplicant.

She is right to be afraid. I have proven, to myself and all the world, that I will do what must be done.

Creator knows, I have proven it.

***

As ever, sleep eludes me. I wish it were troubled dreams, nightmares to survive and overcome. I wish even for fear to seize my soul and leave me trembling in the corner. I wish my mind would race into a dizzying swirl of thoughts and anxious wonderings. But no. I am not afraid, nor am I worried. Sleep eludes me for no reason I can discern. I spend the endless hours of night when all the world is at peace searching for the cause.

I've gone over the memory of Torlas's death so many times that its sharp edges have worn smooth. The look of defiance in his eyes, the resigned anger clenched in his jaw as he stared past me towards the throne, towards his true enemy. I knew, somewhere in my heart of hearts, what would happen the day I went to him in his office. We were children then, even though we thought we were so grown.

"I don't want to do this. But, if I have to, I must. I'm going to pit myself against your father, as much as the thought terrifies me to my core. I won't let you become like him. You need to be more. It isn't just that you can be human and a Shaper; they are one and the same. As long as you let me, I'll be here, reminding you."

I can't help thinking that Torlas would still be alive if I hadn't gone to him. He set himself against my father for me, not for himself. I pushed him down the path to treason.

And he walked it with his head held high, as he always did. Seeing him standing there, unrepentant, so full of hate…

"Do it, and be the monster he wishes you to be."

I flinched the first thousand times I heard those words in my memory, but now they sound less like a condemnation and more like a statement of fact.

I chose duty and responsibility over love, and in so doing I gave my father the tools to extinguish tens of thousands of human souls in a single moment. The cataclysmic wave didn't stop after destroying the army of the Republic, after all. The devastation stretched nearly a hundred miles. Dozens of fishing hamlets and minor ports were washed away in an hour, each of them full of our citizens. Human beings just going about their lives, oblivious to the drama playing out on the Way of the North, trusting their king to keep them safe… I traded the lives of our soldiers for the lives of our civilians. Any sane person would disagree with that arithmetic.

Those actions make me monstrous, but not a monster. What makes me a monster is that I can't find it in me to regret. I mourn his loss; I hate that Torlas is gone from the world, but I would not change the past. I've tried to make myself wish it, but I can't.

I *must* be a monster.

Abandoning the attempt to sleep, I roll out of the stifling cotton sheets. The thick blankets the servants originally placed on the bed rest in an untidy heap halfway across the room. Even with the windows open to allow in the cool breeze off the desert sands, I feel trapped and suffocated, an unwelcome visitor in a stranger's bed.

A startled gasp breaks the silence when I stand.

A figure moves in the darkness, darting towards the open doors of the balcony. Bright green light floods the room as I call to the earth. Strange shadows dance across the walls in forms jagged and monstrous. Before the intruder can reach freedom, spinning blades of glass fill the exit. The assassin lowers his head and barrels through anyway, jerking as two blades cut into his torso, one of them certainly deep. By the time I reach the balcony, though, the assassin has disappeared in the darkness. Either he sprouted wings and flew into the air, or he has the agility, even wounded, to scamper down the side of the smooth marble building. The night is still; the altercation was quiet enough that the Tide stationed outside my door don't bother to check on me.

Eternal damn my weakness. It was foolish to try to restrain him in the doorway. I should have cut his legs out from under him to be certain he couldn't flee. Next time I catch a stranger in my room, I won't be so merciful. My face contorts into a scowl. It's depressing not to have to question whether there will be a next time.

A few spots of blood speckle the balcony, the only proof of the stranger's visit. If he *was* an assassin, he was a terrible one, because he managed to creep unnoticed into my room, yet did me no harm. It had only been fortunate timing that allowed me to expose him at all. If he wasn't an assassin, though, then what purpose…?

The shifting glow of my power is not the greatest light by which to search, but I don't want to open the door to ask my guards for a lantern. I'd rather solve this mystery without involving anyone else. Especially Uncle. If I'm ever to step outside of the considerable shadows of the men who've dictated my life, I

69

need to start solving my own problems.

He began his flight near the oversized cedar desk across from the bed. Was the trespasser a spy? What did they hope to find in my personal chambers? With a slight effort of will, I brighten the light emanating from my shoulder. A scrap of parchment rests in the center of the empty desk. I frown, a bit disappointed. So much for a grand mystery to solve.

Written in flowing script more art than function, the short message makes little sense.

Tragedy is to be blinded rather than born blind.
If you wish to see, light up the night.

What in the Creator's name? What nonsense is this? Whoever he is, he went to the trouble of sneaking into my personal chamber, only to offer me riddles. Yet my heart quickens. A thrum of life pulses beneath my skin. I should probably be afraid that strangers can so easily pierce my defenses, but I want to know. I have no reason to trust a word this stranger might say to me, but, even so, my mind already races to solve this riddle.

Light up the night? There isn't a fireplace in my chambers. A lantern? I won't ask for one; the desire to keep this secret has only grown.

The moon rises. Her light limns the outward edges of the furniture silver just as my light burnishes the inward edges emerald. At the place where they intersect, the light diffuses in stages, a minute vision of the infinite shades of color separating silver and green. An idea strikes me as the pure light plays across the polished surfaces. Years ago, a lifetime ago it feels now, I had to display my power for a parade.

Giddy like a child, I open myself to the earth. Drifting in the wind and stirring in the streets, sand of the desert knows only the aching beat of the sun and the capricious whims of the wind. My will demands it forget its freedom and come together, a fractured whole coalescing as one until a curved edge of glass floats in the air at the edge of my balcony. Colorless, the moonlight burns shape into the invisible arc of shining glass. The light bends as it passes through, returning into itself and reflecting into the night. If I turn the glass just… so.

A beacon of pure white moonlight lances upward, stronger and brighter than I imagined it would be. Joy, unfettered and unabashed, glows in the shadow cast by the brilliant spear thrown into the sky. It has been so long since I've pushed myself for anything but violence. It has been so very long since I've made anything beautiful. I forgot that the power coursing through my veins could be anything more than a weapon.

Distant shouts echo through the streets. The shaft of light paints the sky silver, dimming the stars. It is so obvious a beacon it would be impossible to miss. If this mysterious stranger wanted a sign, I've given it to him a hundredfold. Reluctantly, feeling the moment slip through my fingers like a pleasant dream, I let the glass collapse again into dust. The rush of hopeful wonder recedes as surely as the tide.

In the darkness, I feel the shadows more deeply, as if the light has revealed doors long shut and forgotten.

What right have I to make anything beautiful?

The destruction I have wrought would stain even the purest soul.

What right have I to joy?

I have chosen sorrow.

***

Lentana doesn't come in to greet me in the morning. Dressed for training in a fitted tunic and pants, I hesitate in the empty room, wondering whether I should wait for the girl to show. After a moment standing alone in my silent room, though, I slip into well-worn leather boots and head for the door. Rather than the expected honor guard of Tide, Uncle waits for me outside my door. Towering nearly to the high ceiling, his handsome face does not break into his typical smile. My stomach drops as he folds his arms, feet planted squarely in the center of the hall. He's not the type for social calls, so this probably isn't going to be a pleasant conversation.

"Good morning, Uncle," I say awkwardly.

"Iliana." Creator, he looks like a thundercloud ready to spit lightning.

"There is no court today, Uncle. I had planned on training with the Tide in the grand hall…"

"Would you care to explain the… disturbance in your room last night?" he says abruptly.

"Disturbance?" I ask, knowing full well what he means. I don't know how he found out, but…

"The beam of light you shot into the sky."

"Oh." Relief floods through me. Just that. Uncle's frown deepens, as if he can read my thoughts. "I was experimenting. I didn't really expect to give quite that much of a show to the city, of course."

"Experimenting," he grunts.

"Yes. With how glass can reflect, bend, and actually strengthen light. Like a magnifying glass can focus sunlight into a single point, I crafted a larger lens to bend and focus moonlight."

"Interesting," he says, finally moving aside and opening a path for me to walk. "I didn't know you were working on anything in secret."

"Oh, it's not a secret," I say, struggling not to make it sound like a lie. "Just something I've been playing around with."

We take ten steps in silence. Well, I take ten. He takes four, long and graceful. Creator, is he bigger than he was? As the silence stretches, my nervousness grows. Does he know? Does he realize that I'm hiding something from him? Pressure grows between us, an invisible wave of expectation. I have to tell him, have to open my mouth and say what I know. There should be no secrets between us…

"Am I making you uncomfortable, Iliana?" he asks, not

72

turning to meet my concerned gaze.

"No, Uncle, I—"

Ahead, a young messenger appears, the thick metal anklet of a slave jangling on her ankle. Rummaging through the courier's bag at her side, she doesn't notice us until she nearly runs straight into Uncle. She can't be more than twelve, but already the first blossoming of classic Khalintari beauty glows in her cheeks. The look of terror on her face washes away my nerves in a wave of concerned calm.

"My, oh, your, uh…" she trails off, backing up slowly, her hand forgotten in the bag full of messages.

"Be at ease, child," I say warmly, stepping forward so that she focuses on me rather than the giant at my side. "Do you have a message for me?"

"Yes," she says breathlessly. "A message. For the queen. I'm looking for her."

"Well, you've found me," I say, smiling.

"Okay," she whispers.

"The message?" I prompt gently.

"Oh, right!"

She practically throws her head into the bag, though her exuberance will probably hinder her search rather than aid it. After a few seconds, Uncle grunts impatiently, stepping past the slender girl and moving rapidly down the hallway. He glances back at me, his eyes brooding.

"We'll talk soon," he says before disappearing through the doors exiting the east wing, my missing Tide on either side of the door slamming fist to chest in sharp salute.

"Right, here!" the girl says finally, drawing out a tightly rolled scroll hardly bigger than her hand and presenting it proudly.

"Thank you." A thought strikes me at the sight of her beautiful smile. "Who owns your contract, child?"

"Lady Saran, your Eminence," she says promptly.

"I see," I say with relief, the image of this girl called to the bedchamber of Eledar Cortola fading away. Though I have no idea who this 'Saran' woman is. "Well, thank you again."

"Your Eminence," she says, bowing her head formally before she spins and jogs after Uncle, breaking into a skip halfway to the door.

Unrolling the message, I nearly drop it when I see the same flowing calligraphy as before.

Speak not so loudly in your thoughts, lest they be heard.

To begin again to see, follow late walkers west.

I didn't expect them to contact me again so soon. Was the messenger girl one of them? The thought seems absurd, but I don't know anything about these people. They could be recruiting children as an expendable resource rather than putting their own lives at risk. And of course, they continue to speak in riddles. Speak not so loudly in your thoughts? Who can hear thoughts?

The Master of Thought can. His dark eyes, mocking and knowing, flash across my consciousness. Of course.

"I will be there. In the heart of Coin. Until then…"

Perhaps he is here, just as he promised more than four years ago. And these people are warning me that… what? He is listening? Creator. What a nightmare. I can't even trust that my own thoughts won't betray me. All of my doubts, my fears, my pain… so much of what I once thought sacrosanct can be used against me, if I offer the wrong thought to the wrong person. I haven't seen him. I would recognize his face anywhere now that I've thrown off the mental block he put in my memory.

Frowning, I crumple the message in my fist. Letting my steps carry me towards the hall and the soldiers waiting to spar with me, I start to parse out the second half of the message. The meaning of 'late walkers' seems obvious, but west? The west gate? People walking generally west? If they're expecting me to end up at the west gate of Coin at midnight for a convenient ambush, they had better keep dreaming.

My heart tells me they aren't hostile. No, I bet it's something close to home, probably the west wing of the House of the Republic or nearby.

As we reach the doors into the grand hall, I put the cryptic nonsense from my mind. A dozen soldiers stand at attention in full battle regalia, armor gleaming in the slanted rays of early morning sun filtered through the windows high above. Here, finally, I can let it all go, the sorrow, the confusion, the doubt. I have to be focused, sharp, all distracting thoughts surrendered to the needs of the body. At my signal, they draw their swords, assuming ready stances. Calling to the earth, I leap to meet them.

Chapter 4
Bastian
The Sixty-Fourth Day of Summer
In the year 5223, Council Reckoning

Sweat soaks the cloth wrapped around my face, suffocating, but I do my best to ignore the need to rip it away. As I clench my hand into a fist to stifle the urge, the burning sands shift under me with a thin whisper. The sun looks on as it drifts across the noontide sky, oblivious to its blinding heat. At cursory glance, none of the others are visible, though the torrid haze makes it difficult to see. I can't last much longer, though. If I don't get out of the oven I dug for myself, I'm going to suffocate.

The sand starts to shake and tremble before my nose, and relief pours into my mind like a cooling draft. It's no less hot, but at least the wait will soon be over.

Opening myself to Thought, I reach out and establish a loose connection to the fighters arrayed around the beaten track of earth that passes for a road through this part of the desert. Their cold discipline and unbroken stoicism might make a better man feel shame for his weakness, but that man isn't me. If I have to spend one more minute trapped in the boiling sand, I'm going to burn my own mind out. Whatever passes for my conscience tries to nudge me towards some kind of sad connection between Lav and the errant thought, but I'm spared the introspection by the arrival of the caravan.

They've doubled the escort. More than two dozen soldiers ride on either side of the heavy wagons, their heavy blue armor jangling in an overloaded wagon at the back of the caravan. It's far too hot to wear plate, but the Empire soldiers haven't had time to adapt their fighting style to the shifting sands. As it is, they are vulnerable in sweat-soaked gambesons.

Freeing Commander Ghali, as it turns out, was a stroke of pure prophetic genius. She and her Spearsisters have been the backbone of what resistance we've managed to mount. The Khal coerced or purchased elements of the Steed and wisely placed every military asset under Ghali's command. It was Ghali's idea to harry the supply lines, and her knowledge that led us to successfully take half a dozen caravans filled with the foodstuffs earmarked for Empire use. I brush my consciousness across her mind where she waits across the road. Unfathomable and impenetrable, the lightning-quick path of her thoughts is calculating a thousand variables in an instant, each coming together to choose the perfect—

She slows her thoughts to a crawl to mentally shout the command to attack. An accommodation for me, of course.

Instantly, I echo the pulse of urgency to the others. The sand explodes around the caravan in unison as our fighters heed the silent command. The horses rear and startle, spilling several riders to the sand. Before they can begin to regain their composure, the Spearsisters are among them, their silver blades soon glistening red. A half step behind, the Khal of Nothing brawlers fall on the remaining soldiers, their methods brutal but no less effective. Agile men leap onto the backs of horses and go to work with short daggers.

A soldier bursts from the bedlam on a black horse and gallops directly towards me. The sword she raises is already red, matching the bleeding cut across her ribs. Her thought is of escape, not revenge, but she knows that running me down will allow her the space to flee.

The coolness of her reasoning would be impressive if it wasn't leading directly towards my death. A blast of chaotic thought scrambles her focus, and the sword falls from her limp hand. Absent her direction, the horse, trained for war, lowers its head and charges.

Ah. Shit.

By the time I think to move, it's far too late. A thousand pounds of angry horse fills my vision. Somehow, all I notice is how beautiful the sun glistens on its ebony flank.

A flash of blurring movement to my left. A lithe woman, curled into a tight muscular ball, slams into the horse's shoulder. I stare, dumbfounded, as the massive creature hardly checks its stride. She must have deflected it somewhat, though, for its head turns at the last instant. One moment, I'm staring death in the face, and the next I'm eating sand, the world tilting underneath me.

Groaning, I roll onto my side, my ribs spiking agony with every shift. Someone might tell me I'm lucky to be alive, but, from the pain in my chest, I'd tell them to fuck right off. My spinning vision settles eventually.

It hasn't been more than a few heartbeats, and the conflict is all but ended. The only remaining Empire combatants are a pair of soldiers who managed to break free and gallop towards the horizon to the east. A few Spearsisters pursue on horseback, but more as a herding measure than to catch the panicked men. The Khal's people will ensure they never reach the Way.

Peeling away the sweat-soaked cloth, the sweet relief of open air caresses my face. Its tender touch does little to dispel the deep ache in my chest. The scalding sand of the desert wars with the angry gaze of the sun for which can be the first to wring the last drops of sweat from my body.

Creator, Eternal, whoever might be listening, I hate you.

After a moment, a silhouette blocks the sun. Commander Ghali crouches on the balls of her feet. Without bothering to ask for permission, she reaches over and sticks a finger in my side. I flinch with an involuntary whimper, but she pokes around despite my feeble protests. She sits back on her heels and watches with a disturbingly satisfied air as I writhe in pain and clutch at my ribs.

"Why are you so cruel?" I mutter.

"Quit being a baby," she says finally. "Your ribs might be cracked, but you'll be fine."

"It feels like I'm dying," I groan, glaring at her.

"You probably should be," she agrees, her lips twisting into a frown.

A bit of blood leaks from the corner of her mouth, and her shoulder hangs a little off. A bruise already discolors the side of her face and arm. Even in my pain, I put two and two together.

"Thank you," I say, meaning each word despite the pain.

"You're too valuable to lose this early on," she says simply, shrugging with her good shoulder. "Seems foolish to lose the Master of Thought to a runaway horse."

"I have to agree."

"Regardless, I'm sending you back to Coin," she says, offering me a hand. I ignore the offer, quite comfortable on the sand for the moment. And I know damn well she plans to yank me to my feet. Instead, I shoot her a curious look, to which she shrugs again. "You have no training and no experience in combat. I've had to keep my eye on you in every fight, attention I could have spent protecting my sisters. The coordination you offer is valuable, but I don't think it outweighs the risks."

She turns her head and tilts her chin towards a Spearsister lying on the sand, two of her brethren wrapping cloth around her midsection. She may live, but only the Creator knows which way the scales will tip. Her thoughts are overwhelmed by pain. Ghali chooses that moment to deliberately slow her thoughts and show me a memory.

My eyes flick towards the Shaper, standing frozen and alone off to the side. A rider bears down on his position, blade raised. Twisting my spear free of the dying soldier in front of me, I spin away from further combat and burst away. A cry of anger and surprise erupts behind me. Reila expected me to be there, defending her. Already regretting my choice, but too late to take it back, I plant my spear in the sand at full sprint. It bends, creaking in protest, then snaps forward, launching me into the air. Curling to protect myself, I brace to slam into the horse's flank...

"I can fight," I say defensively, offended in spite of the inner voice screaming agreement to her every word. "I could burn away their minds far more easily than you with your silly spears."

"Which we already agreed is a waste of your talent, and a risk that we shouldn't take. I already indulged you by bringing you out here in the first place."

She sighs as a Spearsister approaches and offers her a questioning look. With an impatient gesture, Ghali gives her assent, and the woman takes a firm grip on her arm. With a sharp jerk and an audible crunch, Ghali's shoulder snaps back into place. Aside from a single hitch in her steady breathing, she doesn't react. Eternal's forgotten tomb, I'm glad she's on our side. Even reading her thoughts, I can no more fathom her mind than I can the soul of a rock.

"Well, damn," I say softly. "I guess I'll take that hand now."

"Why did you want to come out here, anyway?" she asks, lifting me to my feet. I can't restrain my yelp, though she doesn't comment. Of course, she doesn't have to. "This doesn't seem like the battlefield you would choose."

"It was Tana's idea," I admit, shaking my head. "She can be extremely persuasive when she wants to be. Something about broadening my skillset or learning or something. To be honest, I was only half-paying attention. I didn't want to be there. Coin, under the tyranny of another... it's sickening, you know? And I feel..."

"Culpable?"

"Maybe."

"That's fool's talk," she says, rolling her shoulder. "I didn't take you for a fool. My predecessor, on the other hand..."

The previous Minister of Spears had been the driving force behind our foolhardy commitment to the war against the

Kingdom of the Sea. Though the Khal of Nothing and I both agreed with the sentiment, we didn't imagine that she would convince the others to throw the Shield into the fray. Ghali's words rest uneasily in my thoughts. I *am* at fault, at least partly. I forced Cortola to overstep his words, to lose his momentum and stray into hypothetical fears... fears which turned out to be well-founded.

I was only partly honest with the commander. Part of me despairs at seeing Coin brought low, but, more, I just can't sit by as others deal with the problems I helped create. I want to *do* something, damn it, and there is little I can do in Coin. The Empire presence there is far too strong. Out here, at least I can feel like I'm getting something done, taking the fight to our enemies.

She's right, though. I'm more of a liability than an asset out in the desert. My arena is crafted of silk and song, not blade and blood. Though I may make a show of resisting, I'll follow the caravan east. The Khal's forces and the Spearsisters strip down the stolen goods and disguise the wagons with remarkable efficiency, so I imagine I won't have to wait long.

Glancing up at the glaring sun, a smile cracks the grime and sweat caked on my face. At least I'll be able to take a bath again.

***

The thick wheels of the desert wagon roll smoothly over the sands behind the plodding backs of the draft horses. Bred for wide hooves and unflagging strength, the quality of even these simple beasts of burden are a testament to the long bloodlines of the Steed. The reins dangle loosely from my hands; the horses know their business far better than I do. The thin wagon cover, designed to block the sun but permit the breeze, flaps to an unseen gust. I let my head loll against the wooden headboard. Worn smooth by countless riders doing the same, the wood feels both comforting and disconcerting. Just like the ancient doors of

Coin, the smooth contours of the wagon speak to age beyond measure.

Though some of the supplies were sent to rebel bases throughout the desert, most of the wagon train went north after the ambush. We don't actually want the people of Coin to suffer from our predations. Rather, the vast majority of the supplies are smuggled into the city at night and quietly distributed to the populace. Officially, our raids will slow the flood of supplies to the capital to a trickle, but, if we do our job right, only the Empire will feel the bite of their lack.

Threading the needle between the Vein and the Way, a week's journey will bring us to Coin. Trapped in the silent desert of this unmarked land, however, an echo of disquiet whispers through my mind. My half dozen men, Hands under Gabriel's command, avoid me, their thoughts practically shouting their fear. They've been warned of who and what I am, and they have no desire to fall under my sway. Not that I'd bother. The fanatics surrounding the Khal would notice any irregular behavior, and the Khal herself seems to have a preternatural ability to detect lies and deceit. And what do I have to gain? She is, at least for now, my staunchest ally.

The two Spearsisters traveling north, on the other hand, could care less about my presence. They go about their tasks with quiet efficiency, keeping company only with each other. They ignore me and the Khal's men in equal measure. So I'm left to my own devices. Never a good time. My thoughts, especially surrounded by the uncaring expanse of nature, always turn the same direction.

What am I before the endless dunes? No matter what I do, I will be forgotten. If I am even marked in the first place.

For some reason, the thought doesn't fill me with the despair it once did. The certainty I felt standing in a half-forgotten alley in Coin still lingers. Though the emptiness of the endless sands creeps into my very being, nuggets of certainty stand like river stones against the current. Coin is my home, and in it are the only people I care about. Jynn, her tiny body unable to contain the extraordinary strength of her personality. Lav, the brother who loves me despite my sins, who knows me through the tide of madness I wrought. Even Saran, the cold woman others know as Khal, who allowed me past the walls of the fortress she built around herself. And, of course, there is Coin itself, the gorgeous Jewel of the West, glittering in the midst of desert sands and defiant of the scouring wind. If there is anything from which to take inspiration, it is my impossible city.

The prospect of their company is enough to hold back the ennui of the sands.

What would Te'ial say?

Thriska Cursed. Your soul knows sadness because it is tainted. You deserve to feel this way.

The thought, echoed in the derisive tones of the captain, brings a smile to my lips. Even if she hated me on a fundamental level, she still took care of me and chose to set me free. I will die unsatisfied if I never see her disapproving grimace again.

"Coin!" one of the Khal's men shouts ahead joyfully.

That single syllable drags me upright and forward, lassitude forgotten.

Not Coin. Home.

***

The Way of the West continues north under the great southern gate of Coin. A line of traffic waiting to be let into the city moves forward in fits and starts. Soldiers of the Wave stand conspicuously under the shadow of the gate in their brilliant azure armor. Though I'm sure it gleams prettily, they may as well set themselves on fire as spend an hour under the sun trapped in that metal prison.

The draft horses pulling my wagon fall in line with the traffic without my input, lazily plodding forward. I'm alone; as soon as the city came into view, the stolen caravan split into a dozen individual or paired wagons so as not to arouse suspicion. The soldiers wave me through after a thorough investigation of the wagon's contents. I'd be nervous, but there's nothing illegal to find. Everything was already meant for Coin before we stole it. It just won't arrive where they think it will.

It might be subtle to a foreigner, but the streets feel empty. Soldiers in various states of broiling stand at every corner, and their oppressive presence joins the scorching late Summer sun to suppress the boundless energy of Coin. It's a blessing; now that we're in the city, I have to take an active hand in guiding the horses, and I don't trust myself not to run over some poor pedestrian. A few blocks into the city, I leave the Way of the West and head east towards the appointed rendezvous. A brief brush of power wipes any interest from the soldiers' minds along with the memory of my passing.

A few blocks later, trundling along a less-traveled street, a man in dark clothing steps in front of the wagon. The deep shadows of his hood hide his features even in the bright afternoon sun. I pull on the reins, bringing the wagon to a halt before I run him down. When I reach out with my mind, his thoughts are an empty hole in the fabric of space, not like he doesn't exist, but rather as if a wall has been erected around his consciousness. I stretch out my senses in all directions and feel another of the aberrant voids coming up behind me. Even if I can't feel them, maybe I can still…

Sending out a sliver of will, I try to deflect the figure's attention, imparting the urge to step aside, to let me pass. He steps forward instead. He doesn't appear to move quickly, but he's next to me before I can react, a short blade held in his hand. I start to scramble away, but a second figure appears on the other side of the wagon. Fuck. I should have just run him over.

"Bastian Batir," the first man says, tilting his head so I can see his face. He is Donirian, bland, unremarkable, but nonetheless frightening in his lack of expression. "You will come with us."

"Listen, guys, I don't know who you think you've got here, but…"

"Do not try to resist," the other figure, a woman, says flatly. "Your death, here in the city, would be inconvenient."

"Inconvenient?" I say incredulously. "The potential shattering of thousands of minds is *inconvenient?*"

"Yes."

The flatness of her response is all the more terrifying. I send another burst of thought into the void, more powerful than the first. Neither shows any sign of even noticing the attack. Panic claws at my stomach as the man levers himself up next to me. His dagger presses to my side, and I freeze.

"Our master would like to speak to you, Batir," the man says firmly. "But it is a desire, not a necessity. Do not get any ideas of escape or resistance, for I will not hesitate."

"Who is your master?"

"You will see soon enough."

The woman slides onto the wagon bench on my other side, her dagger replacing the man's as he takes up the reins of the horses. We trundle forward, the sharp point of the knife pricking my side with each jostling step. Warm blood trickles down my side.

Their minds remain voids to my senses, unnatural pits from which no thought escapes. Whoever their master is, he has some knowledge of Thought and how it works. While most of my consciousness devotes itself to shouting a litany of terror, the puzzle of it all lurks beneath the surface. The walls set up around their thoughts block me out too effectively to be anything but deliberate. An Ensouled of Thought, like Jynn, must have crafted this impenetrable wall. The more I think about it, and the more my senses scrape along the edges of their defenses, the better I understand it. Much like how Ulia blocked me from my power in the Isles, if I could set up a shield around a person's mind, I might be able to create a similar effect, but it wouldn't last very long.

85

The thought gives me a spark of hope.

If I can delay them, distract them, perhaps… but no. The point of the woman's dagger is already wet with my blood. I believe them when they say they'll kill me, damn the consequences. Yet they haven't, which means their master would prefer me alive.

Steeling myself, I loosen my limbs and let my body sag against the headboard. The point of the dagger digs into my side, but the woman removes it before it can scrape along my rib. The fresh wound leaks blood more freely than the last. The pressure of the dagger's point returns, lighter than before. As the wagon rattles across a loose stone in the street, I clench my jaw and let the momentum carry me towards the woman. The dagger bites into my side for an instant before she pulls it away, cursing.

"Are you trying to kill me?" I groan, clutching at the wound. I wish the performance was pure theatrics, but that last one really hurt. "I'm doing as you ask."

"Sit up straight," she snaps in annoyance.

"I am," I say.

"Quiet," the man says, his eyes scanning the crowd.

"I'm doing what you want," I say loudly. "And you stabbed me."

A few passersby glance up in alarm. The assassin's blade appears like magic against my throat, though the way he holds his arm conceals the weapon from easy view. A large man in the silks of a noble house steps forward, but hesitates as the woman turns to face him.

"I said quiet. I know what you're trying to do. Word will never reach your friends in time for them to save you."

"I'm not trying anything," I say weakly, raising my hand and waggling my blood-drenched fingers. "It hurts."

"It'll hurt a lot more if you don't shut your mouth," he says evenly.

"Fine."

His dagger disappears again, and he returns to guiding the horses. I make a show of favoring my side, satisfied. It might be a small victory, but the blade's pressure is absent. I've got room to work. The thought nearly draws a snort of derision out of me. Here I am, thinking like I have any chance of escaping these people. They're clearly professionals, and I barely know which end of a knife to hold. Not that I *have* a knife to hold. I just know that, wherever we're going and whoever they're taking me to, I don't want to go. Better to die here by my own choice.

Trying not to show it, I shift into a position where I can see the woman out of the corner of my eye. The dagger rides in her lap, ready for use but far enough that I've earned myself a split second. Maybe, if I throw an elbow at her head, I can surprise her…

The warning look she gives me as I start to tense is more than enough to deflate what little courage I've managed to gather. Creator, what was I thinking? Overpower two prepared assassins with my imaginary physical prowess? I have far more dangerous weapons. Sweeping my senses in all directions, a dozen minds are within easy reach of my power. Flitting from one to another, searching…

…three silvers is all I need, but if this greedy bastard will give me four…

…half-rotten already, he'd be lucky to get a few coppers…

…can't watch where he's going. What an ass, doesn't care where people are walking…

There.

Jumping from the indignant pedestrian to the object of her ire, my consciousness settles behind the eyes of a weary farmer prodding uninterestedly at a donkey hooked to his wagon with a stick worn smooth with use. He doesn't notice anything past the animal's back, dull eyes staring sightlessly ahead. His wagon, empty after a long day's effort selling to merchants of the city, rumbles carelessly over the stones. He's going too slowly to reach the intersection in time to matter. All it might take, though, is a little motivation.

The crack of the farmer's stick striking the donkey's flank echoes through the quiet street. Startled braying shatters the peace of the scorching afternoon. Driving the farmer to smack the donkey once more, I take control of his hands and drag the reins sharply to the right before jumping back to my own body. The assassins have stiffened at my side. The farmer's wagon rumbles across the intersection, careening back and forth under the panicked power of an irate ass. A slave throws down a heavy parcel and dives out of the way just before the wagon tramples over the box. The farmer, shouting curses, desperately saws at the reins.

The assassin pulls on reins of his own, though his intervention isn't necessary. The well-trained horses of the Steed have already stopped. The donkey crashes into a stall selling bananas with a splintering crack. The wagon lurches to a halt halfway up the stall, a broken wheel spinning uselessly in the air. The snap of taut leather heralds the frantic beast's escape, though the clatter of its hooves is lost to the shouts of outrage from the people on the street. As all humans are drawn to catastrophe like flies to honey, a crowd forms like magic.

"Cern..." the woman says, glancing across to meet her companion's eyes.

"Is this your doing, Batir?" the man growls, his dagger snapping back to my throat.

"Me?" I feign surprise. "That's way outside my range."

"Eternal damn it." The farmer's wagon rests halfway across the road, but the crowd of people gathered has grown to several dozen, completely halting all traffic. "We'll walk. Stay close."

It's tempting to complain, to grab my side and stagger, but even without the ability to read their thoughts I gather that any more setbacks will turn our relationship lethal. That doesn't leave me entirely powerless, though. Any overt use of power will lead to a knife through the ribs. I have to be subtle. And break my mind in two so that I can walk and Shape at the same time.

As we push into the densely packed crowd, I open myself to the power. A dozen thoughts blossom at once, worries and joy and annoyance. To swim against the tide would be to drown in it, so I surrender, flowing along with the current of annoyance and breathing in the eddies of curiosity. Taking complete control would be tantamount to suicide, as my body would lose all grace and coordination the second my attention leaves.

No, I have to try something else, something new. I developed the ability to passively divert attention in dangerous areas over months of intentional concentration and effort. I'm now skilled enough at it that I'm rarely memorable to anyone I meet in passing. What if I just... reverse it? Concentrating on my steps, grounding my soul through the firm grip the man has on my arm and the dagger pricking into my good side, I send out a pulse of power.

Look over here.

The two shielded minds at my side don't react, of course. In this, their greatest weapon is also a weakness. As the power washes out, heads begin to turn. First one, then another, then half a dozen. Too many. Shit. Too many.

Don't look over here.

The attention in our direction wavers and returns to the crash. Okay, 'looking' might not have been the best idea. What will attention do but earn me a shallow grave in the desert? I need to delay our progress, slow us down, allow time for the protection these two have to fade.

Provided I'm right about how the shield was created. For all I know, the wall around their consciousness is a permanent alteration. If that's the case, of course, I'm as good as dead, so it's not really worth dwelling on.

Closer.

89

The pulse of intent ripples through the crowd. Half a dozen take a step forward. A man stumbles into my captor, who shoves him aside while keeping a firm grip on my arm.

Closer.

The crowd tightens as more people unwittingly push towards the crash. Weaving through the press becomes difficult. People are reluctant to move aside, especially after they see under the hoods and recognize the Donirian faces glaring at them. I welcome the feeling of claustrophobia that rises in me as the people press in around us. The day is hot, and the heady scents of sweat and perfume twine together into a sickening miasma.

"Cern..." the woman says again, shoving aside a slender man and glaring at her companion.

"Quit saying my name. We're almost there," he mutters, though his voice is nearly lost in the press.

Closer.

Movement becomes impossible. The crush of bodies unnaturally drawn together is suffocating. In desperation, Cern lashes out, his blade returning red. The initial cry of pain is drowned by shouting. The victim, a woman with a fresh gash across her chest, screams again in pain and horror as his dagger cuts us a bit of breathing room. People turn at the sound and finally notice the blood decorating my side and the red daggers in my captors' hands. The mood turns ugly, as the heat, the excitement, and the sudden presence of hostile Donirians set fire to the drought-laden field that is the people of Coin.

As Cern brandishes his blade threateningly, a man steps up behind him with a rock grasped in his fist. Cern's partner stabs through his forearm before he can bring the stone down, but takes a vicious blow from someone else in return. The two Donirians exchange a look fraught with meaning. In one moment rendered glacial by terror, their eyes flick to me.

I've made a mistake. I wanted to slow our progress, not incite a riot. The anger of the people is far more potent than I realized. The assassins know they won't make it out of here, not with me slowing their progress. So they'll cut the anchor.

My denial surges forth in an explosion of power. The hostile crowd disappears as a torrent of fear blasts through their minds. Some fall to their knees, though many more flee blindly, all thoughts subsumed beneath a rising tide of panic. Cern and his compatriot, damn it all, do not waver. He tightens his grip, tensing to strike, any thought of dragging me onwards gone.

I shout into his face, a meaningless final gesture of despair.

His facade cracks, his eyes widen in terror, and he spins to sprint away, stumbling over bodies of people paralyzed by fear.

I stand, dumbfounded, as he scrabbles on hands and knees in his haste to flee. He's gone before I can think to turn and see what his partner is doing. She cowers on the ground, her dagger forgotten at her side, head clasped in her hands. Slowly, carefully, I step beside her to retrieve the weapon. She whimpers at the sight of my dusty boots.

The street looks like it suffered from an invisible explosion. People lie in a circle about me, draped over one another like matchsticks. Many sprinted blindly in their fear until they ran into something solid. Several lie unconscious with bleeding head wounds, while others writhe on the ground with limbs twisted in unnatural angles. Surrounded by carnage of my own creation, I can do nothing but watch as the world returns to life. The thoughts of the assassin whimpering on the ground are clear as day; whatever protection she had is broken.

A stranger turns a corner ahead, features contorting with confusion. The distant thought to flee the scene flits in and out of my consciousness. Part of the strength of my power is in anonymity, and I can't get much farther from secrecy than this. Yet here I stand at the epicenter of the mental explosion, curiously staring at a victim.

"Bastian!"

The sound of my name recalls my wayward focus.

"Bastian! Move!"

Ah. Right. Someone is calling me. Thinking feels like trying to shove a palace across a river. The world is a collection of whites and grays, colored and yet colorless, moving and yet frozen. By the time my eyes move to see who is calling my name, a decade has passed, but her frantic motions are lightning-swift, hands blurring.

"Jynn?" I say, or try to, at least.

The second I catch her eyes, she appears at my side.

"That's a neat trick. When did you get so fast?" I ask, puzzled. "Your legs are too short to teleport."

"Did the sun addle your brain?" she snaps, this child who is most definitely not a child. Her tiny elfin features crinkle into angry disbelief. "What are you doing just standing here?"

"A woman wanted to hurt me," I say, gesturing vaguely. My hand is covered in blood. "Oh! She *did* hurt me."

"Bastian," Jynn says, laying her small hand on my cheek and turning my face towards hers. Recognition blossoms in her dark eyes, and she shakes her head slowly. Or quickly. Hard to say right now. The solemn concern on her face doesn't fit the stature of her body, and I laugh at the sight. "Not all there right now, are we?"

"Hah! I'm not the one who teleported in the middle of the street."

"Sure, sure," she says, pulling my hand. She sounds like she's talking to a toddler. "Come on, buddy. I'll teach you how to teleport later."

"I don't know if you can teach me," I say, the words leaving my lips without any conscious thought behind them. "I'm normal sized."

"Right, I forgot." She sounds like she's trying not to laugh. I get the vague feeling that I should be offended. "I can get you a grown-up teacher later."

"Thank you. That would be nice."

The problem of my education solved, I let her lead me away from the fallen people. I'm not sure if I believe her. Teleporting would be nice, though. Walking is such a bore. And exhausting. It'll be good to get away from all the shouting. It makes my head hurt. I don't know why everyone is always so angry these days.

Following Jynn into an alley, we appear in front of a door that, in my estimation, is halfway across the city. The feeling would be off-putting if I hadn't just learned that Jynn can teleport.

"Wow!"

"What?" she asks warily. It makes me wonder what else I might have said.

"I didn't know you could take me with you!"

***

It feels like morning. It's hard to tell, since I woke up in one of the endless basements connected to the Khal's secret tunnels beneath the city. How I got here is less material than why I can't remember. My nose wrinkles. I got used to my stench out in the desert, far from civilization and the comforts it offers, but the contrast with the clean scent of incense and freshly brewed *shial* brings reality crashing home.

Staggering up the stairs, feeling strangely untethered from the world, I pause and listen at the sound of feminine voices. I recognize each of them, though they speak too softly to be understood. Normally, I'd listen through my power, but my very being shies away from the idea of tapping Thought right now. Yesterday's explosion clearly did something to me. Instinctually, like a broken limb, I know it's better to limp right now than to run.

The voices halt as I push open the door.

"In here, Bastian," Jynn calls from the living area near the front of the house.

The furnishings are spare and unappealing, little more than a broken divan and a few boxes shoved against the wall, a far cry from the sumptuous decor in the Khal's personal safehouse where

I first met her. Even so, the Khal looks closer to royalty than poverty, even sitting on a dusty crate. Her simple vest and pants appear to fit the setting, but the richness of the finely spun linen would put kings to shame. The golden script traced along each hem tells a story I wouldn't dare look close enough to read. If she thought I was checking her out, she might just follow through with her promise to bleed me out in the desert.

Jynn sits carelessly on a broken end table, swinging her legs and evidently oblivious to her seat's alarming wobble. Every time I see her, I have to remind myself that she's a five-thousand-year-old warrior so legendary that the world still remembers her name. Mostly, at least, which is still a tender subject. She nearly spoiled the literal purpose for her existence and doomed the world to death and darkness because she couldn't control her anger when she saw a statue bearing her name and a male likeness. She does not take kindly to jokes about that night. Just because she happens to inhabit the body of a twelve-year-old doesn't make her any less dangerous.

I'm surprised to see Tana sitting stiffly on the divan, a hand pressed to her side. When I left for the desert, Jynn and I had just managed to get her chosen as the queen's personal servant. Getting her to open up her thoughts enough to doctor her memories had been a trial, but ultimately worth it if our suspicions about the Lord General are true. Ever since the parade at Midspring when he seemed to notice my examination of the queen's mind, we've been on the lookout for signs of our power's use. Servants with gaps in their memory, fanatics blinded by faith, people agreeing to things outside of their character… Though subtle, we've seen enough signs to assume that he probably has an Ensouled of Thought working for him. Considering my experience with the assassins, I think any doubt can safely be set aside.

"All there, Batir?" the Khal says, a smile in her voice if not on her face.

"Sure you didn't just blink your way up the steps?" Jynn asks smugly, a sadistic grin twisting her adorable face.

"Way to kick a man when he's down," I groan, settling onto the cool stone floor with my back to the wall. "Was it that bad?"

"You asked me three times if we could *think* ourselves onto a star." Jynn's tinkling laughter is far too malicious. "Classic."

"What happened to me?"

"You gave up too much of your soul," she says, her smile faltering. "Most Shapers just get sleepy before they can get too close to the edge. If you push past your natural limit, either through stubborn will or, like in your case, burn your energy all at once, strange things happen as your body starts to shut down. Your muddled thoughts were a sign of how close to death you really were."

"But I feel fine, neh?" I glance between them, eyebrows raised. "It was that close?"

"It's been three days," the Khal says simply.

"Ah. Right. Okay," I say, coughing into a fist. I glance between them, a sudden doubt rising. "Can I ask a question?"

"You aren't hallucinating Tana," Jynn says, any last trace of her humor disappearing. "She nearly died last night to deliver a message to the queen."

"She reacted quickly," Tana says, utterly failing to hide the pain lurking behind her words. "I thought I could get in and out without her noticing, but, apparently, she's a light sleeper."

"You interrupted our discussion of what to do next," the Khal says. "Since the girl *you* demanded that we try to save, based entirely on a chance meeting years ago when she was barely fifteen, nearly killed one of our own."

"Hey, I just wanted to give the girl a chance," I say, turning up my hands. "And it's not based entirely on that meeting. You can't feel what she's been through like Jynn and I can. No one deserves what that girl has endured."

95

"We have—had—Lentana at her side, with easy access to her bedchambers. We could have killed her a dozen times over by now." The Khal leans forward, her elbows on her knees and her eyes smoldering. "Isn't our goal to drive the Empire from our land? What better way than to remove one of the very pillars of their power?"

"And if we could turn her to our side? Wouldn't it be even better to ally ourselves with a Shaper as capable as she is?"

"Better to take her off the table entirely. We could never trust her, even if we did manage to pry her from the Lord General's side," the Khal counters.

"I say she's worth trying for."

"Would you trade her life for Tana's?" she asks as if she's genuinely curious as to the answer.

"Of course not, but—"

"He isn't wrong," Tana says softly. "There is so much about her that I like, so much that demands to be respected, even followed, but I can't figure her out. In one moment she is kind and caring, but in the next she threatens the death of innocents. She… defended me… when she had nothing to gain by doing so."

"And she did light up the night. Super bright," Jynn says, crossing her legs at the ankles. "Even if she nearly killed Tana, it was probably in self-defense."

"I need to return to her side," Tana says firmly.

"She'll make you the second you show up with those wounds," the Khal says, waving her hand dismissively.

"Not if Tana forgets how to feel pain," Jynn says cheerfully, like it's the most natural thing in the world.

Chapter 5
Kettle
The Forty-Sixth Day of Spring
In the year 5223, Council Reckoning

The soldiers decorating the manicured yard in front of Hona's estate fall silent, heads to the ground, hands outstretched. Towards me. Their whispered reverence lingers on the air like the melody of wind through the trees. The shadow blades in my hands dissolve into smoke and creep away from the rising sun under my disheveled clothing. Suddenly self-conscious, I pick unsuccessfully at the twisted straps.

"Um, Hona?" I say after a moment, trailing off as the sound of my voice sends a trembling ripple through the backs of the soldiers.

When he doesn't respond, I glance at him sidelong, trying to keep the soldiers in sight. Blood leaks from his nose where one of the soldiers struck him, but he doesn't seem to notice. His eyes are wide and staring, his expression shocked and disbelieving, his mouth gaping open.

"Hona?" He doesn't react to his name, nor to the sudden presence of the Family as they file out of his house. "Hona."

"Eshani!" he says, scrambling until he can press his forehead to the ground in the same posture as the soldiers. "Forgive me."

"Hona, get up." He tenses, but doesn't lift his eyes from the ground. "Seriously. We broke bread together last night. You helped me fix my broken wagon. Do you really think this is necessary?"

"But…"

"Get. Up."

Hesitantly, he climbs to his feet, eyes still cast to the ground. The soldiers remain motionless. The tips of their spears sparkle like edged diamonds in the morning light. Aurelion sprints around the corner after a moment, bare chested and sword in hand. He skids to a halt at the surreal sight spread before him. Ezil steps up beside me, eyeing the waiting soldiers warily.

"Do you have any idea what is happening?"

"They've been saying that word," I murmur, trying not to let my voice carry. "Eshani. Didn't Hona say something about that last night?"

"Are you telling me they think that you're some sort of god?" she asks.

"Surely not..." Staring at the sight of the men with their faces pressed to the earth, the morning air charged with expectant energy, my stomach drops. "By the Depths, maybe they do."

One of the men lifts his head from the ground, though his face remains down, and begins to shout in his native tongue. After his outburst, he practically slams his forehead to the ground, every limb trembling.

"Hona?" I ask, voice rising. "I could use a little help here..."

"I... I am not worthy to—"

"The man begs your forgiveness for daring to speak without leave, but humbly desires to know what you wish of your servants, lady Eshani."

Myn, face down just outside the door, speaks confidently, fluidly, her tone deferential yet still bearing the steel it held last night. The top of her head bobs once, her black hair streaked with thin tendrils of white. I can hardly believe that this proud woman would bow.

"Myn, look at me," I say, my voice echoing as if traveling down a long tunnel.

Her eyes, dark pools of midnight, shine with unshed tears. Her lip quivers, not with sorrow, but with suppressed joy. What little remains to tether me to a world resembling mine snaps at the sight.

"I'm going inside," I say, feeling suddenly dizzy.

"What should I tell the soldiers, Eshani?"

"Tell them whatever you like."

I nearly stumble as I try to walk, but Ezil catches my arm, leaning close.

"Straighten up. Look regal. I don't know what in the Eternal's name is going on, but I do know one thing," she hisses in my ear. "We need to look the part."

Meeting her eyes for the barest glimmer of a moment, I give her a subtle nod. Lifting my chin, concentrating on putting one foot in front of the other, I manage to stride with some measure of confidence into the manor. The second I make it to the sitting room, I slump into one of the soft leather chairs. The distant sound of Myn calling in her native tongue is answered by one of the soldiers. After a quick conversation, she enters and comes to stand in the doorway. Her eyes do not lift from the floor.

"Myn, I'm going to need an explanation about what just happened out there."

"The good soldiers of Dusk have pledged their allegiance to the Eshani," she answers promptly. "As is right."

"And by Eshani, you mean..."

"Yes, my lady. You."

"I'm not who you think I am," I say immediately, shaking my head. "And I don't want their allegiance."

"Do you possess living shadow?" Myn says softly, her eyes peering up at mine. "Does it answer your call?"

"Yes, but—"

"Then you are the Nightmother, the queen prophesied to return darkness to the light."

"Myn, be serious." She opens her mouth, probably to

confirm how serious she is, but I hold up a hand to halt her. "What kind of figure of prophecy am I? Your husband helped fix my wagon on an abandoned dirt road because I have no idea how to. I am a thief, no more, fleeing east with other thieves in search of a better life."

"None of the details of your previous life matter," she says firmly. "All you have been through merely led you here. To your kingdom. To your home."

"You dined with me last night. You were afraid yesterday that we were desperate bandits come to rob you!"

"And yet the stars shine brighter for lack of the moon," she says, the cadence of the words marking the phrase an aphorism, some local wisdom that the people of Eshan would know in an instant.

"What's that supposed to mean?" Hom grunts. I almost jump, having forgotten anything outside of this bewildering conversation.

"Just because truths were once believed does not make them true," Myn answers.

"Well, just because you give me a title doesn't make me whatever you say I am," I say, squeezing my eyes shut. "Creator, I can hardly *think*."

"You are the hope of Eshan. You must go east and take your rightful place on the Throne of Night. The Amanu will step down and become your servant. Together, you will usher us into an age of prosperity and plenty."

"This is getting stranger by the second," Inia says, wide eyes locked on Myn.

"I don't want to be a queen," I say. It's the first thing in this entire conversation that I'm certain of.

"But you are," Myn says, clenching her fists. "You don't have a choice."

"Like hell I don't," I growl, anger surging in my chest. I don't remember standing, but I'm looming over the small woman.

"No one tells me who or what I am. I can go south, or north, or any direction I please. Whatever you may believe, I am not your queen. Everyone, pack up. We're leaving."

As I turn to go, Myn drops to her knees and clasps my hand in both of hers. Desperate fear trembles through every line of her body. Unnoticed tears streak down her cheeks.

"Please," she whispers, her voice breaking. "Please. Do not leave."

"I am not a queen," I say grimly.

"My father ruined himself for you." The words make no sense, but their anguish claws at my heart nonetheless. "He was a Star of Eshan, and he gave it all up. For you."

"I don't know what you're talking about."

"I can't *make* you understand," she whispers, her hands dropping into her lap. Her shoulders heave beneath a sob. "But give me the chance to try."

"Kettle..." Aurelion starts to speak, closing his mouth as I turn a glare his direction. He doesn't have to finish his thought. He wants me to hear her out. Aurelion of the A'kai'ano'ri, honorable beyond all reason, heart as soft as drifting clouds. Part of me hates him. I want to say the words, to push him as far away from me as I can, but I can't make them pass my lips. Because the larger part of me agrees.

"At least stay the night," Myn says softly, hopelessly. "If you still feel the same way in the morning, I won't stop you."

Meeting the eyes of each of the Family in turn, the burning anger in my chest falls away. They each impart their own bit of wisdom in their silent looks, each as plain as day. The sisters are tired of running, and, whatever the cost, wish to stop their roving feet. Hom and Yelden, fools that they are, see a kingdom for the taking. The awe these strange people feel has begun to wear off on Sario by the glazed look in his eyes. Kit appeared at some point in the commotion, and he watches me with clever eyes, as if he knows what I will decide.

Corna is the only one who shows concern, but I can tell it isn't for the situation. We're the Family. We've been and done whatever we need to survive, and this is no different. No, she knows my heart and knows this is the last thing I want.

And Aurelion... damn it.

I feel like a child, standing on the eastern shore of the Isles as the tide draws out to sea. Each wave steals a bit more of the earth beneath my feet, my balance growing more precarious with each departing grain of sand, until it feels like there is no way I will not fall...

"Fine," I say finally. "One night."

***

The others respect my wish that I be left alone. I retreat to the children's bedroom, empty but for eight small beds. I can tell who slept where purely by the state of the sheets. Rin is the last on the left, the sheet rumpled but spread smoothly, her best attempt at the crisp sheets her mother used to make as a maid. The two beds pulled together are definitely Elan and Tera, inseparable since their earliest days with the Family. Orn, the son of a mason, always folds his pillow in two, and Lesi sleeps on the edge like even the tiny bed is too extravagant for her. I don't know how many other children slept in the cramped basement where I found her half-dead, but she's always treated space like a scarce commodity worth preserving. The bed without a pillow, looking untouched, is of course where Milen decided *not* to sleep. Whatever happened to him in the past, he wouldn't be caught dead in a bed.

And, finally, there is one bed that appears wholly untouched, as perfectly made as the moment we entered the room. Even though I watched Kit climb into it the night before, I would be hard-pressed to find a single bit of cloth out of place. He made stealth a habit before, but he's turned it into art ever since he found the ring.

Found... him.

Kit hasn't ever told us his name. I'm not entirely sure Kit knows it. There is a chance that, lost and alone as long as he was, the soul inside the ring has forgotten it as well. All we know is that he has a power that does not fit into our understanding of the world. Though he has no strength of his own, he can give strength to others, as he did to me to lift the weight of an empire's wealth. A Source, as Kit called it.

Ever since, I've been watching my son, searching for any sign that the soul inside the ring has changed him. Kit might be quieter, but he's always been a serious boy. He might be sneakier, but he's always wanted to be better than me. If there is any influence the ring has had on him, it is to manifest his personality even further.

The mystery of the ring isn't exactly important right now. Sighing, I sink down onto Kit's perfectly made bed. The thin mattress offers little comfort.

In the Creator's forgotten name, what have I gotten myself into?

The strange people of Eshan look nothing like the people of the west. They would appear almost Khalin, but the liquid straightness of their hair and the sharp beauty of their features is wholly exotic. The People may trade with Eshan, but in what port I have no idea. Perhaps their lands extend south all the way to the sea.

And now these people are trying to claim that I am their queen.

Me, an exiled Islander who forged a family through theft and desperation. I am as far from royalty—in blood and in deed—as one can get.

The weight of their eyes, their awe, and their bowed heads already settles about my shoulders like a leaden cloak. I have no desire to be *seen*. I live in shadow and darkness, content with the family I chose. Like a hare creeping through the tall grass, instinct urges me to flee before the snare can close about my foot.

Na'epaiw'ian.

It is time to come home.

The words drift through my memory, unbidden. Words spoken by a stranger, in the language of a people I left behind, from the lips of a woman who stood by when my comrades tried to cut out the one thing that made me special.

Words of prophecy.

Most of the world would disregard any talk of prophecy as the ravings of a lunatic. There is only one person who can see the future, and the Master of Time has not been seen in five thousand years. For me, though, prophecy was as essential to my upbringing as manners and martial prowess. The People know the Seer is never wrong. She sent those words ahead through time, years before I was even born, just so that I would hear them as the sun rose on the most dangerous day of my life.

It is time to come home.

What had Myn said?

"All you have been through merely led you here. To your kingdom. To your home."

I've known only two homes in my life, one which cast me out and one my enemies burned to the ground. Was this what the Seer intended? I thought I was breaking away from her vision, disregarding her words in one final act of defiance. I should have known better. Any choice I make is as she has foreseen. I am helpless before the current of the future.

Or am I reading too much into this? Did she think I would come back to the Isles?

Groaning, I bury my face in Kit's pillow. I could think in endless loops and never come to any reasonable conclusion. Rationality and prophecy rarely go hand in hand. I don't resist as exhaustion seizes my mind and drags me under.

***

The sun's rays slant through the western-facing windows when I awake. Motes of dust trace golden symbols in the sunlight.

Their dance is somehow comforting. They don't notice my quiet watch, nor would they care if they could. I wish to be like that dust.

I lift my hands above my head and stretch until my joints pop, and a sigh escapes my lips. The current scatters the lazily swirling dust. By my interference. By the Depths, I need to stop seeing symbols in everything.

Scowling, I head for the door. The scent of Myn's cooking in the air sets my mouth to watering. I slept right through lunch, and the chaos of the morning robbed me of breakfast. The others have already taken places around Hona's long table when I arrive. The spot at the head of the table, once occupied by Myn and Hona, has been conspicuously left vacant, but I ignore it in favor of settling in next to Corna. I return her faint smile and take in the room. Hona himself is absent, no doubt still standing outside staring at the ground. My family watches me seriously. They've been with me for years, through theft and sorrow and loss. I don't need to say anything for them to know my decision.

Myn bustles in, eyes popping wide at the sight of me. Bowing, she turns and disappears deeper into the house, shouting almost before she's out of sight. I open my mouth to speak, but she reappears before I can say anything, her older children filing in behind her. If yesterday's meal was a feast, the spread laid out before us befits a royal banquet. Dozens of earthenware platters heaped with food both familiar and unfamiliar decorate the long table. By the time Myn finally comes to stand at my side, the table groans under the weight of it.

"Myn, you really shouldn't have done this," I say, frowning.

"I will not disgrace my table by allowing the Eshani to go hungry," she answers.

"We could fatten our children on this spread for a month," Corna says, trying unsuccessfully to hold in a laugh. "I think you overdid it."

"Nonsense." Myn's lip curls as she looks at Corna. The

disdain is new; she listened raptly to Corna's stories last night. I get the feeling it has something to do with her closeness to me. "Eshani, companions, please eat your fill."

"Join us," Aurelion says, gesturing towards the head of the table. Myn looks scandalized.

"We won't eat a bite of this until you do," I say firmly. I'm over this subservient nonsense. "You and Hona both."

"Is that your command, Eshani?"

"No." Corna rolls her eyes. "Just do it."

"Very well," Myn says stiffly, disappearing to retrieve her husband.

"I could get used to this," Hom says with a grin, grabbing a spoon and shoveling a mountain of rice onto his plate. He's three bites in before he realizes that no one else is eating. "What? You really gonna let this go to waste?"

"Ass," Corna says mildly, looking at her fingernails.

"Hey, don't go—"

"Ass," Koli echoes, scowling at him.

"Fine, fine," he says, pushing his plate towards the center of the table. There isn't much room, but the gesture is more symbolic than anything. "Seems like none of you been hungry before."

"You'll get to eat soon," Yelden says, patting his shoulder. "Just don't reach for it until her highness does."

"Corna, what do they call it when you murder your brother?" I ask lightly.

"You don't have to get your hands dirty," she says, smiling. "Just ask, and your wish is my command, my liege."

I bury my face into my hands with a groan. The sound of footsteps approaching brings my head back up. Hona shuffles in, his eyes downcast, Myn following. She guides him to a seat, then takes one herself. Our brief levity fades like starlight before the dawn. I stare at them for long moments in silence, but neither will meet my eye.

"Enough," I growl finally. "I promised to stay the night and hear you out, so I will. But I won't let you talk to the ground or serve me like I'm anything special. You speak to me like a human being, or we walk right now."

The pair exchange a look before reluctantly lifting their faces.

"Alright. Now, everyone, let's eat."

My friends jump to it with gusto, and the sound of friendly banter and scraping forks fills the silence. I deliberately look anywhere but at our hosts, talking and laughing with my family. I notice Myn flinch when Hom makes a crass joke at my expense, but I laugh with the rest of them. The spice reminds me distantly of the Isles, and the comradery of good times in Donir. Despite our valiant efforts, we hardly put a dent in the mounds of food.

"Myn, there's no way your children are going to be able to eat all of this," I say, frowning at the table.

"They have food of their own."

"This is *just* for us?" I glance around in disbelief. "Are the soldiers still waiting outside?"

"From what I can gather, they were going to set camp in the lawn out front," Myn answers solemnly. "They wouldn't leave."

"Kit! Get your butt in here!" I shout. There is a brief pause as everyone glances around in confusion. I just smile grimly at the door leading from the sitting room. "Don't try to creep away now. Just come in."

The door opens to a sheepish Kit, his face reddening under the weight of the adult attention.

"What gave me away?" he asks, trying to keep the whine out of his voice.

"You didn't make a sound," I say graciously, opening my arm for him. He hurries over and accepts the gentle hug. "I just know you better than to think you would be sitting quietly with the other children. Now, do me a favor. Gather the others, Hona's and ours, and bring them here."

"Yes, Mother," he says dutifully, if reluctantly.

A moment later, the children file in, a diverse group of faces drawn from half a dozen cultures.

"Children, if you would be so kind, please take this food out to the soldiers camped outside."

Myn opens her mouth to protest, but shuts it at the expression on my face. Her children look confused, so I raise my eyebrows at her. She finally repeats the order in her language. In seconds, the table is bare of food but for the occasional forgotten grain of rice or splatter of sauce. I put my elbows on the table and lean forward, planting my chin on my hands.

"Alright, talk," I say flatly. "What is this prophecy? Where does it come from?"

"The prophecy is old," Myn says, eyes drifting. "It comes from the time before even the Eternal's kingdom, when the world was balanced between day and night."

When Ezil scoffs in disbelief, I make a sharp gesture of quiet. It isn't that I disagree, but I'm polite enough not to voice my skepticism. More than five thousand years?

"What do you mean, balanced?" I ask instead.

"There was a time, known here as the Age of Sun and Moon, when days did not pass. Light and darkness did not alternate, as we know it now, but remained constant, dividing the world into two mighty kingdoms: Light and Shadow." Myn pauses, as if expecting us to challenge her claim. When we remain silent, she continues. "The world passed in turn between war and peace as the two nations strove against one another. Even as detailed as our histories are, much has been lost in the millennia since. We do know, though, that Light created the days as we know it, and in so doing won the war."

"You're saying *man* made day and night?" I ask incredulously.

"Not the concepts themselves, but the cycle of them, yes.

108

Our histories are clear. I know it sounds unbelievable to those raised elsewhere, and there are times I've doubted it myself. Not anymore," Myn says, glancing down at her clasped hands. She doesn't say why she no longer doubts. She doesn't have to. "Regardless, the prophecy was given by the final Empress of Shadow, R'hea, Blessed by the Darkness, as her kingdom fell to the coming of day."

The name hits me like a punch to the stomach. I gasp, my chest suddenly tight. Corna looks at me in concern, but I can't look away from Myn. By the ruined Depths. By the majesty of the Creator. R'hea of Darkness. The legends of my people press against the edges of my mind. The name came from somewhere, from *someone*. She is not just a cautionary tale, but a woman made true by history. Feeling faint, I motion for Myn to continue.

"Await my successor, the mother of night, who will bring shadow fully into the light." Myn pauses, closing her eyes, a look of rapt fervor stealing over her face. "The last words of Empress R'hea. The prophecy Eshan has been waiting to come true since the fall of our kingdom. We have endured through several ages of man, our histories preserved, our borders secure, our faith unbroken. And now." She opens her eyes, filled with tears, and stares at me with joyful hope. "Now, our faith has been rewarded."

"Myn…" Hona says, eyeing his wife with concern. He shuts his mouth at her glare.

"What is it, Hona?" I ask, looking between the two of them. "Speak."

"You are not the first who has come bearing the Blessing of Darkness," he says, spreading his hands. "Three times, others have come to claim the Throne of Night."

"What happened to them?"

"They were charlatans," Myn grits through her teeth. "Seeking power only for themselves and not for the good of our people. They followed in the steps of the Empress, and they did

109

not return."

"There's something you're not telling us," Corna says, narrowing her eyes. "If there have been others, why do you believe so readily that Kettle is your Eshani?"

"It is her father," Hona says, refusing to meet his wife's scowl.

"You said that he ruined himself for me," I say, leaning back.

"Do you wish me to tell it?" Hona asks his wife.

"No," Myn says, settling trembling hands on the table. "I'll tell the tale. My father was an Oshei of Eshan, the Lightning Lord, respected and feared throughout our kingdom."

"What is an Oshei?" Corna asks.

"A Star, in your language. Ancestral warriors granted the power of the Creator through lineage and loyalty to Eshan."

"Granted?" I ask, my thoughts going to the boots on Aurelion's feet. And whatever Kit has.

"The Stars are each granted marks of office that contain the Creator's blessing. My family, the clan Aryal, has borne Oshei warriors for generations. My great grandmother was first granted the Lightning Mark by the Amanu of her time, and its power has stayed with my clan ever since."

"So what happened?" I ask, trying to keep the strange names straight. These warriors, the Oshei, are most definitely Ensouled, just like Tecarim in his boots and the mysterious spirit Kit found in the sewers. The fact that the Ensouled are common knowledge in this kingdom is surprising, as I'd never heard of them in all my travels until I ended up in Gordyn's secret vault. "If your father was so honorable and respected, why did he give it up?"

"When I was a girl, not yet ten years old, a stranger came to our estate. He was foreign, with darker skin than any I'd seen. He asked for my father by name. Respecting any traveler's right to hospitality, my father took him in for the night. He sent me to bed late, but I remember the sight of him sitting in his favorite chair, a glass of dark wine resting in his hand, firelight reflected in his eyes. When I woke the next morning, he was not the same man."

"What do you mean?" Aurelion asks, but I already know her answer. I've seen what happens when the Seer meddles.

"He was always a passionate man. After that night, though, he became obsessed. He made preparations to travel immediately, though he would tell no one where he was headed." Myn opens her clenched fist and stares down at her empty palm. Her hand shakes. "He placed the mark of his office in my hand that day, and he left me with a hope that nearly broke me, as well."

"Hope?" Yelden asks, frowning. "How could hope be something bad?"

"Hope is the most dangerous thing to give to a desperate man," I say quietly. "For in hope, there is strength to continue, to fight, to resist. Hope can overcome all reason and thought. It is a blade with two edges, and both are sharp."

"True, Eshani," Myn says, and her eyes do not speak sorrow. "My father told me that the Eshani would come in my time. A stranger, she would come from the west accompanied by a family stranger still, and… and I…"

"It is why we moved out here, of course," Hona says when his wife falls silent. "Everyone called us crazy for leaving the security of the kingdom behind. This life suits us, though. We have had no cause to regret, even if Myn's faith has… wavered, at times."

"Twenty-five years is a long time to wait," Myn says quietly.

"How long?" I ask quickly, stomach clenching.

"Twenty-five years," she says again. "Not so long, now that my faith has been rewarded."

And now that her father has been proven sane. She doesn't

say it, but we all hear it.

"Wait, Kettle, aren't you—"

"You've given us much to think over," I say, cutting Corna off before she can say anything else. Creator, it must be as obvious as it seems. "Myn, Hona, if you would give us the room?"

"Of course, Eshani," Myn says, and she and Hona quietly file out.

I give them enough time to get out of earshot, then motion Sario to check. He slides the door open and glances up and down the hall as Inia does the same thing at the other exit. Both flick their fingers in denial, but I don't allow myself to relax. Motioning the others close, I speak barely above a whisper.

"We leave in the morning," I say firmly.

"I figured as much," Aurelion whispers. "I told Kit to have the children quietly ready the wagon. It should be good to go."

"Thank you," I say, though I don't meet his eyes.

"Why are we leaving?" Sario says in disbelief, louder than he should. "You are... I mean... the prophecy!"

"I grew up around prophecies and portents," I whisper fiercely. "I know the hand of the Seer when I see it. I don't care what she wants or what she's seen. We don't know these people or their culture. We can't even speak their language. Do you really think this Amanu or whatever is just going to quietly step down when an Islander with a magic trick shows up?"

"She's right," Corna says, patting Sario gently on the back. "Men in power never give it up easily."

"Only a fool walks into a nest of scorpions," Ezil says, nodding. "If we move forward, we will be devoured."

"We haven't even unpacked yet," Hom says sadly, though not in argument. "I wanted to see this kingdom. Their food is good, and I bet it's beautiful."

"And it would remain so until we woke with daggers at our throats. Or choked on poison in their delicious food. Prophecy be damned, holy men are not immune to the blade. We leave at

112

dawn. No, before dawn. If anyone tries to stop us, we do not hesitate." I glance around at their faces, filled with resolve and acceptance. "Thank you, my friends. I'm glad to have you at my side."

"Where will we go?" Sario asks, his expression glum. I can tell he's thinking of the endless sea of grass we just crossed to reach this kingdom. I'm trying not to think of it myself.

"Somewhere where no one will recognize us," I say, shrugging. "South, I think. I don't want to see snow again this Winter. Quietly, now. Make ready to go."

***

I don't sleep. Even if I hadn't slept the day away, I wouldn't be able to sleep now. The children's room feels cozy and warm with the chorus of their soft breathing led by Elan's gentle snores, a balm to my frayed nerves. Rin's head lies in my lap, her body half-curled around mine. From across the room, I occasionally get a flicker of white light, starlight reflected in Kit's watching eyes. The night passes at a crawl, the thin sliver of moon cutting a slow track across the patch of night visible through the window.

It is for them, as much as for myself, that we walk away. They will be targets should we become involved in the politics of this strange kingdom. They deserve the chance to grow, safely and freely. I'm beginning to fear that, staying with me, they won't find that safety. All we've done is run from one danger to another. Tears prick at the corners of my eyes. They deserve better.

Creator, let me give them a place where they can be safe.

The door opens silently, and I tense before Aurelion's tall silhouette comes into focus.

"It's time," he whispers.

The children awaken without complaint, quietly filing into the main entrance to the manor. Any sense of comfort the old leather brought me last night has dissipated, stolen by the vagaries of a fate I plan to flee. There is no sign of Hona, Myn, or any of their children, and all of my family is accounted for.

Opening the door, we file into the predawn light. The sun has just begun to lighten the edge of the plains to the east. As the sunrise casts the horizon into relief, it doesn't look smooth and flat as it has for over a season. The jagged teeth of distant mountains mar the clean line of the earth. Stepping quietly towards the barn, I freeze at the sound of movement, the rustle of clothing and moving feet and growing whispers, which then give way to burgeoning shouts, which quickly become a roar loud enough to drown out thunder. Turning towards the road, my heart falls.

The sun crests the horizon. Its uncaring light spreads across Hona's land… what little of it is visible beneath a sea of faces so vast that its end disappears up the road. People stand on one another's shoulders for a better view, more pouring onto Hona's farm by the second. Hundreds of people lift their hands to point, their faces contorted in joy and rapture, some opening weeping.

"Shit," Corna shouts next to me, her voice nearly crushed by the roar of the crowd. "What do we do now?"

Myn and Hona appear at the door, their faces opening in surprise and wonder. Soldiers, dozens more of them, stand at the ready and keep the surging crowd at bay, their strange spears held horizontally. The hands reaching over their tenuous barricade are numerous, but no one tries to push past the line of warriors. Even in their zealotry, the people of Eshan seem to be in control.

The nearest ranks quiet after some minutes, the silence racing like wildfire through the people. As they look at me, only at *me*, looks of fear and wonder and awe and suspicion, their regard sharpens and the air fills with heightened expectation. My family step closer to me, eyeing the waiting crowd with wary distrust. In the unnatural silence, free of birdsong or human speech, Aurelion's solid shoulder presses against mine.

114

"Show them, Kettle," he says, his voice gentle.

"No. If I show them, I've accepted this…"

"We don't have a choice," he says, ensnaring my eyes in his. "Look at them. The word of your arrival, whatever we may have wished, will have reached their entire kingdom by nightfall. If you don't show them what they want to see, they may well tear us apart."

"I won't," I say, pleading with the world as much as the man before me. "I can't. I'm a thief from Donir. I'm a mother to orphans. I am not a queen."

"Even so," he says, his fingers reaching for mine. I let him take my hand, his steady strength a foundation upon which to stand. Whatever lies between us, his loyalty is beyond question. "The only way out is through."

The truth of his words doesn't make them any less heavy. My fingers wrap with his, my knuckles whitening. I raise my open hand to the sky. Against every instinct screaming for me to hide, to run, to disappear, I open my heart and call to shadow. It is difficult, like reaching my hand across a chasm towards a friend, but eventually it answers.

The darkness traces lines along my skin as it pools in my hand, a sphere crafted of the void. There is no shine from the orb, no glimmer reflecting the sunrise. The morning light disappears into the blackness, which remains unsullied and impenetrable.

As one, with a shake that sends a tremor through the ground beneath my feet, the people of Eshan fall to their knees, pressing their faces to the earth.

***

"You were going to run, weren't you," Myn says, her face alight with victory. We've retreated to the relative safety of Hona's home, though the rumble of conversation outside is audible even through the thick wooden walls. "But you cannot escape your destiny."

"Just tell me what I need to know," I say tightly, clenching

115

my hands into fists. "What am I walking into?"

"Honestly?" she says, losing her deference the longer she's around me. "This is where the prophecy ends. You are supposed to bring shadow into the light."

"What does that even mean?" I ask in exasperation. "I have traveled through much of the lands to the west, but I've never encountered anything else like my shadow."

"I don't know." She puts a finger to her lips. "The previous three Blessed by Darkness each followed in the footsteps of the Empress. I imagine, after you are introduced at the capital, that you will do the same."

"Footsteps? What footsteps?"

"How far is this capital?" Aurelion asks.

"The capital of the Dark of Eshan, Yohru, was built on the foundations of a mighty fortress high on a mountain. A fast horse could take you there in twenty days. The location was partly chosen for the defense of the last remnants of our kingdom, but more because the Empress made her final journey to a valley at the base of the mountain. She walked into the valley and disappeared, taking the veil of darkness with her. That valley has been sacred ever since."

"You mentioned the Amanu before," Corna says, her tone clipped and professional. Now that we are committed to this, she's gathering as much information as she can. "And not in the kindest light. What do we need to know about him?"

"He's young, for the Blessed," Myn says, her mouth twisting in distaste. "Less than thirty Winters. But he is powerful, both in name and in truth. His family, the clan Ihera, already possessed six Stars before their youngest son was discovered to be Blessed. It was almost absurd to think of anyone else for the position when the last Amanu died."

"His death was unexpected, I'd guess," Ezil says sourly. "Sudden sickness? Fall off a horse?"

"A bandit's arrow," Hona says grimly. "Far from any

prying eyes on her morning ride through paths believed safe."

"The murderer was executed for the crime, of course," Myn says. "The trial—"

"Was quick, because of course he confessed," Corna says, rolling her eyes. "And your people went with this?"

"How do you say no to the strongest clan in the kingdom?" Myn asks, raising her hands helplessly. "Not just in power, but in wealth, in connections, in soldiers, and with a Blessed of the Creator sharing their name?"

"This is exactly as I feared," I say. "This family—the Ihera, you called them?—is never going to step down to a millennia-old prophecy. Especially not to a stranger."

"We are in a war against an enemy with every advantage," Aurelion says, rubbing his hands across his face. The ugly burn bisecting the tattoos marking him as Shorn no longer makes me flinch, but only just. "And, beyond that, we don't even know the rules of engagement."

"There will be no rules," Corna says, offering a dark smile. "Or, if there are any, there's no way we can follow them. Not if we want to survive."

"Ours is a culture built on honor and respect," Hona says defensively. He eyes us like we're insane, but Myn stares at him with a look of fond disbelief. "The Ihera will follow—"

"Oh, *arin*," she cuts in, patting his shoulder gently. "I love your optimism, but the Eshani's companions are correct."

"So, as I said before, tell me what I need to know," I say, meeting her eye.

"If you arrived unannounced, they might just try to make you disappear," Myn says thoughtfully. Now that she's faced with a problem, any vestige of her servile demeanor has disappeared, and her keen mind has returned. I much prefer her this way. "But that sheep has wandered. They won't be able to attack you outright. Don't eat food served by anyone you don't trust. Don't walk alone in secluded spaces."

117

"Or ride on paths thought safe," I say wryly. "I don't trust anyone outside of this room. And, no offense..."

"You'll need Stars if you wish to be taken seriously," Myn says, ignoring my concern.

"Stars are Ensouled, right?" Ezil says. "So we have Aurelion and—"

"We have one Star." I give her a warning look. I don't know what Kit is capable of, but I won't have him be even more of a target than he already is. "It will have to be enough."

"No, it won't," Myn says, spinning about and disappearing on rapid steps. She returns in less than a minute with a small wooden box of polished wood. With trembling hands, she opens the lid to reveal a pendant of burnished bronze, inlaid with a symbol I've never seen before. "All of Eshan believes that my father took the mark of his office with him when he left. They are wrong. It is time for the Lightning Lord to return."

Chapter 6
Jace
The Seventy-Second Day of Spring
In the year 5223, Council Reckoning

"Your news is out of date," the woman says, shaking her head. "The *Kingdom* is no more. All hail the Emperor Helikos the Sealord, conqueror of the Khalintars and ruler of the Empire of the Sea."

The declaration settles a blanket of silence over the blanket of snow covering the ground. The Khalintars conquered? We've been out of touch less than a year. We left Donir in flames from open rebellion. How is it even possible?

"How?" Locke sounds like he's speaking around a dagger lodged in his stomach. "The Republic is... was... strong."

"It happened in a moment," the tall man says, his face set in grim lines. The woman looks sick, and the pain in her eyes feels *personal*. "The Republic attacked across the Way of the North, sending every able-bodied warrior they had. The Sealord summoned a wave large enough to touch the sky and swept them all away."

"Not just the Khalintari army," the woman says bitterly. "The wave drowned dozens of villages on the western coast of the Kingdom. The bastard murdered thousands of his own citizens."

"Is the war lost then?" Juliet says, folding her arms across her chest. "Was our journey here pointless?"

"I'll stop fighting when the Sealord breathes his last, or I do," she says, voice shaking with passion, her hand dropping to the hilt of her sword.

"Regardless," the man says, eyeing his companion out of the corner of his eye. "Though I am inclined to trust you, we survived so long out of an abundance of caution. You have followed the path, but you haven't reached its end. Wait here."

He disappears into the trees like a wraith, invisible before I can think to track him. We stand awkwardly, shivering now that we've stopped moving. The chill in my chest grows by the second. Juliet's power can only hold the ice at bay for so long. We need a fire, a safe place to sleep, and a chance to rest.

"You guys live out here?" Locke asks, his expression grim as he surveys the wintry landscape. "How cheerful."

"Don't be rude," Juliet says, stepping forward now that she's finally caught her breath. "We are the guests here. My name is Juliet, lady. It is wonderful to see new faces after being surrounded by nothing but snow for a whole season."

"Poline," the woman answers, though she doesn't smile. "A pleasure."

The words are empty and cold. It feels like the world is likely to end before this woman smiles. Locke looks at her with renewed interest, his face turning thoughtful.

"Poline..." he says thoughtfully. "Were you, by chance, in the Tide?"

"Once," she says stiffly.

"I seem to remember a soldier with red hair who traveled with the princess, and—"

"Don't." A subtle shift, and her stance is suddenly threatening. "Who are you?"

"My name is Locke," he answers easily.

"The world is small indeed," she says flatly. The aura of menace around her fades, though its memory lingers. "I spent half a season trying to track you down after Firdana. We hit a dead end when you disappeared from your prison cell. I thought you might have escaped."

"If only. I was taken into Kranos' secret dungeon and...

yeah."

"How did you escape?" a voice calls, deep as the mountain roots.

Held appears between the trees, followed by a man with shoulders nearly as broad as Bota's, sporting a deep brown beard below a cleanly shaved head. His blunt features and rugged appearance are in stark contrast to the bright sparkle of his warm brown eyes. Despite his craggy face, it feels like he's always about to break into a smile. As he moves closer, I realize he isn't really that large, perhaps a head taller than I am. His presence, though, swells to fill the air. I feel compressed, crushed, like there isn't enough room for me in the open forest. It's difficult to stand up straight before him.

"If you are who I think you are," Locke says, shrugging. He appears utterly unfazed by the man. "You probably already know that."

"I am," he agrees, showing white teeth in the middle of his thick beard. "And I do."

"Uh," I say lamely. "Who is he?"

"That's the Mason, Jace," Locke says, shaking his head. So *that's* why he has such a presence. "His likeness was spread to every person in the Deep on the off chance we crossed paths. Standing orders were to try to end him at any cost."

"I don't see you moving to attack," the Mason says, his eyes twinkling.

"The throne betrayed me before I ever betrayed it." Locke's lips move into a thin smile. "You're safe."

"Glad to hear it, Locke of the Deep." The Mason's piercing gaze flits around the rest of our party, settling briefly on Juliet before coming to rest on me. "Welcome, comrades. I am Itolas, known—absurdly—as the Mason. I know most of you, by reputation if not by name. Alice, who speaks louder than those with a voice." Alice grins impishly, making a show of flipping her hair... which promptly avoids her touch. "Bota, mighty and loyal."

121

Bota thrums with pleasure. "Jace of the Simply, Reknor's ward." I hold his gaze until it shifts to Juliet. "But, my lady, I do not believe I have any intelligence of you."

"I am Juliet, formerly of the merchant family Perrea." She bows with such precision it feels like the trees are pillars holding up a high royal hall. "Exiled, I use what knowledge I have to heal."

"And how did you come to be a part of this eclectic group?" he asks, his eyes boring into her. His presence sharpens, pressing against Juliet like a palpable wind. My hand twitches towards hers, but she stops me with a flick of her eyes. I feel like I'm watching a duel, helpless to intervene. Something lurks beneath his attention, a mistrust that Juliet hasn't earned. The longer he stares, the more something builds in the pit of my stomach.

"They rescued me from slavery under the Master of Beasts," she says, refusing to wilt before his gaze. "I owe them my life."

"And we her," Locke says, stepping up next to Juliet and laying a hand on her shoulder. "Without her talents, we would never have made it here through the cold."

"I see," Itolas says, his face unreadable. A bitter wind whistles through the clearing. Eternal's kiss, if he makes a move on her... My hand drifts to the hilt of the saber at my hip. The Mason doesn't appear to relax, but the moment passes. His face breaks into another broad grin. Opening his hands, he beckons us onward. "Welcome, all. This is no place for friends to gather. Let me show you to a fire and a hot meal."

"Itolas, if you can deliver on that promise, I'll kill for you," Locke says, the joke falling somewhat flat considering who he is. I don't move as the others set off.

"Wait."

Everyone pauses and turns to look back at me. It takes me a second to realize I spoke the word.

"I am not..." I grit my teeth, trying to still the tremble in my limbs. "I have questions of my own."

"I'm sure you'd rather ask them after we—"

"No." Itolas looks surprised at the interruption, but shuts his mouth without complaint. I'm angry, Creator knows how much, and it isn't just about how he looked at Juliet. It's so much more. "Where... where have you been? What have you been *doing?*"

"Careful, Jace," Locke warns, easing away from the Mason.

"You know more than we do," I say slowly, trying to get my thoughts in order. "Your people told us that the Kingdom conquered the Khalintars in the time we've been traveling here. If you know that... why haven't you been helping us? How have you let... all of this... happen?" I take a deep breath, searching for calm. I don't find it. "You let Reknor be taken. You left me and the Enclave to rot in the sewers. Creator damn you, we brought Donir to its knees! There was open rebellion in the streets! If you know so much, *where were you?*"

"Calm down, lad," Itolas says softly. The gentle firmness in his voice works, at least enough for me to listen. "Do we need to do this here?"

"Yes," I say stubbornly, crossing my arms. Juliet places a light hand on my back, but I ignore her. "Right here."

"Fine," he says, running a hand across his smooth pate. "We know more than you, but at the same time precious little."

"Don't dodge the question—"

"Let me finish." The command in his voice brings me up short. For a second, I lost sight of who I'm speaking to. The Mason, nearly a century old and a living legend, does not like being interrupted. "We used to know a lot more. Helikos is a crafty devil. He put the princess in charge of rooting out rebels, and she was remarkably effective. Too effective. Over the last few seasons, she's killed or captured most of our operation in the city, starting with Reknor. We've ordered the few that are left to go

123

dark just to survive." He sighs, his expression falling. "We haven't dared try to sneak anyone in since. We're nearly blind out here."

"Nearly?"

"We have an ace in the hole, so to speak," Itolas says, his eyes flicking towards the sky. "But he only has one set of eyes."

"I still think…"

"I know, lad," he says, his voice weary. "I've known Reknor my whole life. If there was any way we could have gotten him out, we would have."

As my anger fades, my exhaustion returns in full force. Staggering, I lean on Juliet's arm to stay upright.

"Alright," I say finally, though I know some of my questions remain unanswered. "Take me to a damn fire."

As we walk through the frozen trees, it's hard to imagine any encampment this far out. There are no signs of humanity anywhere; no smoke, no sounds, no dwellings… this walk, aside from the new company, is no different from any of the endless days trudging through the endless snow. Large boulders encased in ice, left by a rockslide from higher up in the mountains long ago, appear out of the uniform blanket of white. It's only as a woman in furs steps from a near-invisible crevice in the rock that it dawns on me… we're already there.

"Held, run on ahead and make a fire in one of the bigger ones. East bank, I think. Your section. Poline, show them around. They are welcome, by *my* word." Held shoots the Mason a look of confusion, but doesn't protest. Itolas squints at the sky again, then turns to us with a welcoming smile. "I have things I need to do, and Al should be informed. Get settled in, and we'll talk later."

Poline leads us around the camp, which turns out to be much larger than I imagined. The rebels have spread across a pass between two peaks, little known and rarely traveled, as there are easier, more accessible passes through the Claws to the north and the south. Twin mountain streams, coated in ice, wind through the center of the camp. Distant mountains and sheltered

124

valleys stretch away out of sight without any sign of man's interference.

For the rebels' sake, the location is a godsend. They have access to both sides of the mountain, far from any prying eyes that might reveal their location. Technically, the land is owned by Duke Paloran, but only in name. No one save for the insane and the desperate would call such an inhospitable land home. The dwellings are set up for both defense and stealth.

"There are guard posts and small armories there and there," Poline says, gesturing towards two unremarkable boulders. "Those willing to defend the people here actively watch the west, where our enemies are gathered, though we keep a light watch on the east as well."

"Have you ever been discovered?" Locke asks.

"Not yet." Poline stares west for several steps, her eyes distant. "Who would come up here?"

"People looking to find rebels," he says wryly.

"As far as we can tell, they don't have the resources to spare." She indicates a slope leading upwards to our right. "The noncombatants have their own space there along the south wall of the pass. If you need clothes mended or a warm drink, head that way. But be polite. They expect you to work for your trouble."

"Noncombatants?" Juliet says. "Isn't this a military camp?"

"Maybe once," Poline answers, half-glancing back. "But soldiers have partners and children. Were they supposed to leave them behind?"

"Of course not. But still... if you're attacked..."

"They know the risk. When the time comes, we may all end up with a sword in our hands..." she trails off.

A squad of soldiers, dressed in white furs and carrying bows, stop their march and turn to stare as we go past, some with open horror on their faces. Shit. I may have gotten used to the Enclave, but strangers... Poline signals something with her hands, and the soldiers relax somewhat, though they continue to stare.

Another squad approaches from the south, a ruddy glow to their cheeks despite the early afternoon.

"Eternal's shriveled tits, what is *that?*" The man who spoke drops a hand to the hilt of his sword. His squad spreads out behind him, their faces turning hostile.

"New arrivals, Karl," Poline says patiently. "Welcomed by the Mason himself."

"Says you, *Tide*," he growls back, tightening his grip on his weapon. The first squad tenses at his words. "You ain't exactly proved yourself yet, neither."

"Keep that sword in its sheath," she says softly. "We're all on the same side."

"Are we, *Tide?*" he says, his mouth twisting the word unpleasantly. "I ain't so sure."

"Is there a problem?" Held calls, jogging up to the group. At the sound of his voice, the soldiers stand at attention, all but Karl, who continues to glare. Held narrows his eyes. "Report."

"Monsters in the camp, Captain," Karl says, not looking Held's way. "And traitors."

Held steps crisply into Karl's line of sight, forcing their eyes to meet. The look on Held's narrow face makes the frigid air feel colder.

"The Mason himself declared them welcome less than an hour ago. They have been through more to get here than any of us, and have greater cause to fight as well. The Master of Beasts broke their bodies, yet they had the strength to come here. Through the Winter." Held steps close, lowering his voice. I'm close enough to pick out the words, but only just. "And if you question Poline's loyalty again, I won't answer with words. She has contributed more here in a half a season than you have in years."

"Aye, Captain," Karl says, a muscle in his jaw clenching. "I stand corrected."

"You're on duty tonight, soldier," Held says, stepping back

and raising his voice. "You shouldn't be drinking."

"Aye, Captain," Karl says again, continuing west with his squad of soldiers. The look he gives us is nothing short of lethal. Some from his group look like they've swallowed something bitter, others look apologetic. "Won't happen again."

As the soldiers depart, I try not to sag to the ground.

"I'm sorry…" Held begins, but Locke holds up a hand.

"Not your fault. We figured that's how most people would act when they saw us. Trust is earned." Alice nods sadly, and Bota thrums low enough to rattle bones. Locke bares his teeth in something that could, conceivably, be called a smile. "Especially for monsters."

"True," Poline agrees, her face stone.

"What's to the north?" Juliet says, her voice a bit strained.

"Mostly the other peak guarding this pass," Held says, falling into step with Poline. We reach what seems to be the crest and begin walking downhill for the first time in what feels like forever. Thank the Creator. "There is a narrow path leading upwards to a ruined keep. Whoever built it, they built it to last, but nothing survives up here forever. That's where the Vengeance and the Mason stay. What they do up there… harder to say. Ah, here. We're coming to our little neighborhood."

A dozen of the ancient, crumbled boulders lie scattered about a glade. Even though it's probably my imagination, this side of the mountain feels a hair warmer. Soldiers stand at our approach, their expressions stoic. They have the look of true fighters, not just people with swords. Each has a certainty to their movements, the earned grace of warriors that do not waste motion. My people.

"*These* are your new recruits?" a man says in a voice somehow familiar, his handsome face falling into a lopsided smile. An image of flashing steel… he's shaved the beard, but… "Held, I'm impressed. There hasn't been a gathering so terrifying since we tested him."

"I don't track, James," Held says, glancing at our motley group.

"You're telling me you don't know who you brought in?" James Elthe, Blade of the A'kai'ano'ri and one of the masters who tested me, winks at me like we're old friends. "That's the youngest Blade in a hundred years."

He steps forward as Poline and Held gape, taking my proffered hand and grinning. With Juliet's aid, he helps me to a fire, putting a hot bowl of stew in my hands. The Enclave is treated with the same genuine warmth and welcomed heartily. Apparently, the Mason knew exactly what he was doing when he placed us here. Each of the warriors sitting around these fires, nearly twenty strong, is Shorn.

The stew does wonders towards reviving me, though it can't quite touch the weariness that has settled into my bones. I don't feel much up for talking. Luckily, I don't have to. James Elthe immediately regales the others with the story of my test, speaking in amazed tones about my defense against Benko while my sword was still in its sheath. The others look at me skeptically, and I don't blame them: huddled in my tattered furs, hands clutched greedily around my soup, I probably look more urchin than swordsman. Every time they look at Elthe, though, they're reminded that this story comes from the lips of a Blade.

He gets to our fight, my initial defeat, his bemused shock when I put my right hand behind my back and fought better with my left, and his disbelief that he lost to a boy using his off hand. The amazement on their faces only grows, both Enclave and Shorn alike.

"And then…" he sighs dramatically, his face losing some of his animation. "It's lucky he already passed the test. Because then he fought Ke'sti'ra."

"Shit," Held says, with feeling, glancing at me in sympathy. Several of the others look like they've seen a ghost. "How'd it go?"

"About like you'd expect," I say, shaking my head ruefully. "She trounced me so easily I still dream about it sometimes."

"Who is Ke'sti'ra?" Locke asks.

"The Ghost of the Rak'a'to," Elthe says, his smile grim.

"Oh." Locke's expression falls like the others. "*Her.*"

The only sound in the glade is the crackle of the fire. A log pops loudly. James Elthe jumps and deliberately shivers like he's trying to shake off a bad memory.

"Well then." Elthe stands and lifts his hand towards some nearby stone dwellings. "You can call those two home. They've got cookfires going, so they should be nice and cozy. And, Jace?"

"Yeah?"

"We train at dawn."

***

The next few days pass pleasantly, despite the ever-present chill of the Claws at this altitude. Bota, Locke, and I take one dwelling, while Alice and Juliet take the other. The inside is larger than I expected, with enough room for each of us to have our own space. A small firepit in the corner keeps the temperature perfect, and, through some means I can't figure out, the smoke is whisked away through a chimney that doesn't lead into the sky. If nothing else, it is a welcome reprieve from trudging uphill every day in the snow.

Each dawn, I wake up and join the Shorn in training. We begin with the same stretches Reknor taught me years ago, the movements a welcome return to those nostalgic days spent smelling the dust of Reknor's storeroom, laughing and sweating and cursing through another long training session. When we are fully warmed by the movements, we fight, first unarmed, then working our way up to swordplay.

I'm rusty at first. The time spent working with the hewn wood in the sewers helped stave off the inevitable decline of any skill left dormant, but it couldn't take the place of real practice against living opponents. Elthe, remembering our previous duel, procures a single-edged sword from their armory that fits me better than the cavalry saber. I throw myself into the training, clawing for the invisible edge of heightened readiness I once held. The discordant song of swordplay fills the glade every morning for several hours. It is… peaceful. In the best way.

There are no arguments; no one gets upset when they lose. Rather, there is quiet conversation, the wisdom of those higher in the ranks imparted to those still seeking strength. It's disconcerting how everyone listens to what I say, held rapt by any minor advice I offer, even those more than twice my age. I guess, even rusty, I *am* a Blade, fast, strong, and getting faster and stronger by the day. Above all else, though, I have control. Just as Reknor taught me.

To be honest, I learn far more than I teach. Reknor was a capable tutor who made me into a confident swordsman, honing my natural skill into a sharpened weapon. Here, I get to train with others, peers, warriors dedicated to the elusive goal of perfection, offering their own perspectives and tactics. Each person, regardless of their skill, brings their own unique cunning to the task of war. Reknor may have laid my foundation, but with these people, I can build something else entirely.

There are none more dedicated to the craft than the former Tide Poline. She throws herself at every opponent, filled with seemingly endless drive, training into the afternoon when the rest of us break at midday. Her body shouldn't be able to handle the abuse, but she rises every morning with the rest of us, mouth set into a grim line. Whatever happened in her past, she is preparing for her future. I can't tell whether I admire or fear her… or both.

In less than a tenday, we grow comfortable among the Shorn. The supplies are fairly lean. Though there is game in abundance this far from civilization, typical luxuries like bread are largely absent. A small balding man, who turns out to be Held's father, Aldan, does his best to cook for us all.

Alice and Locke, the most 'normal' appearing of the Enclave, fall in with the scouts and hunters. Alice was already a master of silent communication and raised in the Kinlen Forest, and Locke made a living out of silence. They disappear for days at a time with Held and a select group whose job it is to range out and return with news and food. When I see Alice, she's always grinning.

Bota rarely leaves our shared dwelling. He seems to have made himself something of a burrow in one of the rooms, from which he only exits for mealtimes. I don't know how he can stand to spend so much time alone.

And Juliet, of course, heals. In the course of intense training with edged weapons, injuries happen no matter how skilled the combatants. I never see her use her power; it seems like our powers, both hers and mine, are a secret we have collectively agreed not to share. Even so, concussions heal overnight, cuts that require stitching scar up in days, and bruises miraculously disappear.

Of the Mason and the Vengeance, there is no sign.

***

One morning in early Summer, after nearly a season spent among the Shorn, James Elthe calls us together before we stretch. Juliet wanders over curiously, sitting down against a tree off to the side to watch.

"My friends, at her *insistent* request, Poline desires to be tested and prove herself Tempered. As we have three Tempered gathered in one place, we will grant her request." The air is still cold enough this high up that white fog eclipses his face with every word. "Though we should need no reminder, the rules remain the same: one duel, no blood, two of three to advance."

Held, a dark-haired man named Dilner, and a woman in her middle years with steel-gray hair called Crallia rise as one, blades presented. Poline stands in the center of the glade, the tip of her bared sword an inch from the earth.

"Alec Held," Elthe continues, his typical merriment replaced by solemnity. "You are called to question this Fold and see if she is worthy of the Tempered. Your sacred task is before you. You are the test."

Elthe begins the chant, a mantra I've gone over in my mind a thousand times since my test.

"We are the children, yet we seek to learn. We are the ore, yet we seek the hammer. We are the soul, yet we seek purification."

"Begin."

Held steps forward, drawing his blade and casting the sheath aside. His weapon is identical to Poline's: a double-edged longsword of hardened steel favored by the Tide. He offers her a formal salute, which she ignores. Held grins a predatory grin as he closes.

"I was always better than you," he teases, circling to her left. She slowly pivots to face him without moving from the center of the clearing. "All the way through training. I helped you get into the Tide in the first place."

Poline doesn't bother to answer. It's part of the test, of course. The A'kai'ano'ri is about more than just swordplay; it is about discipline and self-control. It is seeking perfection in all aspects of life.

"I was always going easy on—"

Poline springs forward, her blade leading. As Held moves to block, she twists her body into a kick, her boot slamming against the meat of Held's thigh. Wincing, he staggers back, fending her off and shaking his foot. In the short seconds of Poline's duel with Held, I learn several things. She uses her sword as a distraction more than a weapon. Its threat always looms, but the majority of her attacks come from elbows, from knees, or from the pommel of her weapon. The edge of her sword is a gleaming feint disguising a dozen other methods of attack. Held manages the blows well. He rolls with the punches, turns solid hits

132

into glancing blows. Just like her training, though, her indomitable spirit wears him down. The end is evident long before she manages to end the fight with a thunderous elbow across his temple.

"Dilner Smithsson," Elthe continues after Poline has the chance to catch her breath. Held was the best of the three; the remaining fights are a foregone conclusion. Anyone can slip, mistakes can happen, but Dilner is a straightforward power fighter. Half of the tricks Poline used on Held would have felled him in half the time. The woman's hard work has definitely paid off. "You are called to question this Fold and—"

Wind cuts through the glade without warning. Snow whips into our eyes, and I throw a forearm across my face. I glance at Elthe. He's smiling, clearly unconcerned at the sudden change. The wind dies quickly, and the falling snow reveals a man standing in the clearing near Poline. Slender and tall, but powerful, his short blond hair matches the clean beard on his face. A sword hilt pokes over his left shoulder, the craftsmanship evident even from a distance. He drops a pack carelessly at his feet. Elthe stands and approaches him, offering his hand in welcome. As he gets closer, I notice spots of red flecked across the stranger's green jerkin. Blood?

"Welcome back, Altos," he says. "You're just in time to witness the second bout of a Fold seeking to join the Tempered."

The stranger ignores him. His eyes search the clearing, taking in the scene in seconds. Poline stands awkwardly to the side, her test suddenly and strangely interrupted.

"Where are the newcomers?" the man asks finally, his voice flat and deadly.

I stand before I can think, my body urging me to be ready. Whoever this man is, and I have a sinking feeling I know exactly who he is, there is a latent threat in the air. I keep my hand off my sword, but only just.

"About," James says cheerfully. "Telias's ward has fit in

133

nicely, and the others—"

"You," the stranger says, lifting his hand and pointing at Juliet where she sits to the side. Her mouth falls open in surprise as he shifts to offer her his profile. As if he is preparing to defend himself. Or to attack. "You do not fit any description of the Enclave. Telias told me nothing of you."

"I am Juliet, once of the merchant house Perrea," she says, slowly rising to her feet. The man shifts his weight onto his back foot at her motion. "I came here with the others of the Enclave, having been rescued from the dominion of the Master of Beasts."

"You're coming with me," he says curtly, his hand rising to the blade over his shoulder. A hand that gleams with a symbol of purest white. "Slowly, or I won't hesitate."

I'm between them in an instant, my hand deliberately distant from my weapon. His piercing blue eyes bore into mine. Reknor taught me that an opponent's eyes can tell you much of their intentions, their plans, even their motivations. From this man, though, I get nothing.

"Step aside, boy," the man—the Vengeance, for it can only be him—says flatly.

"Wait just a second," I say, fighting to keep the desperation from my voice. "What do you think she's done?"

"I won't ask again," he says, his body tensing.

"Just wait," I say, lifting a hand and fighting to keep it from shaking.

"Boy..."

"Altos, what's going on here?" James Elthe asks carefully, keeping his distance from both of us.

"You've welcomed a viper into our midst," the Vengeance hisses, his eyes snapping to Elthe. "This girl, or one of her fellows, tried to lead them right to us."

"What?" I ask dumbly, the accusation so absurd that I can barely register it. "That's impossible."

"I have to echo that sentiment, Al," Elthe says, eyeing

Juliet skeptically. "She's been a model citizen since she got here. Damn, more than. She's healed us, better than any of the others in the camp."

"We've been hidden here for almost twenty years. Twenty years, Elthe," the Vengeance growls. "These idiots have threatened everything." I open my mouth to protest, but he continues before I can speak. "First, they leave a trail in the snow wide enough for a blind dullard to follow. I could see it from a mile in the air, drawing a line straight to us. Worse, I spotted scouts, enemy scouts, following it into the mountains. They won't report back."

"An honest mistake," I say helplessly.

"So I thought," the Vengeance snaps. "Until I stopped to question one of them. They weren't just following the trail, which fresh snowfall would have covered eventually. They were following these."

He bends to reach into his pack, pulling out several misshapen balls of bent and broken twigs. I don't recognize them at all until Juliet gasps from behind me. Oh. Shit. The little shapes she was weaving all the way here. The careless hobby she picked up to pass the time.

"No, no way," I say firmly, shaking my head. "Again, an accident…"

"Not according to their scouts."

"And you trust what they said?" I ask in disbelief.

"I can be quite persuasive when I need information quickly." My skin goes cold. That explains the fresh blood sprayed across his clothes. "Now, for the last time, step aside."

"Jace," Juliet whispers behind me. Her hand, light as a feather, comes to rest on my shoulder. "Move."

"No," I half turn, trying to keep an eye on the Vengeance. "This is absurd—"

"Is it?" she asks softly, her face lost. "Maybe… maybe he's right. Not on purpose, but… we know what Kranos is capable of.

135

Why was I weaving those little things? Creator, Jace, I've never wanted to play with my hands. We didn't question, didn't wonder why… I think I *should* go with him."

"That's insanity." I take her by the shoulders, turning to face her fully. "This is insane. You would never betray me… us."

"Would I?" she asks, reaching up to my hands. Not to hold them, not to reassure me, but to pull them from her shoulders. "How can we be sure? What if this isn't it, and he's done other things to my mind… more dangerous things."

The Vengeance's footsteps are nearly silent, yet they seem loud in the stillness. They are the only sound in the glade but for the racing beat of my heart. Helpless. I'm helpless to stop this. Is she guilty? Not intentionally, yet even so… can I let her go with him? There is something off about his eyes, a frightening coldness barely human. He doesn't care that blood crosses his chest and legs, human blood he shed…

I can be quite persuasive when I need information quickly.

"No," I whisper, meeting Juliet's tearful gaze.

"Jace…"

My sword leaps into my hand. The tip points unwaveringly towards the Vengeance's throat. His eyes register the briefest surprise before they freeze over again. His blade comes up, its edge glittering strangely in the light of the rising sun. Almost like diamonds…

"You can't have her," I hear myself say, distantly, my conscious thoughts racing into the fight to come.

"I gave you a chance, boy," the Vengeance says, his voice dull and emotionless. "You chose poorly."

"Altos, Jace," Elthe calls in alarm. "Just wait a damn minute…"

I barely hear him. My focus is on my opponent. His eyes are pools of still ice, so I ignore them, reading his shoulders, his hips, the shift of his feet. If he's going to attack, he'll have to—

He *moves*. My sword screams across in a parry. There was

no sign, no tell, just a blistering thrust faster than thought. Our weapons should ring at the contact, but he's already retracted the thrust before the sound can reach my ears. Blood blossoms on my thigh as I block his second attack, too slowly, his blade already flashing for my shoulder. Spinning aside, I throw a desperate elbow at his head. He's gone, dropping into a—

His foot slams into my chest and lifts my feet off the ground. I crunch into the frozen ground. My breath explodes from my lungs. Get up. *Get up.* I find my feet. He steps forward, confident. Arrogant. Fuck. My turn. Feint an elbow. Feint a thrust. Commit with the feet, but not the hands.

My blade flicks laterally under his block, his instincts fooled, my footwork shouting lunge, my attack anything but. Still he *moves.* My blade tugs on something, but he's gone. His sword bites into my left shoulder. I need space. He lets me have it.

Blood flows from a shallow cut on my leg, more from the gash on my shoulder. I can fight, but the more I press my body, the quicker I'll lose blood. Not that it matters. This will be over soon, one way or another. He looks at me in disbelief, his strangely glimmering blade gleaming red with my blood. He favors his leg, though. He's bleeding, too. Fast as he is, I can't imagine the last time he's been hurt in a duel. I can barely accept that I'm the one who did it.

His eyes change. They aren't focused on me, not at all. Something else...

A gust of wind slams into my back, a solid fist of air. I stumble forward, lungs aching again. I start to regain my balance, and an invisible hand yanks me to the left. I resist the pull. The pressure flits to the other side in an instant, and I nearly fall at the sudden change. I duck, instinct taking over, and feel a rush of air ruffle my hair. Another fist hammers into my wounded leg, and I collapse to a knee.

This isn't fair.

I force my head up to meet his eyes as he walks towards

me. Air condenses around my arms, strong as steel. I can't lift my blade, can't regain my feet. Damn it, no. Not like this. He can't...

He can't have her.

The world ignites. The deep umber of the trees, the pure blue flame of the distant snow... and a shocking torrent of white flame tinged with metallic intent. The air is alive, darting and weaving to this man's call. His form is a flame too bright to look at directly, the silhouette of his body alive with blinding fire pouring from him in streams of light. His will fills the air in the glade completely. His sword glows a strange mixture of light, ochre and emerald and gray. At his will, white fire encircles my arms and wraps around my chest. I can almost read the intent in the metallic glow.

Stay. Resist. Hold.

It isn't natural. Not to the air. It will listen to the man who bears its mark, but reluctantly. The white flame longs to be in motion, to dance to its own melody.

Then... *dance.*

A line of pure golden light cuts across the space between us. In its wake, the white flame floats away, untethered, set free from the metallic fire of intent. My arms jump forward, my sword free. The glowing weapon in his hand moves in a blur of flame and slams against mine. A spark. Golden and true. Drifting down towards the emerald fire of the earth, flickering in the coldness of the white flame of air, its life the span of a second.

I can feel it, *hear* it, this tiny spark. If I call... it will answer.

Lifting my open hand, golden light pours from me. The spark leaps through the air onto my palm, taking the light into itself and growing. Coldness spreads through my chest, and I gasp. The Vengeance flicks my forgotten sword from my hand. His energy relaxes, his furious light dimming. He believes he's won.

My other hand lurches forward, crackling light exploding outward. A stream of fire washes over him, red and orange and *hungry.* My brain distantly imagines him collapsing to the ground, his clothing aflame and his skin scorched. The Vengeance does nothing of the sort. Somehow, someway, a sheet of white fire blocks the scouring flame. He had no time to react, no space to move, and yet the air pushes back against my fire.

Throwing myself to my feet, I pour more into the fire, more of myself. My limbs go cold, my legs shake. The shield of air shrinks. He leans away, white flame flickering. I feel Juliet behind me. She will be safe. I just have to finish this.

"Stop! Jace, stop!" I would recognize her voice anywhere. The words, though, don't make sense. I'm defending *her.* Why should I stop?

Crimson light engulfs my outstretched arm and yanks it away. My fire blasts harmlessly into the air. Shock snaps my connection to the flame. The world returns to dull color. The fire dies, leaving nothing but a shimmer in the cold Summer air. Juliet stands, her own arm outstretched, the blood red symbol of the Master of Beasts bright on her arm.

"Why?" I ask dully, too spent to fear the Vengeance still standing behind me.

"I can't let you kill him," she says, the glow of her mark fading. "I can't let you kill your own father."

Silence roars throughout the forest. The world seems scared to breathe. Time slows to a crawl.

"That... what?" I ask finally, shaking my head, trying to make sense of her words.

"How *dare* you." The Vengeance spits the words. He's looking past me to Juliet. Burns and blisters decorate his cheeks and outstretched hand. He doesn't notice. He doesn't even seem to remember I'm here. "My daughter was stolen from me. *Stolen.* And now you come here with these lies."

"It isn't a lie," Juliet says strongly. "Jace is your son, or may the Creator strike me down, here and now."

"Abomination," he hisses, his eyes locked on the smooth

skin of her forearm where the red symbol once stood. He raises his sword. "You should not exist, for Kranos lives. You are an affront to the Creator and his works. You must be cleansed, in his name."

My thoughts run slowly. I have no weapon to stop him with, no energy to defend against his rage. I will my limbs to move, to get in the way one last time. I fall to a knee instead. He flows past me, steady and smooth as always. How does he have the strength? A grunt of surprised pain echoes over my shoulder. I barely have the energy to turn, but I do.

A great bear of a man grapples with the Vengeance.

"That's enough, Al," a deep voice growls. The Mason. "You don't have the right. Not anymore. You're not—"

"I *am* the Vengeance!"

His thunderous shout echoes. He spins, ripping himself free of the Mason's grip. The sword in his hand flashes across. A dull ring, the sound of steel against stone, reverberates through the clearing. The sound grows, on and on, a sonorous bell tolling the end of the world. The Vengeance freezes, a look of horror spreading across his face. His sword falls to the ground as the ring dies, his hands reaching out, trembling, towards the Mason.

"Itolas, Itolas are you…?"

"I'm fine, Al," the Mason says, his voice gentle. "No harm. No blood."

"I… I…"

"I know, friend," he says, carefully placing an arm around the Vengeance's shoulders. "Save your apologies."

The Mason leads the Vengeance out of the clearing, murmuring all the while. Neither looks back.

"Creator help us all," James Elthe breathes into the emptiness that follows. "What just happened?"

Chapter 7
Iliana
The Sixty-Ninth Day of Summer
In the year 5223, Council Reckoning

"Come on, princess," he calls from somewhere ahead, his voice filled with mocking laughter. "You're faster than that."

The swaying greenery of the garden blocks any sight of him. I scowl anyway. I'm being careful not to step on any of the flowers I've worked so hard to grow. He, on the other hand… I kneel in the rich earth. Petals of vibrant pink lie crushed in the sharp impression of his boot. Their half-shattered parent tilts dangerously. Forlornly.

"Princess?" he calls. "Iliana?"

He keeps shouting, sounding more and more distressed by the second. Serves him right. It gets hard not to giggle as he searches frantically through the thick greenery. I press both hands to my mouth to hold it in.

"Iliana!" he shouts in agony.

"I'm right here, silly," I say playfully, standing up a few paces away.

He jumps halfway out of his boots. Relief floods his face, though it is quickly replaced by anger.

"Why didn't you answer me?" he asks, stomping over. His hair, in desperate need of a cut, flops down over his eyes. Dirt and sweat streak his face, and rich soil covers the knees and elbows of the fine clothes he wore to the palace today. He must have fallen trying to look for me. He doesn't seem to notice that I watch his feet, which, miraculously, manage not to crush any more of my flowers. "Well?"

"I was punishing you," I say, smiling.

"Punishing…?" His chubby cheeks crinkle in confusion. "For

what?"

I point down to the crushed peony at my feet. He looks down at the earth, then at his boots, then back to me. He has the decency to look ashamed.

"Oh, Iliana, I'm sorry," he says, bending down to look at the broken flower. "Is there anything we can do for it?"

"I don't know," I say, crouching down next to him. "Maybe if we can get it to stand, it'll have a chance."

"Great! I'll be right back," he says, jumping up and nearly crushing the plant again.

A warm breeze filters through the leaves and stirs my dress. With it comes scents, strange scents foreign to the fresh smells of soil and life. Things both beautiful and ugly, delectable and sickening. My feet guide me over to the bars marking the edge of the palace gardens. Down a slope and between some trees, I can just see the nearest estate's fence. Beyond it, the distant shape of the city proper, filled with buildings and people I've only seen from the back of a carriage.

"Iliana!" he shouts again, already exasperated.

"I'm over here," I call patiently.

He comes to stand next to me, a broken wooden training sword in his hand. He looks down at his estate and frowns.

"Why are we looking at my house? It's boring."

"Not to me," I say quietly. "I want to go there. And everywhere."

"You're ten years old," he reminds me, smiling a taunt. "They'll never let a kid like you go anywhere."

"Torlas Graevo, you are so mean," I say, stomping my foot. "I think I should be able to go wherever I want."

He looks thoughtful before glancing around at the greenery. Though we know there are guards lining the perimeter of the garden, none are currently in sight.

"Come on, princess," he says, taking my hand. "Let me show you something."

Torlas leads me along the edge of the garden. He moves slowly, *his eyes following the black iron bars of the fence. He stops twice and grips a particular bar, but nothing happens. The third time he pauses, the bar rattles in its housing. Glancing around again to make sure we can't be seen, he fiddles with the bar until it comes off entirely. The space it leaves is just wide enough for me to squeeze through.*

"There," he says, satisfied.

"There, what?"

"This bar has been loose for years. I used to be able to climb through it, but I've gotten too big. It looks right for a munchkin like you, though." He stares down at the opening, his expression glum. I get the feeling he once used this gap quite a bit. "If you ever want to get out of the palace without being seen, just come here. That fence is my estate. There's a bar I made loose a while ago there, too."

"But I'll be caught," I say, suddenly afraid. "The soldiers will tell Father."

"You know they let you stay in the garden all you want," he says, flipping the mop of his hair out of his eyes. "Tell them you'll be here, and you can leave whenever you want. If you want to see me, you just have to ask. Just be careful if you go alone. People might report a little girl wandering around by herself. Here."

He disappears into the brush. The gap in the fence feels as wide as the horizon. A way out of the palace? A way to see the city? To talk to strange people? It takes everything I have not to dart through the narrow exit right away. Torlas returns with a ball of earth in his hands, from which sprouts a slender green stalk, a bud just beginning to open. A lily. Using the broken sword, he carves a narrow hole large enough for the roots. When he finishes patting the soil smooth, he stands and makes a vague gesture.

"Do your thing. Make it grow."

Scrunching shut my eyes, I try to find the earth, breathing slowly like Father always says. It's hard to find the feeling most places, especially in the palace. Here, though, the earth wants to talk. It likes to listen. I ask it, as nicely as I can, to help the little plant to grow. To bring it water and make it comfortable.

143

Green light flickers under my eyelids. I open my eyes to see Torlas looking at me in amazement. The earth has flattened around the plant, and moisture squeezes to the surface. It might be my imagination, but it already looks happier.

"Now you'll never forget where it is," Torlas says, smiling at me. "If you ever need me, just find the white lily."

***

"Your Eminence?"

Morning light bathes my room. I slept. By some miracle. But that dream... that memory... Torlas's death may no longer hold any edges, but this sweetness is sharp enough to cut. Deeply.

"Court is in an hour, your Eminence."

"Lentana, they can wait a few minutes," I murmur sleepily, stretching luxuriously in the soft sheets.

A shaft of sunlight lances through the balcony window and burns into my eyes. The last bit of sleepiness fades. Groaning, I sit up. The tangled mess of my hair drapes over my shoulders and down to the sheets. Apparently, I forgot to put it up before I fell asleep. I climb reluctantly out of bed.

"What dress would you like today?" Lentana asks, voice disappearing into the closet on the opposite wall.

"How about a dress of... your people?" I feel awkward asking, like I'm crossing a line that shouldn't be crossed. Steeling my resolve, I push forward. "Of Coin?"

Lentana's face appears around the closet door for a moment, her expression unreadable. Abruptly, she grins, the corner of her mouth nearly reaching her ears. Creator, she's gorgeous. Her eyes sparkle as she disappears back into the closet.

"I have just the one!" she calls happily.

She's back before I finish standing up. A thin sheet of coral fabric drapes over her arm. That must just be the slip... right? She's going to get the rest of the dress? She doesn't seem to be going back into the closet...

Her attendants gather with a comb in hand and go to work

on the snarls in my hair as Lentana slips off my night clothes and slides the coral dress up my hips. It isn't silk, but whatever it is, it slides along my skin with supple softness. Asymmetrical, draped over just my right shoulder, the dress flows to the backs of my ankles, rising to my knees in the front. It is entirely modest and entirely provocative all at once. My bare shoulder feels exposed, my legs open for all to see, the material itself so thin it feels like I'm wearing the air.

At a signal from Lentana, the servants spin my hair into a high tail. Lentana herself slips two golden torcs onto my arms above my elbow. She takes locks of my hair and draws them through cunning loops in the burnished rings.

The woman in the mirror staring back at me looks nothing like me. The wide fan of shining hair, the bright color of the dress that brings out the blue shimmer in her eyes... my skin has always been a shade different from the people of Donir, my hair an exotic color. This dress just *fits* the woman in the mirror as the style of the east never has.

"Lentana, this is…"

"Tana," she murmurs, her smile wide and genuine. "Only my mother and the Minister ever called me by my full name."

"Tana," I say, meeting her eyes. The difference fits her perfectly. "How do I look?"

"Like a queen of the West."

***

If my sudden change of attire causes a stir, the whispers are outside my hearing. The Tide in the hall are too disciplined to waver, and the supplicants are worried more about themselves. The only person who eyes my new look with anything resembling concern is Uncle. Court passes in a blur, finishing sometime past the ringing of the noontide bell. I struggle not to hurry my steps to match Uncle as he escorts me out of the hall.

"Going native, Iliana?" he asks, glancing at me once we're alone.

145

"The dresses we brought from Donir are too hot for this place," I answer honestly. The material of the Khalintari dress makes the air in the grand hall feel positively cool. "It means nothing."

"It suits you," he says, his face stern. "You look more like your mother now than you ever have before."

"Truly?" I ask, unsure how I feel.

I have no memory of my mother, nothing to tie the comment to. No likeness, no feeling, just the distant secondhand memories Father and Uncle have shared with me through the years. He continues without bothering to answer the question.

"So you sent Cortola to weed out the rebels to the south," he says slowly. I brace myself for a reprimand. "An inspired play. He will join them, and thereby show us his true allegiance, or he will die, giving us a martyr to sway the populace, or he will succeed, removing a thorn from our side and proving his loyalty. Any outcome serves us well."

"Thank you, Uncle."

"You are your father's daughter, whether you know it or not," he says, smiling a strange smile.

A memory wells to the surface, a moment I don't know if I truly lived. A man writhing in pain, held up by chains, his face broken by torture. His eyes blaze as they meet mine.

"Your Tide is safe. Your father spared her the moment he realized you cared."

Pain lances into my brain in a sudden spike, scattering my thoughts. My eyes clench shut against the agony, tears leaking from their corners. A name briefly flits across my thoughts before the pain rises to consume it.

Markis Calladan.

"Iliana, are you well?" Uncle asks, his voice devoid of any real concern.

"Fine," I gasp, shaking my head. The pain disappears as I let the memory go. The memory? The dream? Impossible to say.

146

"I'm fine."

"I have business this afternoon. We will dine together this evening," he says, turning to leave. "The new Minister of the Ram has matters he wishes to discuss away from the eyes of the court. I agreed on your behalf."

"Of course, Uncle," I say automatically, Tana's words, her questions, lurking in my heart as I watch him leave.

Not towards the entrance of the House, though. That way lies to the south. His business, whatever it is, lies to the west.

***

Follow late walkers west.

The moon passes the window and casts my room in darkness. Throwing back the sheets, I silently stalk over to the closet, drawing on a simple dress of white. It isn't a perfect match for the servant's attire, but it will have to do.

Walking unnoticed in the House of the Republic won't be as trivial as it was back in the palace in Donir. There, I knew the halls and the rooms like the back of my hand. With a superficial disguise, I could walk with the confidence of any other servant. I have none of those advantages here. The ever-vigilant Tide won't allow me to wander, and here there is no garden, no loose bar, no white lily. I'll have to get creative if I want to pass unseen. The only thing I have going for me is that so few of the natives have seen me up close.

Last night's intruder unwittingly offered the perfect path. My balcony opens onto a drop that would be death to any who missed a single step. Luckily for me, I don't have to climb. Wrapping a scarf around my shoulder to hide the light, I call on the earth. Shards of glass slide into place, a near-invisible staircase hovering in the air. My connection with the earth allows me to practically run down the floating steps. Any misstep I make, the glass shifts to correct.

As I descend, I keep an eye on the smooth marble wall. There was no report of a broken body found outside the House, so the stranger must have found some way to disappear… there.

A window, arched and split down the middle into two swinging doors, reflects the silver light of the stars. At my command, the glass creates an easy path closer to the wall, the shards higher up flowing into place beneath my feet. A dark smudge marks the sill. Blood. Creator knows how they managed to reach this window without my advantages. Set below and behind the outer edge of the balcony, they must either have sprouted wings or done some absurd acrobatics while bleeding from fresh wounds.

Sorry, whoever you are. I hope you don't hold it against me.

The window opens easily at my touch. Slipping through the narrow opening is no problem. Wherever I am, there is absolutely no light. Calling the glass to me, I slowly unwind the thin scarf until a bit of emerald light peeks through. A narrow corridor stretches forward, rough-hewn and unfinished, perhaps a servant's hall that the builders decided not to spend the money to complete—slim chance in a city named Coin—or a hidden passage not meant to be found. Either way, it is a perfect way to move west.

I walk for a while in silence before the sound of low voices reaches my ear. Slowing, I edge forward, casting about for the source of the sound. By my estimation, I should be leaving the east wing of the House of the Republic and approaching the central hall, though this thin hallway shows no sign of ending. The voices, though… It's almost like I'm in the room with them.

"…quiet as a Temple of the Unknown. I don't know why they make us watch this hallway."

"Whatever, it's easy work. Better than guarding *that* door. The things I've heard…"

"Don't tell me. I'd rather sleep well at night."

Their voices, clearly two soldiers of the Wave on watch, echo from my right. A solid wall of rock. I edge closer to the wall, and a narrow crack appears, only visible with my face nearly pressed against the stone. I can just see light, filtered cerulean... a piece of cloth... a wall hanging. Right. The colors of the sea are only hung where the public can see them. My guess about nearing the center must be accurate. Leaving the bored soldiers to their watch, I press on. Several passages leading off to the south and north loom in the darkness and disappear. I ignore them for now; I need to keep heading west.

The longer I walk, the stranger I feel. Do these hidden passages honeycomb the entire building? Do they grant access to my chambers? Have I *ever* been safe in the House of the Republic? I haven't seen any exits aside from the window I came in. If that is the only entrance, this passage can't be very useful.

The narrow corridor winds to the right in a gentle curve before coming to a sudden end. A ladder stretches upwards, though only a short distance. So much for this passage being a mistake or unfinished. Picturing the curve of the wall, how far I've gone... ah. I'm following the wall at the entrance of the grand hall. The ladder must lead up and over the high doors, then back on the other side. Climbing, I can picture the doorway in my mind as my feet touch down on the other side. Into the west wing.

As interesting and disconcerting as this little jaunt has been, though, I'm going to need to find an exit eventually. Whatever my mysterious messenger wants me to see, it probably isn't inside these walls. The rough-hewn stone smothers the sound of my footsteps. Trailing my fingertips along the wall, my feet slow almost of their own accord until I come to a stop.

I should turn back. There's nothing worth seeing here.

Shaking my head, I cast the errant doubt aside and force my feet forward. In seconds, I come to a stop again, no more than a few paces farther on.

I should turn back. There's nothing worth seeing here. No one should be wandering the halls this late.

That last thought sends a spike of adrenaline racing

through my veins.

No one should be wandering the halls? Why would I think that?

With the thought comes awareness. Something presses against me, an unseen force almost like a hand against my chest. Now that I'm aware of it, the deterrent feels frail, a suggestion rather than a command. My awareness robs it of its power, and the desire to turn back disappears. Forcing myself not to hurry, I walk carefully forward, eyes wide for any movement.

A distant scream echoes through the hall.

That scream, so terrible, so filled with horror... I've only heard its like once before. It isn't the same scream, not from the same person, but there can be no mistaking it. The last time I heard such utter anguish was when I pressed my ear to the stone of the dungeons below the palace in Donir... a secret passage behind a cell that prisoners disappeared from... agony splits my head in two as the memory spills out into living color.

He jerks to the side, flying through the air and slamming into the bars of the cell, his armor screeching in discordant protest. Out of his control, his head turns slowly, deliberately, to face the occupant of the cell. He lets out a whimper as his face moves forward and presses against the bars. I can see his muscles straining to run, to hide, to flee, but nothing happens. Nothing can resist the power of the Master of Beasts.

"What are you doing here, little man?" Uncle's rumbling voice echoes down the hall.

Tears stream unchecked down my cheeks, arcing lightning jumping through my brain, black torment eroding my will. I push against the pain like a wall of thorns, cutting myself to press through to the memory.

Terin. His name was Terin. A Wave assigned as a guard at the entrance to the dungeons, young and earnest and...

My hand presses against the wall, the only thing keeping me from falling. The pain recedes as I let the memory fade.

150

Something lurks in my mind, a panther stalking my thoughts and guarding certain memories with claws and teeth. What else have I forgotten? What else have I done of which I have no memory?

The screaming trails away. A presence, unseen but palpable, flows through the corridor on the other side of my palm. Heavy steps, too far apart for any normal man. As he passes close on the other side, the air shivers and is still. The echo of his steps fades, and air brushes against my cheek. Pressing my face close to the stone, another crack beckons.

A corridor, nearly identical in appearance to the passages in the east wing, stretches out of sight in either direction. Across from my vantage, a woman with brown hair and bland features sits with her legs crossed on top of a small table, tossing a dagger into the air and catching it effortlessly. Dark clothing covers flexible leather armor, and her boots look well-made and well-used. There can be no doubt. She is a member of the Deep. A season or two ago, she'd be answering to me. If she is in any way bothered by the screams, she doesn't show it. The urge to leave, to turn back, still plays unending in the back of my mind. The feeling seems to be coming *from* this woman.

Footsteps sound in the hallway, different from before. The woman perks up, the dagger falling easily into her hand. She relaxes as whoever it is comes into sight.

"Took you long enough. It's past midnight," she says, stifling a yawn.

"You patrolled recently?" a man asks from my right in a familiar voice.

"Didn't need to." She stands and stretches, jerking her head towards the hallway leading west. "The big man himself just finished up."

"Damn," Silken says, striding into view. "They're always riled up after he stops by."

"Better you than me," she says carelessly, patting him on the shoulder and disappearing back towards the center of the

House.

The man stands in the middle of the hallway, the cant of his shoulders screaming reluctance. Finally, he sighs, straightening up and striding onwards. The second he does so, the urge to turn back, to return to bed, picks up again, a shade stronger this time. I take two steps back before I realize what I'm doing. Shaking my head, I hurry after him.

The walls are thick, and his footsteps fade quickly. Pushing forwards, I keep my eyes open for any potential exits. Every ten steps or so, the sound of his footfalls returns stronger. I guess the spying seams lie at those regular intervals. After the pattern repeats four times, I expect to hear him again ten paces later, but I'm greeted by silence. Slowing, I search out the crack. The corridor beyond is dark and motionless. He must have turned.

Backtracking, I return to the last passage leading south. There have been none leading north for some time, as no walls have bisected the wide corridor proper to offer a path north. I just have to hope he's gone south. Fear hurries my feet along. Whatever is going on here, he's my best chance of finding it.

Something echoes down the hallway, so faint at first that I can barely hear it. A melody. A voice lifted in song. The song draws me forward, familiar and haunting. I've heard it before, I know I have, but I can't place it. The strange pain lurks in the recesses of my mind. Experience tells me the memory lies somewhere beyond its rending wall.

The song grows in strength and beauty. It is a song of healing, of forgiveness, of spirits soaring to the heavens. I can't understand the words, yet I know them all the same. Closing my eyes, I let my hand trail along the stone and drift with the current of the music. I am walking through the trees along a stream, the tinkle of water, the urge to swim and forget my sorrow. A tightness in my chest, a tension I've carried so long I'd forgotten it even existed, eases. My lungs draw in a breath fuller than any I've felt in a long time. There is pain, but the pain of a stretched scar, not a fresh wound.

A discordant clang shatters the song and sends me crashing back to the present. My lungs constrict, my heart beating wildly in my chest. Even so, the pressure does not feel so immense. The edge isn't so sharp.

"Cut that out, old man." Silken. Close, like we're in the same room. "No one wants to hear your shite."

"I disagree. Even someone as hopeless as you might benefit, Silken."

That voice. The soft warmth of it, like it might break into laughter at any moment. Like it cannot help but impart wisdom.

"Shut up," Silken growls.

A flash of silver illuminates the crack to my left. Silver light. My pulse quickens. The Master of Thought? Hurrying over to the crack, I peer into a room filled with shadows. Silken stands near the doorway, a silver symbol illuminating his silhouette from the side of his neck. Another man stands opposite him, his shoulders thrown back and his long hair wild. All of the furniture has been removed, but this room was probably meant to store goods for the upkeep of the House of the Republic. A few metal bars run vertically along the walls, all that remains of racks meant for food or wine.

"It will take a greater will than yours to cow me, Silken," the man says, stepping forward. "If your master hasn't done it, what makes you think *you* can?"

Fear crosses Silken's face as he realizes how close he's allowed the prisoner to get. He hurriedly slams the door. The sound of a key turning in a lock fills the sudden quiet. The prisoner stands motionless in the middle of the room, some distant filtered light offering just enough to discern his outline. Without warning, he throws his head back and shouts.

"Live, friends! Your souls cannot break unless you lose the will to fight! So fight!"

Weariness slumps his shoulders after the declaration. His

voice moves in my chest, knocking on doors closed and locked. The way he moves, the beauty of his song…

"Telias?" I whisper aloud, an ache building in my head.

He disappears in the darkness. For a moment, the room is still. Though his outline doesn't reappear, his voice whispers back to mine through the crack.

"I may finally be going mad. Princess?"

"Is it…" I stop, claws of agony rending at my thoughts, trying to scatter them before I can think. "Is it you?"

"Yes…"

The way he says the word carries so much more meaning than any simple affirmation. It is relief, joy, welcome, agreement, and, yes, affirmation. Telias.

"How did you…?" I stop, fighting back tears that fill my eyes, desperately holding in sobs that tremble through my chest.

It doesn't matter how he got here, just that he is. Our conversations in the dungeons back in Donir play through my mind, his confidence, his surety. For once, my head doesn't hurt. For once, my heart doesn't ache.

"There is always a choice. Always. A choice to follow or to lead. A choice of loyalty or love. A choice to live… or to die."

"I chose wrong, Telias," I say finally, the words catching in my throat. "So wrong."

"I'm sorry," he whispers, with all the understanding in the world.

"I… I'm so… *afraid.*" My fist slams against the stone. The sound doesn't carry; the stone doesn't care. "Something is *wrong* with me."

"What do you mean?" he asks gently.

"I keep… remembering things. Things that didn't happen. Or maybe they did. People. Conversations. It's like I've forgotten half my life. And when I remember…"

"What happens?" His voice is louder. He presses against the crack on the other side of the wall, as if his nearness can lend

154

some comfort.

"It hurts," I say helplessly. "Like a monster stands between me and what I should know. Like claws rip apart my mind if I try."

"Creator damn him," Telias growls, rage abruptly burning in his voice. "Curse the man that died and left this power to *him*."

"Who?"

"He's destroying everything, spitting on the Creator and nature." His forehead thumps against the wall. "I feared something like this, but I didn't think... not to you of all people..."

"What are you saying?" I ask, the tightness in my chest returning a hundredfold. "What did he... what has been done to me?"

"Iliana," he says, his voice losing its angry edge. "Kranos... isn't what he is supposed to be. He is not the Master of Beasts. Or at least, not *just* the Master of Beasts. He has been... experimenting. Under the cover of the Sealord's power, he is fighting to bend and break the laws of nature. It started in Tarin, before the Council even fell. He stole the power of the last Master of Thought."

"That's... that's not possible. It can't be."

"I would have agreed with you a season ago," he says softly. "There's a reason Helikos let Kranos take me across the Way of the North. They both know I won't tell them anything through any measure of torture. But every few days, he comes to this room and tries to break me. He tries to push into my mind, to learn what I know. It is... insidious."

"You're saying..." I gasp, the implication of his words slowly dawning on me.

"Yes," he says slowly, sadly. "It is the only explanation I can imagine. Kranos is abusing his power to control your mind."

"No, I—"

I can't believe it. I won't believe it.

Or is this exactly *why* I won't believe it?

My legs drop out from under me, my clenched fist

155

remaining stretched over my head. The air moves slowly to the uneven hitch of my breath. My skin burns where the cloth of my dress touches me. My mind… my thoughts…

What is me? What is him?

Who am I?

Telias begins to hum, the soft sound a gentle caress. I can feel his need to reach out, to take me in his arms, to lend what comfort he can. His presence might be the only thing standing between my sanity and…

"You said… you said before Tarin?" I whisper. My whole life. My whole life he's been around me, training me, pretending to *care* for me. My whole life. "Do you think… who *am*… can I trust…?"

"You are still yourself, Iliana," he whispers, understanding my half-completed thoughts. "No one has the strength to control another completely."

"I trusted him," I say in wonder. "I trusted them both. Against every instinct. Against everyone… everyone who actually *loved* me."

"This may be why," he answers gently.

"Father…"

"I'm sure he knows. It may even have been his idea." Telias sighs, an expression of such world-weariness it hurts to hear it. "I'm sorry, Iliana."

"The things I've done…" I collapse completely, wrapping my arms around my legs and burying my face. "I am their puppet."

"No," he says fiercely, pressing his face against the crack. "No. Never that."

"It is that, or I am a monster in truth."

He is silent for a time. My mind is empty, drifting, waiting for this man to answer. I'm drowning, dark water closing over my head as surely as the proud soldiers washed from the Way of the North.

"We all have it in us to be monstrous," he says finally. "Goodness lies in resisting that monster. In chaining it up, in keeping it at bay. The greatest among us have mighty chains indeed." He pauses. Takes a breath. "Yet all chains are breakable. Especially if someone does their best to weaken them. You are not a puppet, Iliana. And you do bear some guilt for your deeds. That guilt, though, this pain, shows me that you are most definitely not a monster. Monsters do not feel regret."

"Then what am I?" I ask desperately, helplessly.

"You are a young woman who must fight if she wishes to be good."

"How? How can I fight against my own mind?"

"I will teach you."

***

"You look tired, Your Eminence."

"It's nothing, Tana," I say, smiling at her through the mirror as she runs a comb through my hair. Studying her for a moment, something seems strange about her. When she bends, she looks stiff, her normal confident grace absent. "Are you alright?"

"I'm in perfect health," she says quickly. "I'm more worried about you. Did you sleep last night?"

"Of course I did," I say just as quickly.

"Good. The Lord General wants to see you in his rooms."

My stomach falls to the soles of my feet. There's no way he knows what I got up to last night unless I can't trust my thoughts from him at any distance. No, no. That path leads to paranoia and madness. There have to be limits to his connection to my mind. There *have* to be.

"It is the most basic of techniques, but remember. If you try not to think about something, it will inevitably rise to the surface of your thoughts. Instead, choose to think about something else. Anything else. Something fascinating, intriguing, even something distantly related to what you wish to hide. Think like the Maelstrom, which no ship has

escaped. *Circle around those thoughts, over and over again, and let him be trapped in that current. Fill your mind, and you can hide your true feelings.*"

I'm not ready to face him. I haven't slept, haven't practiced...

"I can tell him you're indisposed," she says, reading something in my face.

"No, it's fine."

It'll have to be.

His rooms are directly below mine, a symbol of my place as queen. It is only symbolic, though. I try to marshal my thoughts on the short walk to the stairs. Swirl my thoughts. Concentrate on anything *but* the fact that I know he's been messing with my mind.

Now I'm thinking about it. Okay... my duties?

My brain goes dull even as I think of sitting on that graceless glass throne. And, now that I know what he's doing, I'll never feel comfortable with him at my side again—

Eternal damn it.

A Maelstrom, a Maelstrom... what intrigues me? What can I think of so deeply as to drown out everything else?

Emerald eyes and fiery hair.

No. Not that mystery. Anything else...

"Do you think you'll be long?"

"What?"

Oh, Creator save me. We're at the door.

"Should I wait for you here, or...?" Tana says, eyeing me strangely.

"Oh. No. You can go about your duties, just be available should I need to find you."

As she turns to leave, she whispers something under her breath, something along the lines of 'you *are* my duties,' but I don't pay her any mind. I can't.

The door swings open to reveal Uncle's stern visage. I cast myself into a Maelstrom of thought, though I've no idea if it will

158

protect me or drown me.

"Iliana, come. There's much to discuss," he says, moving aside to allow me forward.

"Of course, Uncle," I say, but my thoughts are far away.

I think of Father, his stoicism, his pride, his joy in me and sorrow for my mother, his stern visage breaking into a smile...

"Did you hear me, Iliana?"

"Hm, what?" I ask vaguely, dazed, my vision blurry as it settles on his broad face. Tears. "I'm sorry, Uncle. My mind was elsewhere."

"Indeed," he grunts, leaning forward. I sit in a chair while I try to remember what he was saying. A series of maps lie spread across the surface of the broad table that occupies the majority of his sitting space. It is exactly like the war room from the palace. The map of the Khalintars is largest and most predominant, and there are a hundred notations in Uncle's tight script. He taps the table to bring my eyes back to his. "We must keep our eyes forward, not backward, if we wish to advance. Focus on the here and now."

There. The compulsion. An invisible wave of intent, insinuating itself in my thoughts. The urge to forget, to think only of the present. His eyes narrow, and I give in to the urge.

"Yes, Uncle," I say hurriedly, pasting a smile on my face.

"As I said before," he begins slowly, suspicion still written across his face. "I'm leaving you for a while."

"What?" I say in surprise, sitting up straighter in my chair. "Why? Where are you going?"

"After your move with Cortola, I have faith that you'll manage in my absence," he says, an excited gleam entering his eyes. "I've found something to the west. Something we've sought for years."

"What is it?"

"I suppose there is no harm in telling you," he says, standing and pacing about the room. I've never seen him so agitated, so animated. "There is a thief on the border of the Western Khalintars. A leader of some bandit tribe; what they call themselves is irrelevant. The victims of their thefts all share a similar story: each of them goes suddenly blind just before the thief strikes. Everything goes dark."

"Kettle!" I say, though the conflicted emotions that well up at the mention of her name are hard to name.

"She has loyalty. She loves. She is willing to do whatever it takes for her friend to be safe. Why should we punish her for that?"

Who said that? Whose voice...?

"I don't think so," he says, frowning as his long steps devour the length of the room and return. "Though now that you mention it, I guess it isn't impossible. But no, I think it is the Master of Light."

"The Master of Light can strike people blind?"

"Iliana, please," he chides, turning to me as he continues to pace. "Imagine for just a moment what you could do with light."

"I guess you could stop the light from reaching their eyes..."

"Yes," he says impatiently. "Or bend it around them, or deflect it away from them. Either way, it is a rudimentary use of the power at best, but it fits. There have been no other witnesses. No one has seen a suspicious figure, nor have they noticed anything strange, even though the thefts have all been conducted in broad daylight."

"They are so bold?" I say, not having to feign interest. "They must be far from here if they are taking such a risk."

"Yes. Near the border to the west, as I said. It will take me some days to make it there and track them down. I wouldn't expect to be gone much more than a fortnight, however."

"Fourteen days?" I ask skeptically. "To reach the western border and return? That must be what... five hundred miles?"

"Closer to seven, to reach the villages I'm discussing. Don't worry. I have methods of travel that are both quicker and more reliable than horseback."

"I would never worry about you," I say honestly, though I try to keep the edge out of the words. "I'm sure you'll be back, safe and sound."

"Yes," he says, halting his pacing and facing me completely. "Iliana, you're acting strangely this morning."

"Am I?" The question is more to stall than anything.

"Your... words... feel off."

"I'm distracted," I say, allowing the heavy sorrow of Torlas's death to rise to my mind. His pride, his anguish, his words, cutting me in places I didn't know could be cut... "I'm sorry, Uncle."

"When I get back, we'll talk about this further." He smiles slightly, his handsome face blossoming with confidence and power. Though now, staring into his eyes, I can't help but see their cruelty. "Until then, be careful, Iliana. The people of Coin are not to be trusted. Though I've done my best to weed out any potential insurgents in the House of the Republic, there are ten thousand people who'd love to see you dead in this treacherous city. Stay with the Tide, keep to the House, and you'll be fine until I get back."

"Of course, Uncle," I say automatically.

"Then I'll see you on my return."

I stand at the dismissal. He turns immediately to the maps, his eyes scanning his route. When I reach the door, something makes me pause.

Leave, you fool. You survived. You passed the test. He's not even thinking about you anymore. Just leave.

"What are you going to do if you find them?"

Creator, I'm an idiot.

"What?" he says, glancing up.

"I said, what are you going to do if you find the Master of Light?"

The pause before his words is nearly imperceptible, and

161

yet...

"Recruit them, of course. If you were a bandit on the outskirts of society, wouldn't you want to be raised to a high position in the Empire of the Sea?"

I offer him a sickly smile and a nod, ducking through the door before I can say anything stupid enough to get me caught. I almost jog through the halls back to my rooms, closing the door firmly behind me and leaning my back against the warm wood separating me from the rest of the palace. Hope and fear fight for my attention, my stomach roiling. Fourteen days. I have fourteen days to speak to Telias, to learn what I can of the world.

Fourteen days to take back my life.

Chapter 8
Bastian

The Seventy-Seventh Day of Summer
In the year 5223, Council Reckoning

"I can tell you're worried about her."

"I'm just so bored," I say, planting my chin on my hand.

"Liar," Jynn says, skipping past. "Regardless, there's no sign they suspect Tana. Relax."

"All I've been doing is relaxing!" I stand, wearing away at the barren stone of the little hideaway with my steps. Maybe if I'm stuck here much longer, I can pace my way into an escape tunnel. There isn't even a decent window in the safe house where the Khal has us stashed. "This is entirely unnecessary. I'm leaving."

"Be patient," Jynn says in her too-high voice. She moves to block the door. "We don't know enough about those people who attacked you."

"I beat them, didn't I?"

"Only because they were stupid enough to try to take you in alive," Jynn says, her childlike face looking at me like *I'm* the immature one. Okay, fair, but still. "And you almost killed yourself to break through whatever wall they had around their minds. If they were planning murder, you'd be one dead hunk of meat."

"I..." I trail off, knowing that every word she's speaking is the truth. I don't have a decent argument to make. Honestly, I don't even have a bad argument, or I'd be making it. Sighing, I force myself to sink down onto the threadbare couch. The Khal could have at least given *some* consideration to my comfort.

"Listen, I get it."

"Do you?" I say sullenly, leaping to my feet and pacing

again.

"Bastian, if anyone gets you, it's me. I lived in your head, remember?" Jynn walks over and takes my hand, leading me gently over to sit again. I resist her pull easily, rooting myself in place. She looks up at me sympathetically. "You've been working alone for your entire life. You've never had to rely on anyone, and you never wanted to. Now you have people, competent, capable people, who are working on your behalf, and you don't know what to do with yourself."

"Yeah, but—"

"You also take orders about as well as an abused mule, because you're an arrogant prick who thinks he's always right." I regard her flatly. She looks up into my face, her eyes luminous pools of innocence. "So, be patient. If people are armed against our power, let our friends handle them. Our time will come."

"Fine," I say, relenting to her pull and collapsing bonelessly onto the couch with a sigh. "But I'm not waiting here much longer. In fact, if we don't hear something from the Khal soon, I'll go find her, or Gabriel, and *demand* some... are you even listening to me?"

"No, sorry," she says distractedly. "Your wait might be over. We have visitors."

"Are you sure?"

A complicated knock in the appropriate rhythm sounds on the wood. As I stand to face the door, I regard Jynn out of the corner of my eye. The symbol of her power, conspicuous on the edge of her palm, doesn't show even a glimmer of silver. How did she know? I always keep a tenuous grasp on the power so that I can read surface thoughts around me, but I have to focus to feel Gabriel's thought patterns on the other side of the door. He isn't alone. His companion is not from the Khal of Nothing, but his thoughts are familiar all the same.

"Oh," Jynn says quietly as she identifies the second presence as well. "Well, this is going to get interesting."

164

"Uh…"

"Don't worry. She wouldn't bring him here if she didn't think… well, there's always prayer, right?"

I don't have time to answer before a key rattles in the lock and the door swings open. Gabriel leads, his darting eyes taking in the small room before he moves aside to allow our visitor to enter. The second figure, hood up and face covered, slides past him. The Khal of Hands scans the street carefully before finally closing the door.

"Creator protect and keep you," Gabriel says, his face flat and stoic.

"And you as well!" Jynn says cheerfully, though her eyes flick maliciously between the hooded figure and me.

I meet the piercing eyes under the hood, careful to keep a neutral expression on my face. His slender hands rise to uncover his face, his eyes never leaving mine. He's older than I remember, still youthful and strong, but definitely older. The gray at the temples of his midnight black hair only lends his handsome face wisdom. Well, it would be handsome, if it wasn't currently twisted into a look of such utter disdain and hatred.

"You would bring me before *him?*" Eledar Cortola, the disgraced Minister of Finance, hisses, turning his glare on Gabriel. "Had I known your Khal of Nothing was this piece of Creator-cursed filth, I would have spit in your face before taking this meeting."

"Shouldn't you be showing a little more *fear*, Eledar?" I say evenly, a feral smile growing on my face. "When last we met…"

"Bastian."

Jynn folds her slender arms across her chest, one eyebrow rising in a look of reproach.

"Don't. You aren't that man anymore."

Says who.

"Says you, you stupid ass."

Jynn's voice is different in my mind, still high and girlish,

165

but with an edge that will only come as her body ages. My eyes flick back to Cortola and the look of pure rage spread across his features. Hate fills his eyes, so much hate that I don't bother reaching out to feel it. It would be like welcoming poison into my mind. But... below the anger, below the rage, lies something more primal, hidden by the bluster of his emotions. Fear.

You deserve his hatred. You earned it. What are you going to do now?

Get out of my head.

"I didn't say anything," Jynn says, confusion spreading across her face.

I stifle a groan. When did my weak little conscience adopt her voice?

Cortola watches the exchange between us, his face falling to stone. Feeling Jynn's gaze, ethereal and literal, boring into the side of my face, I sigh and relax. My shoulders fall. I didn't even realize they were tense. I guess I need to offer him something. I guess.

"Minister," I begin, doing my best to keep my voice from sarcasm. From the way his eyes narrow, I can't be sure if I succeeded. "You are... just... in your anger. What I did to you was, for lack of a better word, evil. I was young then, and naive, and stupid. So I guess... I'm sorry?"

"This is just another manipulation. Another abuse." He edges towards the door, his hand reaching for the handle behind him. "I told myself I would die before I let you anywhere near me again."

Anywhere near my daughter *again.*

Oh. Fuck, I forgot completely about the threat I levied on him when last we spoke. Something about forcing his daughter in front of him... man. I was nine colors of asshole back then.

"Oh come on. At least ten colors! Give yourself credit," Jynn says unhelpfully.

Thanks.

166

"Minister, I know you have no reason to take me at my word, but I promise you that I am a changed man." I run my hands through my hair, trying for some semblance of steadiness. "I have been through things that shaped me into something… else. I won't touch your thoughts. I… promise?"

"Then let me leave," he says, his eyes darting between me, Gabriel, and Jynn. He doesn't seem to know what to make of her. It's not surprising; I barely know what to make of her either.

"You are free to go at any time," Gabriel says smoothly. "Though I request that you wait until the Khal arrives. She would be disappointed if you didn't stay to hear her offer."

"He isn't your Khal?" Cortola says, his expression bewildered. "Then why is he here?"

"He served me for some time," Saran's rich voice calls from behind me. I jump, half-spinning. I've been trapped in this place for days. I would have staked my life on the fact that there was only one way out of the cramped little house. Damn woman and her hidden passages. "Now, our relationship is more of a mutual understanding."

"Served?" Cortola asks skeptically.

"Served." She says the word with such quiet confidence that challenging it would be like questioning the color of the sky. Cortola glances at me, and I shrug and nod. "Even knowing your prior relationship to this man, I brought you here for a reason."

"And what is that?"

"The foreign queen has sent you on a mission to root out rebels to the south," she says, not pausing for confirmation. "You stand with the leaders of those rebels. We would, for obvious reasons, not enjoy being 'rooted out.'"

"So you are the fools disrupting our supply lines," he says, somehow finding his confidence again as he stands straight and proud. "You realize that our people will suffer, not the Empire."

"If that is your conclusion, then you are considerably worse informed than I thought," she says, sharing a look with

Gabriel.

"What am I ignorant of?" he asks, offended.

"Those supplies are being smuggled straight into the hands and mouths of the populace of Coin."

"So you're not really cutting the supplies to Coin at all," he says slowly, stroking his thin beard. "Just to the official sources."

"Which any well-informed citizen of Coin should be well aware of," she says flatly. "If you are this incompetent a politico, I may as well remove you from the table."

"Are you threatening me?" he asks, puffing his chest. Wrong woman to get uppity with, my friend. "I have never responded well to threats."

"Minister, please. I wouldn't stoop to anything so childish." Right, thanks for the not-so-subtle dig there, Saran. "If I wanted to kill you, you would never have woken up this morning."

"Uh, Khal, I thought you weren't threatening him," Jynn says nervously.

"I'm not," she says evenly. "I'm making him an offer to keep his life."

"Um, well, okay," Jynn says, exchanging a side eyed glance with me. Sure. Definitely not threatening. "Carry on."

"So, Minister," Saran continues as if Jynn hadn't spoken. She clasps her hands behind her back and lifts her chin. "You are tasked with taking the loyal remnants of the Steed and getting rid of the disruption to the supply lines from the west. I want you to do exactly as you are supposed to do. Take the Steed, gallop around the sands for a few weeks, and come back with trophies that I will provide you. Declare the rebels vanquished."

"So you get to continue to operate in secret..."

"And you get to remain in your position and accept the acclaim of the imperials."

Cortola stares steadily at the Khal, his expression unreadable. She knows better than to speak any longer. Even though she's questioned his competence already, we all know he's more than capable of coming to the correct conclusion on his own.

"Give me a moment," he says finally, turning and walking towards the corner. Even though the room isn't very large, he offers the traditional sign of trust in turning his back on us. The gesture is as surprising as it is pointless.

"Batir," Saran says, turning suddenly to me. I don't like her tone. "I have news that, while significant for all, pertains particularly to you."

"Go on," I say, an unconscious dread spreading like acid through my gut.

"There have been abductions throughout the city. Of the orphans and the disabled."

"No," Jynn gasps, her voice speaking for me as the word sticks in my throat.

"The home where your brother lived stands empty," she says.

Perhaps anyone else would have spoken the words with some level of understanding. Not the Khal of Nothing. Any honey she has ever spread over words was purely to attract flies.

"Who?"

The word echoes as if drifting through a long tunnel. Movement in the corner of my eye. Cortola. Irrelevant.

"It was all done in the night, so stealthily that my eyes saw nothing." Passively, distantly, muffled by the storm building in my chest, I faintly detect twin notes of emotion from the Khal as she says those words. Disgust, that anything could happen in Coin without her knowledge, and grudging respect, that someone managed to pull it off without her knowledge. "From what I've gathered, though, the people who did this are akin to those who tried to accost you as you reentered the city."

"When?"

"Six nights past."

So long. He could be buried in a shallow grave already,

little more than food for the gardens outside the walls. But why? Why would they take people who are harming no one?

"Where?"

"Again, our information is very limited, but they were last seen in the vicinity of the Plaza of Stars."

"Maybe this has something to do with the west wing," Cortola murmurs, his expression turning thoughtful.

I barely hear him past the roaring in my ears.

"You're right," Jynn says, answering Cortola's unspoken thoughts. "I tried to get close a couple times, but they've got the west wing locked down tight."

"You've been in the House of the Republic?" Cortola asks, looking Jynn up and down.

"I've met you twice, Minister," she says, rolling her eyes. "You should really learn the names of your servants."

"What—" I swallow, trying to push the words out. "What about the west wing?"

"Shortly after the imperials arrived, the Lord General claimed the west wing for his own," Cortola answers. "I haven't been able to get anyone close. Anyone sent that way returns with inane claims of seeing and hearing nothing out of the ordinary. It's almost like they've been brainwashed."

"Don't look at Bastian," Jynn says sourly. "Though you aren't wrong in your assessment. The Lord General can control Thought."

"Impossible," Cortola says automatically.

"We don't have the time to explain," I say. Something in my voice brings him up short, and he closes his mouth. "We know where they have him. It's enough."

"Bastian, wait," Jynn says, shifting to stand between me and the door, even though I haven't moved. "We *don't* know. If we go in blindly, we might stumble around until the entire Empire army comes down on our heads."

"You've killed armies before."

"That was a long time ago," she says sadly. Cortola stares at us like we've just declared ourselves part of a new race of chicken. No one deigns to explain. "And time exaggerates every story that survives. I want to rescue Lav as much as you do..." She holds up her hands at my glare. "Maybe not *as* much. I'm just saying we need a plan. Whatever that plan is, even if it *is* just sprinting up the steps and burning the guards away, I'm with you to the end."

"He may not have time for a plan," I growl. "Every second could matter."

"And he might be dead already," Saran says, lifting one slim eyebrow. "Or he may be languishing in a cell. The fact remains that we don't know enough to move."

"I can't take that risk."

"At least wait for nightfall," the Khal says, turning to Gabriel. "How many can we muster by sunset?"

"A few dozen. More, if we commit your personal forces." Gabriel's eyes roll towards the ceiling as he calculates. "The Empire has at least a hundred soldiers on hand at the House of the Republic for just this kind of thing, many of them elites, with thousands more spread throughout the city. In a pitched battle, we wouldn't last longer than a few minutes."

"We won't be going to give battle," she says, her dark eyes turning to me. "Just to hold the door open."

"Thank you," I say, throat suddenly thick. The Khal of Nothing, risking lives for my brother? She tips her chin in a short nod of acknowledgement.

"Are you fools thinking of striking at the House of the Republic? The seat of Empire power?" Cortola asks, doing his best to follow along.

"Yes," Jynn says, putting her hand in her pocket. "What's it to you?"

"I have information that, for all your vaunted 'eyes,' you apparently do not," he says smugly.

"Is it true?" Jynn whispers, her eyes unfocusing. "The timing couldn't be more perfect."

"What is this child talking about?" Cortola says, frowning. "Is she a bit touched in the head?"

"Kranos is gone," she says, turning to us with a hopeful smile. "Out of the city, even out of Coin's province."

"The Lord General is out of the city?" I ask. At Jynn's nod, my jaw clenches. "Pity."

***

The sun's last rays paint the eastern face of Coin golden. Though there isn't any official curfew, the streets are nearly empty at this hour. Coin used to be a bustling city, a place of grandeur and life. The Empire has drained the vibrancy from a city of rainbow color. There is still beauty in the glow of the walls, but a quieter beauty, a silent beauty. Like a tomb lost under the shifting dunes.

Jynn crouches silently at my side. Though the Plaza of Stars is barren of traffic, the dozens of alleys and side streets leading to it are filled with all manner of cover. A marching patrol of enemy soldiers rattles past, their eyes straight ahead and their steps in perfect unison. I can sense Jynn scoff next to me.

"All spit and shine and polish. Pretty, but useless. They won't find anyone who doesn't want to be found."

I don't reply. My mind is still, quiet. I may have felt rudderless since the war was lost, but not anymore. I know what I want and what I'm doing. Woe be to any who stands in my way.

A jagged line of dark shadow creeps up the golden walls to the east, the western skyline cast in silhouette. Not long, now. My patience holds the reins of my need for the moment, though it strains to run free every time I think of Lav.

I may not be much of a man. I may not have done much worthwhile in my life. Yet I've always looked after Lav, always done my best to serve him.

Even if I'm the reason he needs it.

172

"You're going to have to open up to someone about that someday."

With the barest concentration, I wall Jynn off. She glares holes into the side of my face. I don't care. Once we move, I'll let her back in, but we have some minutes yet, and I don't need her running commentary on my life. As if she's got everything figured out. Of course, with her knowledge of the Eternal's visions, maybe she does.

It doesn't matter. Lav, I'm coming.

The second stars appear in the sky, I spread my senses over the area. Wells of thought from my various allies appear like beacons of life in the darkness. The nearest patrol walks three streets away. The four soldiers standing at attention at the main doors to the House of the Republic feel relief at the disappearance of the glaring sun, longing for their cots back at the barracks. They must stand watch for two hours yet. Luckily for them, we don't plan on using the front entrance. For their sake, they had better be careful what noises they investigate tonight.

"It's time."

I know.

"Be careful, Bastian. We don't really know what we're walking into."

I don't respond. Be careful, she says. Only once Lav is safe.

A pulse of intent ripples into the night from Jynn. Gabriel's people go to work, each heading towards a different part of the House. Jynn and I move with Gabriel himself around the entrance to the left, sticking to the shadows. I stumble over an errant stone, the sound echoing into the Plaza. Before the soldiers on watch can even react, Jynn scours the alarm from their minds. I shoot her a grateful look and press on. The open stretch of street separating the House from the rest of the city looms empty in the darkness. Even though I know that no one is watching, I feel exposed as we run like scuttling beetles across the stone and into the shadow of the House.

Gabriel hurries us along with a few flashing movements of his hand. Any gesture he makes is pointless; we're already attuned to his every thought. I crouch at the base of the wall, making a cup with my hands. I'm not strong enough to lift him, not even close, but he uses me like a human ladder to reach the thin ledge of the lowest window. I do my best to be a steady foundation as he goes to work, feet planted firmly on my trembling shoulders. After a moment, his whispered curse breaks the silence.

What is it? I send towards his open mind.

He doesn't answer, though his thoughts open even further to mine. He returns his thieving implements to hidden pockets inside his clothes and instead draws out a dagger. The point digs into the seam underneath the window, scraping away some kind of substance, which flakes colorlessly into the night.

"They've sealed the windows," Jynn says, frowning. *"Is this a Republic practice, or…?"*

No, that's new. The imperials must have done it.

"They really *don't want anyone getting into this wing."*

How long? I ask Gabriel.

He gives the impression of uncertainty. It could be minutes, could be hours, depends on how careful and meticulous they were, and it *definitely* depends on how few interruptions…

I take the hint, even though I'm reluctant to let go. Focusing on Gabriel's mind took the edge off the burning fire building in my shoulders. Thankfully, he is a slight man, built for agility and acrobatics. Even so, I've never been the most physical of humans. The night drags on, silent but for the distant tramp of boots and the soft scrape of Gabriel's knife.

"We can talk, if that will help," Jynn says suddenly. She doesn't turn from her lookout perch at the edge of the building.

Sure, I say, latching onto the sound of her voice. *What about?*

"You have to stop blaming yourself for Lav."

Nevermind. Silence is golden.

"I'm serious, Bastian. What happened when you were a child was not your fault."

Since I, well, did it, it's kind of hard to believe that.

"And what did you do?" She glances back at me, though her expression is unreadable in the darkness. "Seriously. What exactly are you blaming yourself for?"

I broke his mind.

"Did you mean to?" She doesn't wait for me to answer. "Of course you didn't. You didn't even know you were a Shaper. Children feel things so much more deeply than we do. Anger, fear, hunger, they don't know how to manage any of them. You were a child, and you were afraid. You just wanted him to stop."

And I made him.

"Yes, you made him stop. You lost control, as children do. And what have you done since?"

Making sure Lav doesn't die isn't penance for what I've done. Eternal damn my mind, it might have been a mercy just to let him die.

"You don't believe that," Jynn says sadly.

You don't know what I believe, I snap back. *I'm just about tired of—*

The rasp of metal on metal heralds the end of Gabriel's work. His weight disappears from my trembling shoulders as he clambers through the open window. Jynn, not meeting my eyes, walks to me and climbs, accepting Gabriel's help and vanishing into the darkness. Gabriel reappears and offers me his hand. I don't have time to parse through the roil of emotions churning through my heart. Jumping as high as I can, I barely reach Gabriel's outstretched fingers. His iron grip makes the most of the tenuous purchase, and he lifts me with fluid ease until I can grasp the window frame myself.

Bare of furniture or ornament, the dark room we find ourselves in returns the echoes of our breathing strangely. A door looms opposite outlined in light, but I don't pay it any heed for the time being. No, the walls hold all of my attention. Or what is left of them. Jagged gouges scour the marble like a thousand bolts of lightning, some reaching nearly to the ceiling where it stretches to twice my height. The claw marks—which feels impossible, though I don't have any better explanation—cover every inch of the room. Glancing back at the window, I frown. Why did... whatever this is... leave the glass? If it can dig furrows into solid marble, why would it ignore thin panes of glass?

Gabriel stalks to the door and begins working on the lock. His muttered curse is louder this time. Whoever designed the security seems to be seriously pissing Gabriel off. His tense shoulders and jerky movements tell enough of a tale. Leaving him to his work, I spread my senses out. From the west, a strange collection of pain, misery, and anger pool from a dozen, two dozen people, it's hard to tell. There is little rational thought in that direction, much like what I felt from the heavy covered wagons the imperials brought with their victory parade.

To the east, I feel...

I should turn back. There's nothing worth seeing here. No one should be wandering the halls this late.

Jynn?

"*I feel it. Someone, who is most definitely not the Master of Beasts, is using our power. Seems like he's giving it out to subordinates now.*"

Something lurks underneath her surface thoughts. Normally, her emotions are about as intelligible as sheet music read by a blind man, but whatever she's feeling has cracked her near-perfect control. Pressing against the edge of her thoughts, I flinch away. *Anger.* White-hot, righteous, unrelenting fury. The idea that *anyone* would taint the Creator's holy power by creating *abominations...*

Jynn... I begin in warning.

"*Find your brother, Bastian,*" she answers shortly, tightly. *Help me find him.*

176

"You'll manage."

"Gabriel," I whisper aloud. "Don't open..."

The door creaks open with a groan. Before I can say anything else, Jynn darts past him and disappears to the east.

"Follow her. She's so angry she isn't thinking straight. Try to... I don't know, rein her in."

"Me?" he says, his expression skeptical. "Her?"

"Do your best."

Following him out the door, I turn left as he goes right. All I can do is find Lav, and quickly. Whatever Jynn is about to do... I can't worry about it right now. As I walk to the west, towards the lower quarters for the respected slaves, the cloud of anguish and terror grows stronger. The emotions feel untethered from their source, like a drifting miasma of horror. Laughter, hatred, elation, terror, anger, contentment, fear. Each step brings a crashing, disjointed rush of emotion.

I step forward.

—my legs Creator my legs Creator—the lilies of the meadow spread so beautiful, their white—no red not again not the red no red no red—kill me kill me kill me—deliver me from this shame, take me—

I retract my senses, wincing, my heart twisting strangely, my thoughts fraying. Alright, stay close. Don't lose yourself. You are Bastian Batir, and you're here to save—

I step forward.

—damned, as the Eternal is damned, as the Creator is damned, as—laughter is moonshine, her smile a ray of sunlight after—fuck fuck fuck fuck fuck—Creator please, please, let me die—orn shall sound and the sky shall break and the Creator shall come—

Staggering, I sever my connection with Thought. The air feels like molten desert sand in my lungs. Cut off from my power, the hallway returns to focus, smokeless lanterns illuminating spotless white marble and wall hangings in cloth-of-gold. A normal man might walk this hallway and believe it the height of opulence and luxury. He would not feel the fractured agony, the shattered anguish pressing, pressing... I'm used to all the sordid and distasteful thoughts humanity offers, and I thought I'd tasted all the flavors of love, sorrow, and pain. But there is nothing to prepare me for this.

Lav.

Taking a deep breath, I force myself forward. A closed door appears on my left. How am I going to...? Fuck. I take another deep breath. Steeling my will, focusing my thoughts like the point of a dagger, I reach into the room.

—*heart! Stop heart! Stop*—

Not Lav.

Drawing in a shuddering breath, I let my eyes drift down the hall. A dozen doors on either side loom like gateways to the Eternal's own prison. My heart beats in a staccato rhythm, and sweat beads on my brow. In the Creator's forgotten name, how am I going to make it through them all?

Lav. You're doing this for Lav. You aren't important.

The next door.

—*LET ME FREE LET ME FREE LET ME*—

Heat. Blinding light. Truth burning in my veins, the awful truth that Lav is dead. She stares in a malicious glee, fading as silver light threatens the sun.

LET ME FREE. LET ME FREE. LET ME FREE.

She staggers and falls, her hand reaching out to follow my command even as her body succumbs to the pressure...

I blink away the vision, the awful memory and the broken mind screaming words so similar to mine. When I was certain Lav was dead, when I knew that it was my fault. Shaking off the memory, I shove myself off the wall and stagger to the next. Deep breath. Hone your focus. Dagger, not net. Lightning, not cloud.

—*shadows, just shadows, not him, not him, not him, just shadows*—

Next.

Again.

And again.

Each a new nightmare, a broken window into a fractured life. Strange bodies, definitely inhuman. Madness, always madness. No thought like the other, no pattern familiar, no mind approaching normal. And none of them Lav.

I can barely think. My conscious thought is a kaleidoscope of broken images and words, darkness, flashes of light, strange landscapes I've never seen, angry faces of people I'll never meet.

The hallway swims before me.

I blink.

—*A bolt of lightning arcs across the sky above a strange mountain that reflects the light—*

I step forward.

—*My leg, a squelching tentacle, flops across the stone—*

I close my eyes.

—*Colors I've never seen, colors for which I have no name, colors he forced me to see, dance in memory. Burning crimson, pupils swimming, my eyes an ocean of writhing flesh and fire—*

I sit. The stone is cool against my back. Sweat drips down my nose, stinging my eyes. Eyes that see a hallway, a hallway of white marble and tasteful decoration. Wearily, warily, I lift my eyes to check my progress. My heart falls. My spirit trembles.

Eight.

I've made it through eight doorways. There are a dozen more, and the hall turns ahead... How many more? How many more until I find him? How many more until I lose myself to the darkness I feel waiting impatiently at the edges of my mind?

At least one more.

Heaving my leaden body forward, I manage the next door. Concentrating is pointless. Focusing has only brought madness closer to my door. I'll be quick.

—*a grand staircase curves upwards and out of sight. Mother walks ahead, her shoulders back, her soft dress whispering against the stairs. Her hand holds mine, warm and strong. I want to run up the stairs, but she told me to be good. We meet the Minister today and—*

No. Not Lav. I try to let go, but—

—WHERE ARE MY ARMS WHAT DID THEY DO—

No, no, n—

—smiled at me. She must want to be with me. No one has ever smiled at me like that. She just couldn't get away from her family. It's okay. I've rescued her. I don't know why she keeps crying. Why she tries to run. She smiled at me. We are made for each other. She'll see. All I want is to see that smile again. I love—

—IT'S IN MY CHEST IT'S IN MY—

—serenity shall always—i'll kill you fucking prick i'll rip off— after Father left, we—STAY BACK PLEASE CREATOR PL—sunlight in the darkness, a ray of ho—it hurts, why does it—peace, Master of Thought. Peace—rip off his fucking—

That voice. So calm. Speaking... to... me?

"Don't struggle, Master of Thought. Drift with the current."

—hurts, by the Creator, what have they—

I'm lost. I can't...

"Don't fight. Come to me. Follow my thoughts."

—the itch, maddening, I just want to scratch my face, why did he take my fingers—

"Follow my thoughts. I will shelter you."

The voice entrances as capably as my own, drawing me through the chaos. Abruptly there is silence. At least it seems so at first. Music, calming and yet powerful, surrounds my fractured mind in impenetrable harmony. The inmate's madness lurks at the outskirts of this man's mind, but the music holds it at bay. It holds mine at bay.

Who are you?

"A friend, it would seem," he says, his mind's voice rich and mirthful. *"I haven't felt power such as yours for many years."*

You know my power?

"I was friends with your predecessor. We often stretched the limits of what Thought could do. When you push the mind too far, it

180

can have dire consequences. I do for you what I did for him whenever he reached his limits."

It's... nice... here.

"Yes, he always said my mind had a particular music to it. I have no idea why. I never met a Master of Tones in all my time, so I never got an answer."

Tones has been gone for...

"Yes, over a century. There are other parts of the world, other civilizations beyond the Ways. So long as they don't disrupt the balance, we let them govern as they see fit. I'm sure the Master of Tones lives somewhere beyond our reach."

Who are you?

"A friend, as I said." He seems distracted, his attention wavering from me. Distantly, a shout ripples through the harmony, harsh and commanding. *"There may be trouble. Where is your body?"*

Nearby. I think. Are you a prisoner here?

"Yes. Though I am kept in better quarters than the rest of my fellows." He exudes sorrow, deep and regretful. *"I do what I can, but there is only so much a body can take."*

Have you heard of a man named Lav, or Lavilion? He's my brother.

"I'm sorry, but I haven't. They don't let us talk to one another." A distant crash breaks through the peaceful music. *"I believe our time may be up, Master of Thought. You need to return to your body. Now."*

But I like it here.

"I appreciate your fear," he says, seeing straight through me. *"But soldiers are coming. There are screams, shouts, the clash of weapons. If you were in your body, you'd hear them yourself."*

I don't know if I can make it back.

"Nonsense. A Shaper's connection to their body is too strong to be so easily severed. Reach out with your mind. Feel for it. There is a path, a tether, holding your soul to its source."

Following his words, I reach. The cacophony of insanity grows louder, but so too does a comfortable silence, a welcoming harbor amidst the storm. Narrow and straight, a path does seem to lead back to the empty well of my body.

How do you know all this?

"*Do you feel it?*" he asks impatiently. "*If they find your body, unconscious as you are… Concentrate. Follow the path. Listen to no other thoughts, entertain no other fancies. Straight as an arrow, and you'll return just fine.*"

Thank you, friend. I will come for you if I can.

"*Worry about yourself, Master of Thought. I am where I need to be.*"

The harmony of this man's mind suffuses me, settles me, grants me the focus I need. My body. The silence. Listen to nothing else. Steeling my will, I throw myself from the peace.

Distantly, I hear them, their anger, their madness, their broken sorrow. I ignore them, driving forward, blocking them out, walling them off. Then—

—*A child's face, my face, young and twisted in pain*—

I open my eyes.

The hallway is still empty, for now. The sounds of combat echo through the corridors, shouts of pain mixing with agitated shouts of lunacy from the prisoners. Still, I surge to my feet with renewed hope. Lav is here, here and *alive*. I just have to find him. A shout of pain cuts short, seemingly right around the corner. People are dying.

Lurching to my feet, ignoring the weariness that has settled into my bones, I stagger down the hall. I don't bother being careful. Jogging towards where I think his mind was, I turn a corner. Another long corridor, one that used to house the slaves held in the highest esteem, stretches away to the north. My heart quails. There are at least a dozen doors on either side, each reinforced by makeshift contraptions to serve as holding cells. It would take me hours to safely search the prison for Lav, and too much time even unsafely.

A pair of soldiers dressed in dark leather skid around a corner on the opposite side, their swords red with blood. Fuck.

I don't know if I can focus enough to hurt them, if I can even touch my power without falling again into madness. They hesitate for the briefest moment when they spot me, their eyes flicking over my empty hands, the helpless look on my face. A hand motion shifts their run, one falling back behind the other, their eyes narrowed on me with lethal intent...

Lav is close. I can feel it, I know it, somewhere beyond any explanation. If I could use my power... but no.

Heart breaking, I turn and run.

The clash of steel on steel resounds everywhere in the House, its echo so loud I can't hear the footsteps of the enemy soldiers chasing after me. Sliding back around the corner, I put everything I can into a sprint back towards our entrance. If I get there fast enough, I can get out before—

Something punches me in the back. I stumble, my feet nearly slipping on the smooth marble, but I regain my stride. A weight drags at the back of my shoulder, heavy and... I glance back for the briefest instant. They're close behind, faster than me and closing, and... oh Creator there's a dagger in my back, one of them threw a fucking dagger and it's sticking out of my shoulder. Seeing it makes me dizzy, and the pain roars into being like a bear prodded from hibernation. I pass the swinging door we entered, knowing I'll be caught if I slow, probably be caught even if I don't.

A pair of double doors swings open ahead of me, some distant part of me recalling that they open to the main foyer looking out on the front entryway. A figure lies on the floor before them, writhing, gibbering, mind little better than the mad fools behind me. The target of Jynn's ire, if I had to guess.

A man steps through the doors ahead, his face blackened, a curved dagger held backwards along his forearm. Relief, terror, both at once. Either he's going to kill me, and it will all be over, or

183

he's going to save me. Regardless, I'll look death in the face.

His eyes widen, flicking over my shoulder towards my pursuers. His arm pumps back and forward twice in quick succession. Glittering steel flies towards my face, and my eyes close against my will. So much for the whole looking death in the face thing...

The hiss of flying steel whispers past my ear, eliciting twin grunts of surprised pain behind me. I don't slow, can't slow, and my savior jumps to the side right before I would have bowled him over.

The grand entrance hall is chaos incarnate, slick with blood and broken bodies. The half of the hall leading back towards the Conclave chamber is lit by glowing braziers, but the other is a horror of flickering shadows and bits of flame as men and women fight with only overturned coals to guide them.

I stumble to a halt and try to make sense of the chaos. A force of Empire soldiers led by a man in aquamarine armor presses against a smaller number of dark shapes trying desperately to hold open the front entrance. I need to get to the entrance, and now, for the Khal's fighters are meant for stealth and sabotage, not outright fighting. Even as I watch, the line buckles and gives way before the disciplined and armored force, sealing off that exit. The man who saved my life launches himself desperately at their backs, cutting down two before the others surround and butcher him.

Despite standing in the middle of the hall, it doesn't look like anyone has noticed me. Trying not to draw any eyes, I slink towards the scribe's entrance I took at the end of Autumn last year. The door I took when I helped to cut the legs out from under the Republic and leave it open for the Sealord's conquest.

There's no sign of Jynn or Gabriel, and I belatedly think about the window we entered through. It's too late now. I'm going to have to find another way out. Opening the door as quietly as I can, I slip through into the cool darkness of the grand meeting hall. The closing door swallows the sounds of fighting completely and leaves me in shocking silence. The words of the Ministers, especially when the doors are closed, are not meant to carry to unwelcome ears, and apparently that barrier works both ways.

I need a second to breathe, to think, but I don't have one. Warm blood leaks down my back. Visions of slamming the handle of the dagger into one of the heavy wooden seats to dislodge it flash briefly through my mind, and are just as soon discarded. I'm more likely to ruin something important. As it stands, I don't *think* anything critical has been damaged. I need to keep it that way long enough to get out of here.

I head towards the back of the cavernous room. A throne of glass sits near the northern edge of the room, glittering in the dim moonlight filtering in through the windows high above. Though a beautiful, flowing construct of the queen's Shaping, it doesn't fit in here. Without the Ministers' chairs spread throughout the hall, the room looks empty and forbidding. Passing the throne, I run my left hand along the glass, staining the pure crystal with fingerprints of blood. It seems somehow fitting for this empire forged in the blood of my people.

Hopefully, the imperials haven't discovered the tunnel carved into the back of the hall. Originally meant for the Ministers to escape should violence threaten, the passage has remained a closely guarded secret for centuries. When I monitored Cortola in my early years, I was delighted to discover that, not only had it never been used, Cortola himself had managed to hide its existence from every other Minister. As far as I know, the secret passages between the walls are known to four individuals still breathing: Jynn, Saran, Cortola, and myself. If I can make it into the passage, they'll never find me.

A scrape of stone on stone echoes weirdly through the empty space. Ahead, a slender figure appears, a loose gown floating ghostlike about her. Emerald fire banishes the moonlight and the shadows alike. Twirling glass tumbles through the air behind her in a dizzying pattern, like a peacock's tail in challenge. If she's surprised to see me, bloody and stumbling through the dimness, she doesn't show it. A blade of glass flicks towards me faster than thought. I drop to the marble, the deadly shard knifing through the air above my head.

She stalks forward silently, glittering death rising to rain down on my head. Desperate, I lunge into my power, throwing forth the first piece of it I can, the only memory I have of her.

"Perhaps, when you're older, you'll come visit, neh?"

Her eyes meet mine in the darkness. She raises her hand, the blades of glass twirling higher. It isn't enough. She doesn't remember, or doesn't care.

The emerald light winks out, glass tumbling to shatter on the marble with a tinkling echo. Absent her light, the room feels dark indeed. Her desperate whisper carries.

"Help me."

Chapter 9
Kettle

The Seventieth Day of Summer
In the year 5223, Council Reckoning

A bright flash, and the air cracks in two. Thunder rumbles into the pristine blue sky, rebounding off the high peaks of the mighty mountain range surrounding us, paced only by Corna's delighted, and perhaps malicious, laughter.

"How about that, stodgy?" she cackles, prancing over to the smoking ruins of a boulder that likely lay peacefully alongside the road for centuries. "And you said I couldn't do it."

Dyed black and yellow, her vibrant silk shirt and pants flow in the wind of her passing. The fashion in Eshan is one of comfort and ease; men and women alike wear open shirts and flowing pants cinched by belts of flexible silk which they call a *dimina*. I find it far more sensible than the Donirian fashion of skirts and corsets and stiff collars, though I miss the comforting tightness of my old leathers. The pure black silk wrapped loosely about my body does offer me some small nostalgia for the Isles, for it is the same, as I suspected when we set out east.

Corna pauses, her grin faltering, before scowling down at the pendant on her chest.

"Don't try to change your tune now, buddy. You did *not* say shouldn't. You definitely said couldn't." She looks contemplative. "Didn't you?"

Not for the first time, though maybe the hundredth time, Myn turns a concerned and disapproving look my way. It's gotten easy to ignore, as many times as I've seen it. I don't blame her, really. I took a priceless gift, an artifact that represents not only her family's might and ancestry, but her father's honor, and gave it to an unpredictable and overly dramatic thief.

Her capriciousness is partly why I gave it to her in the first place. Whatever normal humans might think to do with the power of lightning, Corna will undoubtedly do something flashier and scarier. The bigger part of why I gave her the pendant, of course, is that I trust her completely.

Even if she does spend half the time arguing with the ancient and honorable spirit housed in the pendant.

I glance around at the forbidding peaks stretching to the clouds on all sides. Dawn lightens ahead, though it will be hours yet before the sun crawls over the wall of rock. It's been many days since these mountains—the Kevagul, which apparently translates roughly to Shadow Wall—haven't dominated sight in every direction. The name feels ironic, as the stone that makes them up is the purest white.

East, ever east. It feels like we really will hit the edge of the Khalintars soon, but we haven't even made it halfway through Eshan. Though a 'fast horse' might take you to Yohru from the western edge of Eshan in under twenty days, we've taken the journey like we're riding sea tortoises on land. Apparently, their Dawn kingdom stretches just as far in the other direction.

I sigh, returning my eyes to the immaculate, well-crafted work of art these people call a road. Broad enough for four wagons to pass abreast despite following a narrow pass through the mountains, no stone is out of place.

As soon as we passed the outlying border of Dusk a few miles east of Hona's farm, the roads began. The Arurama, or the Moon's Walk, they call it. They are not timeless and unnaturally perfect like the Ways. Rather, skilled artisans from Eshan cut the pristine stones so perfectly that the broad pavers seem like they grew naturally from the earth. It is more impressive than the Ways in some respects. Though the Ways have stood the test of millennia, the roads of Eshan are maintained with unceasing effort and care. The masons who repair the roads hold places of high esteem in these lands.

It's a good thing the roads are so broad, otherwise we would never make any progress. The way forward would be completely blocked by people seeking to catch a glimpse of the Eshani.

We've passed hundreds of hamlets, dozens of villages, and several towns large enough to get lost in. Each time, the citizens turned out in droves, eagerly craning their necks for a glimpse of me, waiting for a demonstration of my power. When I inevitably relented to the pressure of their silent and solemn faces, they bowed, faces pressed to the ground, as I passed. It hasn't gotten any less strange, no matter how many times I've seen it. I chose a life of obscurity in the shadows; I hardly wanted to be *known*, let alone *worshipped*.

The architecture of these lands doesn't match anything in my experience. Each building is constructed with a tiered ceramic roof that always, without fail, slopes away to the south. It makes the structures feel strange and half-finished, like they would be complete if reflected over a mirror. Myn told me the odd choice was made due to the Barhaze, or Bitter Wind. Apparently, each Winter brings cold winds so strong they've warped the architectural knowledge of an entire civilization. She said it like I shouldn't be concerned at all, but, well, I am. Summer is passing, and Autumn's presence is all-too-fleeting.

"Corna," I call, giving in to Myn's frown. "Could we save the big booms until we're in a safe space? I'd rather not have your thunder bring an avalanche down on our heads."

"But you told me to practice," she says with the barest hint of a whine. She scowls down at the pendant. "*You* told me I need to practice, too. What do you mean, wasteful? That tiny bolt? We've got plenty."

"Corna..."

"Yes, mother," she says, drooping her shoulders and

sulking over to Aurelion, who is in the process of starting a fire. His *dimina* is black silk slashed with violet. At Myn's direction, my Stars wear the color of my clan along with markings of their power. The children, the triplets, and the other men each wear white silk with black seams to denote their place in my personal circle. Corna shoots Myn a sideways glance. "Did you ask her dictatorness why we stopped so early? The sun won't set for hours yet, and I'm totally over the road."

"I will not tell you why," Myn says stiffly. "Suffice to say, I have my reasons, and that should be enough for you."

"It isn't."

"I trust Myn's judgment on this one," I say, breaking in before their bickering can blossom into an argument.

"Not like we have a choice," Corna groans, unhelpfully picking up a smoldering stick from the beginnings of the fire and waving it about.

Aurelion looks pained, his eyes following the glowing ember as it sputters and goes out. With a sigh, he returns to work, muttering something under his breath. The children have taken the early break to wheedle Hom and Yelden into an impromptu swordplay lesson, and Sario listens with no less attention. Ezil, Inia, and Koli immediately set up their tent and disappeared inside. They've been working on something in secret, or so they say, though I have my suspicion that they're just taking the chance to rest and relax without childcare responsibilities.

Corna's complaint is true enough. We've had to rely on Myn for basically everything. It isn't just that she is our translator in a foreign land. She's chosen the pace of our advance, the route we've taken, the clothes we wear, the soldiers who guard us. How we greet people, how we take our leave, when I show my power, how I sit and when I stand. She's kept us from ever taking the hospitality of any of the multitude of strangers who've offered their homes, so as not to show favoritism or offer any unintentional message in my choice. It is as tedious as it is vital to

190

our survival and success. We would be a leaking ship trapped in the middle of shark-infested waters without her to serve as sail and rudder.

Corna hates to rely on anyone, and she's managed to spread her discontent to Hom and Yelden, who have never been the most accepting of men. My heart, aided by the calming advice of Ezil and Aurelion, believes in Myn and the faith she has in me.

And then there's the timing. Twenty-five years. Her father sacrificed their collective way of life to... I don't even want to think it. Part of me yearns for it to be true, for the woman riding at my side to be who I think she might be. I almost feel ashamed to wish it, for it feels like a betrayal of the family I forged by choice.

"Creator's hairy balls I'm bored," Corna gripes, offering the spent stick to Aurelion, who takes it wordlessly.

"Use the time," Ezil calls from within her tent.

"I was trying!" she protests, wiggling her fingers. "No booms, remember?"

"Etiquette, Corna," Ezil says flatly, her face sticking out briefly between the flap of the tent to offer her a look of reproach.

"But... but..." Corna glances about for help. Aurelion focuses intensely on the fire, and the men are too caught up in fixing Tera's grip. Her eyes go suspiciously round and innocent when they turn to me.

"We're going to reach the capital tomorrow," I remind her gently. "It can't hurt to brush up."

"I could use the refresher, if you'll practice with me," Aurelion says graciously, still focused on the fire, which has just begun to crackle to life. Corna shoots him a betrayed look.

"Fine," she sighs, defeated. "Myn?"

"As an Oshei, you must always stand precisely..."

***

The soft scuff of sandaled footsteps outside my tent finds me awake and alert. Tension and nerves have kept me up all night, my mind racing through a thousand possibilities, none of

191

them good. It's been hard to sleep the entire journey, and not just because of the incessant murmur of life and sound from the train of followers stretching out of sight behind us. In all the discussions and arguments we've had on this long journey, we've never thought for a single moment that the powers that be would surrender to some ancient prophecy. We've been waiting for the Ihera to make their move...

And more, Hona's insistence of demons in the darkness has stuck with me. I am never alone, not really, but I often see flickers of movement in the corner of my eye, like something stalks my steps. Perhaps the stress of this past season is making me paranoid, but I can't shake the feeling that I'm being watched, that, impossible as it is, someone dogs our path east. The feeling has faded now that we're in the mountains and the narrow pass.

For some reason, I miss the shadows at the edge of my vision. They felt familiar, like a half-remembered melody. They made me feel less alone.

Their absence since we reached the mountains makes it more likely I *wasn't* just imagining things.

At the soft sound outside by tent, my shadow flows into readiness with difficulty, invisible in the darkness. It takes enough effort that my hands tremble. By the Depths, it's getting worse, not better.

"Eshani," Myn whispers softly, and I relax, letting the shadow evaporate along my skin again. Even that small moment of connection leaves me feeling strained.

"What is it, Myn?"

"There is something you should see."

Slipping into the black silk marking my status, I step out into the darkness. If dawn is coming, any sign of it is hidden by the silent mountains looming to the east. Myn beckons silently and moves further down the road. We pass Koli and Hom on last watch. At their questioning looks, I flick them a few signals with my fingers.

No, there's nothing wrong, but yes, be ready just in case.

Continuing on, we pass an outer ring of soldiers of Eshan, their uniforms proudly declaring their allegiance to a dozen lords and provinces, one from each of the lands to the west, and, not to be outdone, several sent on fast horses from the king of Dawn to the east. They shift to form ranks about us, but Myn stills them with a snapped command.

She leads me forward, alone, into darkness broken only by stars peeking sullenly from between gaps in a ragged blanket of cloud. My heart beats faster. For the first time since I learned of this cursed prophecy, I'm alone, separated, vulnerable. But this is Myn, who I have chosen to trust. I can't imagine she would lead me into an ambush, at least not intentionally. I force my hands to relax, though I don't let go of that edge of wariness.

The road curves to the north, then bends back to the east around a shelf of rock. A mountain comes into view, taller and wider than any other, towering so high that its tip disappears into darkness. I've caught glimpses of this mountain a few times through the peaks: Darker, broader, and untouched by snow. Myn stops, and her hands disappear into the wide sleeves of her *dimina*. Her eyes remain fixed firmly on the mountain. I follow suit, gazing at the mighty monolith dominating the east.

The sky begins to lighten behind it, limning its upper slopes in golden light. I squint closer at those slopes. They look regular, unnaturally so... the light grows, the sky burning orange, and my jaw drops.

It isn't a mountain at all. It's *two*... and between them...

The sun crests the horizon, lower than should be possible, rising between the twin mountains I thought were one. Suspended over the peaks, a city floats among the clouds, darkness cast in harmonious angles. Rays of fire silhouette the massive supports holding the city aloft, the sight so strange I have to force my mind to accept it. The sun, rising *beneath* a city...

And that city.

Tiers of sloped ceramic climb into the sky, piercing the clouds and disappearing from sight. The city rises like a mountain in and of itself, no less mighty than its natural brothers and sisters. No light burns among the mighty structure, no cookfires or lampposts. It holds the beauty of a statue, lifeless and frozen in time, a relic of a forgotten age where the impossible was the norm. Everything feels frail before its might.

Something tears my awestruck gaze away from the high city, a feeling I've felt only a few times in my life: dangling from Aurelion's arm over the edge of the Abyss in Donir, calling for aid in the dungeon of the Master of Beasts… The road forks ahead, one branch winding up the northern edge of the mountains towards the city. The southern road, though, slopes down into a valley between the peaks. As the sun climbs higher into the sky, the depths of the valley remain shrouded in darkness. A darkness that does not dissipate. My shadow stirs beneath my clothes, writhing along my skin.

"To the north, the road to Yohru and the Amanu," Myn says, though she, too, looks down into the valley. "To the south, the Valley of Shadow, the final path of the Empress."

"Is it always…?"

"Yes," she says. "It is always covered in shadow. None who venture there have ever returned."

"Why not?" I ask breathlessly.

"They were not the Eshani," Myn says, turning to me with hope shining in her eyes. "They were not you."

★★★

"Creator's shapely ass," Corna whispers for the seventh time, head craned back to stare up at the citadel looming over our advance. She frowns and glances briefly at the pendant on her chest. "No, I will not watch my language, stodgy."

The road leading to Yohru snakes around the mountain pass, ascending towards the mighty structure floating high above our heads. The rising sun reveals an artistic elegance to the dark

194

silhouette. Each structure fits the whole seamlessly as dozens of ascending spires, their tiered roofs like the edge of serrated blades, strive for the heavens. Yet none can match the central tower, a dark monolith of deep gray stone edged with silver.

"We'll reach the lifts by noon," Myn says, her concerned gaze resting on the wagon in front of us. Sweat gleams from the flanks of the pair of mighty draft horses that the King of Dusk offered from his stables. "We look foolish, riding this shabby monstrosity. Why do you cling to it so tightly?"

"I'll tell you when it matters." I offer her a look of reassurance. "Just know that it's important. I'm not one for grandiose gestures anyway. More of the slink about type, if you catch my drift."

"You need to shed that attitude," she reminds me impatiently. "The more people who see you, the more who believe in you, the harder you will be to unseat."

"I could care less about the seat," I mutter, letting my eyes drop. Like iron to a lodestone, my gaze drifts to the shrouded valley growing smaller with each passing mile. There is shadow down there, living shadow, more than I thought possible, more than I ever imagined existed.

We fall into relative quiet as our train marches on. When we round a final bend, the road straightens towards what appears to be a wall of solid rock arcing high into the sky, so high that cloud partially obscures its edge. The city is nearly directly above us, most of its majesty hidden by the mountain stone. Soldiers dressed in livery of silver and a blue so dark it is nearly black line the road, long spears pointing out to form a tunnel of deadly steel. I don't need Myn to tell me they are the Amanu's personal soldiers, nor that the color of their attire is an insult to me. No one, and I mean no one in miles and miles of travel, has dared wear black.

"Into the maw of the beast," Aurelion mutters from my right, his face turning grim at the sight of the soldiers.

"Hom?" I call, glancing into the back of the wagon where he, Sario, and Yelden sit with the children.

"I've got a plan, but it's pretty shit," he says matter-of-factly. "You've seen these mountains, Kettle. You have a better chance of marrying the Sealord than any of us have of making it out."

"Seconded," Yelden says, his expression sad. "When we robbed the Kingdom, I pictured a dozen ways we might die, but I never imagined we'd walk straight to death with open arms."

"Come on, brother," Sario says, slapping him on the shoulder. "We're still breathing, hey?"

"For now," Yelden says gloomily.

"Keep working on it," I say softly, my eyes falling to the children.

Most of them are old enough to follow the conversation and its implications. They show no fear, though. They continue to trust, continue to believe in this fragile dream of family we've carved from the world. Kit meets my eyes coldly, almost in challenge.

"You're wasting us back here with the others," he says flatly. "We can turn the tide."

"Trust me, *Kit*," I say, deliberately emphasizing his name. He doesn't react. I don't know if he even realizes he spoke in the collective. "Should things go to the Depths, you'll get your chance."

I face forward as we pass into the ranks of the soldiers. They stand in silent salute, their discipline immaculate, the points of their spears unwavering. As the last of our party enters the tunnel, the soldiers collapse behind us, forming a wall of steel to keep our long train of followers at bay. The tide of humanity has been an incessant annoyance throughout the long road here, but I still can't shake the feeling that the jaws of a trap are closing behind us. Shivering, I force my eyes forward.

Massive metal chains dangle from the cliffside ahead,

easily as wide as the horses straining to move our heavy wagon. I can't imagine how we're to ascend the sheer rock face, let alone how we'll get the wagon up.

The moment we reach the halfway point across the straight stretch of road, the chains stretch taut and slide into motion. A broad metal platform, easily large enough to carry us and the contingent of soldiers both, appears at the top of the cliff and drops smoothly towards the road. The contraption, crafted of solid metal, must weigh half as much as the mountain itself, yet its descent is even and steady.

A man stands alone in the center of the platform, arms folded in a pure-white *dimina* that shimmers silver depending on the angle of the light. In his middle years, he has the appearance of a panther at rest, the strength in his frame evident even through the loose silk. A curved sword decorates his hip, its hilt shining with silver wire. The platform lurches to an abrupt stop, and he does not so much as sway.

Aurelion and I share a glance. This is not a man to trifle with.

"The head of Yohru's Stars, Baeda Sonjur," Myn whispers. "An honorable man. His *keishi* is Master of Metal."

Sonjur steps forward and offers a bow that is little more than a tilt of his head. The pilgrims trapped behind the wall of soldiers voice a collective cry of outrage. Clearly, the bow was not exactly respectful.

"Greetings, Kettle of the Isles," he says in lightly accented Donirian. "I am told this is your preferred language."

"Gree—"

"Bow before the Eshani," Myn snaps, coming to her feet. "Your rightful queen."

"Her status remains uncertain," he says evenly. "Perhaps, a demonstration?"

"This is ridiculous," she says, her hands balling into fists.

"And not unexpected," I say, laying a hand on her arm.

197

She looks at me with barely concealed fury and offers me a tight nod. "Greetings, Baeda Sonjur. I am glad to learn that there are those in Yohru who speak the tongues of the west."

"My *keishi* traveled to many lands in her long life." His hand goes to the hilt of his sword, an unconscious gesture. "Through her, I have learned much."

"Then offer her my thanks, as your conversation is welcome. What kind of demonstration would you prefer?"

"A simple call to shadow will do," he says.

Trying not to grit my teeth, I force the shadow to boil out of my clothing and form into a blade of darkness, the same symbol I've crafted a hundred times now. Sonjur's eyes trace the symbol of power on my face impassively. I swing the blade once, allowing the shadow to dissipate and flee the brightness of the sun. Sonjur bows at the waist, his head nearly touching the stones of the road.

"Do you consider yourself a warrior, Kettle of the Isles?" he asks as he stands.

"I have many enemies," I say carefully. "Yet I still stand."

"A warrior is measured by her enemies," he says cryptically, though he bows again, perhaps even deeper this time. "Welcome to Yohru, Kettle of the Isles."

"Eshani," Myn snaps, as if she can't help herself.

"That remains to be seen," he says simply. "But come, you must be weary from the road. It is my honor to serve as your host until the legitimacy of your claim can be determined."

"We are not to see the Amanu?" Myn asks in surprise.

"His will is that our guests learn of the ways of Eshan before they present themselves to the Tower of the Moon. You will have an audience with the Amanu in ten day's time," he says, a glimmer of emotion stealing into his eyes. "I was told to relay to you that this delay is not meant as an insult."

"Of course not," I lie, certain that the solemn man doesn't find the situation *funny*, even if that's the read I'm getting. And the delay is most definitely an insult. "We are happy to accept your hospitality."

I climb down from the wagon and take my place at Sonjur's side on the platform. Any wariness I might feel towards the contraption disappears as our entire group and a dozen soldiers pile on without causing even the slightest tremble. Sonjur gestures towards the massive chains as they spin into motion.

"Long ago, two Shapers were born to the people of Eshan: one of Metal, and one of Stone. They lived for centuries, devoting themselves to the betterment of our land. The lifts are a result of their collaboration."

"Have they ever broken down?" Nolan asks, a sheen of sweat decorating his forehead. His eyes are locked on the platform, as if to avoid the ever-increasing drop in his periphery. I've never seen the man shaken, not even during the hectic escape from the city. I didn't think it would be heights that did the job.

"Yes," Sonjur says. "Though rarely. We are lucky enough to have the knowledge to repair them."

"Your *keishi*?" I guess, glancing at the sword at his hip.

"Just so," he says, a brief smile gracing his lips. "She was one of the original inventors."

"A blessing, to have such wisdom passed from hand to hand," Aurelion says.

"Indeed, warrior," Sonjur answers, his eyes flicking across Aurelion's broad shoulders and narrow waist. "Perhaps you will honor me by sparring once you are settled in."

"Of course," Aurelion says, bowing the appropriate height, as Myn taught him to. "The honor would be mine."

"Men," Corna says, rolling her eyes and dancing over to the side of the platform, where she leans precariously over the edge. Nolan makes a small noise in the base of his throat, and she turns her back on the drop and offers us all an impish grin. "It's all swords and... swordlike things."

The rest of the ascent passes in silence, the view stealing the words of everyone who can stomach it. The mountains fall before us, the distant road rendered insignificant, the world spread out in pristine perfection. We float up and through a drifting cloud, the remarkable silk of Eshan unaffected by the brief, and cold, dampening of the air. Sonjur seems content to allow us to drink in the sights. He stares stoically at the rock wall, though I feel his eyes on me when I look away.

When we reach the top, a short stretch of road leads to a pair of gates, wrought of black iron, standing ominously shut. More soldiers line the way, many more, enough that a tremor of fear ripples down my spine. If the Ihera want to do away with us, now is the time, surrounded as we are. I might cut my way free, but to what end? To die alone on a mountainside? To watch as my friends fall to flashing spears? No, if this trap is our end, I will share it.

At Sonjur's brief nod, though, the soldiers snap into salute, a shout of welcome echoing into the valley. In unison, their discipline perfect, they bow at the waist, eyes cast to the ground. The gates open silently, identical slick metal chains drawing them apart. A contingent of soldiers wearing the silvered sheen of clan Baeda march forth, collecting us at the gate. If possible, their precision is even greater than the Ihera, not a single step out of place. I have not known him long, but I would expect nothing less from the command of a man like Sonjur.

As we pass through the gates, Sonjur steps back to allow me to lead the way. My stomach clenches, but I force myself forwards alone. Under the shadow of the gates arching high above, I can't help but wonder what, exactly, they're for. Why would a city in the clouds need walls? No army could possibly climb the slick cliffside without the aid of the lift, especially not if defenders harried them along the way.

The mystery flits from my mind as the streets of Yohru come into view. Muted colors dominate the architecture, grays and whites and silvers in various shades. The road ascends as it moves on, eventually winding to the left and out of sight, presumably to a higher tier of the city. A few brightly colored stalls pop against the uniformity of the background, evidence that a market routinely lines the open courtyard before the gates. Not so now.

Citizens fill the street, silent. Dressed in the various colors of their clans, each *dimina* distinctive and sharp, the crowd of men and women stare at me like an object to be examined. In contrast to the common folk below, there isn't a whisper of sound. As I walk, alone, into this city full of strangers, they do not wave or cheer. The noontide sun, bright this high above the earth, shimmers in the black beauty of their hair, in the dark stillness of their eyes. I come to a halt, unable to force my feet to move. I do not know these people, and they do not know me. It was a mistake to come here. We should have...

Sonjur steps up at my left shoulder. He shouts with the voice of a battlefield commander, words cracking against the crowd like a whip. Their eyes return to me, an edge of hunger burning through the air. I don't need his nod to know that a demonstration must follow. The shadow arcs through the air and forms the same blade in my hand, the mark of my shadow blossoming on my face. The people still do not speak, still do not utter even a whisper. The citizens of Yohru match the silent majesty of their city... but they bow.

***

Sonjur's home is a towering edifice three tiers above the common gate. There is no more room to build in Yohru; the only way to add space is to ascend. Someone in Sonjur's ancestry must have been absurdly wealthy, for his estate's height is matched only by its elegance. The same tiered ceramic tiles, silver-gray in color, indicate no less than seven floors before coming to their peak. I expect servants to flood out at our arrival, but he walks up to the doorway as if any other man, opening the door for himself.

The first floor is actually three, a ceiling of dark wood stretching several stories into the tower. A set of stairs winds up the inside of the tower towards a balcony circling the room before disappearing into the floor above. A low table, meant for kneeling, rests on the right, upon it a quill and parchment ready for use. Intricate tapestries, surreal and abstract, decorate the walls in subtle white and silver threading. If they have a story to tell, I can't understand it. The floor is polished black stone threaded with white, not marble but something akin to it. There is no other adornment, just open space and quiet.

Of course, that's the point. In a city of limited area, to have such *space* is pure luxury.

A man in a matching *dimina* to Sonjur's steps crisply across the stone without a whisper of sound. He may as well be Sonjur's younger twin, clearly a scion of the Baeda. He bows, honestly and respectfully, before coming to quiet attention. Sonjur offers him some quiet commands, and he nods, turning to my companions as they file in and bowing in welcome.

"My son, Baeda Iyuro, will take your companions to their lodgings," Sonjur says.

I glance at Myn, and she nods. Sighing, I wave my friends to follow the man, though I motion for Corna and Aurelion to stay. Myn, of course, doesn't budge. My inability to communicate on my own is frustrating at best, and could well prove deadly. Myn tried to teach me at least the basics of the *hitaan*, their lilting language, but it is a tricky and abnormal beast. The verbs seem to go everywhere, the words always in an order I don't expect, strange nuances applied to phrases and inflections that change the meaning in unexpected ways. I imagine learning the tongue of Eshan is like trying to learn the *I'wia* from scratch.

"What is next, Baeda Sonjur?" I ask as the others follow Iyuro up the stairs. "You've managed to get us into your home. I assume the ten days are meant to give the Amanu and his house an opportunity to sound me out and determine what kind of threat I really am."

"You are direct," Sonjur says, his expression unreadable. His silence stretches just long enough to be uncomfortable before he smiles. "I appreciate directness. Yes, the Ihera wish to know who you are, and how dangerous you could be to them. You do not have a home in Yohru, at least not yet, so I offered to serve as your host until such time as your claim can be judged." His smile broadens. "The Ihera, of course, wanted to take you to their estate and maintain full control over the potential Eshani. I still have some pull among the Stars, though, so I spared you that fate."

"How generous of you," Corna says, barely concealing the edge of sarcasm in her voice.

"Oh, no," he says, eyes flicking to Corna. "It was a pragmatic move. *I* now have the Master of Shadow under my roof, a situation that will only elevate my clan and name. You should be thankful, though. I plan to give you open access to the city, in so much as you desire it, and my home can serve as a neutral site to meet with both the kings of Dusk and Dawn and the representatives of the greatest clans. I do not think you would enjoy the same hospitality trapped inside the Ihera estate."

"Which will conveniently mean *you* get to attend all those meetings," Corna says, folding her arms across her chest. "And thereby know more about our dealings than anyone else in the city."

"Why, yes," he says innocently. "I would assume, as host, that I will be granted a seat at the table."

"How have the Ihera reacted?" I ask, narrowing my eyes. "This seems like a dangerous move for you, political power or no."

"Oh, I'm certain they are quite upset at this turn of events." Sonjur blinks once, slowly. "How tragic."

"That is not your only reason," Myn says, staring at Sonjur's face.

"No," he agrees, the levity falling from his face. His dark eyes meet mine. "My family believes in the return of the Eshani, as did Aryal Jeshar, Myn's father. Not all of his friends abandoned him when he left. Some believed in the words he carried with him."

"Creator help us, another zealot," Corna groans.

"Not so," Sonjur corrects firmly. His gaze turns piercing as it bores into Corna. "A loyal friend, who chooses to honor his friends. That pendant you bear is the legacy of clan Aryal, woman. Do not dishonor it."

"Though she speaks like a child, Baeda Sonjur, Corna is a loyal friend as well. Kettle chose her to wield this power, and wisely, by my estimation," Aurelion says, smiling.

"I can't tell whether to be complimented or insulted," Corna says mildly.

"Both."

"Very well," Sonjur says. "You asked for what comes next. I will bring the influential members of society here, as many as I can in the next ten days. With the aid of both Aryal Myn and myself, we will try to help you navigate the winding maze of Eshanian politics."

"I do not know how much help I'll be," Myn says, frowning. "I have been away from Yohru for a very long time."

"I remember a girl with a keen and fearless mind," Sonjur says, raising his eyebrows. "Have you lost those?"

Myn dips her head in embarrassed pride.

"What kind of reception can I expect?" I ask.

"That depends mostly on you. There are several honorable clans, like my own, who will undoubtedly support your potential ascent. The majority, though, will have to choose. Do they support the Ihera and stability, or do they wish to follow a ten-thousand-year-old prophecy into potential chaos and civil war?"

"When you put it like that..."

"I hope you are not weary of climbing," Sonjur says, a glint in his eyes. "For there is a long way yet to go."

***

"Umbral, to me!" I shout, twisting aside as a maw the size of my fist flashes past. "Umbral!"

A pair of fangs slam into my calf, piercing the hard leather of my boot. Before it can fling its coils around me, I snap a kick to the base of its skull, tearing out the sharp points in a brief flash of agony. Warm blood drains down my leg and into the sole of my boot. Reacting to a flash of movement, I spin into a kick, slapping another serpent aside as it lunges up at me. One of its fangs breaks with a sharp click. The angry hiss of the snake is echoed by others, many others. The ground is alive with them, twisting and turning through the roots.

"Umbral, to me!" I shout again. "Umb—"

A bot'yal slams into me, its fangs fastening on my shoulder. Before I can fight, another clamps onto my boot. Already, coils begin to wrap around my arm and leg, squeezing tightly. Blood leaks from the bites, but far worse is the pressure, the scales wrapping around my chest and pressing, an ache already building in my lungs. My scream is strangled in my throat, hope fading with the darkness creeping into the edge of my vision.

Strangely, my heart turns to a mystery in my final moments. The strange cloud of darkness, blacker than the night sky, drifting purposefully over the water. So familiar, like it would answer if I called. If I call...

Energy floods into my limbs, a rush of power setting my veins afire. A presence touches my mind, alien and inscrutable. Darkness, limitless darkness. Avoiding the hateful touch of light, the dangerous heat of fire. Fear, hate, mistrust, and... loneliness. Aching, unending loneliness.

A sudden light. A call. A beacon in the dark. For a split second, it hesitates, as if unsure whether or not to answer.

Please.

A sense of rushing wind, urgency, eagerness. Not emotion as a human might feel. Something else, hardly recognizable.

205

The pressure eases on my chest. Air rushes back into my lungs in desperate gasps. I fall to the ground, coughing, choking. My trembling hands fall upon the writhing snakes. Fear seizes control of my limbs. I lunge backward, forgetting where I am. The rock, on the edge of a cliff. I can't even shout my despair as I cast myself into darkness.

And do not fall.

Something cushions me so that I drift gently back to rest on the earth. Shakily, I stand, glancing back towards the pack of bot'yal. There is no motion from that direction. I stagger over, giving way to my curiosity, a shield so I don't have to face the nature of my salvation. The snakes are scattered about the rock, or what's left of them. Something sliced them into pieces, the cuts impossibly clean.

Taking a deep breath, I turn back the way I came. Floating there is a void, a nothingness beyond the light of the stars. If the night is dark in the jungle, this is the shadow cast by that darkness. A formless cloud, it floats in the air, exuding something strange... nerves? Is it... anxious?

The thought is so absurd that I almost laugh. A black slash of the Depths themselves, nervous to meet... me? It has no reason to be. It just saved my life. Twice.

At the thought, the shadow swirls in on itself, pleased. I smile in spite of myself. Lifting an open hand, I beckon it over. Slowly, carefully, it floats to me, a tendril curling towards my hand. Remembering the sliced pieces of snake resting a few steps away, I almost flinch away. I force my hand to hold firm, and the darkness slips around my arm like the tail of a cat calling for affection. So soft as to make silk feel coarse, the shadow slides across my skin with infinite tenderness. My heart swells, a hole I didn't know existed filling with—

A gasp, his gasp, so unnatural to the night, spins me around.

Invisible in the darkness but for his eyes, Sanar must have come to find me. Those eyes, normally filled with laughter and love, hold nothing but horror.

***

Sunlight slants into the wide window of my quarters at the

Baeda tower. I overslept. I force myself upright, groaning at the stiffness in my back. The low bed in my quarters is firmer than anything I would choose. Considering I've spent more than a season sleeping on stones and dirt, it shouldn't be, but I still long for the softness of my original feather bed, now ashes with the rest of our house back in the Corpses in Donir. Stretching, I stand and head to the breathtaking view of the mountains, dwindling to the west until their foothills fade to the sea of grass separating the Empire of the Sea from Eshan. With the right spyglass, I feel like I could pick out Hona's estate somewhere along the edge of the plains.

The Baeda clan, ulterior motives aside, are the perfect hosts. I would be a fool to trust him completely, but Sonjur has been a blessing sent from the Creator himself. He keeps the general public away and saves my finite time for the people who matter. His knowledge and advice are more than I could ever have hoped for. My instinct is to slink about the rooftops, listening in on conversations of the elite as they scheme for or against me, and I would, were it not for the tiny, insignificant obstacle of language. I'm reliant on Sonjur and his clan's hospitality entirely. It isn't a good feeling.

Mostly because it feels very much like my path has been ordained.

Go home, she says, in the voice of a man sent forty years into the future. She must have known it would send me straight the other direction.

I walk in from the west, and there is Myn, strong and capable and loyal, sent by prophecy twenty-five years ago to wait for my coming.

And now, Sonjur, who may be my lost father's best friend, an accomplished politician and honorable warrior, is my most valuable ally. The Seer's fingers are all over Eshan, and all she did was send a man with a few choice words.

The sharp clang of steel on steel echoes up from below

and shakes me from my reverie. I hurriedly throw on my *dimina*, darting out of the room and down the stairs. Bared steel in hand, Sonjur and Aurelion square off in the center of the empty stone floor. They pause as I race down the stairs and slide to a halt. Aurelion offers me a brief smile, and a flutter runs through my heart. I don't know what I feel, not really. I mean, I know what I *feel,* I just don't know what I *want.* I mean…

I kneel to the side of the room, an echo of a memory ghosting through my mind. I knelt like this a hundred times, a thousand times as I trained to become Umbral. I grew up at the practice ring, beside it and inside it. My memories are of pain, but the best kind. The pain of growth, of experience. Of… Sanar. Pushing his memory back into the dark corner where it belongs, I blink to keep the unexpected burn of tears at bay. That dream must have loosened the tight hold I keep on the past.

Sonjur and Aurelion circle, their styles near-mirrors to one another. They come together like dancers in matching graceful steps and sinuous speed. A dozen heartbeats pass before they pause, the soft whisper of their feet counterpoint to the discordant rasp of steel. As a Tempered of the A'kai'ano'ri, there are few breathing who can match Aurelion Kraft, but the Baeda patriarch holds his own. The tempo of the fight picks up, their swords flashing, blurring. Sweat breaks out on my forehead as they move faster again.

By the Depths, they're holding sharp steel. If one of them makes even a slight misstep at that speed… it happens. Sonjur's foot slides a few inches too far, not enough to even be called a stumble. He reacts instantly, calmly, his sword whipping back to close the tiny window of vulnerability. Aurelion, though, is already past, the edge of his sword hurtling towards Sonjur's unprotected leg. I gasp, half-standing, as the blade closes the gap… and stops.

The men stand, each offering the other a nod of respect. I release a breath I didn't realize I was holding. How…?

"My *keishi* is Master of Metal, lady Kettle," Baeda says, not

208

bothering to look my way. "There is no danger."

"Oh. *Oh,*" I say, mind racing through the possibilities. "That is a remarkable training tool."

"I have found it most useful," he agrees, a slight smile creasing his face.

"Again, Sonjur?" Aurelion asks, hefting his sword. "I haven't fought so worthy an opponent since…"

His eyes slide to me, his words fading into silence. I wince. Of course, the only time we fought, he'd been wielding the power of Light, and I'd done my very best to kill him. In the process, he'd destroyed some of the last living shadow left in existence. Or at least, so I thought. I can feel the shrouded valley so far below us, like a distant call just at the edge of hearing.

"You fought the Eshani?" Sonjur asks, his eyes flicking between us. "In earnest?"

"It was another time," I say softly. "He was doing a job."

"And who was the victor?"

"I was, but…" Aurelion looks sheepish, his eyes falling to the sword in his grasp. A weapon of vulnerable metal, not unbreakable Light. "I do not think the result would be the same, should we face one another again."

"The Eshani must be formidable indeed, for you to say so," Sonjur says, offering me a slight bow. He turns back to Aurelion, raising his sword. "Again?"

Chapter 10
Jace
Summer's Dawning
In the year 5223, Council Reckoning

I've grown used to the gentle curve of the gray stone walls of my prison. After Alice dressed my wounds, she offered to bring my meals so that I didn't have to venture out into the camp. Not knowing what else to do, I accepted. I haven't left since. Days pass without word, either from the Mason or the Vengeance.

The longer the silence stretches, the stranger I feel about it. On the one hand, the anticipation grows to near-unbearable levels, my mind filling in the gaps with fears great and small. On the other, at least the greatest swordsman of an age isn't coming to finish me off. Perhaps it will give me the time to figure out what I feel about... everything.

The worst part is that I can't talk to Juliet. Shortly after the fight ended, she followed after the departing Shapers. I had raised a hand to stop her. Exhausted as I was, she'd just smiled, held my cheek for a moment, and walked past without a word. The questions I have for her, her fears, her outlandish claims... they all rattle around in my chest, growing into a storm I can hardly contain. I don't even know if she's still alive. And this nonsense about the Vengeance being my father...

Each of the Enclave has stopped by to see me, often with a reassuring word. They are just as in the dark as I am, though, even Locke. He seems wary of trying to spy on the Vengeance. The Shorn ignore me. I can't tell if it's because they believe I've betrayed them or if they're just giving me space. No one expected that they'd witness a duel between two Blades firsthand, let alone

one between Shapers. In the days following the fight, Elthe and the more senior members analyzed the duel for the benefit of the others. Since then, though, their silence has echoed as loud as thunder. Which makes the sound of soft footfalls outside my abode all the more surprising.

"Jace?" a hard woman's voice calls from outside. The former Tide, Poline. "May I?"

"Sure," I find myself saying. "Why not?"

Ducking into the low entrance, the crimson haired woman puts her back to the wall and slides to the earth. She doesn't speak, though her eyes take in the grease in my hair and the dirt on my clothing. I haven't changed since the fight. The realization brings a frown to my face. Poline's nose wrinkles slightly as she takes in my no-doubt impressive odor.

"You know, I used to spend a lot of time inside, too," she says, her eyes roving around the gray stone encasing us. "When I first got here, I did little else but sit and brood. And train."

"Congratulations," I say. She tilts her head quizzically, seemingly unsure as to whether or not to be offended. Realizing how it sounds, I hurriedly gesture towards the bandage wrapped around her wrist. "On your ascension. You deserve to be Tempered."

"Oh," she says, relaxing again. She glances down at the wound where a second scar will match the two remaining tattoos. "Thanks."

Silence grows between us, thick enough to cut. I think to speak, to ask her why she's here, what it is she wants, but I don't want to drive her away. Something about her silence settles me.

"Why?" I ask finally.

"Most of the people here have lost something, or had it taken from them," she says, understanding the intent of my simple question. "Families, loved ones, livelihoods. I won't pretend to compare my tale to theirs, or yours. My loss, though... perhaps it is worse because it is not so final."

"What did you lose?"

"Love," she says, dropping her eyes to the packed earth floor. "She... left."

"And this is somehow the Sealord's fault?" I ask, confused.

"Yes." Her eyes come up, anger blazing to life in their emerald depths. "He twisted her mind. He took the woman I loved and tried to rob her of everything that makes her great. In the end... he succeeded. She left me, not because she wished to, but because she was afraid he would kill me if she didn't."

"This sounds... personal," I say slowly.

"It is. By the Creator it is." Her slender fingers wrap around the well-worn hilt of the sword sheathed at her side. "Why do you think I train so hard? I want to be ready should I get the chance."

"You realize he's never going to fight you with a sword," I say, a sourceless bitterness rising to the surface. "You'll never get close enough to hurt him."

"Probably," she agrees evenly. "But all men bleed."

Silence falls again between us.

"You've got a strange way of cheering people up," I say after a moment.

"That's not why I came." She stands, folding her arms across her chest. "None of us know the future, nor would I guess at yours, considering you tried to kill the damn Vengeance himself."

"I was defending myself," I start to argue, but she holds up a hand.

"Regardless, wasting away here serves no one. The Vengeance might be a cold bastard, but the Mason would never let him lay a hand on your friend. She'll be back soon, safe and sound."

"It's nice of you to say so," I say, unable to keep the biting skepticism from my voice. "But you saw the blood on him, the look on his face."

"You're not a prisoner here, Jace." She glances out the door, painting a look of confusion on her face. "No one is standing guard. If those old Shapers were going to punish you, they already would have."

"I..."

"Just get off your ass, Blade," she says, turning and disappearing before I can answer.

***

Whether it's Poline's words, or just the recognition her visit forced on me, a restless vigor takes hold of my mind. Rising before dawn the next morning, I skulk down to a mountain stream and carefully break a thin layer of ice that night froze over the water. Stripping out of my grimy clothes, I plunge into the icy waters and gasp through a thorough scrubbing. The cuts on my shoulder and leg burn for a moment before the cold numbs the pain. My muscles relax for what feels like the first time in days. Rinsing my worn clothing as best I can, I scramble out of the creek as dawn begins to lighten the eastern sky.

If the Shorn are surprised to see me line up for training, they do an admirable job of hiding it. Elthe offers me a smile and a brief nod before taking the lead. Moving slower than normal, careful not to reopen my wounds, I gently glide through the stretches before sitting to the side to watch the others. The symphony of steel on steel is comforting in a way that silence and solitude can't match.

As the practice ends, the Shorn do not disperse, as they normally would. None of them look at me, but I can feel their attention all the same. Elthe glances about, a faint smile creasing his lips.

"Cowards," he says mildly. "They're too afraid to ask, so I will. We want to hear about it, from your eyes. How was it, to face the Vengeance?"

"I..."

"You don't have to, obviously," Held interjects quickly.

"No, it's no trouble," I say. Before I can blink, the assembled Shorn form a ring around me, like children waiting for a story. In some ways, they are, for are not the stories we tell our children meant to teach? "I guess… you might think that his speed is the problem, but it's his eyes…"

They listen, rapt, the best audience a man could ask for. Several ask questions, pointed questions that make me evaluate the fight again: my mistakes, his, what I could have done. Held serves as the Vengeance as I work through the feint that fooled him, the others nodding along to my explanation. As we reach the part where he, well, *cheated*, I find myself with nothing to say. I barely know what he, and I, can do myself. How could I possibly explain it?

"Let's go over the thrust again. One more time," Elthe says, his eyes troubled. "I saw him do it, but I still can't figure out how he managed to hide it…"

"Altos has an unfair advantage," a rich voice rumbles. Engrossed in the discussion, none of us noticed the Mason's approach. He stands at the back of the group, his powerful arms folded across his broad chest. My heart rises at the slight figure of Juliet standing at his side. Free, unfettered, unharmed. She smiles, and my breath hitches. "He's almost two hundred years old. The old bastard has had a long time to practice."

"How's his leg?" Elthe asks.

"Good as new," Itolas says, his eyes straying to Juliet. He turns to me. "As are, hopefully, his manners. I'm sorry, Jace. If ever you could count yourself safe, it should be under my care. I'm sure that you wish to speak to Perrea, but join me for the evening meal tonight." He glances again at the woman standing at his side. "She knows the way."

With an affable wave to the assembled Shorn, he turns and ambles away. I catch Juliet's eye and tilt my head towards the open forest.

"Another time, James," I say, setting off. If he says

214

anything in reply, I don't hear it.

I walk in silence for a time, enjoying the sound of her steps next to mine. Her presence, after the fear that's owned my thoughts these past days, is a soothing salve. When we make it far enough that we won't be overheard, I turn to study her. She stands easily, no sign of pain or discomfort in her stance or face.

"You're...?"

"Yes, I'm fine," she says easily, her hand rising to brush my arm. "All we did was talk."

"And?"

"That's a bit too vague of a question to answer." She frowns. "They are satisfied that I'm not a threat, at least not intentionally. And they believe that, from their knowledge of how Thought Shaping works, it is unlikely Kranos was able to implant anything more serious than an unconscious desire to leave a trail. They're pretty sure that he wasn't even attempting to find this place, but rather to avoid any more escaping prisoners after the Enclave."

"What about you?" I ask, concerned. "What he said, what he called you..."

"Still in the air," she says, offering half a shrug. "Itolas seems far more accepting, which is no surprise. I imagine I swayed Altos a bit when I healed the cut you gave him. It was nasty, by the way."

"Is that reproach in your voice?" I ask, incredulous. "I fought him for *you*."

"And I told you not to," she says flatly. "I have a mind of my own, and I can damn well think for myself. If I was a threat, I needed to be dealt with. You weren't thinking rationally."

"But you aren't a threat," I protest, but she's already shaking her head.

"What you did was noble, I guess. It was also incredibly stupid and shortsighted."

"Wow," I say, my face growing hot. "I was just..."

215

"Acting like a child," she says evenly. I can't meet her eyes, though I feel them boring into me. "I need you to trust me, Jace."

"I do," I say, but it comes out sullenly, just like the child she's named me. I force my eyes up to hers. Rather than the anger I expect, there's a vulnerability to them, an uncertainty. She needs something from me, something I haven't given. My anger slowly dissipates. Taking a deep breath, I try to let the embarrassment go with the air in my lungs as I blow it out in a cloud of white. "I trust you. Promise."

"As far as stupid things to do, it *was* pretty impressive," she says, face softening. "Few would throw themselves in front of the Vengeance for a friend. Especially not for me. Now, come here. Alice probably did a decent job, but there's no need for you to suffer."

She raises her hand, the crimson symbol of Beasts glowing to life on her arm. I catch her before she can touch me. She tilts her head in question.

"I'll keep them," I say firmly. "The pain, and the scars, will be a reminder."

"Of?" she says, raising an eyebrow.

"You."

"Just what a girl wants," she says, laughing. "For scars and pain to be her mark."

"You, and the wisdom you've given me," I say solemnly. My thoughts turn to the Enclave, and the echo of her words. "When I first met you, you opened my eyes to a new perspective. You tried to teach me not to assume, to know before I judge. I've tried to live that lesson ever since."

"Trusting me is hardly the same."

"Trusting friends, then." She closes her mouth, thoughtful, before finally offering a grudging nod. I let loose a breath I didn't realize I was holding. "Now, about this whole... parentage thing..."

"Right," she says, leaning back and looking me up and down. "The family resemblance is there, in your build, your nose, maybe the jaw…"

"You're sticking with this?" I ask incredulously, shaking my head. "The Vengeance, *my* father? And *he* bought it?"

"He's hard to read. I think I got through to Itolas though."

It's strange to hear the Mason's name run so easily off her tongue. A sense of vertigo twists my eyes, and the earth feels unsteady beneath my feet. I met Juliet as a leper, an exile, a blind girl cursed by the Creator to suffer and quickly die. Now, she's conversing with the greatest Shapers of our age, personally gifted power by the Master of Beasts, on a first-name basis with the Mason and the Vengeance. How far we've come.

"How?" I ask finally, the question too big to put into words. "But… how?"

"When Kranos found me, when he made me what I am… he believed he had me fully in his thrall." She glances down, clasping her shaking hands together to steady them. "Why wouldn't he? He saved me from blindness, from my disease, from certain death. He offered me strength, and a life I could never have hoped for, with the only price my obedience. And if not obedience, then fear." She begins to pace abruptly, her footsteps crunching through the icy snow. "He sealed my mouth to control me, to remind me of his power over me."

"I'm sorry."

"I can handle it," she says, though she doesn't meet my eyes. She walks for a moment in silence, the only sound the soft crunch of snow. "Jace… I think he's lonely."

"Kranos?" I say in disbelief. "Juliet, he's insane."

"Maybe," she half-agrees, turning to face me. "But even so, he has no one to talk to. You'd think he and the Sealord were enemies, the way he talks about him. He has no one to vent to, no one to hear his fears and understand his perspective." She swallows, her expression hollow. "For a while, I was that person

217

for him. The perfect audience: silent and attentive. Who would I ever tell? He literally sealed my lips. I needed him to *eat*. Believing his secrets safe, he told me things that I'm sure he has never uttered to another soul."

The thought is staggering. The Lord General had always been a relative mystery to the public. Unapproachable, terrifying in his competence in both healing and battle, his actions in the war to unify the east under the Sealord were ruthless and precise. He managed to kill whoever he thought necessary and squash any organized rebellion in less than a year. I met him myself, at the King's Ball, and I found his presence off-putting and, for lack of a better word, frightening.

But to know his thoughts, know his secrets...

"He thinks the Vengeance is my father?" I ask, frowning.

"He suspects. He spoke of a rumor, a story that he and the Sealord worked tirelessly to suppress. On the night of the coup, they mysteriously came into custody of a newborn Master of Earth. It is somewhat of an open secret at court that the princess is the Vengeance's daughter. Everyone who lived before those times knew of the Sealord's obsession with Altos's wife. She chose Altos, but the Sealord got his revenge by claiming their only offspring. She died that night, most say in childbirth."

"Most?" I say, head swimming, trying to keep up with the flood of revelation.

"Yes, most. There is a story, swift execution to any who voice it, of something else happening that night. Kranos was there at Iliana's birth, in case his healing powers were needed. He told me... he told me he could sense another. A twin. The Sealord gave him instruction to take the girl, but nothing else. So he left, leaving soldiers behind to deal with the grieving mother. He never figured the boy would matter, for he would follow his mother quickly into death. But there was a fire, mysteriously set, that burned their home to the ground, soldiers and all. Just before the home collapsed, a woman was seen fleeing with a baby wrapped in her arms. A woman named Rosaline."

Rosie. Her face, damp with sweat from the Summer air, a ringlet of brown hair plastered to her forehead. Smiling, caring, tender. My mother.

"They thought they lost track of you then, that you died or fled Donir entirely. Rosaline disappeared so completely that they never heard another word. I guess they never thought a highborn servant would end up at a place like the Simply."

"She was only Rosie to the other girls," I say woodenly. "She gave the men a different name, different *names*, always new."

"Smart. They'd nearly forgotten about the story before you attended the King's Ball," she continues, unrelenting. "When the Sealord saw you next to the princess, he couldn't help but recognize your kinship. They tried to find you, but you eluded them, even as they took your home. Kranos wasn't convinced, and he still isn't. Now, I know. The second you Shaped fire at the Vengeance, everything clicked into place."

"Why didn't you say anything before?" I ask, the implications of her words too large to accept right now. Maybe ever.

"Before, it was the wonderings of a madman about a secret so big it would be death to utter it," Juliet says, shrugging helplessly. "I didn't want to offer baseless hope, or whatever you might have felt. The second I knew, though... I couldn't sit by and let you kill your own father."

"I... I need some time," I say, turning and shambling away without another word.

The air presses in on me, suffocating. My father's element. The thought makes me dizzy. Staggering, hardly knowing where I'm going, it's only after I reach the curving gray walls of my little home can I breathe again.

The embers of the fire glow a sullen red. I slump onto the earth, struggling to carry any thought past inception.

Rosie. My mother. My protector. My... savior?

The Vengeance. Cold. Terrifying. My... I can't even think it.

Wheeling images, a caring face I've never seen, a woman who died to birth me. A woman who died, *after* giving birth to me. Died in a fire...

The thought lurches in my gut. I spin to the side, heaving bile onto the earth. My legs curl to my shuddering stomach. I can't muster sorrow, at least not for a faceless woman I will never meet. But for the life I might have led... staring into the coals, cheek pressed to the earth, I can't picture it, not really. But I try.

Stability. A home. A father of limitless power. A mother who might have loved me. A sister... Creator, she was familiar, like I'd known her from another life. Perhaps in her face, its lines, its shape... I was simply seeing myself.

The earth shifts beneath me, shuddering under a great weight. The hand that comes to rest on my shoulder engulfs it entirely, fingers reaching nearly to the floor. A deep thrum reverberates through my chest, almost below hearing. Though I have heard Bota's anger and his frustration, his joy and his sorrow, I've never heard this.

Gently, so gently I barely feel it, he lifts me from the earth and wraps me in his mighty arms. His scent is earthy, pleasant. Nothing like I would have expected. He cradles me close as if I'm nothing but a child. I have never felt so small. The shock of his strange tenderness is a whisper amidst the roar in my mind. Any other time, I might push him away. Not now.

"Peace," he whispers, the word felt more than heard. "Peace."

The deep rumble of his voice rattles through my skin and into my bones. His command is simple, and has no reason to work. Yet the storm in my chest quiets. The sharp edges of my thoughts soften. Eventually, warm and safe, my eyes close, and sleep takes me.

***

A gentle hand shakes me awake. The fire is spent, the small space nearly black. The dim red light illuminates Juliet's face as she looks down on me, eyes dark pools of sympathy. My mind is quiet, still.

"It's time," she says gently.

It takes me a second to remember. The Mason. Dinner. I rise silently and follow her into the night. The cookfires burn brightly, larger than normal, like the people seek to stave off the darkness. We thread through them like ghosts fluttering in the night. We pass out of the camp proper, following a thin trail to the north. Even in the dark, Juliet steps confidently, our feet following a path half-hidden by snowfall and pine needles. The ascent is steep, and the exertion reopens the wound in my thigh.

We reach a small clearing, a fire burning in its center. A pot hangs over the crackling flame. The flickering light shows angles foreign to nature: sharp, broken stone. Some kind of ruin sits above the mountain pass. Judging by the space within, a tower once stood here to guard this seemingly inconsequential pass. Some ancient civilization must have valued it highly. Perhaps an old border between warring nations, or a final redoubt in the face of invasion. Whoever brought these stones to rest atop each other, even their memory has long since passed.

The Mason sits across the fire. The flame's reflection dances in his eyes. For a moment, he blends in with the ancient stone, still and solemn and old. Though his beard yet runs a bright russet brown, there is something ancient about this man. His eyes flick to us, and the illusion breaks as he offers a warm smile, welcoming and true.

"Welcome, friends," he says, standing and opening his arms. He gathers a few earthen bowls in his massive hands, ladling in portions of the steaming stew. "Please, have a seat. Here, and here."

"It smells wonderful," Juliet says, closing her eyes and breathing in the steam.

"An old recipe," he says, his smile intact, though his eyes go sad. "From an old friend. He always used to brag about his mother's cooking." He puffs out his chest, adopting a short, haughty way of speaking. "I'd hold Mam's cooking up against any of your fancy chefs! Best in three hundred years!"

Juliet laughs, but I don't feel much like smiling. The soup is excellent, some combination of cheese and potato that truly approaches the divine. We eat in silence, perhaps not a companionable silence, but there is little tension. The Mason moves with the genial grace of an aristocrat trapped in the body of a kodiak. As my spoon scrapes the bottom of the bowl, I glance around the clearing, empty but for us and the ancient stone.

"Is he..."

"No," the Mason says, his smile fading. "We thought it better if I speak to you first."

"Alright."

"There has been a lot to take in," he says, shaking his head. At my incredulous look, he laughs, his humor restored in an instant. "I can't imagine how you feel right now."

"Hard to feel much of anything," I say wryly. A sudden urge rises in my chest, the pressure of it nearly making me gasp. I try not to give the desire voice. It feels like a betrayal. Of Rosie, of all she did for me... yet I can't resist long. "Will you tell me of... her?"

"Ah," he sighs, his gaze drifting to the stars. "Nadine. She was a light in a world falling to darkness. She held the love of all who knew her, and the two greatest men of our age besides. Altos could hardly believe she chose him."

"You call the Sealord great?" I ask.

"Greatness has little to do with righteousness," he answers seriously. "It is impossible to argue that Helikos has not achieved great things, even if we don't like them. Unless my brain has fallen to dotage, I have memories of a very different Helikos than the one the world will remember. When he was younger, he was a

222

good man, a curious man." He seems to give himself a shake, his eyes focusing on us for a moment. "But that's not what you asked. You asked of your mother."

He speaks for hours, late into the night. Most of the stories he tells are of small moments, gestures, kindnesses, and arguments. He doesn't make any claims about her, doesn't try to declare who she was. Rather, his memories paint a woman in all her faults and graces, fiery and impatient, kind and welcoming, sarcastic and cutting, loyal and protective. Juliet speaks more than I do, her questions casting more light on this faceless silhouette looming in my thoughts.

The moon has set before he falls silent in the darkness, the fire having collapsed to embers. I can hardly remember a single story that he told. There were too many, one after the other, the names and faces too foreign. I'll never have a chance to know the woman who gave birth to me. Through the Mason's memories, though, her outline is more distinct.

"On the morrow, I'd like to see you both again," he says after a moment. "I am sure there is much you wish to know. And there is much I can teach." A grin splits his beard as he glances between us. "How'd you like to learn how to really Shape?"

***

Itolas collects us after morning training. Spurning the ruins from last night, he heads towards the center of the sprawling camp. As I've spent most of my time in the little niche the Shorn have carved on the eastern slope, I don't really have an understanding of how many souls the rebel Shapers have gathered. The communal cookfires in the center of the camp each hold lines of people, young and old, waiting patiently for breakfast. Several offer shouted greetings as Itolas passes, and he gives them a friendly wave.

Harsh shouts and the sharp clack of wood on wood fill the air as we approach a training ground where recruits toil under the watchful eye of a few experienced soldiers. The trainees are

223

uniform only in their uniqueness. People from all walks of life, the old and the young, washer women and callow farmhands, scarred sailors and unblemished youths, all grit their teeth and stab determinedly at one another with blunted spears. Itolas studies my expression and grunts.

"Not exactly the fearsome army you expected?" he asks wryly.

"No," I agree, shaking my head. "You won't win against the Empire with soldiers like these."

"Our war is not with the soldiers," Itolas says easily, waving the soldiers away. "Altos and I only seek the death of two men."

"Yet they have tens of thousands of spears at their command. How many can you muster?"

"I have a thousand I would rely on in a fight." Itolas slows in his walk, turning back to watch the people toil. "These people may surprise you. They fight for themselves, not for me or Altos or anyone else. They chose this life. Besides, Helikos's armies will disperse like smoke before a strong breeze if their leaders are taken from them."

"And they are spread thin," Juliet says, nudging me in the ribs. I straighten at the gentle rebuke. I hadn't even realized my shoulders were slumped. "How many soldiers does it take to police two continents? Especially when both are ready to rise against them."

"Sounds like the time to strike to me," I mutter.

"Soon," Itolas says, continuing on.

"If not now, when?" I walk quickly to keep up with his long strides. "They *are* stretched thin. Donir nearly fell without our help. We may only have a thousand spears, but we have several dozen Shorn, three Blades, three... Creator, four Shapers under one command. The Empire couldn't muster an army that could halt our attack. Not with all the might they have to be spending in the Khalintars, and the princess and the Master of Beasts are both in the west."

"And then what?" Itolas ask softly. "We may be able to take Donir with martial prowess. But there is the Sealord to contend with."

"One Shaper against four?" I ask incredulously.

"Have you not heeded recent tidings?" Itolas leads us into another of the innumerable stone dwellings as he speaks, though the rough-hewn stone steps wind down into the earth deeper than any I've entered. He gathers a lantern as we descend, deftly lighting it on the move. "Shapers come in all forms. Some, like me, are straightforward in our strengths. I can Shape stone and Shape it well. It comes easily to my call. I struggle, though, to be precise. I am like the mountains, strong and bold, but also clumsy. In contrast, the Master of Beasts has a weak soul. He—"

"What now?" I interrupt.

"It's true, Jace. He was always the weakest on the Council. He was known as the Healing Hand because that is the simplest power of the Master of Beasts: encouraging a creature to resume its natural form. Despite that weakness, though, he has always been the most surgical. He can focus down to levels I can't even imagine."

"Where does the Vengeance fall?" Juliet asks.

"If Kranos is a candle, and I am a torch, Altos is a bonfire. He can do things that are hardly rumored in myth, with precision and power. What he imagines, the air does its best to achieve. Now Helikos... he was always strong, but the events at the Way of the North put things into a new light. He may well be something else entirely. Ah. We're here."

The Mason stops at an unremarkable expanse of stone wall, appearing no different from any other. Without warning, a seam appears in the stone, a line so straight as to defy nature. A ponderous square of rock, deeper than my shoulders are wide, swings silently aside. No rumbling, no shaking... a dozen oxen straining couldn't shift that colossal stone. But this man... he glances at me, baring his teeth in a grin.

"Benefits to being famous," he says, winking.

A startled laugh bursts out of Juliet. I just shake my head as he gestures us onward. A short passage leads to a small room, perhaps ten paces square, with a ceiling of rough-hewn rock and a floor of polished stone. A rectangular table rests in the center, crafted of some red-veined rock I don't recognize. The Mason settles the lantern on the table and then points wordlessly to the bench across from him. The flickering lantern casts his face in shadow as he regards us with all the patience of a mountain. The longer he sits, the less he seems human, and the more he seems like another part of this subterranean space, one with the depths of the earth. After a few minutes spent in silence, I shift uneasily. He comes alive, his expression opening.

"Sorry," he says gruffly, thick fingers rising to rub the bridge of his nose. "I was thinking back to when Altos taught me. It's been a decade or eight, so I ask that you bear with me."

"You learned from the Vengeance himself?" Juliet asks. "What was he like?"

"Hah, he was a sprightly man of a hundred Winters back then. Still in love with the world. Altos was a prankster, a trickster, a man always ready to laugh. That was before he took on the mantle. The burden." Itolas frowns, and for a moment I fear he'll slip back into the silence of the rock, but he shakes himself and continues. "Regardless, I'll start at the basics. I imagine some of this will tread old ground for you, Perrea. Forgive me."

"I am sure there is plenty I don't know," she says graciously. "The Master of Beasts only wished to know if he had correctly implanted his power in me. I don't think he ever meant for me to grow into it."

"So," he says, leaning forward. "Shaping is limited by three things: your will, your element, and your imagination. The first and greatest is will. Some Shapers describe commanding their element like a general his army, while others speak of asking respectfully like a child their teacher, and still others have a friendship, an understanding, with their element. Often, these are the greatest among us."

"You speak as if the elements are alive," I say slowly.

"Of course they are," he says, as if I am the idiot for doubting. "I can hear the stone sing around us. You may have heard its voice in its groans and grumbles, the strain of holding up so much ponderous weight. Imagine how your bones would feel if you weighed as much as the mountains."

"But stones don't have bones," I say impatiently. "Stone doesn't feel pain, or think."

"I'd kindly ask you not to insult my friend so," he says, lifting a hand, not towards me, but towards the ceiling above. The rock promptly groans, a sound filled with discontent. "Normally, the stone ignores people like you. When I'm around, though, it listens closely. Careful lest you offend it."

"Uh, well," I say, glancing upwards apprehensively as the stone groans again, dust hissing down in an angry whisper. "Sorry?"

"I've heard my... element... speak so," Juliet says slowly. "I am most used to its screams."

"You're a healer," the Mason says softly. "It is easy to forget that flesh exists without pain."

"Okay," I say, running my hands through my hair in frustration. "You're telling me the elements can speak. But I don't hear fire." I lean in, careful not to get too close, and offer my ear to the lantern. "What was that, buddy? This is nonsense?"

"They don't speak as we do," he says patiently. "But every Shaper will tell you their element has a voice. You need to open yourself to its song."

"I don't believe..." I trail off as Juliet puts a hand on my forearm.

"This was easy for me because I spent my life healing. I knew the song of the body before I ever got the chance to hear

227

it." The bright red mark of power glows into being on her arm. "Keep an open mind."

I stare at the flame, its sinuous dance mesmerizing even as my pulse quickens. I made myself believe that I left the fear behind, that the beauty I found when I touched this strange power cured me. Now, feeling the heat, gentle as it is, still I have to fight the urge to shy away.

Creator, I'm safe. It's just a bit of fire. Just a fire, safely contained in glass.

"Why do you fear it?" the Mason asks suddenly, eyes boring into mine.

"I'm not afraid," I say automatically. He merely stares. Juliet glances between me and the lantern, realization dawning on her face as well. "Listen, I'm not afraid of the lantern."

"It's okay, Jace," she says, offering me a warm smile.

"Ugh. Fine. I... I don't know why," I say, grinding my palms into my eyes. "I just... am."

"Is it a memory?" Juliet asks, gently rubbing my back.

"No. Yes. I don't know."

"There is nothing to fear," the Mason says softly. "Nothing at all. Not for you."

I raise my eyes to stare into the lantern's flame. A scream, so distant yet so close, burns in the fire. Pressure builds in my chest. I just want it away, away from me, *away*. The fire reacts, dancing feverishly, pressing against the far side of the lantern. It looks almost afraid, like a beaten animal, backed into a corner and cowering. Afraid? The fire is afraid of... *me*?

I barely notice as a new light, the purest orange of the brightest flame, glows into being in the dimly lit room. I hear it. The fire. Or rather, I *feel* it. Its sorrow, its fear, its confusion. For it longs to come to me, to answer my call. Yet all I command is that it cannot.

"Good, Jace." The Mason's voice. "Open yourself to it. For now, that is enough."

I hardly hear him. The fire has settled as I have. As I breathe in and out, it pulses in time, a slow, silent duet. It wants to serve, would love to serve, to live and breathe its brief life with me, in me. When I close my eyes, I still see it, dancing in time to the beat of my heart. It will not burn me; it cannot burn me. Why have I been so afraid?

At my silent call, it comes, passing easily through the cracks of the lantern and flying to my grasp. It burns there, merrily. I know instinctively that, as fire ever does, it needs fuel. My body, my soul, will serve. The fire crackles along my skin, though I feel nothing but a gentle warmth. With a thought, again acting more on instinct than conscious thought, I draw the flame into my hand. A burst of energy floods my veins, weariness washing away before the warmth of the flame.

The others are talking, I think. My vision has shifted again to the other sight, the other existence where the world is awash in flame. And by the Creator, there is *light.*

A fire above all else, like none I've seen, a brilliant swirl of silver and gold and crimson and gray, a gorgeous maelstrom almost too bright to look at. My hand rises, my will beckoning to the flame. It responds, though sluggishly, as if reluctant to break from its formless shape, but still it comes. The second this new fire touches my skin, a bolt of lightning crackles across my very being.

What I *thought* life to be was a dull shadow, a pathetic excuse for existence. This…

My skin burns with life, my back arching in such a torrent of power I can hardly stand it. More. Creator, give me more. My outstretched hand is both plea and demand. Give me *more.*

The tongue of flame, a brilliant marriage of color and light, grows, flowing into me and setting my body alight. I become something new, something more. I learn what paradise can be.

The fire blurs and moves, breaking its shape entirely. Yes, more. Come to me…

Something blasts into my chest, lifting me from the bench and slamming me against the wall. The world dulls to stark and colorless gray. Gray, because I've taken the natural fire, and a symbol of power on the Mason's bared upper arm offers our only light. He stands across the room, arm outstretched, trembling. Rock grips my body, immovable and inexorable. Stone fingers wrap around my head and squeeze. Like a cracked branch laden with snow, my bones, my *skull*, creak under the pressure.

I blink, trying to clear my thoughts. The light of life still burns through my veins, though already it has begun to fade. Its absence hurts far more than the joy its presence offered. Sorrow replaces ecstasy, the memory of that shining moment growing more distant by the second.

The Mason takes heavy, shaky breaths in the silence. Sweat beads his bald pate. His eyes are haunted, enraged, and, above all, terrified. Juliet stares at him with horror, though she seems frozen in shock.

"What..." he begins, then pauses, gulping down another deep breath. "What did you do to me?"

"He didn't do anything," Juliet says, finding her voice in my defense. "He just—"

The Mason's gaze flicks to her, and she closes her mouth immediately, glancing at me in alarm.

"I asked you a question, boy," he says, his voice like rattled stone before a rockslide, ominous and inevitable. "What did you do to me?"

"I..."

I can't force my lungs to work. I barely have the will to consider his question. The world feels empty, meaningless, this mundane life such a tragic disappointment. I've already forgotten the feeling that sent me to another realm, a blessed realm, a different world of light and life and awareness. Yet the memory of its memory is enough to mourn.

"This is your last chance, Jace," he says, his outstretched

230

hand tightening slightly. The fingers of stone press against my skull so tightly he wrings a shout of pain from my tortured lungs. The immediate pain distracts me from the pain of what I've lost. Though part of me would welcome death rather than live in this existence. "Tell me what you just did."

"I called to the fire," I say softly. "And it came."

"We saw you call to the flame of the lantern," he says, a touch impatiently. "We saw you absorb it. This is natural, normal. Telias could do the same. What did you do after?"

"It felt... good," I say, the word so inadequate I nearly choke on it. "I saw more fire, brighter and stronger, and I... I called to it as well."

"There was no other fire in the room," Juliet says.

"You're wrong," I say, the memory shaking through my core like the aftershocks of an earthquake. "You are *so* wrong. I called to the flame, and it came. This life... this world... there is so much more. So much more to feel and to see. This... I..."

"Itolas, what is he talking about?" Juliet asks, though she doesn't stop eyeing me with concern.

"I don't know," he says, the fear finally seeping through the cracks of his facade. "It felt like a hand reached into my body and... Creator protect me. It was like my life, my soul itself, left me."

"Truly?" she asks, finally looking his way.

"I think..." he trails off, staring at me. His lip twitches, and a shiver arcs down his spine. His outstretched hand, though, does not waver. He visibly steels himself, taking a deep breath and releasing it slowly. "I think I know, even in part, what death feels like."

"I must have... the fire I saw... it must have been *you*," I say slowly, a sudden fear of my own subsuming the sorrow. "How is that possible?"

"I don't know," he says. "I've never heard of anything like this."

231

There is a threat in his words, one he doesn't need to voice. Whatever just happened, I've shaken him to his very core. I took the very fire of his life and stole it for my own. If I can do that... if I *wished* to do that... I might be too dangerous to leave alive.

"I'm sorry, Itolas. I didn't know. I would never... I just wouldn't," I say, trying to mean every word. Trying, and mostly succeeding. But the memory of that exalted joy...

The Mason stares at me for a moment in silence, once again more stone than man. Juliet seems to recognize this moment of decision, her silent plea loud in the stillness. I let my limbs relax, and the stone holds my body in an embrace that may well be final.

Finally, he sighs. His hand drops to his side. The stone releases me, and I slump to the earth.

"We'll... we'll talk later," he says, turning to the dark doorway. "Don't... we'll talk later."

I ignore Juliet as her hands come to rest on my shoulders, offering me a wordless comfort. Comfort I can't feel. I have no energy, no will to stand. I can't tell if I am relieved that the Mason let me go... or ruined because he didn't take from me this desolation I once called life.

Chapter 11
Iliana

The Seventy-Seventh Day of Summer
In the year 5223, Council Reckoning

"I'm afraid," I whisper.

"I understand," Telias whispers in turn.

My back is pressed to the wall in the darkness of the hidden hall, and, from the sound of his voice, he mirrors me on the other side. Though it nears midnight, I have no urge to return to my bed. The moments I spend with this man are balm enough.

"He's going to know as soon as he returns." I hug my knees. "How do you hide from someone who can read your mind?"

"Kranos is not omnipotent, Iliana," he says a little louder. "He may be monitoring your thoughts at times, but he can't read your deepest secrets. Much of the power of Thought is stolen the instant the subject is aware. He can't touch you now that you know. Focus. The damage done to your mind is unnatural, and ultimately superficial. These wounds will heal. Delve into your thoughts. Peel away the layers of deceit. You will know what is real, and what is not."

"How will I know?"

"There is a game I used to play, with the last Master of Thought," he says, a smile in his words. "He described our minds like a forest, with our memories the trees. He would try to hide a memory in my thoughts, a false memory. There is a quality to false memories, a hazy ephemerality. Rather than having roots, they simply lay on the surface of our minds. If we focus, we can tell the difference."

"And what about memories that have been taken?"

"Memory can't be destroyed. Merely suppressed. Look in your mind for the holes, the voids. Rather than seek a memory, seek its absence. Now, breathe with me. Slow, and deep. Slow, and deep. Slow..."

I let the cadence sweep my conscious thought away. The impenetrable darkness in the hidden passageway robs my eyes of meaning, and the only scent is of clean, untouched stone. There is nothing to distract me. Drifting, I flit through memories as they come.

Father, his smile, his pride. All false. Even now, though, the thought feels dissonant, wrong. Father cares for me. He's only ever done what is necessary to rule. He is everything a good king should be... tears pool in my eyes from emotions felt and unfelt, contradictions and broken promises, love and burgeoning hate. I release another slow breath and try to let his memory fade. I let my mind follow him tangentially. His commands, his orders, the task he gave me...

The Oaxl. Mielina. Jahana. My time with the tribes, however brief, was pleasant. Their's is a simpler life, a life of honor and survival. A life spent earning a Name. Rielspar, they called me. Shimmerthorn. A name I did not earn, a name given to me in desperation, Jahana using me like an arrow shot at the heart of the woman who took control of those lands.

A woman traveled north with me, guided me. Ina. I had nearly forgotten her. Her sharp wit, her ruthlessness, the surprise in her eyes when my glass cut her down...

Why did I kill her? I can't imagine that I would kill without reason. What drove me to it?

A void, much as Telias described, lurks at the end of that question. Frowning, I push, scrabbling at the edges of the emptiness. Pain, all-too-familiar pain, rips into my mind. Knowing what it is, what it represents, I shunt it aside, gritting my teeth and attacking the empty wall again. Tears spring to my eyes, but I

234

don't relent. Just… a bit… more…

"There is nothing in this world that could make me forget you."

Poline.

I killed for *her.*

Her perfect eyes, her gentle arms, the softness of her lips… I choke back a sob.

Images flicker across my consciousness.

Poline walking stiffly down the Way of the West, our shared laughter at the absurdity of it.

The twinkle in her eyes as she protected the secret of the white lily.

The firmness of her back as I curled around her, half-broken by a nightmare.

The set of her shoulders before she lunged in our sparring, the surprise in her eyes when I finally read her attack.

The warmth of her lips as they brushed against my ear, wishing me happy birthday in the midst of an endless blizzard.

The look on her face when I told her—

Even through the agony, she is perfect. This pain, so natural, clean, and true, is pain I relish. Her memory is solace and sorrow. Poline. How could I… how could *he.*

Fury such as I have never felt, rage at once hot and caustic, surges in my throat and overwhelms the pain. He took her from me. It is bad enough that he took her from me in truth, but to rob me even of her memory…

My anger is not enough. The pain, unceasing, claws at my consciousness, ripping at my focus and striving to slam closed the door I've fought so hard to open. Stubbornly, I cling to her, her memory slipping away no matter how tightly I clutch.

The feel of her lips on mine…

And she's gone.

The pain fades. Tears, unknown and unheeded, trickle from my eyes. I'm gasping.

"I can't," I whisper, my voice raspy like I've been

screaming. Maybe I have. "The pain... it's too much."

"Don't give up," he says firmly. "You are strong, Iliana. That you fight at all is worthy of song. Don't lose hope."

"I..."

"Quiet," he says, his voice suddenly fraught. A rustle of a movement as he climbs to his feet. "Something is happening. I hear... shouts. Fighting."

"Rebels?" I ask, scrambling up and wiping away my tears.

"Maybe. I can't be sure."

"I'll find out."

"No, Iliana." His voice is close again. "If they've come for you, you're safest here."

"If they've come for me, they've made a mistake," I answer, turning and hurrying down the passage.

"Iliana!"

I ignore him. I reach the ladder in moments, but pause with my foot on the lowest rung. I glance back. A passageway leads north, no doubt following the walls of the throne room. Trusting an instinct I barely understand, I leave the ladder and go north. It almost feels like I'm pulled forward, a silent need burning through the night. The passageway narrows, constricting until I have to turn my shoulders. Just when I think I can't continue, it ends. Scowling, I draw more deeply on the earth, and the green of my power brightens.

A lever, hardly distinguishable from the wall, casts a shadow in its light.

Without pausing to think, I lift it. Stone grates on stone, and a hidden door springs open. The throne room opens dark and empty in front of me. I'm near the back of the room. Blades of glass flit to my will, detaching silently from their hidden places about the throne. I step forward, and my light illuminates the startled face of a Khalintari man. He is bloody, surprised, and his attire does not match a servant's. An enemy.

He drops gracelessly to the ground under the blades of

glass meant for his chest. I stalk forward, determined to end him quickly so that I can aid in the battle in the hall. He raises a hand in silent denial as his eyes, dark but for my light, reflect the blades rising to end him. I think—

"Perhaps, when you're older, you'll come visit, neh?"

The beard is new, the face hardened by time and hardship, but still I recognize the Master of Thought.

Panic sparks in my chest. I can't let him touch me. I can't let him touch my mind.

The glass begins its lethal movement before *hope* arrests their advance.

The Master of Thought... the natural born Master of Thought...

My connection to the earth fades, and the glass falls to the marble floor with an echoing tinkle. This man, this mystery, can...

"Help me," I whisper, falling to my knees.

He seems stunned for a moment, silent and still in the darkness left in absence of my light. A scream from the entry hall, loud enough to cut through the heavy stone, seems to revive his urgency, and he scrambles to his feet.

"There's no going that way," he says softly, his offered hand scarcely visible in the gloom. "Perhaps we help each other, neh?"

***

The battle is over before I slip through the doors of the throne room. The entry hall is frozen chaos, an image of the unmoving dead cast against the fitful embers of overturned braziers. A group of soldiers stand watch at the entrance. One turns and jumps at the sight of me. They surround me in an instant, a cordon of steel and flesh between me and the harmless air. Captain Silken enters the hall a moment later.

"Where were you?" he demands, storming over.

"I do not answer to you," I say resolutely, letting a piece of my anger free. "And you'd do well to remember it."

"Forgive me, my queen," he says, offering a lazy version of the Tide's salute. "I was worried, is all."

"I thought it best not to expose myself to the enemy's strength. I was seeking rebels in the shadows," I say, pretending to be mollified. A chill catches my skin as he regards me. This man can read my thoughts, if given the chance. But there is no sign of silver where his neck glowed as he stood before Telias. "The throne room is clear, if you had bothered to check."

"Thank you, my queen," he says, bowing his head. "Mayhap we should get you back to your chambers, 'case any more are about."

"Agreed."

Without delay, the Tide march me through the corridors to the door of my chamber. Tana waits outside, an anxious expression on her face. I turn back to the Tide.

"Thank you for your diligence. That will be all."

"Do you think that is wise, my lady?" a soldier asks. His eyes are on Tana. "Are you... sure... you will be safe?"

"I will be fine, Tide."

"At least let us check your rooms," he says, his voice nearly a plea. Too stubborn to refuse, but too loyal to push.

"Very well," I say, pushing down a spike of anxiety. The man better be ready to use his power, because they will be thorough. "But be quick."

"Your Eminence," Tana says, stepping close. For a second, it seems like she wants to offer me a hug. A faint smile pulls at my lips at the thought. "Are you well?"

"No, Tana." I eye the closed door carefully, bracing for startled shouts and muffled violence to break the silence. "But perhaps I will be soon."

The soldiers return without issue. The Tide does his best to hide his displeasure when I direct them to stay outside. He continues to eye Tana with mistrust.

"Return in the morning," I say to Tana as she moves to

follow. "Tonight, I'd like to be alone."

She looks like she wants to say something, but a single glance towards the Tide is enough for her to hold her counsel. Instead, she bows and retreats, though she glances back several times. I put her from my mind as I step into the cool darkness of my room. In the stillness of the night, separated from the reckless impulse of the moment, a sudden fear strikes me. This man is the Master of Thought. Have I traded one master for another?

"I get it," he says in his light accent, stepping through the doorway leading to the closet. He has a torn strip of silk wrapped around his shoulder and chest, already stained with blood. "But you have nothing to fear from me."

"Then get out of my head, and stay out of it," I snap, trying to still the tremble in my voice. And failing.

"Forgive me," he says, raising his hands. "It is hard... forgive me. It is self-preservation. Yet I will stop, for you."

"How's the shoulder?" I ask, nodding at the bandages.

"Not bad," he says, looking mildly embarrassed. "I thought it had stuck me deep, but it caught in my shirt. Mostly just a scratch."

We stand in awkward silence for a moment. The shouts of soldiers running past echo up to my balcony. They are searching for the rebels, though, from the sound of it, without much luck. I walk over to the window and gaze down at the soldiers scurrying about the streets.

"Were they with you?" I ask.

"Yes," he says, moving closer but halting a respectful distance away. "We came to save—" He stops himself, and I glance at his face. In the darkness, it's hard to tell, but it looks like he's in pain. He swallows thickly and shakes his head. "We came to save my brother."

"And who was your brother to be brought here?"

"He is not... capable. He was being cared for in a home, but he was taken. By soldiers in your employ."

"Not by my command," I say, turning to face him fully. "I have heard about these abductions. I haven't yet been able to figure out the why."

"They are being broken," he says harshly. "Their bodies twisted and warped. Not just invalids. Children. Orphans. Experiments for your mad general."

"I'm sorry," I say softly, afraid that, should I speak louder, my composure will break. "I didn't know."

"I know you didn't," he says, running his fingers through his hair and pacing nervously back and forth.

"Of course you know." I can't keep the bitterness out of my voice.

"Pah," he says, tossing up a hand in disgust. "I don't need to read your thoughts for this. The Master of Beasts rules here, whatever your title. Though the years have been long, you did not seem so cold when last we met."

"You met me for a few moments, at best," I protest. How much does this man know about me? How much could he have really learned in those few seconds? From the look on his face, enough. "And... you may be surprised. About who I really am. Creator, what do I even call you?"

"I am Bastian Batir," he says, bowing formally. "Once scribe to the Minister of Coin. Now... more."

"I guess you know who I am," I say, trying to make a half-hearted jab at humor. "But nice to finally meet you anyway. You know, it took me years to break through whatever block you put on my memory."

"You spared me," he says suddenly. "And you asked for my help."

"Yes."

"What do you need help with?"

"Don't you know?" I ask, more challenge than question.

"No," he says simply. "I am not in your mind, as you asked. I do, however, have my suspicions. But it would be easier if

240

you told me."

"I…"

I turn to look back out the window, trying to compose myself. Fear steals my voice, robs me of reason. To give my truths voice is to give this man, this stranger, power over me. More than he already has. I can hardly remember half of why I wanted his help in the first place. Uncle would never seek me harm. I am valuable, capable, his very—

"He's done something to my head." My voice, trembling, defies the thoughts creeping again into my mind. It is like being stretched between two horses galloping in opposite directions, stretched to breaking. I can't tell if at any moment I will suddenly split asunder. Only knowing that his influence is there allows me to resist it at all. "Even now. Creator, right now. I know what he's doing, to your brother and to so many others. I know he's using his power to control me. I know he's stolen memories from me, memories that break my mind with pain to seek. Even as I know these things… I can't stay angry. I can hardly feel fear. I can't make myself hate him. I should hate him, shouldn't I?"

"You said it is happening now," he says slowly. "But he is not here."

I let out a shaky laugh.

I have no idea why.

"I just thought the words 'he would never seek me harm.' Does that sound like a reasonable thing to think right now?"

"You asked me…" he pauses, silence filling what space the darkness leaves in the room. "You asked me not to read your thoughts. To understand this, though…"

"Do it," I say quickly, before I can change my mind. "Just don't…"

"I won't," he says softly.

"Okay. What do I…?"

"You can sit, and close your eyes, and think of whatever suits you." As I take a seat on the bed, he settles into the chair at the desk, careful to keep the distance between us. "I will join the flow of your thoughts, and perhaps learn something of what he's done."

"Anything? Anything I want?"

"To start," he agrees, closing his eyes. I hurriedly follow suit.

Naturally, my mind goes blank immediately. What do you think of when someone asks you to think? After a moment, though, like a dog worrying a bone, my thoughts spin back to the void. The nameless void trapped somewhere deep in my consciousness. A void Uncle put there to defend me—no, damn it, to *steal from me*. I know, if I push, that pain waits for me there, but something tells me it is *worth* the pain. I *want* what is trapped down there. I want... *her*...

The pain, sickeningly potent even familiar as it is, surges up to claw away my reason. I flinch back, the memory of the agony stronger than the memory it hides. Bastian makes a quiet sound. I open my eyes. His face is contorted into a painful grimace, a tear squeezing out of his left eye. He looks at me with sympathy, and I give a shaky shrug.

"How long has this been happening?" he asks.

"I can't be sure, but I don't remember it until after I came here." I fold my arms to fight a shiver. "Maybe he's been tinkering more with my mind now that we're away from Father."

"Tinkering? *Ayra na arivar!*" He turns to the side and makes a show of spitting. Whatever he said in Khalin, it wasn't a compliment. "No, this is not tinkering. This is disgusting. This is..."

"What?" I ask, as his face turns contemplative.

"This is something I would have done when I was younger. Had I known how," he says, frowning.

"So?" I ask, leaning forward slightly. "Can you fix it?"

"I need to know more, to dive deeper. But initially, I would say, with enough time, perhaps."

"Perhaps?" I whisper incredulously. "With enough time? We don't have time! The second Uncle returns…"

"You know, you shouldn't call him that," he says mildly. "I only got broad strokes, but I did learn that. The names you think of them… that is part of his control."

My stomach lurches. Their *names?* How I think of them? I've thought of them as Father and Uncle since I was a little girl…

"And," Bastian continues, eyes staring into the distance. "I may need to consult with a friend."

"No," I say quickly. "No one else can know."

"She can help us," he says, his expression reluctant and glum at the same time.

"How could a friend help with a problem of the mind?"

"She knows more about Shaping Thought than any soul after the Creator," he says, returning to pacing around my room. I might be imagining it, but he seems happy to have such a large space to walk in. He mutters to himself as he walks. "After five thousand years of practice, she damn well better know *something*…"

***

When someone knocks respectfully on my door, my eyes snap open.

Morning. I slept. Somehow, I felt *comfortable* enough to sleep.

Lurching upright, I frantically search the room. Asleep, he's vulnerable to being found. Another knock, equally gentle and respectful. Bastian is nowhere to be seen. Frowning, I move to the door and open it.

Tana stands at the door, radiant in white. She raises an eyebrow when I don't move aside. Careful. This is Uncle's—Kranos's—personal choice for my servant. I can't act suspiciously, or she might run to Silken or get a message to… Kranos… to return. I fake a yawn and stumble back towards the bed.

"Morning, Tana," I say, flopping back onto the bed. "I may

get off to a slower start today. With all the chaos last night, I didn't sleep a wink."

"I'm sorry, your Eminence," she says, though something in her voice draws my gaze back to her.

She's taking in my face, the disheveled sheets, the time of day... her expression hardens, and she steps closer, eyes searching all about the bed. She mutters something to herself, too low to hear, save for something about the Creator and needing saving. When her search proves fruitless near the bed, she turns and moves towards the closet.

Which is when I finally see him. Some time in the night, Bastian dragged the heavy blankets from my bed into the corner and made a nest. Swathes of thick cloth obscure most of him save for his face and a single hand clenched around his chest. Tana stiffens, spotting him at the same time I do. She immediately bursts into motion, *towards* the sleeping man.

Quietly, I call to the earth. I've no desire to kill her; I *like* her. To protect this secret, though, I have no choice.

"Careful, Tana," Bastian mumbles, raising a halting hand my direction. "You're making our princess think some dangerous thoughts."

"Tell me you didn't do it," she growls, stamping up and kicking his foot under the blanket.

"I didn't," he says defensively, trying, and failing, to kick her in return.

"She never sleeps," Tana grits, glancing briefly back at me. "And it's clear she slept."

"Nothing to do with me." He rolls over and snuggles into the corner. "Let me be, neh? We still have an hour until Jynn is supposed to get here."

She kicks him again, and he gasps in exaggerated anguish.

"Swear it," she grits, fists tight at her side.

"I swear, okay? I swear by my family and my good name..." He trails off as she leans forward menacingly. "Fine, by

244

Lav. I swear on my brother's life that nothing happened."

"What is going on here?" I ask, finally finding my voice. "You know each other?"

"We're friends," Bastian says breezily. He doesn't wilt when she offers him a flat look. "She saved my life, I saved hers, and we've been boon companions ever since."

"Twice," Tana says, nudging him again with her sandaled foot. "I've saved your life twice now."

"Who's counting?"

"Me."

"Petty."

"Necessary."

"How did you manage to get appointed by my uncle... I mean... Creator damn it. By *Kranos*?" I ask, frowning. "Is it only my thoughts he can read?"

"No," Bastian says irritably, crawling out of the tangled blanket and stretching. "We had a suspicion that he could use our power. So we planted false memories and thoughts into Tana to make her particularly appealing for a tyrant keeping tabs on his underlings."

A pulsing headache forms behind my eyes. I can't help feeling betrayed. That Tana is one of my supposed saviors should be a welcome truth. That would be rational, though. I wanted her to be someone who respected *me*, trusted *me*. The way she made herself vulnerable, the way she looked at me dressed in the style of her people...

"I always figured you were spying on me," I say, a pit opening in my stomach. "For Kranos. But how you've acted, what you've said... I guess part of me had started to hope that you were more."

"I am," she says, with such surety it is hard to argue. "I only ever gave Kranos false reports, and I meant everything I've said to you. Even if you did try to kill me."

"The message at night," I say, realization dawning. "I told

myself that I'd ask for forgiveness if I ever met... you."

"There's nothing to forgive," she says, waving her hand carelessly. "I would have killed anyone creeping about *my* rooms at night."

She comes to sit on my bed, gathering my hands in hers. The casual touch startles me. She touches me every day, combing my hair and preparing me for the day. It never felt strange then. This is different.

"Iliana," she says softly, meeting my eyes. It's the first time she's ever said my name. "I have gotten to see you in the last season, really see you. And, despite whatever has been done to you, or whatever you've done, I like you. I see your struggle, yet you get up every day and, even though many of them hate you, you do your best by the people of this land. That is not false. I am sorry that I had to deceive you. I promise not to lie to you again."

Before I can react, she pulls me into a hug, arms about my shoulders. It is a long moment before I can bring myself to return it.

But I do.

Tears suddenly blur my vision. Pressure builds in my chest, though all that escapes is a hollow sigh. A part of me feels, not healed, but mending. I feel, for the first time since Torlas's death, like I am not alone.

"Not to break up the touching scene, but Jynn's outside," Bastian says, stifling a yawn. "Princess, I have to warn you. *I* might have the willpower to stay out of your thoughts, but Jynn, on the other hand..."

"Prick."

I jump as a voice, high and feminine and flatly sarcastic, echoes in my mind. Who?

The door opens, and a tiny girl skips into the room, twelve years at most, her servant's uniform only accentuating her youth. The bag flapping at her hip finally allows me to place her.

"The messenger..." I say, frowning. "You brought me the

message to head west."

"Guilty," she says, grinning. "And saved you mental torture in the process. A simple 'thank you' will suffice."

"I… don't understand."

"You're welcome," she says, grin widening. "Now, I heard Bastian's inadequacy has led to our formal introduction. Thank the Creator, then, that the man's an idiot."

"Don't let her adorable appearance fool you, princess," Bastian says, narrowing his eyes at the girl's back. "Those tiny dimples hide a war criminal."

Though her smile remains in place, some of its luster fades at his words. There is a hard edge, an edge that doesn't belong in the voice of a child so young, when she speaks again.

"Let's get to work, shall we?"

***

I do not think I'm meant to be awake.

Darkness presses against my eyes, and someone's will, gentle and benign, urges me back to sleep. As Telias said, though, awareness steals much of Thought's power. And I haven't slept well lately.

"What is it?" Bastian's voice, recognizable for its arrogance even in a whisper.

"I've never seen its like," Jynn answers, a faint awe in her voice. "It is a work of art. Painted by a madman."

"It runs deep," he agrees. His feet whisper across the floor as he paces. "Deeper than I imagined it could."

"You're thinking of Elina and Nomman, aren't you?" she asks.

"Who are they?" Tana's voice.

So that's why they're bothering to speak out loud. Tana had left to see to her duties and deliver messages on my behalf, so as to keep up appearances. She must have returned while I slept. They've 'worked' for the last three days, though I felt little of their attempts to take my mind apart. Well, as Jynn put it, they weren't 'tinkering' just yet. That would come after they understood what *Kranos* has done to my mind. The more I've tried to alter how I think of him, the more I've come to recognize the subtle, treacherous pressure to think of him as Uncle. To think of him as loyal, as benevolent, as incapable of doing wrong.

The only moment of terror in the last three days had been when Silken came to the door demanding to know why I had canceled court. Tana had glanced at the Shapers, who briefly concentrated before giving her a nod of approval. When she explained that I was Shaping a gift for the Master of Beasts to welcome him when he returned, he accepted the story immediately. If, as Bastian and Jynn suspect, he is in on the secret of my manipulation, such vapid endeavors to earn Uncle's favor would only seem natural.

"Bastian's parents," Jynn answers after a moment. "In his ignorance and immaturity, he sought to control them in much the same way."

"Really?" Tana sounds mildly disgusted, though thoroughly unsurprised. "That's evil."

"I was doing it for a good reason, if that makes you feel better." He stops pacing somewhere near my feet. "You waved Lav before me like a carrot on our journey here. You have an inkling of how much he means to me. Well, I just wanted them to take care of their son, neh? Is that so evil?"

"Yes," Jynn says wryly. "It is pretty damn evil to burn people's thoughts away, seek to control them entirely, and research different 'flavors of love' to implant in a misplaced effort to keep them together, even if it *was* for your brother's sake."

"When you put it like that…"

"There isn't another way to put it. What you did was wrong, and evil, even if it pales in comparison to what this bastard has done to her. Regardless, if you'd known me back then, I could have told you that love is not something that can be falsified. Lust, sure. Attraction, definitely. Attachment, of course. But the secret of love? Why we love? Why it's so powerful? You were digging for a treasure that no man, Shaper or otherwise, has ever found."

"You can stop pretending, princess," Bastian says suddenly. "Why do you think we speak your bastard language?"

Oh. They wouldn't speak Donirian if I wasn't listening. Next to these two Shapers of Thought, I may as well be an open book. I push myself to a sitting position and try to shake off that disquieting thought. Jynn sits on the floor with her back to the wall, Bastian's nest of blankets a cushion at her back. Bastian stands quietly, arms folded across his chest. Tana sits at the desk, the heavy chair turned to face the others.

"So, what did we learn?" I ask eagerly. My question is met with a silence I recognize from my days leading the Deep in Donir. A deep silence, a silence of tension and fear. A silence of people who have nothing good to report. I still the tremble in my hands and try to steady my heart. "Tell me."

Still, Jynn and Bastian exchange a glance, silent conversation passing between them. I clench my jaw and force myself to wait. These people will be my salvation, if any is to be had. I can bear a few moments of silence. Finally, Bastian nods, and Jynn stands.

The little girl is a walking mystery. I haven't quite gathered who she is, or was, but I have learned that her soul is old, old enough to make offhand comments about places that, so far as we can trust our histories and legends, *might* once have existed. Even so, it's hard not to trust her earnest little face. She comes to sit at my elbow, her eyes meeting mine with terrifying sympathy.

"Iliana, you may not know me well. We've just met, after all. But I know *you*." She searches for words as if trying to frame a shapeless painting. "I have followed the flow of your thoughts, traced their pathways to places you do not remember. I will not claim to have seen even a fraction of your memories. Yet still I know you."

"Get on with it," Bastian says from the side, his expression dark. When Jynn twists to glare at him, he waves his hand dismissively. "If you know her, as you claim to, you know she's strong enough to take it."

"Ignore him," Tana says, offering me an encouraging smile.

"He's right," I say evenly. "Tell me."

"Alright," Jynn says. "Our power is hard to explain to those who haven't experienced it. So I will rely on metaphor. If you grow confused, stop me." She pauses. Even at my nod, she still doesn't speak, but takes a moment, marshaling her thoughts. "Imagine your mind is a garden. Your thoughts, your memories, are the green things that grow…"

She describes a world not unlike my garden back in Donir. The undergrowth is that which we no longer remember, yet still shapes our lives, a background of verdant life that exists en masse rather than standing on its own. The flowers are memories of happiness and hope, each their own color and shape. The dead spots are places where tragedy has poisoned memory, tainting all it touches. Just like in any forest, there is life hidden beneath the branches, memories buried or forgotten, beautiful or terrible when unearthed.

What Uncle has done to my mind is much like those memories we forget until we lift a branch and are suddenly reminded of them in all their vivid glory. Around the memories he wishes to bury, he has grown brambles to inflict pain if I wish to see them. He has done his best to prune my garden, to shape it to his liking like a noble his country estate in Firdana. Yet, for all his efforts, there has been growth he could not control.

The twitching limbs of the assassin's torture.

Torlas's friendship, his love… his death.

The horror of the cataclysmic wave, sweeping away so many souls before its power.

"And there is more, things he's managed to hide, to tuck away in guarded recesses of your mind," Jynn says, her lips twisting together. "There is a man, Markis Calladan, who told you the Sealord was not your father. That memory is guarded very well. We missed it a dozen times following the channel of your thoughts."

"So is he?" I ask, trying to wrestle with my wayward thoughts. Thoughts telling me that, of course, Father is my father. What else could he be? Grimacing, I force myself to remain in the moment. "Is he my father?"

"We don't know," Bastian says gently. "Though, since he has allowed this... it is hard to imagine that he is your blood."

"Rich, coming from you," Jynn retorts.

He doesn't respond, but merely nods, his troubled gaze turned inward.

"There is more," Jynn continues. "Most of the memories he guards share the same roots. A woman, a protector. Named Poline."

"I know that name," I say softly, too wary of the pain to approach the place in my mind where she resides. "I can picture emerald eyes, a feeling of safety, but little else."

"He has spent significant time and effort to hide her from your thoughts, and for good reason," Jynn says, sighing. "She is anathema to everything he wants you to be. Your love for her nearly shook you free of his influence."

"Love?" I whisper, the thought absurd and tragic at once. "He has managed to take a person I loved from my memories?"

"There is nothing in this world that could make me forget you."

The words echo like a haunting melody through my thoughts. They are spoken in my voice, but I do not remember speaking them. And they are wrong, so wrong. For an empty space lurks in my mind, a space known only by the hole left in its absence.

I once knew love? Who was she? Did I hold her in my arms? Did I press my lips to hers? Did she know the monster I am and love me anyway?

251

"Can you… can you help me?" I ask, terrified to hear the answer I can feel lurking beneath the care with which Jynn chooses her words.

"I'm not finished," she says grimly. "At first, we didn't even realize his influence, subtle as it was. Bastian noticed it, though, based on something you said. We passed a surface thought, one you've had a dozen times in the past few days: anger and revulsion that your father allowed this to happen."

"Did he?" I ask. "Perhaps Uncle is working alone. Father would never…"

"Creator," Bastian breathes in awe, stopping his pacing to stare at me. "She told me it was happening, but I didn't really believe it."

"What? What is happening?"

"You just called him 'Uncle' again," Jynn says gently. "Two days ago, you hated your father for encouraging Kranos to meddle in your mind. Yesterday, you were sad that he allowed this to happen. Today, you're making excuses for him, your mind returning to the same patterns, the same impossibilities."

"No," I whisper.

"Your garden looks healthy on the surface," she continues relentlessly, laying a hand on mine. "But it is an illusion. Something grows beneath the surface, something invasive and poisonous, twining its roots around yours, choking and binding. We believe that, if left alone, you will return to the shape it desires for you. No matter what you experience, love and loss and everything in between, you will always return to that shape."

"And what shape is that?"

"Loyal. Trusting. Free of doubt or question. A willing prisoner wearing invisible shackles."

It can't be true. I won't believe it. The longer I've talked with these people, the more they've forced me to doubt and mistrust my family. I am a princess of Donir, a queen in the Empire of the Sea, and they are merely some desperate rebels

252

seeking to overthrow my father. They won't succeed.

"Careful of your thoughts, princess," Bastian says. "Already, his influence tightens."

No, perhaps *their* influence is what makes me doubt. Why did I ever trust strangers, especially strangers with such power? I need to get away from them, to...

"Stop," Jynn says sharply, her hand burning silver.

My thoughts quiet. These people are here to help me. I *want* them to help me, because there is something wrong in my mind. I *know* this. Why am I doubting now?

In the silence, I can feel it, like a snake coiling around my mind, constricting, suffocating. The urge to flee, to seek out Uncle for protection, remains, but I can also feel that it is foreign. The thought feels untethered, sourceless. It is logical and foolish at the same time. Horses galloping in opposite directions. Part of me hopes they will succeed in tearing me apart.

"Sorry," I whisper finally.

"Nothing to worry about," Jynn says with forced cheerfulness. "Are you ready to continue?"

"Can you help me?" I ask again, tears pricking at the corners of my eyes.

"Maybe," Jynn says, the bright gleam in her eyes dimming. "But there will be no guarantees. I have never seen an influence of this kind. We believe that the Master of Beasts somehow entwined his power with ours. We've independently concluded that there is no way we could accomplish a similar effect. And Bastian has certainly tried."

"What use is a guarantee?" I stand, lifting her easily to her feet. "Do your best, and quickly. You will not always be here to show me when my thoughts are not my own, and Un... Kranos could return at any time. Do what you must."

"There will be consequences," Jynn says softly.

"I can handle them, whatever they are," I return, steeling my resolve and holding to this purpose.

253

To be free of him, of *them*, to think thoughts born solely of my will. To make decisions without this silent weed choking away any it doesn't like. What could be worse than to lose control over my own thoughts? What would I give to feel safe again in my own mind?

"We can't be sure," Jynn continues. "Either of success, or even of what will happen to you."

"Just tell her, neh?" Bastian says, though he refuses to meet my eye.

"In my own time," Jynn says firmly, ignoring him and pulling me back to the bed. "Picture your garden. The one you always remember back at the palace in Donir. Think of the greenery, the flowers, the trees. Can you see it?"

Of course I can see it. It is the only place I've ever felt at ease.

"Now imagine that a poisonous weed has tainted their roots and contaminated the earth. It has grown deep and strong. Every inch of it is tied to the healthy growth above, inextricably tied. How do you get rid of it?"

"You'd have to get rid of everything," I say, the weight of her words dropping on me like a cloak of lead. "All of it."

"The healthy and the sick alike," she agrees, in the same tone I would use to calm a horse.

"So what will be left? What will I remember?"

"We don't know," Bastian says, finally lifting his head. "Perhaps a few snippets, names, places, events. Perhaps nothing at all. From my experience, though, the mind heals. Even from grievous wounds. I tried a dozen times to burn away the parts of my mother that made her hate my brother, but they always returned. You, your true self, will grow from the ashes."

I should be afraid to lose everything, every memory, every experience that makes me who I am. The reality, though, is that I don't know who I am. I only know the woman that Kranos… and Helikos… have created.

I can't remember the woman I once loved, but my memories of murdering my best friend are all too vivid.

What do I have to cling to? A litany of tortures, of death, of bodies broken in my wake?

What happiness?

What joy?

"I'll do it," I say, more certain about this than anything I've ever done. "I just have one request."

Chapter 12
Bastian
The Eightieth Day of Summer
In the year 5223, Council Reckoning

In the countless hours I spent in the House of the Republic, it was always filled with light, torches and braziers and sconces burning from dusk to dawn. Now, the thin corridors of the House of the Republic would be dark but for the emerald light of the princess's power. Its perfect purity should be comforting, as all light cast by Shaping should be, yet her light makes our shadows monstrous and strange. It sheds no warmth, offers no solace. If anything, I feel colder in its presence.

Perhaps it's because I can feel her struggle not to fall to the Master of Beast's sway with every step we take. As much as we would like to think we could handle her, her will is strong. Jynn and I might not be able to break her concentration if she suddenly decides that we're enemies in these close confines. It is a risk, as everything is these days.

"I have her," Jynn whispers in my mind. *"If she falls, I will do what must be done."*

Somehow that isn't comforting.

"You know why it isn't."

Because, for Creator knows what reason, I care about what happens to her.

It is why the four Empire soldiers of the princess's personal guard lie unconscious in the chambers she claimed from the former Minister of Finance. It is why we're heading towards a group of people with defenses against our power that leave us vulnerable. It is why we're returning to the prison filled with broken minds that nearly drove me mad. We won't be able to use our power lest we risk our sanity.

At least I'll get another shot at finding Lav.

The braziers in the main hall have been righted and lit, the floor scrubbed of the blood and ash that decorated the shining marble last I saw it. The blue dress Iliana wears is more appropriate for a Spring fete than a midnight stroll, but the soldiers standing guard salute the princess without comment. Their thoughts echo their gesture: they would rather not know what she's doing or where she's going if she's heading across the hall, and especially if she is going without a proper guard. They were instructed, in no uncertain terms, not to concern themselves with the defenses of the west. They've been soldiers of the Empire long enough to know not to toe the line around the Lord General.

It is surreal to pass openly through the doors out of which I burst in headlong panic a few nights ago. The long corridor stretches out before us shrouded in shadow. Tana closes the door behind us, and we return to the princess's cold light to guide our steps. As we approach the first turn to the left, a subtle pressure washes over us, urging us to return, to turn back. During our assault, Jynn claimed to have rampaged through any undefended minds bearing our power; clearly, she didn't get them all. And, since I can't feel anything of the will behind the pressure, this one bears their master's protection. The depthless sea of broken suffering, though...

Time to shut it down. You don't want to touch these minds.

"I hate being blind," Jynn answers, her surliness a thin facade veiling her fear.

Letting the power go completely, I return wholly to my mundane senses. To me, it's like shutting your eyes and trying to navigate a darkened room. To Jynn, it must be like losing your legs and trying to run. Her tiny shoulders hunch in on themselves, and her confident stride falters. With a visible effort, she straightens her back and forces herself onwards.

"You're up, princess," I whisper in the silence.

"Stay behind me," she commands, lifting her chin imperiously and striding forward with confidence.

The woman seated halfway down the next corridor scrambles to her feet, surprise and terror warring on her face. She recovers enough to offer the princess a sharp salute as we approach.

"Where does the prisoner Telias rest?" Iliana calls, far too loudly in the silence.

"My lady, this is, this is most strange," the woman stammers, eyes darting about the empty corridor as if searching for an escape. "I wasn't told—"

"You are not privy to our innermost council," she says coldly. "So I will forgive you your impertinence. Once. Where is the prisoner Telias?"

"By your leave, I will speak with my captain," she says, saluting again and turning to go. "My lady."

A flicker of glittering glass, and the woman slumps to the ground. A brief flash of silver burns spots into my eyes as she dies and her power releases. A headache forms at my temples as a silent cry of denial echoes through the air. Tana winces at my side, though Jynn and the princess seem entirely unaffected. A chorus of muffled grunts and cries of anger and anguish echo down the corridors as the prisoners voice their displeasure. This soldier was not exactly a mature Shaper, so her death brought no cataclysm. It would be wise, though, to remember the consequences of killing Shapers without knowing what destruction their death will cause.

"We should probably get moving," Jynn says idly. "Though the protected ones might not have felt that, everyone else in range just woke up in a cold sweat."

The princess doesn't hesitate or comment, but continues on her way as if she didn't just summarily execute one of her own soldiers. Inwardly shrugging, I step over the body and follow. The soldier chose her loyalties. After a moment, Tana's steps join mine. I don't have to read her thoughts to know that she doesn't like what just happened. Another day, I might let her try to be our conscience, but there is no time for doubt.

At the edges of my sense, I feel a touch, feather-light, as if someone wielding our power doesn't want to be known. It is subtle, capable. Someone with practice.

"Care," I say softly.

"What?" Jynn asks, glancing back at me.

"Someone knows we're here, and they're smart enough to hide their presence."

"Strange," she says, glancing up and down the empty corridors. "I didn't feel them."

"It was quick." I allow in the faintest hint of my power, ignoring the miasma of chaos and sorrow permeating the air, and briefly search for them. "They've cut themselves off, but I'm sure they know we're here."

"Then there's no time to waste," Iliana says, setting off in a graceful jog, slippered feet whispering across the bare stone. "He should be this way."

As we hurry after her, a sense of sourceless dread washes over me, and not from any conscious awareness. Something opposes us, lurking in the dark corners of these tainted halls. I don't dare reach out and find it, not where we are, but its presence is felt all the same. Jynn glances behind us a half a dozen times in as many strides. She must feel it too. Iliana leads us down a new corridor, smaller.

"He's in one of these, but I can't be sure which," she says, sticking close to the northern wall. She knocks on the first, listening carefully for a response before whispering. "Telias?"

A roar of primal anger rips through the silence. The door shudders, once and then again, the hinges creaking from the blows. Iliana steps back carefully, glancing briefly at us.

"Wrong door," she says simply, moving to the next in line.

At the second and third, she is met with silence. At the fourth, though, a warm male voice answers. A voice I recognize, though I've never heard it.

Iliana raises her hand, and a blade of glass floats to her grasp. With tiny brittle cracks, it breaks into smaller shards. The shards fly into the keyhole on the door, and she closes her eyes in concentration. Clicks and softly groaning metal sound from the door for a moment before the bolt turns. From the other end of the prison, the sound of guttural rage echoes down the corridor. Something, or someone, is provoking the prisoners. Jynn and I share a worried glance. With a forceful crunch, the door swings wide.

A man emerges from the darkness, his long hair dark but for streaks of white. One of his eyes burns with life and piercing wisdom, while horrific violence claimed the other long ago. He grins through a wild, unkempt beard. The clothes he wears were once finely tailored, and have mostly survived his ordeal, though they have grown threadbare at the knees. Iliana throws herself into his arms, and he holds her close with all the tenderness of a father his daughter.

Over her head, his gaze rakes over us with palpable force. He pauses on me.

"Good to see you made it out," he says, dipping his chin in respect.

"Only with your help," I answer honestly. Creator knows how he recognizes me when he's never seen me in the flesh. "I guess I'm here to return the favor."

"Did you find him?" he asks, glancing up and down the corridors.

"No," I say quietly.

Inexplicably, tears blur my vision as a foreign emotion abruptly fills my chest. It takes me a moment, powerful as it is, to realize that it is thankfulness. This man, trapped and tortured for days on end, victim of assaults physical and spiritual, asks first not how we will escape, but after me. After my brother. He doesn't know me, yet he asks.

"Then we have work to do," he says.

His presence seems to grow to fill the hallway. He turns to lead us deeper into the prison. A primal cry pierces the night. A hunting cry. We freeze as the murmuring chorus of groaning anguish peaks to a crescendo.

No longer muffled. No longer held at bay. A predator loosed from its cage.

"Does anyone have a blade?" Telias asks, not turning from the darkness in the direction of the cry.

"Not the most martial group, sorry," I mutter.

"Unfortunate."

A shape appears at the other end of the hallway. In the darkness beyond the circle of Iliana's light, its silhouette doesn't match anything that exists in this world. Nothing that *should* exist, all bulges and angles that defy definition and bewilder the eye. For a moment, it doesn't move, though I can tell it watches us. My eyes burn from staring.

I blink, and it's halfway down the corridor, charging before my eyes fully open, its heavy feet or paws thundering. It breaks the circle of the shining light in an instant. Its pale, undulating body makes no more sense visible, a mass of ridges and rippling muscle. It is nothing human.

Telias stands before it, defiant. Perhaps if he had a sword, he might be able to fight it. He certainly seems capable. But bare-handed? Against whatever that thing is? He, and we, will die in seconds.

Blades of glass fly out in glittering arcs of death. The monster roars, blood spurting, and it stumbles before continuing its charge. Iliana meets it head on, dress twirling about her knees, the symbol of her power glowing brightly. A massive appendage whips out to crush her against the wall. She drops beneath it, nearly to the floor, rising just after it passes. She darts in, a pair of longer blades shimmering in each hand.

The creature is brutality incarnate, its blows cracking wood and splintering marble. Iliana sways aside with agile grace, always an inch ahead, blades biting again and again until they are black with blood in the strange light. I have never seen anyone move like she does. The only experience that approaches it was watching Ghali's personal Spearsisters practice at the old fort. Yet they had been following a pattern of moves, a prescribed dance to which they each knew the steps. This... this is something else entirely.

She is driving the creature back, confining its massive strength behind the edges of her weapons. Before the grace and speed of her movements, the monster looks clumsy and slow. As inevitable as our deaths seemed a moment ago, it feels equally impossible that she should lose.

Her foot slips in spilled blood.

The illusion shatters as the monster's fist strikes her a glancing blow. The emerald light flickers as she slams into the opposite wall. Telias leaps into the fray, slamming a kick into the creature's shoulder. Though it towers over him, he drives it back with a series of deft blows. Unarmed, though, no man could stand before this thing for long. Its hand flashes out and lifts him from the ground. Its fingers wrap around his chest and nearly meet at his spine.

The princess's light flashes brighter. Her voice fills the hall with a desperate shout. A blade of crystal the height of a man scythes across. She just Shaped that in less than a second? Telias falls to the ground with the monster's severed arm. It roars in agony, clutching at the flood of ichor rushing from the wound, though its roar abruptly cuts off as the blade sweeps across its neck.

The silence is physical. Immediate danger past, Iliana steps towards Telias, holding on to her shoulder. Blood leaks from the corner of her mouth, and her arm has twisted out of socket and dangles limply at her side. Before she can reach him, Telias gains his feet with eyes only for her. He scrutinizes her shoulder briefly before offering her a silent question.

"Do it," she grits between clenched teeth.

I glance at Jynn. She doesn't bother to watch as, with a practiced wrench, he twists Iliana's shoulder back into place. She grunts, but straightens, offering him a thankful nod. I can't even imagine what pain she's enduring. First Ghali, and now the princess. Jynn would probably suffer the agony in equal silence. I, on the other hand, would no doubt be sobbing on the ground.

Clearly, I'm surrounded by idiots.

Telias steps carefully to the brute lying on the marble. He bends down where the severed head fell and lifts it in his hands. The face, though misshapen and twisted in anguish, is that of a child.

"Kranos is truly mad," he says quietly. He places the small head next to its imposing remains and stands. "But he isn't here. Who would let that monster free?"

"Silken," Iliana says, her voice dangerous. "He guards this place for Uncle."

"Kranos," I say, finding my voice. "Remember to think of him as Kranos."

She glances at me, then back at the abomination lying on the ground. The abomination which was once an innocent child.

"For now, I have no need of the reminder," she says coolly. "Whatever our business, we should—"

A piercing cry, different from the first, blasts through the night. Shortly after, another, guttural and deep, rattles through the halls. Telias and Iliana share a glance, seeming to come to a silent accord. He looks at me, sorrow in his eyes.

"I know," I say, staring deeper into the darkness. "One nearly did us in. Two? Three?"

Death looms in our shadow, but I can't force my feet to

move. Lav… what has he done to you? Would I even recognize you? Would you still recognize me?

"After this… I don't even know if I want to find him."

"Don't say that." Jynn grabs my hand and pulls me towards the entrance. "I'm sure he's fine. And, no matter what, we need to free these people."

"For now, we need to run," Telias says, sprinting past us.

A grunting roar from deeper in the prison lends swiftness to my feet. We burst out of the doors at a sprint. At the sight of the princess, dress torn and face bloodied, the guards move to stop us, barring the door and drawing their swords.

"Open the door!" Iliana shouts.

"My queen, what—"

"If you wish to live, you'll go to the east wing and pretend you never saw us," she shouts, waving them aside.

"My lady, what has happened?" the woman on the left asks, refusing to move aside.

Iliana slides to a halt, and we nearly collide. She looks the soldiers up and down, their turquoise armor gleaming in the flickering firelight. I half-expect her to cut them down, as she did the fledgling Shaper in the prison, but she doesn't. We don't have the time to waste if we wish to escape, but she pauses to meet their eyes.

"The Lord General has gone mad," she says honestly. "He is using his holy power to create unnatural abominations in the west wing. Monsters are pursuing us, and they will kill us if they get the chance."

"We'd heard the rumors, about what happened in Donir, but…" the woman trails off and glances at her companion.

He gives her a nod, and they clasp hands briefly, a warrior's salute. She steps to Iliana's side, sword drawn, and pushes open the doors. We hurry down the front steps of the House of the Republic. The soldiers standing guard outside call a challenge. The Tide snaps a command, and they fall in line in a cordon about us. We all glance back as a bestial roar rends the night. Iliana notices for the first time that the second member of the Tide is not with us.

"He will buy us what time he can," the Tide says stoically.

"What was his name?" Iliana asks as we resume our flight.

"Orbran, my lady."

"I'll not forget it."

Whatever the capabilities of the average Empire soldier, the Tide who stayed behind must be something special. The thunder of beasts bellowing their frustration does not grow louder for nearly a minute. It isn't much, but it is enough. The Khal's people find us the moment we leave the Plaza of Stars and guide us off the street.

Orbran, she says.

Iliana may forget it, in the trials to come. But I will honor this man, who fell so that we might live.

Orbran.

***

Iliana could be carved from stone, how still and majestic she appears in the dusty tunnels beneath Coin.

Jynn bounces from foot to foot, her elfin face smiling, her eyes speaking to the ancient soul residing within.

Saran leans against the stone wall, arms crossed, only the tightness in her shoulders betraying her facade of calm.

I glance between them uneasily. There is a depth to the power these women hold, a weight, that makes me feel like a fly hoping to avoid a crushing slap.

It is not a pleasant feeling.

Telias, standing at Iliana's right shoulder, looks completely at ease, of course. Despite his ragged clothing and unkempt appearance, he looks like he could stand with kings and argue with philosophers. The bastard.

"From what I gather," Iliana says, suddenly breaking the silence. "You're responsible for the death of many of the soldiers under my care."

"A paltry number compared to the many thousands murdered by your king," Saran returns immediately, pushing off from the wall and unfolding her arms.

"An invading force."

"Provoked by your aggression."

Silence falls again. Not a good start. The two stare like duelists into each other's eyes, searching for weakness. I almost want to shrink against the wall.

"This anger you hold for one another is misplaced," Telias says. They both snap glares on him, but he doesn't wilt. Brave man. "The Sealord and the Master of Beasts are at fault here. They began this war and all of the sorrow that has come of it. They deserve our ire, and only they."

"He's right," Jynn says like she's chiding wayward children. "Be mindful, Iliana. Make sure your anger is your own."

"I..." The princess grimaces and brings her hands to cover her face. "I hate this."

"Jynn, take her three doors down on the left," Saran says, face softening. "The sun is cresting the horizon. She should rest." Jynn nods and takes Iliana's hand. Telias moves to follow, and the Khal holds up a hand. "Stranger, I would have you stay."

"Very well," he says, though he doesn't look her way. His concern lies down the corridor, following her steps until she finally disappears through the doorway. Only once she's out of sight does he meet Saran's gaze. "You're wondering who I am."

"And why my allies felt the need to risk themselves for you," she agrees.

He debates for a moment, some internal struggle. I'm too tired to put forth the effort to figure out what he's thinking, not that I have the urge. Though I barely know him, I would trust him with my life.

"I am not sure how well my name has survived the years," he says slowly. "Especially considering how little time I spent in

266

the west. But I am Telias, once Master of Fire."

"Your name survives," she says evenly. She glances at me, a question in her eyes.

"What reason does he have to lie?" I ask, though I'm dealing with my own surprise. The Warmheart?

"Then welcome, Telias," the Khal says, shaking her head in mild disbelief. "It seems it is my fate to gather legends under my wing."

"I wouldn't call myself legendary *yet*," I mutter. Saran blinks slowly, unamused, though Telias has the grace to smile. "You laugh, but I did save the world. Apparently. Ask Jynn."

"Who is that girl?" Telias asks, eye flicking again to the door Iliana disappeared through. "She is more than she appears."

"If you'll believe the pair of them," Saran says, gesturing towards me. "That is the Mind Razor reborn."

"Wait, *Jynn?* Jynn Dioran?" Telias seems both troubled and invigorated by the prospect. "Impossible ramifications aside, I have so many questions for her. Creator, a soul who *remembers* the time of the Eternal. The mysteries she could solve…"

"Can wait," Saran says flatly. "Bastian, that exchange between Jynn and the princess… it is worse than we feared."

It isn't a question. Perceptive, as always.

"It is more than simple tampering, yes," I say, scratching at my beard. "What he's done to her… it is hard to explain, but she is a danger to all of us every minute until she's cured."

Though Jynn would have explained it better, I do my best. Both of them take in the information stoically. Even if Telias is seething beneath the surface, he doesn't flinch as I finish.

"It is likely that, when we remove, well, if we *can* remove the control he's implanted in her, there will be little of her left. Memories, experiences, personality… his power is wrapped up in everything."

"So you're saying that she will be a blank slate," Saran says, struggling to hide her interest.

"No," I answer, careful to watch Telias. The look he offers the Khal is empty of emotion. Underneath the surface, however... Saran may hold every advantage, but I wouldn't want Telias as an enemy. I hurry on before she can speak again. "She will be a forest after a fire. Some of the mightiest trees may survive, and there may be life below the char. It is possible that her mind shatters, irrevocably, and she never recovers. I don't *think* that will happen. From my experience, the mind is resilient. Faced with unimaginable trauma, we may take time to recover, yet recover we do, if given the chance. Whatever grows from the ashes will be Iliana herself, her truest self, without foreign influence."

"She will risk it," Telias says with certainty.

"So she said," I say slowly, a realization dawning. "I think, Telias, this is why she demanded we save you."

"To guide her. To teach her. Yes, I think you may be right."

"She trusts you, in ways that she'll never trust me. Or Jynn." I'm pacing again. I force myself to stop. "Rescuing you wasn't the reckless command of a girl, as I assumed. She was thinking ahead."

"Is there risk to you or Jynn?" Saran asks.

"There shouldn't be. We've never encountered anything like this before, so I can't be sure."

"So she will not be controlled. She will not aid us in our fight. And our only supernatural assets are putting themselves at risk for dubious benefit." I don't think to read her thoughts until after she's made her decision. The Khal steps farther from Telias as Gabriel and three of his Hands appear like magic from nearby doorways. I can sense a dozen more waiting just out of sight. "We will remove her from the board. We have sacrificed enough for this girl, and I'll not risk you or Jynn. Without you, how can we contend with the enemy?"

Telias doesn't move. He doesn't even tense. He regards

268

Saran coldly.

"I understand your fears," he says, voice soft yet dangerous. "But this is not the way. She is being controlled. She is innocent, in every sense of the word that matters."

"Yet she endangers us all. They are seeking her on the streets, soldier and monster alike, door to door. Citizens of Coin are dying for their ignorance, all to protect a tyrant they would happily depose."

"The blame lies with the Empire, not with her."

"And I'm told," she continues as if he didn't speak. "That she is a danger herself. That she may slip under their control without our notice, deciding we are her jailors instead of her liberators. I will not allow a Shaper of such power to threaten my people."

"There is—"

"I didn't ask for your thoughts, Batir."

"Saran—"

"How *dare* you speak aloud what I offered you in secret," she snarls, her eyes flashing. I raise my hands as a dagger appears in Gabriel's hands. "You will address me as your Khal, or remain silent."

"Your Eminence," I say, bowing my head. It takes everything in me not to try to subvert her thoughts. It would be a futile exercise. Like Commander Ghali, her mind works in ways that confound my power. What arguments would serve to sway her? Sentiment and decency certainly won't carry the day. "Let's say that she doesn't aid us. She remembers nothing, has no loyalty to us or the crown. They will devote untold resources to find her. She is, quite literally, priceless. Let Telias take her far from here, away from the Empire and the Republic. The distraction of her disappearance will waste their resources and give us a chance to strike."

"And where will we strike, Batir?" she asks, raising her eyebrows. "Will you slay the Master of Beasts? Will you destroy their soldiers?" She pauses, but we both know it's for effect. I have no desire to tangle with the Master of Beasts, even less so after witnessing what he's done to the princess. And we both know I am no warrior. "I thought not. We do not have the strength to move against them, Master of Earth or no."

Telias doesn't outwardly reveal his hand, but I sense as his thoughts shift. He is about to strike, numbers be damned. He can see it all, how he will move, how his opponents will react, how he will exploit their desire to protect the Khal. His vision of the fight is more harmony than violence, merely a musician following a song to its inevitable conclusion.

My heart sinks. I glance between Telias and Saran, weighing in my heart what must be done. In the end, there's only one option.

Wait, I send towards his mind.

His eyes flick to me, briefly, before he resumes studying his opponents.

Trust me.

He truly is a man studied in my power. He doesn't speak aloud or give any physical sign. But his thoughts answer well enough themselves.

"What if we can ensure that she helps us?" I say aloud.

I can feel Jynn's anger blossoming from down the hall; she must have sensed the conflict and taken interest.

"I'm not angry with you. She's an idiot if she thinks I'll let her hurt Iliana."

So you support this?

"If it saves her, yes."

"What do you mean, Batir? Speak bluntly," Saran demands.

"We've studied what the Master of Beasts has done. We can do something similar. As we get rid of his influence, we can plant our own seeds in the ashes."

"You bastard," Telias growls, surging towards me. The

270

Khal's men grab his arms to hold him back. "She trusts you. Like an idiot, *I* trusted you."

"I'm saving her life, neh?" I turn to Saran, opening my hands in welcome. "What do you say, Eminence? An obedient Shaper of Earth, powerful and true. She may well turn the tide."

"Do it," she says, turning and stalking into the tunnels. In moments, she disappears around a distant corner. Gabriel and the men restraining Telias remain. For the moment, at least.

"You're exchanging one set of shackles for another. She doesn't deserve this." Telias's face is a white-hot volcano of rage, his lone eye smoldering. He struggles futilely against the men holding him, then suddenly sags, the anger leaving him like a snuffed candle. "You have a chance to be a good man, Bastian. Don't do this."

"That ship sailed a long time ago," I say, shrugging. "I am what I am."

***

If chaos reigns in the streets above, as the Khal suggested, there is no sign of it here beneath the earth. Wrapped in the embrace of the cold stone, the sun and sands feel a distant memory. The room where Iliana rests is small, some ancient storeroom emptied by time then filled by modern necessity. Pallets line the walls, a dozen or more. If each of the rooms is furnished similarly, this portion of the tunnels is a hornet hive of the Khal's men just waiting to be stirred to action.

I kneel at Jynn's side. Iliana sleeps, for now. Jynn helped her along, and now keeps her nightmares at bay. It is not easy. They are many, and persistent.

Jynn's slender shoulders rise and fall in a sigh. She turns and meets my eyes, her youthful face looking anything but, for no child's face has ever worn the expression hers now bears. There is no need for words between us. There never has been. Even when I was trapped and dying in a wooden cage, even before we shared a body, we understood each other. In this, there is no argument.

Though we may not wish it, we will do what must be done.

I saw you talking with Tana. Where did you send her?

"The less you know, the less you have to lie about. And you're a shit liar," Jynn says.

Thanks.

"Should we... begin?"

You don't think we should ask her first? One last time?

"She made up her mind. And it's not like she has a choice anymore, does she?"

I guess not.

"We have to be thorough. There can be nothing left of him to grow afterwards. We can't care about what it does to her, or us. I would rather rip it all out than leave a single seed of his influence to once again take root."

Agreed.

"You're stronger than I am. Go after the memories he has fought to strengthen. I will attack it from the other side, and destroy that which is hidden. With luck, we'll meet in the middle, and his influence will be purged."

No time like the present.

Like two children clasping hands before plunging into a pond, we leap together into the landscape of her mind.

***

A man, his eyes fierce, wears a collar of glass. He won't look at us, won't ever look at us again.

"Do it, and be the monster he wishes you to be."

No, we won't. Not this time. we won't.

Our hand comes up against our will.

Please no. Not this time. We can save him, we can make another choice...

Our fingers close.

The grunt he makes echoes in the silent chamber. His head tilts and falls to the side, his body collapsing beneath him. His blood is so red, so vividly red. It is the only color left in the world. And already it cools.

"*Separate yourself,*" Jynn whispers in my mind.

It's just so powerful. I've never felt anything like this. How does she stand it?

"*I don't know. But she doesn't need to suffer any longer. Destroy it.*"

The sorrow is a fresh cut over aching, half-healed scars. Our soul rips. Yet at least she *still lives…*

Taking her sorrow, I burn the memory away. Like a tentacle of some forgotten sea beast, the part of Iliana's mind that is not her own flinches away as the man's corpse dissolves before silver light. It tries to flee, like an animal arrowing for its den. I pursue.

A man, mutilated past endurance, blonde beard matted with spittle and blood. His lone sapphire eye focuses on us with such hatred that we feel small.

"*So the bitch lives,*" *he rasps, launching a wad of spittle that slaps to the stone at our feet.*

We don't want to approach him. We have no desire to be here. This man nearly killed us, put a bolt through our chest.

"*I don't want to be alone with him, Father. He scares me.*"

"*I won't leave you, my dear. We'll punish him together.*"

Father's voice is a warm embrace that drives away the shivering cold. He won't let anything happen to me. He only wants to protect me.

Eternal's curse, I can feel it. Some tendril of power wrapped around this memory, bolstering it, strengthening it. Why this memory? Why a memory of torture and sorrow? The assassin twitches uncontrollably, gibbering in his chains as Iliana relives this moment. The warmth and love of 'Father' would be better served by happier memories, loving moments. So what is it?

Jynn is too busy to respond. Her power flashes again and again, pulsing in this space that is both finite and limitless. I need to focus.

I am a monster.

The words come not from the memory, but from the source herself.

Ah. There, I guess, I have my answer.

The memory falls before a consuming wall of silver light.

The tendril retracts again. The moment it is untethered from a specific memory, it begins to fade from my senses, disappearing into the white noise of Iliana's memory. It isn't dying. Whatever insidious magic Kranos has worked, it feels like a mind opposes ours, that this energy possesses intelligence enough to seek its own preservation.

I chase it across a glowing panorama of memory.

Childhood lessons on the Creator, on his will, on how much Shapers are blessed above the common man.

Moments of tenderness between the Sealord and his daughter, few and far between, yet raised up by Kranos's power.

Occasional moments of peace and happiness, often untouched.

Strengthened memories of violence and death, blending together after a while.

A frozen battlefield, the sight of scarlet blood leaking from severed fingers against the backdrop of snow.

An earthen floor, opening like a maw to crush the life from two men, then the arm of a helpless woman.

Assassins in a dark forest, a desperate need screamed into the face of a dying man whose chest fills with glass.

A hundred more small battles, a litany of broken corpses of men and women whose names she never knew, and never cared to know.

Each disappears under a wave of burning silver light. Take it all, destroy every memory this thing wants her to know. Let nothing remain for it to latch on to. As I work, I get a sense of something else. Beneath these moments of violence, another lurks. Like a wide stone at the bottom of a river, a memory rests, heavy and dark.

A wall of gray stretches across the ocean and into the land, obscuring all sight. It approaches with shocking speed, devouring our sight by the second. Little fishing villages dot the coastline north, and the curtain of gray swallows each of them in succession.

What is this? Fog? A mist to aid in our retreat?

The tremor in the tower grows into a rumble. Stones jump beneath our feet. The brilliant azure light of Father's power flickers, dims, and finally goes out. He drops to his knees, his shoulders slumping even as the rock shudders underneath us.

A roar builds in the air, swiftly drowning out the sounds of battle, a roar of such volume we press our palms to our ears. The sun breaks through with a few sharp rays cast in sharp relief against the backdrop of cloud. The wall of gray races through the blades of light and shimmers blue. Not mist. Not fog.

Water.

So large it kisses the clouds, so wide it envelops the horizon, the titanic wave races towards the hapless men and women stranded on the bridge high above the waves of the Great Sea. The unshakeable stone of the Way of the North offers no warning. Not that any warning would save them. The long line of Khalintari soldiers yet to join to fight recognize their danger, their lines breaking up as they strive to avoid the unavoidable.

But we will be swept away as well. The tower sways under our feet, the cresting flood dragging the seabed and coastline with it. No construction of man can withstand such power. There is no avoiding this cataclysm, no controlling so much primal strength. This flood will drown the world.

The wave races at lightning speed, filling the sky, enveloping the earth.

Thought breaks upon the implacable roar, but still we scream.

Like the wave in her memory, silver fire washes over this world and burns it to ash.

Silence. This memory was seared into her consciousness, darkening every other light. Kranos's power turned her righteous guilt to self-loathing and despair. No longer.

I've toiled through every instance of violence, every moment he wanted to empower in order to yoke her mind to his will. There were many. Kranos wove his influence through the entirety of her mind. He was clever enough never to command; the mind resists direct control. Her choices were her own, but with only the memories and feelings he allowed her to have. Questing about the landscape of her thoughts, though, I can't feel his influence anywhere.

Except for its source. It writhes before my senses, uncertain and fearful. A dark facsimile of the symbol of our power burned into the fabric of her spirit. It is like seeing myself.

"So that's how he did it." Jynn's awareness floats next to mine, exuding exhaustion. *"It's brilliant, in an evil kind of way."*

It is. The creeping tendrils of Kranos's influence are not grounded in any memory, not even in instinct. He's achieved something that no one since the Creator could possibly have managed: he's combined the power over Thought and Beasts to force her own body to sustain the thing which controls her. It draws on her strength, a silent parasite stealing life.

Can we destroy it? Should we?

"Yes," Jynn says fiercely. *"She deserves to be free."*

Her power gathers, a silver light felt more than seen in this strange landscape.

Wait.

"Why? Let's finish this."

I share a thought with her. A question.

"No. You can't be sure you'll succeed. To leave it alive…"

It is what's best for her. You heard the Khal's thoughts. No matter where she goes, people will seek to control her power.

"If you're wrong…"

I'm not.

"How can you be sure?"

You've been in my mind. You know how quickly I learn things.

276

This isn't hubris. I mean, not entirely. Think of Ulia. Think of yourself.
When I see something, I can replicate it. I don't know how, but I just
know.

"She doesn't deserve to be controlled any longer."
Trust me.

She is quiet for a while. She may be silent for a second or an hour; time is meaningless spent in the disconnected realm of the princess's broken mind. Normally, I could use a memory to measure its passage, following the thread of events to keep time. Here, in the empty space that is all that remains, I have no touchstone to orient by.

"Trust is an elusive thing," she finally says.
It is the only way.

"Only fools think there is one way." Her power washes over me, bathing me in her light. I could push her away, but I don't. I let her in, let her see my intent. She returns to herself when she is satisfied. She sighs, though we have no need to breathe. *"Once upon a time, I would have trusted you to look after yourself. I would have trusted your selfish nature. You've changed. I guess I have to trust who you've become."*

Thank you.

Turning to the writhing symbol wrought by the Master of Beasts, I go to war.

***

Even with Jynn's help, I have little strength left when I'm finished. I feel lost in the contours of Iliana's mind, even scoured as it is. She still exists in the way she thinks, the shape of her consciousness, though the empty silhouette of trauma may well dictate what she becomes.

Though memory can be removed, the mind remembers.

Extricating myself from her mind feels less like withdrawing from another and more like splitting myself in two. The thought senses a pulse of alarm through my spirit. How long have I left my body unattended?

Shaking off my lethargy, I pull away as quickly as I can, careful not to do any more harm to the mind I'm leaving. I'm careful, even then, to keep my thoughts close.

For I found her, her conscious self, deep in the throes of my battle with Kranos's will. She spoke to me, words that I will offer no one. Words that I hope, if nothing else, she remembers. She had no memory of the woman she loved, no thought to connect the words to. She was frightened and lost in the emptiness of her memory.

Still she felt regret.

"I am a monster," she had said, even in sleep, her mind a smoking ruin in our wake. *"I don't remember why, but I know it is true."*

No, princess. You aren't.

"I am. I chose poorly. I chose wrongly. Why can't I remember the choice?"

It is not your fault.

"It is. I could have chosen love."

Then remember this. Not the violence, not the death, not the tragedy. Remember.

"Choose… love?"

Yes.

"Okay."

Chapter 13
Kettle
The Eightieth Day of Summer
In the year 5223, Council Reckoning

It is strangely comforting that my attire for our long-anticipated meeting with the Amanu is the same *dimina* that I have worn throughout my time in Yohru. The black silk doesn't wrinkle or crease, but I check myself in a small mirror adorning the east wall of my room high in the Baeda tower. The material hangs as flawlessly and perfectly as ever. I tug at the hem anyway.

I'm ready for this to be over. No more thinly veiled offers of support, no more fake smiles and false stoicism. I've met with what feels like a hundred powerful men and women, from the richest merchants to the most respected generals. The allies of the Baeda clan have given me the appearance of total support, while the houses loyal to the Ihera have been careful never to commit to anything. For all the posturing, though, each has offered me the same message in a hundred different ways: prove you are the Eshani, and we will back you. Fail, and we will forget you.

The kings of Dusk and Dawn are another matter entirely. The king of Dusk, a man known only as Daraneh, is a dour old man nearing a century of age. The king of Dawn, Koa Mikita, is nearly his inverse, a jovial youth barely past his manhood. By appearance, they share nothing in common, and in any other world they would be rivals. The two are instead fast friends. Proud, independent of the politics high on the mountain, they were blunt in declaring the farce of the Eshani. It was pleasantly refreshing to have the words spoken openly to my face.

"These rich fools live up in the clouds, breathing this thin air, and lose sight of reality down below. We defend the borders of this kingdom. We provide them food and water and give them everything they need to play their petty games," Daraneh had said, his expression turning sour.

"If you follow through with this silly ritual and survive, there isn't much we can do about it," Mikita picked up where his counterpart left off. "The people will follow you. Many of our soldiers would as well, as much as we would like to think they would not forget their honor and abandon their duties."

"I have no desire to govern your lands," I said through Myn. "You will remain king, so long as you agree to ally yourself with me."

"We do not appreciate threats," Mikita answered, a friendly smile frozen on his face.

"And I don't make them. I will need you both, when the time comes, far more than you'll need me. I couldn't imagine better friends to have."

They had seemed mollified at my assurances, though I think it came more from their belief that I have no chance of succeeding than any earned respect. Regardless, Daraneh had offered me one final warning as he ascended his palanquin outside the Baeda tower.

"You speak openly, so I will as well." His weathered face, decorated by a scraggly white beard, cracked into a scowl. "Of all the serpents on this mountain, the Ihera are the worst. They are greedy for power. They will consume you, if given the chance."

"Thank you, my lord," I had said, bowing deeper than was necessary for respect.

I tug nervously at the hem of my *dimina* again. If there is consuming to be done, it will be today. Leaving my room, I force my feet down the winding stair. My companions for the short journey have already arrived: Aurelion leans on the wall at the base of the stairs, eyes following Corna as she paces like a caged tiger across the empty marble floor. Sonjur kneels at the only table, writing something with a careful, slow grace. Three sets of eyes pin me as I appear.

"Is everything ready?" I ask quietly, my voice carrying in the cavernous room.

"Ready as we'll ever be," Corna says, beaming. "You look absolutely stunning."

"I look the same as I've looked for ten days now," I say wryly.

"Exactly. The fashion of this land was meant for you."

"I must concur with Oshei Corna," Sonjur says, returning to his writing. "You wear it well."

The sound of children's laughter echoes from the lawn outside. I head that way when I reach the bottom of the stairs even though we don't have much time before the appointed hour. Aurelion falls in at my side as soon as I'm on level ground. His quiet confidence helps to calm the tempest in my chest.

Outside on the lawn, four of Sonjur's children, or grandchildren, it's a little hard to tell, play with Sario. He pretends to be a monster, roaring and plodding after them. They laugh hysterically, tears streaming down their faces as they easily evade him. I wish my children could act so carefree and joyous. Many are old before their time, unable to let go of old fears... or new ones.

"I should never have brought them here."

"You didn't know," Ezil says, waving away my regrets like they're some irritating fly. "How could you know?"

"You'll protect them?"

"You know I will."

"Keep them safe, Ezil. I have a bad feeling about this."

"So worry about yourself. Your sisters and brothers will protect your children."

"If we don't make it out..."

281

"I'll worry about that when it happens. Just... make it out."

The sigh that escapes my lips feels crafted of ice. No, there is no sign of my children here. They've been spirited away in the night, taken to a house low on the edge of the city that Sonjur claims will not be searched. Should the Ihera make their move today, his people will secret them down the lift and out of the city. The rest of my family will have the chance to make a new life.

Ignoring the prick of tears in my eyes, I spin and march across the open floor of the Baeda tower and out the front door, not bothering to check if anyone follows.

A palanquin waits outside, set to carry me up the winding streets to the Tower of the Moon. I ignore it, walking past without comment and setting off up the streets. Corna makes a slight sound of protest, and Aurelion shushes her. At a soft command from Sonjur, the cordon of Baeda guards hustles to catch up to us, their silver uniforms shimmering in the early light. He will wait behind; the Ihera made it clear he was not welcome at this meeting.

Despite Sonjur's claim that I would have a chance to explore the ancient city, I've spent all my time in Yohru trapped in the Baeda tower. There have been too many people to meet and things to learn, the intricate etiquette and honor of what Sonjur calls the 'unseen dance.' Bow this far, step this close, speak this loudly, hold your hands this way... his lessons swim in my mind as we march higher, though that might just be the altitude. Ten days is not nearly enough to acclimate to such heights. My breath comes short enough already that I briefly regret refusing the palanquin, though only briefly. I won't be carried to my fate like some piece of baggage.

Word of my quiet ascension of the city spreads, and people turn out to line the streets. I don't let my eyes wander to them, not now. They will be silent and expressionless. The people of Eshan are intentional in their words, parsing them out like they are in dwindling supply. In my periphery, a few offer the

282

customary bow of respect to the Eshani, faces pressed to the stone. That so few do makes the motionlessness of the rest feel threatening.

The towers grow more varied and gorgeous the higher we climb. Though the entirety of the architecture is crafted in blacks and grays and silvers, the wealthier families manage uniqueness in subtle ways. In one, the curve of each terraced roof curls back in on itself in elegant whorls. Another has balconies wrapping the tower at every floor, the lower levels lined with people to watch me pass.

As we reach a bend in the street, I pause and turn back. The sight steals my breath. Like spears lifted against the tyranny of heaven, the towers stab defiantly towards the sky. Their muted color is stark against the pale stone of the mountains in the distance. Wisps of cloud trail in the subtle breeze, clinging like pennants to the edges of the dark city. The people remain staring after me, and I shiver.

How did we get here? How did *I* get here?

By the Depths, I'm halfway around the world from all I know. For the second time. And these people may well put a crown upon my head.

The thought nearly has me bolting for the closest alley. I can disappear in moments, even in this strange city. There is no man or woman alive that can catch me when I don't want to be found. If I just...

Alright, girl. Steady.

I put my head down and resume my measured march. I let my eyes trail about the city, taking in each sharp edge and gentle curve. I may not want to rule it, let alone live here, but I will do what must be done to protect my family.

The Tower of the Moon is at the pinnacle of the mountain, a monument to human capability and arrogance. As we approach, much of it is hidden in cloud, though I get the impression that we couldn't see the top even on the clearest day. Wide stones overlap, mortarless, in a dizzying pattern of shimmering silver. The tower is free of unnecessary embellishment; the silent weight of it is impressive enough. Should we climb to its apex, I wouldn't be surprised if we really could step from the tower onto the moon itself.

A straight set of wide steps leads to a tall pair of metallic doors. Soldiers in the Ihera colors stand at silent attention. There is more of the midnight blue-black in their uniforms today. Of course there is. The Baeda escort halts at the base of the stairs, and the three of us continue on alone.

A pair of soldiers open the doors as we near the summit. I pause at the entrance, breathing slowly and deeply. Partly, I need to settle my nerves. This will be the most dangerous meeting since I found myself in Jon Gordyn's presence amidst the bungled heist of his secret vault.

The other part, though, is that Corna has been complaining about a stitch in her side for the last hundred steps. I can afford to let her breathe.

The interior of the Tower of the Moon retains the simple, heavy elegance of its facade. The high ceiling stretches into darkness. Lanterns burn silently at a dozen locations on the distant walls, their light feeble before the dim majesty of the vast room. In the tower's silence, there is a weight of stone and, heavier, time, like it has stood here so long that it has forgotten that stone may topple. It merely is, and will always be.

Four Ihera Oshei, each stern-faced and well into their middle years, stand at attention before an imposing set of double doors. There are markings in brown, green, royal blue, and yellow among their *dimina*. A powerful group of Ensouled, if they truly possess Roots, Earth, Water, and Light. Seeing Light among them sends a tremor of fear through my chest.

As we approach, they step forward crisply and bow, deeply and respectfully. The tension clutching my heart eases some at the sight. I feared disrespect, subtle or outright, and underlying hostility. Their bow, though, has their faces pressed nearly to the floor.

The man on the right lifts his face and speaks loudly in the *hitaan*. Myn steps forward and answers in turn. She stiffens when he responds, and he bows again, perhaps lower this time.

"What is it?" I murmur.

"He asks that we leave our Oshei behind," she says slowly. "The Amanu wishes to speak to you alone."

"Do the Ihera not have six? Where are the others?"

"He claims they are elsewhere on business for the clan. He swears by the honor of his house that the Amanu only wants to speak with you."

Corna snorts behind me. She shakes her brown curls at my questioning look.

"'The honor of his house,'" she says sarcastically, rolling her eyes. "Definitely trustworthy."

"What about you?" I ask Myn.

"I will be permitted to join you."

I take a deep breath and glance at Aurelion and Corna. He stares back at me, but her attention wanders about the room, taking in the bare walls and open stone.

"Go on," she says, feigning a yawn into the back of her hand. "We'll be right out here."

"Should anything go amiss, I'll be listening," Aurelion says, offering me a firm nod and a reassuring smile. "Nothing will keep me from you."

"Alright," I say, ignoring the unease spreading in my gut. I hold his gaze. "Listen closely."

We pass through the doors, and my ears pop, like we've risen even higher. The air feels strange, listless and still. The sheen of sparkling gray stone gives way to glossy obsidian. Sourceless light, white and shimmering like starlight, reflects upon itself in all directions infinitely, like we've traded places with the moon to swim among an unending sea of stars. Two thrones rest

285

near the opposite wall, one of shining silver, the other a void of darkness amidst the unbroken tapestry of stars.

A man sits the silver throne, his *dimina* shimmering in midnight blues edged with metallic bronze. He is young, no more than twenty Winters, and handsome, his dark eyes piercing in the strange light. His hair is cut short and styled into rigid waves cresting his brow. He stands as we approach, his face solemn.

"Welcome, Eshani," he says, his voice deep and heavily accented. "It is good that you have finally come."

"Thank you, Amanu," I say, taking in Myn's shocked expression in my periphery. "I have to say, I share Inara Myn's surprise that you speak my language. And even more surprised that you name me Eshani."

"Is that not what you are?" he says, head tilting quizzically.

"So they tell me. I guess you'll want a demonstration?"

"It would be appropriate, yes," he says, the barest hint of a smile ghosting across his lips.

The shadow comes to my call, reluctantly, for the thousandth time, forming the same shard of night in my right hand. The Amanu's eyes widen, and he leans forward slightly, almost unconsciously. My shadow feels at home here, in this place crafted to mimic the darkness between the stars, yet I don't share its ease. The emptiness in my chest feels cavernous enough to echo my disquiet back to me. My soul feels very small and very alone in the strange space Kit's power left in my breast. I let the shadow dissipate, but not before a shiver works its way down my spine.

"Eshani," he says, an unusual note of... something in his voice. "I never thought you would come in my lifetime."

His face remains stoic, but his eyes tell a different tale. He is eager. Excited.

Hungry.

"Neither did I," I say, trying on a smile.

"When did you have the throne moved?" Myn says, her

focus past the Ihera scion. "And why?"

"It is appropriate," he says, not bothering to follow her gaze.

"Not many would agree," she says, taking one measured step forward to capture his attention. "The Amanu sits in front of the Eshani, not beside."

"Once," he says impatiently. "But we have never had an Amanu like me."

"And we have waited for the Eshani for years uncounted," Myn reminds him stiffly. "You know your duty."

"To step aside for a stranger?" His lips twist into a grimace as his eyes flick back to me. "I mean no offense. You do not know our ways, no matter what the Baeda have taught you. You need someone to guide you."

"What do you intend?" Myn asks bluntly.

"Eshani," he says, intensity burning in his voice. "I know that we have just met, and that the Baeda have undoubtedly poisoned you against me and my clan out of jealousy for our strength. Their manipulations will have filled you with doubt. But look at me." He opens his arms as if to encompass his entire body and mind. "I am the Amanu, the regent of Eshan waiting for your return. I am the Master of Forces, able to bend the will of the invisible world. And I am Ihera, a clan known for its honor and might. Our word, my word, is as unbreakable as the steel our people used to build this city."

"It does not sound like you're planning to step down," I say slowly. There's a desperation to this man, mixed with arrogant certainty. I need to choose my words carefully. "I am new to Eshan, yes. But is that not the oath you swore when you took up the title?"

"Yes," he snaps impatiently. "I made that oath, and I will keep it, should that be your desire. Yet hear the opportunity the Ihera offer, first."

"Go on," I say, trying to read the look on Myn's face

without turning from him. *What is going on here?* I'm not sure how I thought this would go, but I feel like I'm treading water over the limitless Depths. Something lurks below, ready at any moment to pull me under.

"You don't know me, Eshani," he says, holding my gaze in the sparkling, otherworldly light. "I am a man of honor, a man worthy of the silver throne. Imagine what we could be… together."

"You dare—" Myn tries to say, but he raises his voice to speak over her.

"Picture it. Your fabled power, the Nightmother, ruling these lands from atop your ancient throne, me at your side, the Master of Forces, heir to the most powerful clan in all of Eshan. The petty kings will be nothing before us; they will fall in line because they will have no choice." He leans forward in his excitement, and an edge of mania taints his voice. "With me at your side, we can expand the borders of Eshan, return even to conquer the lands you left behind. Marry me, Eshani. Join our strength and forge a new Empire of Night. Together, none will stand against us. Together, none *can* stand against us. Together, we can bring back the glory of Eshan, stolen so long ago by the Light."

His words echo briefly before fading to silence. He stares at me with such certainty that he can't seem to imagine refusal.

And I *can* see it. This man, standing at my side. We would be mighty, a force the world must reckon with. The sprawling nations of Eshan could muster soldiers enough to meet the Sealord and his mad general in the field. I could return with the might of an entire people at my back and break the man who tried to break me. To see the Master of Beasts dead at my feet… there have been few men I have hated enough to wish death upon them. Feeling again, in this moment, the phantom of my ribs breaking, my leg snapping like dried kindling… fear and hate rise, inextricably joined, to choke my breath. To be free of that fear…

to avenge my brother, murdered so brutally before my eyes…

It should be tempting. In some ways, it is.

"Thank you, my lord, for your generous offer." I try to inject as much sincerity as I can in my voice. "I'm certain that, some day, you will find a partner worthy of your greatness."

"Some day?" he asks in confusion, like he can't fathom what I could possibly mean.

"She is rejecting your offer, Ihera," Myn says evenly. "That you are bold enough to ask is affront enough. Be thankful that she has the grace to turn you down unpunished."

"Myn, stop," I say, eyeing the Amanu.

His face spasms briefly, his cheek jumping and his left eye twitching open and closed. His mouth firms into a line, the typical stoicism of these people smoothing over his features. His gaze is stone as he stares steadily into my eyes.

"You are making a mistake," he says, barely controlling the rage trembling through his words. "Throwing away the future of Eshan. You think I'm unworthy of you?"

"No, my lord," I say softly. "I am not making that judgment. I don't know you well enough to try."

"Unworthy," he says, more to himself than me. "Unworthy. Am I? No. No. *You* are unworthy of *me*."

"Silence, fool," Myn snaps. "You speak to the Eshani."

"Myn," I begin in warning, but she ignores me this time.

"The Ihera have always been power hungry, but this goes beyond—"

A symbol ignites on the Amanu's forearm, and bronze light floods the room, dimming the false stars into obscurity. His hand snaps upward, and Myn flies into the air, as if the earth rejects her as wholly as it just embraced her. Her body, silhouetted in the false starlight, rises high, higher than I thought the ceiling could possibly be. I nearly lose sight of her as she comes to a sudden jolting halt. Her scream fills the chamber with terror.

The shadow comes to my call, slowly but more easily this

time. I shift my weight to my back foot, crouching to spring. His hand comes up towards me. I tense to dive aside.

"Kneel," he commands, and his hand drops towards the floor.

A weight slams into my shoulders and head, crushing me towards the earth. I catch myself before my face shatters on the obsidian. Barely. My arms tremble under the weight. My neck burns to keep my head from the stone. My joints ache under the pressure. I can't move, I can hardly resist. His hand lowers again, and the weight redoubles, my bones groaning like coastal trees before strong winds.

"Kraft," I try to shout, though it comes out more like a gasp as I fight to get my lungs to work under the pressure. "Kraft!"

"He can't hear you," the Amanu says, stepping over and kneeling next to my trembling forms. "We have means of fooling even Oshei of Voices."

I don't have the breath to reply. My knees are crushed to the stone, my arms demanding rest. I can't lift my head, but he kneels low enough for me to see his face.

"I offered you the world," he says mildly, the anger gone. He looks more disappointed than anything. I grit my teeth and force my eyes up to meet his. "I offered you the world, and you threw it in my face."

"Yes," I force through lungs starved for air. "The right... choice."

"Fool," he snarls, equanimity briefly broken before he smooths his features again. "You are nothing. I've heard your story: an exiled thief, a mother to worthless orphans. What a waste of life. The only reason you're special is due to a quirk of fate. After you die, another potential 'Eshani' will be born. After you die, you will be forgotten, just another ambitious fool in a long line of them."

"Don't... want..." I can't keep speaking, the pressure slowly collapsing my chest. The weight relaxes slightly, and my trembling arms lift my chest a bit higher, my neck raising another inch.

"What don't you want?" he asks, eyebrows raised.

"I never wanted this," I growl into his face. "I would rather disappear. I don't want the throne. I don't want any of this. Let us go. Say I died, say I threw it all away, I don't care. We will leave Eshan, and you'll never see us again."

"It's too late for that," he says, shaking his head. "The people believe you could be her. They must have their hope answered."

"If I disappear..."

"They will blame me, and my clan. That is unacceptable."

"I never wanted this." I clench my eyes closed in frustration as he continues to shake his head, the picture of regret. What words can I use? What can I say to convince him to let us go? "I'll say it was a trick, that I can't really control Shadow. Let them hate me. Creator, let them take me. Just let my family go."

"Impressive," he says, reaching out and patting my cheek. "You reached the right conclusion without help. Don't worry, you won't have to tell them you're false. You don't speak our language, so I'll speak for you."

"I have a translator."

"Inara Myn?" he says, eyes lazily rising to where she floats high in the air. Her breath comes in terrified gasps, her hands clenching at the empty air. "She was disrespectful. No one disrespects the Ihera."

"Amanu, lord, please, don't," I gasp desperately.

"She must be punished," he says, turning his gaze back to me. "Unless you'd like to reconsider? This is your last chance. Join me, and we can forget this ever happened."

"Do not, Eshani!" Myn shouts, her voice strong and true. "This snake can't sit the throne of Eshan. He has forsaken his honor and betrayed his oaths. He isn't worthy of you."

"Myn..."

"I knew this day would come." she says, and, even spoken softly, her voice fills the room. "My father, before he left... he told me this moment would come. He told me that I would... that I would die in the service of the Eshani."

"Myn, stop."

"Deny him," she says firmly. "You are the Nightmother. Do not sully your honor by bowing to this worm."

"How unpleasant," the Amanu says, frowning. "You have chosen your friends poorly. I would be doing you a favor by ending her now."

"Don't you dare," I growl, fighting against the invisible hand pressing me down. I drive myself half-upright, locking my elbows and forcing my chin up.

"You want to save her? Submit to me," he says.

"I trust you, Eshani... Kettle," Myn says, a peaceful smile spreading across her face. "So trust me in return. This is what is meant to happen."

"What is your answer?" the Amanu prompts, raising a hand towards Myn. "This is the last time I'll offer. Marry me, and all this goes away. We can rule Eshan. We can rule the world. Just say yes."

"I..."

My eyes go to Myn. She stares back at me, floating amidst the stars. Her smile brooks no argument. There must be something I can do. Here in the darkness, the shadow comes more willingly to my call. It resists the press of his power, floating out towards his exposed foot. If I can just disrupt his concentration for a moment, I can save Myn and get out of here before he can recover. I don't care if I have to maim him, though killing him isn't a possibility. I don't know what would happen if a Shaper this powerful, a Master of Forces no less, died by violence in the pinnacle of his strength. The tower could fall, or float away. The city itself could crash to the valley far below.

The darkness forms into a blade thin enough to disappear.

292

I'll attack him low. It will sever his foot at the ankle, but he'll live. Who can concentrate on Shaping missing a foot? Gathering my will, I strike. The shadow flickers through the air, faster than light, faster than thought.

Wind ruffles my hair in this windless space.

My shadow catches nothing but empty air.

Impossibly, his foot moves, sliding gracefully aside.

A voice, high and feminine, speaks in their graceful tongue. A girl appears from behind the throne, her navy *dimina* slashed with white. Wind. Of course he didn't meet with me alone. He never planned on dealing fair.

The Amanu glances at me, a look of disappointment on his face.

"You could have been a queen," he says sadly.

"Don't," I gasp, trying to lunge towards him.

Crushing weight slams me to the ground. I turn my face just before my nose would shatter, my cheek cracking against the obsidian. Stars flash before my eyes. I can't lift my head. Myn's scream, abrupt and loud, cuts off with a hideous crunch. Something wet sprays the back of my head and neck.

My lungs can't give voice to my strangled scream of denial. Tears squeeze from my eyes, slipping down my face far too quickly, the unnatural gravity so great they don't even splash.

Creator help me.

Myn.

I never told her. Never shared my suspicion. Now I may never know. My sister...

The Amanu crouches next to me, blood speckling the perfect silver of his *dimina*. The invisible pressure releases my head, but I don't take my aching cheek off the stone. He clicks his tongue in disapproval, and the force lifts my head against my will. His eyes are dark and empty, the bronze light of his power casting his face in shadow.

"Here is what will happen, *denagri*," he says evenly. "We

293

will walk out of here together. I will declare you a charlatan before the people, and Baeda Sonjur a traitor and conspirator. You helped me there, in a way; always providing the same demonstration, always creating that silly sword. Easily enough faked, with the proper sleight of hand. Do not think to fight. Your Oshei have already been arrested. They, and your other friends, will be executed alongside the Baeda. For delivering the destruction of that particular thorn in our side, I have to thank you."

"The Baeda are an honorable clan," I say, closing my eyes. "You don't need to destroy them."

"Sonjur is too clever by half," he says, shrugging. "I have ambitions beyond merely sitting a lesser throne. New prophecies can be crafted, ancient prophecies, where the shadow must be defeated instead of worshiped. It will take time, but I have time. By the time the next generation has grown, there will be no one left to dispute me."

"Not if I end you first," I growl.

"Careful," he says, stepping back in spite of his apparent confidence. "More lives than yours hang in the balance. To ensure your compliance, I will make you an offer. If you do not resist, I will spare your children. They will be servants in fine houses, and treated well. But only if you do not resist."

I don't answer. I barely hear him. This is what I feared when we came here. This is exactly why I wanted to run at the first hint of prophecy. Damn the Seer and all her meddling. She deserves a place in the Depths with the Eternal.

Still, there is hope. If Sonjur is as good as his word, the children will be out of reach of this madman before he can track them down.

"I see you are coming to the wrong conclusion," he says chidingly. "My people picked up your children, and the five companions guarding them, while you were on your way here."

The last ember of hope dies in my chest. If I could speak to the people, explain the Amanu's treachery... but no. Not even then. The people of Yohru made it very clear that they want stability and certainty, not prophecy and chaos. The only people who would listen are down the slopes camped on the road.

"Come, now," he says.

His power lifts me smoothly to my feet. I nearly collapse, but a gust of wind keeps me upright. I snap a glare on the girl, the Oshei of Wind. She stares back into my eyes, expressionless. I don't hold her gaze long. Myn. The ruin of her body rests, still and silent, on the stone. Her blood darkens the stars around her in a growing pool of crimson. Half her face shattered on the obsidian. What remains, though, retains that beatific peace that overcame her before she fell.

The sight of her, broken and alone, settles my heart even as it breaks it. She knew. She knew she would die in the service of the Eshani, in *my* service, and she came willingly, without question. I'll not let her life be spent for nothing.

The doors to the throne room swing open to an empty hall. A distant boom, somewhere higher in the tower, trembles through the stone beneath our feet. After a single glance upwards, the Amanu moves forward, but I can't take my eyes off the ceiling. Give me another. Come on. Do it. A second bone-shaking rumble shakes the tower again. The Amanu glances up again, then motions to the Oshei of Wind to investigate.

Arrest my Oshei, have you?

Give them hell, Corna. Break them, Aurelion.

The Amanu leads me through the front doors and to the top of the steps. A sea of faces stretches as far as the eye can see, every citizen of Yohru staring expectantly up at us. The thick stone of the Tower of the Moon stifles any sound of the combat between my friends and the Ihera Oshei. A line of Ihera soldiers stand at attention at the base of the steps. The Amanu leans close and grabs my arm.

"Remember your children," he growls. "See them? Look.

I've brought them in case you think to defy me."

And there they are, on a balcony of a nearby tower, no doubt owned by some ally of the Ihera. Ezil, Inia, and Koli kneel, hands bound behind their backs. Hom was treated less kindly, spouting bloody cuts and bruises on his face. Of Yelden, there is no sign. The children huddle together, their faces frightened. All of them but...

The Amanu throws me forward onto my knees. I barely catch myself before I tumble down the stairs. He begins to speak, his voice filled with ringing command, his words unintelligible but all too predictable. I am a charlatan, a thief, a foreigner come to steal the holy throne of the Eshani. He declares my life forfeit, my people traitors and renegades...

Will the people swallow the lie?

Of course they will. Who am I to them next to the Amanu? The first angry shouts already ring through the streets. He continues, on and on, whipping the crowd into a frenzy until he can barely be heard over their rage. By the Depths, he won't have to touch me himself. They'll tear me apart.

A guard stumbles back, and a lithe figure darts through the gap. A hand, slender and strong, grips mine. Kit's eyes blaze as he kneels next to me. The Amanu glances down, silent for a moment, then continues, his voice sparking a wrathful outcry.

"Mother, we can help," Kit says, softly enough that I have to read his lips to understand. "We can save everyone."

"How?" I whisper, flinching as the first thrown stone skitters off my calf.

"There is shadow, down in the valley. With my strength added to yours, we can wipe these streets clean."

"Kit..."

"Do you not remember?" he growls fiercely. "We can give you the strength to do anything. With enough shadow, we can destroy all of our enemies. Take our power, before it is too late."

His palm warms, and the place where our skin touches

buzzes as the power snaps at the invisible barrier between us, demanding to be allowed in. Creator, I've felt half a person ever since the streets of Donir. To feel whole again, to feel complete, *and* to save my family? How could I not?

Just as Tecarim taught me in the hidden vault at the top of the Imperial Bank, I take the wall down, and the first flood of feverish energy arcs through our joined hands, burning and glorious. Life, by the Depths, *life*...

The earth shakes beneath my knees, and the Amanu stumbles. Thunder, so deep it is felt more than heard. A flash of light, bright enough to blind. I just manage to get my eyes around before the wall of the Tower of the Moon explodes outward courtesy of a colossal bolt of lightning. A figure wreathed in crackling blue light leaps from the ruin, free falling until lightning tears into the ground and, impossibly, slows her enough to land in a crouch at my side.

Corna.

A moment later, Aurelion lands next to her, a deep whump rippling out from his feet. The Amanu, and the angry mob, sit in stunned silence. A cloud of dust drifts until it is caught by the wind, always blowing this high above the sea.

"Hi, Kettle," Corna says breezily, though her expression is anything but relaxed.

"Corna," I say, shaking my head slowly. "I'm glad you're safe, but..."

"But what?"

"You blew up the Tower of the Moon. That place is sacred to them. If they didn't hate us before..."

"Good," Corna says, her lip curling as she looks down at the mob with eyes filled with barely restrained lightning. "I don't like this place. And I *really* don't like you on your knees. I think it's time we get out of here."

"But, how, the people..."

The Amanu shatters the relatively peaceful moment with a

shout. The mob stirs, fury and shock and sorrow mixing on their upturned faces.

"Let me worry about that." She bends down and wraps an arm about my chest. "Oh, hey, Kit. You want a ride, too?"

"We guess," he says with dubious agreement.

"Creepy, but okay. Jump on my back. And hang on tight."

The second he's secure, lightning ripples out from Corna in waves of flickering blue. I flinch, but the energy dances harmlessly across my skin, toying with the hairs on my arms before dissipating into the earth.

"What about the others?" I ask, struggling to pull Corna's arm from about my chest.

"Aurelion has them," she says, pulling me tighter. "Now, brace yourself, *chela*."

The lightning picks up the pace of its frenzied dance, sparks flitting through the air and ripping chips of stone from the steps. Pressure builds beneath us, invisible yet certain. Is she really going to...?

"Wait—"

A sharp crack. A flash of light. My vision blackens and blurs, unable to keep up with the pressure of sudden acceleration. Wind ruffles my hair and rushes across my face. Blinking madly, I finally manage to clear my vision.

Yohru spreads out below us, rushing past at startling speed. I recognize little in the unfamiliar city, though I get a better appreciation for the order of its winding streets now that I see them from above. The whole city was built in an intricate pattern spiraling inwards with the Tower of the Moon at its zenith.

A glimpse is all I get, though, because we are most definitely not flying, but hurtling. Our trajectory tilts towards the only familiar building in the city, the Baeda tower rapidly increasing in size as we blast towards it on the tip of a bolt of lightning.

Creator, we're going fast. Too fast. There's no way she can

slow us, not in time…

"Corna!"

"Yeah, yeah," she mutters. "This is the tricky part."

Her arm about my chest tightens and we tilt forward and over, our feet heading towards the side of the tower.

"Gonna need some help on this one!" she shouts.

I don't answer, too busy setting my feet to absorb the blow. By the Depths, my knees are going to shatter. They're going to have to clean us off the side with a mop. Corna gives an incoherent shout, and lightning explodes forward into the tower. The bolt slows us some, but it steals my vision, my knowledge of *when* the tower's side—

We slam against the stone, and I flex my knees on instinct. Corna's arm around my chest barely prevents me from breaking my face on the stone. Gravity reasserts itself. We drop in a pile onto one of the tiered roofs of the tower. The ceramic tiles hold up to the impact, and we come to a halt after we slide a few inches.

Below me, Corna begins to shake. Her arm jumps around my chest, still clinging tightly.

"Corna?" I ask. "Are you alright?"

She gasps, and I twist out of her grip, careful not to disrupt our balance on the roof. My eyes race over her body, searching for any damage or sign. She looks whole, hearty. Her Ensouled! She probably gave him too much, let him in too far, and now… oh.

She's laughing.

Kit looks stunned beneath her, though, as our eyes meet, an exhilarated grin spreads across his face. Corna wriggles off him, wiping at her eyes in helpless hilarity.

"You've never tried that before, have you?"

"The Lightning Lord is still berating me," she gasps. "He just told me that I'm the least dignified Oshei who's ever carried him."

299

"Well, that's definitely true," I say, laughing.

"That was awesome," Kit says, turning back the way we came. "Can we do it again?"

"Maybe later," Corna says, pulling him close. "We've got bigger things to worry about."

As if summoned by her words, an earth-shaking boom echoes in the thin mountain air. A distant roar, many voices raised in anger, chases the echo away. Three more booms sound in quick succession, growing closer with each repetition.

"If that's Kraft, then the others have run into trouble," Corna mutters.

"Go help him," I say, mentally prepping a path down the tower. "I need to speak to Sonjur."

***

Baeda Iyuro opens the door as I reach the ground, and one of my many fears disappears. I wouldn't have blamed the Baeda if they locked the doors to their tower and distanced themselves from us. Perhaps word hasn't yet spread this far down the mountain. From the look on Sonjur's face as he approaches the door, though, they've heard. He studies my expression for a moment, then gestures for me to follow. We pass back out to the little courtyard separating the Baeda from the street. He ruffles Kit's hair on our way.

Angry shouts dominate the air, punctuated occasionally by a flash of light or deep boom. Our friends are only a few streets away, but, judging from the noise, our enemies are in hot pursuit. Sonjur clasps his hands behind his back, somber and solemn. He must know what all of this means. Though it shouldn't surprise me, he is remarkably calm for the captain of a doomed ship.

"I'm sorry," I say softly.

"It was always a gamble, Lady Kettle," he says, glancing my way. A brief smile ghosts across his face. "I knew what fire I danced with. The Ihera were growing too strong to resist, so I acted."

"But your sons…"

"Chose this path with me. I am not a tyrant whose command is law in my house." He turns again to the approaching commotion. "We will face our fate together."

In the blink of an eye, the empty street fills as humanity pours out of an alley a few blocks away. At the front, Ezil leads, she and her sisters ushering the sobbing children along. The bright fletchings of an arrow bob over Koli's shoulder, though she doesn't seem to notice the blood pumping feverishly from the wound. Hom and Sario move on either side of the small pack of children, stolen Eshani swords red with blood.

Corna and Aurelion appear last. As they clear the building, Aurelion throws his hand back the way they came. An explosion of sound rocks the alley. As the echoes fade, the screams of pain and anger redouble. I sprint out to meet them. I have no idea what I can do, weak as I am, but I'll not stand by and wait. Ezil shoots me a thankful look as I take over leading the children on so that she can help Inia with Koli. The sight of me gives my children renewed hope, and their little legs pump faster.

Whatever Aurelion did, it must have been effective, for we make the Baeda gates before any pursuit appears. I glance across their sweaty, blood-stained faces, finding…

"Yelden?" I ask hopelessly.

Hom shakes his head slowly.

"The dumb bastard fought like a demon when they came for us at the 'safe' house," he says, turning eyes shining with tears to glare at Sonjur. "They killed him because they weren't good enough to best him."

"I did not betray you," Sonjur says, then drops into a bow so low his forehead brushes the earth. "Though I will forever lament that my incompetence led to his death."

"We don't have time to point fingers," Corna says from the gate. "We should get this closed if we want to survive the next few minutes."

301

At Sonjur's nod, two of his sons swing the delicate iron fence closed. It is a paltry defense, elegant and useless. The stone wall it's anchored to is barely eight feet high, and will not hold them long. Aurelion ushers the children inside, leaving the rest of us to stand in a loose group before the gates. Koli and Inia follow at Ezil's gesture, both to get Koli out of the fight and to keep the children calm.

The mob, whipped into a frenzy by the Amanu and maddened by the blood my friends spilled to escape, marches in from all angles. Their angry faces clash surreally with the elegant silk of the *dimina* gracing their bodies. The stoicism of their people has been shattered, and emotion rules the day. Even so, the first of them balk at the thought of invading the Baeda tower. Whatever the Amanu may have claimed, these people know that Sonjur is a good man. They fall into an uneasy silence a few steps from the gate, filling the street from wall to wall.

"We need to scare them before they find their courage again," Aurelion says, reemerging from the tower. "They aren't soldiers. The mob feels strong together, but few are willing to die for this cause. If we target the leaders, strike hard and fast, the others may scatter."

"No, Aurelion Kraft," Sonjur says firmly. "There will be no more of my people's blood spilled this day. If it is the will of the Creator that we perish, then we must accept it."

"I'm sorry, but that isn't how we operate," Corna says, not bothering to turn around. "We've done nothing wrong. If your people want blood, we'll give it to them."

"I will fight you myself, if I must," Sonjur says, hand falling to his blade.

"Your *keishi* concurs?" I ask softly.

"Yes. The true Eshani would care enough for the people she would rule to agree."

"I..." The words die on my lips. I don't *want* to be their damn Eshani. I don't want to rule anyone. But...

302

"Kettle…" Corna growls in warning, knowing me far too well.

"No more blood," I find myself saying. "Don't kill anyone. That doesn't mean Aurelion's plan doesn't have merit. Scare them. Do you still have any more juice, Corna? Aurelion?"

"I'm nearly spent," Aurelion says, and his haggard face and dull eyes match the weariness in his voice.

"Don't worry, pretty boy," Corna says, stalking over and patting him gently on the cheek. "I've got this."

A familiar voice shouts over the silence. The Amanu, somewhere at the back of the crowd. A few carry the words to the front, and the people's faces twist again in rage. The shout repeats, and one of the men, a hulking brute with a scarred face, steps forward. Like a flood breaking through a dam, the rest follow, surging towards the frail gates.

"Now, Corna," I shout, trying to be heard over the din.

She's already working. Lightning forms between her hands, spreading over her body like living sapphire armor. The strength of her power lifts her from the ground. Electric blue light snaps to the gate, blasting the front ranks backwards into the rest. She shines so brightly I have to squint just to see her. The mob halts, then backs away before the growing storm of power.

One man does not back away. Clad in a midnight Ihera *dimina* slashed with gray, he steps forward and raises his hands. A block of stone the size of a carthorse rips up from the street. With a flash of gray light, the massive stone hurtles towards Corna. I open my lips to cry out a warning, but her lightning has already reacted. Arcing out in a brilliant burst to shatter the stone, her power showers the crowd with harmless pebbles. The man just has the time to look surprised before a bolt of lighting lifts him from the ground and slams him into the front ranks of the awestruck mob.

They're breaking. More try to flee than seek to come forward. Corna's stronger than I ever thought she would be. The

303

Lightning Lord indeed. She's bought us time, time enough perhaps to escape this deathtrap of a city. Even if Aurelion and Corna can't, perhaps I can muster the strength to get us down. They'll be guarding the lifts, but, maybe, a rope of shadow…

A hand slips into mine.

"It's time, Mother," Kit says. "Take our strength. Command the shadow."

Corna shouts in surprise and fear. Without warning, she plummets out of the air like the hand of the Creator slams her to the earth. She crunches into the stone, leg snapping sideways beneath her. With a grunt of agony, the lightning disappears. In the distance, the Amanu floats over the crowd, his hand outstretched in her direction. The people regain their courage the second she's out of sight. Creator damn him.

"We don't have time for hesitation." Kit squeezes my hand with frightening strength. Crackling energy buzzes through my palm. "These people defy you. They wish to kill us all. They deserve to die."

"I…"

I look to Corna, moaning and helpless on the ground. I look to Aurelion, leaning heavily on his sword, bronze eyes staring dully our way. I look to Sario and Hom where they stand shoulder to shoulder near the gate, ready to fight and die to defend the rest of us. I think of Yelden, killed defending my children thousands of miles from his homeland.

Some instinct warns me against allowing this Source, as he called himself, into my soul again. But I think of my children, huddled somewhere upstairs, and the women standing guard over them.

I don't have a choice. Even if I have to go through Sonjur and all of his clan, I will protect my family.

My wall crumbles. Light floods my body. Like the first breath after drowning, like the first sunlight after Winter, the energy fills the empty parts of me and sets my soul afire. The

304

shadow flows at my command, easy as breathing. The strangeness separating us is a distant memory. Through my connection to the shadow… I feel it.

A sea of darkness far beneath our feet. Enough shadow to darken the sun. I cast my senses into the depths and find no end. Beneath the earth, an ocean of living shadow stretches as far as I can feel, and, beyond the edge of feeling, the impression that it encompasses the world.

My shadow is not the last living shadow, as I feared. Shadow didn't die out; it *adapted*. Deep in the earth, in the places where the sun can't reach, shadow thrives.

I almost lose myself in it, but another will directs mine. Foreign, alien, something lurks in the power Kit is granting me. Its mind, its soul, does not feel human. I can't fathom its intent, no more than I can read the winds or the waves. It feels bigger, *greater*, than I can imagine.

But, whatever it is, it reminds me of my task. To take the shadow, to use it to save my family and punish my enemies. With the strength it offers, cleansing Yohru will be trivial.

I stretch out my will, and the shadow below stirs.

Come.

The shadow shifts like a leviathan rousing from slumber. My awareness, sharpened by the energy flooding through me, follows as it begins to rise, to pour out of the earth, abandon its hiding place and return once more—

"No, fledgling."

Far below, the shadow stops. It defies my will. Like waves in an ocean, the shadow forms into… a face. Large as the valley, wise and kind, her mouth, made purely of shadow, turns to a frown.

"This is not the way. Not with that creature filling your soul. Here."

An awareness, staggering in its ancient might, reaches out through the connection to the shadow. The flow of power ceases.

305

The alien presence in my mind disappears. Only I am left, weak and alone, with the mighty strength of shadow.

No, I need him—

"Come to me as you are, fledgling. I will welcome you."

I don't have time. My people…

"Come to me."

I return to my body, forced back by the woman in the shadow.

Chaos reigns.

My brothers hold the gate before the horde of citizens, barely, trying not to use the edge of their blades to remove the hands shoving at the frail gate. Aurelion finds the strength to stagger to join them. Kit lies at my side, staring vacantly at the sky, hand still feebly grasped in mine. Corna has dragged herself to the wall to slump, whimpering, against the tower. Hands are already appearing over the walls, catapulted by the mob.

The first man lands on our side. He charges, face an angry mask. Halfway to me, Aurelion tackles him to the side. But there are more. Many more. Too many. Sario and Hom retreat as people pour over the walls. They throw open the gates, and the mob floods the courtyard.

I reach for the shadow, but I can't feel it. By taking the Source's power again, I've widened the gulf between us. I feel empty, broken, lost in my own body.

So this is it. This is how it ends.

I can't watch as they tear my brothers apart. I hold Kit's hand, and pray. May the rest of the world be right. May the Creator still live, and care. For, after this life, my family deserves nothing but light.

"Umbral'te!"

Umbral, to me.

A voice from my past, familiar, deep, haunting, horrifying. He is not who I wish to reign in my final thoughts.

Light, brighter than the sun, sears through my closed

306

eyelids. The mob screams in fear and shock.

I open my eyes.

A man, limned in golden light, stands before the open gate. The black leather wrapped around his body is matched only by the majesty of his skin. Tall, strong, beautiful, he faces the crowd alone. They wilt before his gaze.

Though I can't see his face, I would know him anywhere.

Sanar.

Chapter 14
Jace

The Seventy-Ninth Day of Summer
In the year 5223, Council Reckoning

"Slowly now, Jace," Juliet warns. "You know what happened last time. And the time before."

The fire glows in tantalizing bursts of orange and red. Like a lover beckoning from the warmth of a bed in Winter, its glow calls to me.

Take me. Use me. Wield me.

My arm, against the demands of my mind, rises to offer an open hand, welcoming, to the flame. It leans forward, an enraptured audience, clinging still to the bits of wood it has charred nearly into oblivion. Its heat on my hand is a desperate peace. I have been cold for so long. If I just…

"Careful," Juliet whispers.

My hand trembles at the word, trembles in time with my soul. I want it. Creator damn it, I *need* it. The world's flame returns to my sight in all its glory. The air in shades of white, the earth beneath my feet in shades of green and ochre and brown, the flame a brilliant golden orange. The fear racing through my veins is not of the flame, but of what it can do to me. The joy it can offer. The warmth.

The *life*.

"That's enough," she says softly.

"Just a little." I try to sound strong, confident, but the words come forth like the desperate beggars I once scorned on the streets of Donir, on their knees in the snow, outstretched hand shaking, not with cold, but with desire. With need. "I can stop myself."

"Enough," she says more firmly. "Not yet."

A tongue of flame lifts from the wood, floating like a ribbon through the air. I can take it, just this little bit of flame. I can take into myself and nurture it, let its flame add to the embers nestled in the center of my chest. Its heat will spread, and life will return to limbs that have been cold so long they've forgotten what it feels to be warm. Just this little ribbon of flame. Just—

My hand is ripped aside. Juliet's crimson power wraps about my arm, stealing me from the flame. I snarl and turn. My hand snaps towards her throat. Lurid red light pulses. The fire of her power, tainted by the metallic light of intent, ensnares my hand. Growling, I drive against the crimson flame wrapped around my arm. For a moment, she resists, but only for a moment, as my hand inches forwards. Her face, cast in scarlet and silver, contorts in fear. The savage joy of victory floods my heart as, trembling, I get close enough to touch her.

That happiness, however primal, pierces the haze of anger shrouding my thoughts. The flames of life fade, leaving behind the dull colors of the mundane forest. Juliet stares at me, eyes wide. My fingers are wrapped around her throat.

With an effort, I drop my hand to my side. The second I release her, she takes a step away from me, crossing her arms over her chest.

I should feel shame, remorse, *something*. But the emptiness left in the absence of the flame does not fill. The coldness in my chest doesn't relent. The only emotion lingering is the bitter aftertaste of anger coating my throat. I could almost feel it again, that life burning through my veins...

"I don't—" Juliet stops and coughs, her hand rising unconsciously to rub at her throat. I must have squeezed harder than I thought. "I don't think we should continue, Jace."

"Not today," I agree, resisting the urge to glance at the still-burning fire. I can hear it, calling to me, longing for me.

309

"Not ever," she says hoarsely.

"What?" I focus on her again, ignoring the siren's call of the flame. "Why? We're making progress. I've never held out that long before."

"You could have killed me, Jace," she whispers, eyes shining. Creator, have I ever seen Juliet cry?

"But I didn't," I say, though the words sound strange and callous in my ears.

"And the next time?" she growls, her voice a challenge. She blinks, and the tears are gone as if they never existed in the first place. "Because there always will be a next time. I've dealt with people like you before, Jace. Dozens of times."

"No, you haven't," I shoot back, turning away from her. "You've never met anyone who has this power."

"Don't pretend you're better than any other addict." I hear her move behind me, but I don't turn. I can't. "I've seen you gaze longingly at the fire. You told me you feel dead without it. You told me you're cold all the time. You try to hide the tremble in your hands every time we come near a cookfire. You might hide it from the others. But not from me. You're an addict whose favorite drug just so happens to be magical."

"You don't know what it's like," I whisper.

"I know how deeply it has you in its thrall," she says, her voice closer. "This is the third time you've convinced me to come out here, and it's the third time you've lost control."

"I just need more practice…" I trail off, unable to convince even myself.

"You need to put it behind you, Jace. Like a drunkard his favorite drink, the only way forward is away."

"I don't… I don't know if I can."

Juliet walks around to stand before me. Dark marks have already begun to blossom on her throat, a testament to my inability to control myself. That sight finally stirs my heart to shame. My hands come up ineffectually, rising halfway towards

310

her before falling hopelessly back to my side. Following my gaze, she reaches up to caress the tender skin and winces.

"I'm sorry," I say helplessly. "I…"

A brief glow of crimson paints the bright green growth of the forest red. The marks fade, her skin returning to its pristine state. The image of their stain remains burned in my memory.

"It is nothing," she says, sweeping her hand through the air as if to cast aside this memory. "Jace, I don't think you should use this power. There is too little we understand. The way it makes you feel is bad enough, but the rest of it… what you did to Itolas… I won't help you control it. Not after this. But I will help you control the urge to *use* it."

"I don't…" I start to say, staring hopelessly into her electric blue eyes. "I don't deserve you."

"No," she agrees, lips pressed into a thin line. "You don't."

She turns without another word and gathers late Summer snow from the shadows of the trees to cast sizzling onto the fire. The desperate edge of sorrow that springs from the fire's death nearly drives me to my knees. Her eyes flick my direction, pity shining from their azure depths. She moves to the trail leading back to the camp and wordlessly offers her hand. After a moment, I take it.

We walk in silence for a half a mile, accompanied only by the sound of songbirds returned from the south, greeting the sun rising over the mountain. Winter never fully releases its icy grip this high into the mountains. The camp is below the snowline, though, so the only white still clinging to the earth rests underneath the eaves of trees or in the shadow of hanging rocks. There is no transient undergrowth at this altitude, yet life still struggles to fill in the gap Winter has left in its absence. Various bushes and saplings, once frozen skeletons of brown, wear coats of new green broken only by fresh buds patiently awaiting warmer weather to open in all their glory. Warmer weather that may never come.

Bitter anger slicks my throat with bile. None of this would be necessary if the Vengeance or the Mason would just teach me. But now, every time the Mason sees me in camp, our conversation is strained and awkward, and he refuses to meet my eye. His confidence and surety must have just been an illusion if one momentary experience would shake him so. And the Vengeance, well, my 'father' spends so little time in camp his presence is no different from the last two decades of my life: nonexistent.

"You are not who you once were," Juliet says suddenly. She turns to me, but I study the path ahead, unable to bring myself to look into her eyes again. A black and burning acid, shame, eats at my stomach like a cancer. "This power has robbed you of what made you special."

"Maybe I was never special. Maybe I was always this... weak."

She pulls me around, her expression thunderous.

"You're a damn fool if you think that, Jace. Where's the boy who helped a leper with her house and listened when she spoke? Where's the boy who risked his life to steal a painting for a stranger, knowing only that it would bring her joy? Where's the boy who earned the respect, and love, of a living legend? Where's the man who earned the highest title of the Shorn before he even knew their purpose? Where's the man who dared enter the domain of the Master of Beasts to fight a monster and rescue his friend?"

"None of that makes me special," I say, still avoiding her gaze. "I hardly knew what I was doing most of the time. I was young and stupid for a lot of it, and blinded by revenge and sadness for the rest."

"If you don't cut out this self-pitying bullshit, Creator help me, I'll hurt you so badly you'll *need* me to keep you breathing." With startling strength, she wrenches my arm down until I'm forced to meet her eyes. "You saved my life. When I fell to the

312

snow, when I gave everything I could to save you, I felt my soul leave my body. I was at peace. I was *dead*, Jace. I have no doubt. But I *heard your voice*. I felt your will. I came back. I didn't have to, but I did. For you. Can't you see? I loved the man you were, Jace. I still love the man I know exists beneath all this. Eternal damn it, tell me I'm wrong to do so, and I'll walk away. Tell me the man I love is gone."

I can do nothing but stare. Her words fall like arrows from the sky, sharp and deadly. I can't tell whether to embrace them or flinch away. Love? Is that what I feel? Is that what I *felt?* For, standing here before this remarkable woman, I can't stir my tongue to move. I can't stir my heart to beat. The world remains... dull.

"Juliet... I..."

I can't finish the sentence, not even sure what it is I'm trying to say. What I *can* say. She seems to find something in my eyes, though, releasing a sigh and nodding to herself.

"Good enough." She yanks me down the trail by my hand. "I am not so vain as to think you love me, too. Especially not now." She spins back, jabbing a finger in my face. "But, if you care anything for me, or yourself, you won't use that power. It is eating you away from the inside out."

"I..." This is Juliet. The woman I made my moral touchstone before I ever really knew her. If I won't listen to her, who will I listen to? "You're right. This power is... evil."

"What a foolish thing to say," she says, setting off again. "The power isn't evil, but your need for it is. Besides, the only reason I agreed to help you in the first place was because, before you knew what this power was or could do, you used it to *save* a life, not take one."

***

The morning stretches are in full swing before we make it back to the glade I've called home for nearly two seasons. I start to move towards the end of the line when I catch sight of him.

Largely unremarkable from the rest, the Vengeance flows through the movements with the grace of long practice. His eyes light on me, and he steps from the line with a short bow towards James Elthe. The last time I saw him, our blood flowed into the soil of this very clearing. We have avoided each other for over a season.

His expression remains unreadable as he moves into my path.

As we come face to face, I let my gaze rove over his features. Am I there? The shape of my jaw? The curve of my lips? I don't see it. His skin is paler than mine, his hair fair and straight. If this man is my father, there is little that I took from him. He seems to be offering me the same scrutiny, though what he concludes he doesn't say.

"I have need of you," he says finally.

"Come again?" I ask, surprised.

"I offered you the luxury of finishing your ill-advised practice out in the woods," he says coldly. The words imply impatience, but his voice remains flat and empty. "We have precious little time."

"For what?"

"Kranos has left the safety of his armies and travels west alone. He is vulnerable, and exposed. We may never get a better opportunity to take him in the open."

"Wait, wait, wait," I say, waving my hands. "Kranos? The Master of Beasts? Isn't he in the Khalintars?"

"Yes," the Vengeance says, as if he doesn't recognize the extraordinary contradiction he's just voiced.

"I'm going to need some help on this one," I say, turning up my hands.

"Altos can only take one... passenger, for lack of a better word," Elthe says, stepping to the Vengeance's side. "When he came to us, we all agreed that you should go with him."

"Why me?"

"Because you're the best of us," he says, shrugging. "We

can't send anything but our best. If we can take Kranos down, this whole damn war becomes degrees of magnitude easier."

"My information is already nearly a tenday out of date. We need to move now if we're to strike," the Vengeance says.

"You're going to fly us to the western Khalintars to kill the Master of Beasts. That's the plan. The whole plan."

"Yes. Are you ready?"

"Am I *what?*" I shout in disbelief. "Creator, I thought I was just coming back to sword practice this morning."

"And what do you practice *for?*" the Vengeance asks, raising his eyebrows a hair.

"Don't I need, I don't know, supplies? A coat? Anything?"

"You have your blade, which is all you will require." He raises his hand, and a white flash heralds a gust of wind. A small pack flies into his hand on an invisible cushion of solid air. "I have enough food for both of us, and it's quite warm where we're going."

"Do I get a say in this?" I ask, glancing at Juliet, who looks on with concern.

"Of course," the Vengeance says. "But are you willing to risk this opportunity by sending a lesser fighter?"

I don't have an argument for that. Though he doesn't know me well, Reknor must have given him enough for him to know which levers to pull. With a frustrated grunt, I move to stand with him, but Juliet grabs my arm and puts her lips to my ear.

"Don't use it, Jace. We don't know what will happen if you do. No matter how desperate it might seem, *don't.*"

Her sapphire eyes seem alight with a fire of their own, burning into me with unmistakable intensity. I nod, once, and she releases me, pushing me gently towards the waiting Vengeance.

"So, what do I do?" I say, trying to still the whirlwind of my thoughts. After a season of quiet, things are happening far too quickly for me to keep up.

"Turn around." It feels awkward, but I turn. His arm wraps

315

around my chest, a bar made of sinew and steel. "Take a deep breath."

The symbol of his power overcomes the sunrise and bathes the glade in white. Wind rattles the trees, swirling about us like a miniature hurricane. Pressure builds, invisible yet tangible. The wind abruptly dies. The glade feels empty of air, the world holding its breath.

"Try not to scream."

"Wha—"

Wind slams into us. My lungs compress into my feet. Trees blur past. The edge of my vision creeps in, gray and wavering. Against his direction, I open my mouth to scream, but nothing leaves my lips, air flooding down my throat too powerfully to be forced out. My eyes shut against the rushing wind. My thoughts move towards darkness.

We level out, and the pressure eases from my chest. I take in several deep gasps of air, though it feels like I'm trying to fill a bucket one mouthful at a time. The air was already thin high in the mountains, and now it barely satisfies. The wind rushes across my face, but like a heavy breeze rather than a crushing gale. I crack one eye open.

The land is a vista of miniature perfection, like a map made real. The forest stretches as far as the eye can see, one broad sea of waving limbs and rustling leaves. What little air is left in my lungs leaves me in a gasp, forgetting for a moment how much I need to breathe. I heave in a breath and blink away the spots drifting before my eyes as quickly as I can. I don't want to miss anything.

We're flying, as only birds can fly, so high above the ground my mind shies away from the thought of falling. A distant river treks through the forest, glittering in the bright Summer sun. The slope of the mountain falls away until the trees are little more than blurs of green and brown. It's only been minutes, but already a distant plain wavers into view to the south. This high, we can see for miles, yet even so the grassland of Firdana is a hundred miles distant if it's a step. How fast are we moving?

Against my will, my eyelids begin to droop. Whether through the shallow breaths I'm forced to draw or some art of the Vengeance's, the lack of air weighs heavily on my eyelids. I fight to keep my eyes open as long as I can, but darkness creeps in, and I drift to sleep amongst the clouds.

***

My eyes open again to total darkness. A titan's roar fills the air, loud enough to deafen. It's impossible to tell where we are, but I'm flying, effortlessly, floating through the air, with only the Vengeance to… shit. I can't feel his arm. I can't see a thing. An image of the ground rushing up to meet me flashes across my mind.

The world lights up in brilliant white.

A stream of pure fire covers my body, wrapped around each limb in a tight embrace. Terror screams into existence.

The fire is on me, *consuming* me. I need to get it *off.* The bright crimson flame of my arms cut through the white like a headsman's ax. A pulse of golden light breaks up what is left. The metallic sheen in the white disappears, and the fire disperses into the wind. Any last remnant of silver floats up into the night.

When the wind begins to rush against my face from below, two things hit me at once.

The Vengeance was holding me aloft with his power, which I just neatly severed. So I wasn't falling.

And *now* I am.

The darkness of normal sight has disappeared behind a wall of bright fire. The white of the air rushes past at startling speed, laced with a constant rippling echo of purple. I've no idea what purple fire is, and I don't have time to think about it. Below, and growing close by the second, a limitless field of azure flame stretches as far as the eye can see in all directions. For a second, I think that we're over a field of ice and snow, but this blue light is

317

moving, pulsing... rotating.

The Maelstrom. My mind can barely encompass the primordial force playing tyrant to the ocean. The churning waters spin with the ancient inevitability of time. The center, wide enough to swallow Donir itself, rushes faster, devouring the ocean for miles uncounted. High as I am, the near edge of the mighty vortex is just visible, or what I think is the edge. That blue... is it...different?

Creator save my bones, I forgot for a moment *why* I could see so far. I open my mouth to shout, but the wind steals any words I might manage. The Vengeance left me. Surely, there are easier ways to murder me than dropping me into the *Eternal-damned Maelstrom*. As the ocean's surface barrels towards my face, the purple fire burns brighter as my ears fill with the extraordinary, deafening roar of the ocean's fury.

I should probably try to scream again, but instead my thoughts stray to eyes of startling blue, and the words she dared to share with me.

Love...

White fire, burning with the metallic tint of intent, whips around my chest. My head snaps forward as the solid air jerks me to a halt. The spray of crashing waves bathes my face in ocean water. I taste salt. The iron bar of the Vengeance's arm regains purchase on my chest, and his power flares again and again to fight the pull of the earth and climb away from the sea.

After a while, we level out again, nowhere near as high as before. The white fire of his power is dimmer, weaker, a pale imitation of the extraordinary light I woke to. The roar of the Maelstrom cuts off suddenly, the purple fire rebounding from a wall of solid white.

"What did you do?" he mutters in my ear, his voice weary.

"I don't know," I answer honestly. "I woke up suddenly and panicked."

"That's the second time," he says, his words coming

318

slowly. "That's the second time you've cut me off from the wind."

"Are you okay?" I ask nervously, as the light again dims around us.

If he falters, there is no hope for us. Halfway between the continents, caught in a world-devouring vortex, we will quickly be pulled beneath the waves. It takes me a second to realize that we haven't left the Maelstrom behind.

"Yes," he growls stubbornly, though that I get any emotion at all sets warning bells jangling in my mind. "We're in a pocket of natural wind nearly strong enough to carry us unaided. For the time being, we are safe."

"For the time being?"

"I just need to gather my strength." He pauses for a moment, flying in the strange silence of the bubble of wind surrounding us. "And my focus."

"Maybe..." I swallow, fighting the empty hole in my chest. "Save yourself. Drop me."

"No!" he snaps, his arm tightening around me. "I have the strength, damn it. Just give me a moment."

I don't bother to answer, letting the man concentrate. Every now and then, a flicker of metallic light arcs from him and into the air, disappearing as we fly on. The pulses of power are subtle, surgical, so brief I barely notice them. Whatever he's doing, it doesn't seem to be having any effect. After a while, the adrenaline flooding my veins fades, and the fire of the world with it. Below, where the Maelstrom swirls, there is only darkness.

"You weren't supposed to wake up," he says after what feels like an hour. "And even then..."

"Yeah," I say softly. "I... I've always been afraid of fire. When I woke up, I saw your power all over me, and I just... I couldn't control myself."

"You're a Blade of the A'kai'ano'ri," he says flatly, the words as much an accusation as a declaration. "Trained by Telias the Warmheart. Did he not talk to you about control? What did he

319

always say… something about a mason, or an artist, or something."

"Both," I say, feeling the strange urge to laugh. "He said I should fight like a master mason places his chisel."

"Sounds like the sort of thing he would say."

"Is he… have you heard if he's still alive?"

"I don't know." The words stretch between us. Are they a chasm too wide to navigate? Or a bridge to cross the divide? "If he is, he's no longer in Donir. I know that much."

We lapse into silence for a while. My thoughts of Reknor, or Telias, or whoever he really is, are somber. Part of me wants to believe he's still alive, that the Sealord would see value in keeping him breathing. If he's no longer in the dungeons, though… an image of twisted limbs and broken bodies flashes across my eyes. If the Sealord gave Reknor over to his general…

I chase the thought away as best I can, trying to focus on our current predicament. The Vengeance doesn't seem to be faltering. I can't see the brightness of his flame any longer, so it's hard to tell if he's still expending power to do, well, whatever he's doing. The winds remain constant.

Minutes pass. Maybe even an hour. The longer the darkness looms below us, the more terror begins to claw at the edges of my reason. Maybe I'd rather talk about Reknor after all.

"You were friends with him once, weren't you?"

"Brothers," the Vengeance corrects. "I've never known a man I trusted more."

"Then why did you…?"

"He broke our laws," he says, his voice steady. "He, a Shaper of the Council, convinced King Paloran and all of his eastern allies to send an army to unseat Helikos. We were forbidden from leading men, by a law older than any kingdom now in existence, and he chose to break it."

"But he was right," I say angrily.

"That's easy to say now," he says, his voice softening. I

want to turn to look at his face, but I'm afraid I'll disrupt whatever he's trying to do to the wind. "My duty was sacred. *Sacred.* Ten thousand years, there has been a Vengeance, since before the rise of the Eternal. What laws the Shapers agree to follow, the Vengeance must enforce. There can be no exceptions, no leniency given. I swore an oath to my fellow Shapers and the Creator himself the day I took up the mantle, and I followed that oath so long as it had meaning."

"Blindly," I mutter. "Even into the world's destruction."

"Even then," he agrees sadly. "Helikos knew me, knew my loyalty and my sense of duty. Partly, I am to blame for allowing him to play me, but more, he manipulated the others into *deserving* my blade. Many people think that I followed along as a dutiful and naive pawn, too dumb to realize what was happening until it was too late. Few know that, even now, all of the Shapers I executed deserved their sentence."

"What did they do?"

"First was a young Shaper of Lightning. Klor, I think his name was. I'm not sure if Helikos did something to him, or if he was just naturally insane, but he didn't last long enough on the Council for it to matter. Three years after we discovered him, I found him blasting merchant vessels with lightning outside Sail for no better reason than he thought it was funny to watch the humans dodge the sharks."

"How come I never heard about that?" I ask, blinking in surprise.

"Helikos wanted to cover it up as much as we could. Smooth over the grieving families with starsilver, that kind of thing. All to maintain the dignity of the Council, of course."

"Of course."

"The next was Ithira, the Master of Metal, a few days before the Desolation. She had Shaped an extraordinary number of coins, starsilver and gold and the like, into Khalintari currency. Had she been allowed to proceed, she would have ruined the

Republic economy for decades. The Council of Shapers was not to interfere with human civilization unless we all deemed it necessary. When I confronted her, she openly stated her desire to destabilize the Republic. I dismissed her outright when she told me she was following the Sealord's orders. Why would the Master of the Council want to disrupt one of the most stable civilizations in recent memory? It just made no sense."

"That would have made their conquering far easier," I say slowly, realization dawning. "If, right when he took power, the Republic was in economic turmoil..."

"Yeah. Again, easy to say now. She fought me, in the end. The Swordplague, as they call it, luckily only impacted the northern regions of the Republic. The last, of course, was Telias."

"Your 'brother.'"

"Who I spared, despite having committed the most egregious of the sins among the three. The second I left, Helikos made his move. He murdered the Master of Earth personally, and his hired assassins slaughtered the Master of Roots in the southern Kinlen forest. By the time I returned, he had claimed the throne, murdered my wife, and stolen my daughter. In my despair, I walked right into his brand-new throne room and tried to end it there. They were ready for me. I was lucky to escape with my life."

"You fought them both?" I ask incredulously. "Together? What about the Mason?"

"Itolas was out of contact, somewhere in the Khalintari deserts. At that point, I didn't know who to trust, *if* there was anyone I could trust. And I wasn't entirely sane, just then. Nadine..." He trails off, unable to continue for a moment. He coughs lightly to clear his throat. "The ashes of our home were still warm when I returned. What would you have done?"

The final question is spoken in a voice that falters, the Vengeance's flat tones wavering for a moment. It wouldn't surprise me if it was because he hasn't spoken this many words at once in a long time.

"Why are you telling me all this?" I ask finally.

He is silent for a long time, long enough that I begin to wonder if he heard me.

"If what your friend said is true, it is the least you're owed."

"Whoa, listen," I say, wanting to look the man in the eye to impress my sincerity upon him. "Even if she *is* right, you don't owe me anything. I never much cared who my father was, not with Rosie to look after me. I never wanted to go looking for you. I didn't need you before, and I don't need you now."

"Fair," he says, shifting his grip on my chest.

"You owe me nothing."

We drift in silence for a time. I wish we could turn over and fly on our backs. I imagine the stars, here among the heavens over a world of darkness, would be unbelievable.

"I think," the Vengeance says after a moment. "If we're going to try this, we might as well try it now. If we wait any longer... well, let's just say it's time."

"Time?" I blurt out, alarmed. "Time for what?"

He doesn't respond aside from a flash of white light. I squint at the sudden glare. The symbol on the back of his hand burns like a purified sun, white and clean and *bright*. I brace myself for something drastic, an abrupt acceleration to the west like a bolt of lightning, but the Vengeance is after something more subtle, apparently.

The first sign anything has changed is that the pocket of wind allowing us to talk falls away. The wind returns at speed, ripping at my hair and clothing, its ephemeral fingers trying to slow us enough to fall. The rumble of the Maelstrom returns in full force, though there's something different about it. Another sound, lighter and yet more immediate, begins to play melody to the thundering bass of the churning water. My hair, long plastered to my scalp, floats weightlessly about my face. The wind swirls about us like the current of a lazy brook.

And we fly.

"Don't move," the Vengeance whispers, his arm loosening about my chest, then disappearing. "I don't have the power to save you again. If you lose control, I will have to leave you behind. Relax. Sleep if you can. Regardless, *Blade*, control yourself, and *do not move.*"

"Okay," I say dubiously, trying to ignore the gibbering voice in the back of my head screaming terror into the darkness. He let me go. He *let me*— "How long?"

"Until we reach dry land," he says evenly.

I hardly feel anything, but the sound of the Maelstrom fades, then disappears in the space of a few minutes. I don't dare reach for the sight of the fire. I can't risk disrupting whatever he's done. As the roar fades into the gentler whisper of passing wind, a mystery returns to the forefront of my mind. The Maelstrom, thousands of years old and miles-wide, glows with the metallic light of intent.

Someone, alive or dead, created it *on purpose.*

***

The night stretches into an interminable fit of frightened boredom. Every time I take a second to think about what is actually happening, my mind spirals into horrible imaginings of slamming into the inky black water at unbelievable speed. Of surviving the fall, yet knowing I've been sentenced to death, so far from land I may as well swim down until my breath fails me. Each time, I have to force my fists to relax, force my racing heart to slow.

When I can let my mind wander, the fear recedes. Like a wagon following the same track a thousand times, my thoughts circle between three disparate quandaries.

The first is the impossibility that the Vengeance is my father. Juliet's story is a tattered tapestry woven of threads that do not match. It is a tale from the *Enchantress*, one of lost princes

324

and the mysterious and magical power of love. My mind refuses to accept the concept, though it seems like *he* thinks it might be possible. Even though he's talking, sharing things I doubt anyone outside of the Mason knows about his life, he didn't bring me on this journey because of our—alleged—connection. I was just the best fighter available.

Which brings me to the second problem and the entire purpose of this mad quest, that we're to kill the Master of Beasts. I see his towering form and that crimson light in my nightmares. Each detail that comes to mind is more horrifying than the last: the realization that his wounds were healing as fast as I could make them; the strange, gurgling laugh as his cut throat gaped open, something no man should survive; the frightful strength that blasted through my blocking sword and launched me into the bars of an iron cage. The Vengeance is a legendary swordsman, and a mighty Shaper as well. Having fought them both, though, I think I'd fight the Vengeance a hundred times out of a hundred. At least, when he's struck, he bleeds.

The last fear worming in my gut has nothing to do with the others. Juliet said she loves me. The thought is equal parts joy and terror. If the way my breath seems to falter when she smiles is love, then I love her. If the way she makes my heart steady and unsteady at once is love, then I love her. If the way her words burrow under my skin and make themselves a part of me is love, then I most definitely love her.

"The only reason I agreed to help you in the first place was because, before you knew what this power was or could do, you used it to save a life, not take one."

The memory of saving her life feels like a hazy dream. Golden light rising to the sky, dissipating on the wind, my desperate urge to save it, to save her. There was no hunger, no frightful need. I still felt warm afterwards. I still felt alive.

It is with a start that I realize I haven't felt like... that... since we've taken off. The extraordinary sights, the terror and adrenaline, and the startling conversation have brought me the closest to normal that I've felt since the moment I stole Itolas' fire.

The recognition of its absence brings the desperate desire roaring back. The world's fire flickers across my sight, glorious, the white flame of the Vengeance's strength engulfing me. It is beautiful, bold, so much more tempting than the light of normal fire. What would it feel like to taste the soul of the Vengeance himself?

My hand rises of its own accord, reaching towards the white fire burning through the night.

Just like it reached for Juliet's throat.

The look of fear and sorrow etched into her features.

Every muscle in my body flexes at once, from my eyelids to my toes. I drive memories of Juliet like knives into the hunger, strengthened by my shame, tempered by my hard-won control. Slowly, trembling, I force my hand back to my side.

I will not be ruled.

The second I wrest control back from my need, another thought strikes me.

Creator save my soul.

It never occurred to me, so desperate was the need, to consider that I would *die* if I broke the Vengeance's concentration in the middle of the ocean.

***

I blink myself awake, shocked to find the world still dark. I feel strangely rested, like I've slept for hours and have just now awoken at the first touch of sunlight. Slowly craning my head to look between my feet, I can see that the horizon is just lightening back to the east. As I watch, light blossoms behind us, enough to see by at least, and I gasp.

We're only ten paces above the dark mass of the ocean.

The waves whip past in a dizzying blur. Without anything to relate our speed to, I didn't appreciate how damn *fast* we've been traveling. Even as I look, though, it seems like we sink a little closer to the water.

"Uh," I say, thinking to call out, but stymied by what to call the man. Vengeance? Altos? I'll join the Eternal in her prison before I ever call him *father*. I'm saved from having to choose because his voice answers my confused grunt almost immediately. The weakness in it chills my bones.

"Almost," he whispers, his voice breathy in my ear. "Almost... there."

"Close enough to swim?" I ask, squinting forwards. I can't see, but the light is still growing.

"Not... yet."

We sink another pace. The spray from the sea coats my face. At this speed, I imagine we'll skip across the water like stones launched from a sling. I cut off the image with a shudder before I can think about what that might feel like.

"How much longer?"

"Almost... there."

He must be delirious, and for good reason. We've flown from the high peaks of the Claw Mountains in the heart of the Kinlen Forest and crossed the Great Sea to, hopefully, the eastern coastline of the Khalintars. That same journey on foot would take... two seasons? Longer? How much power did the man expend to take us so far so fast? How much power does the man *possess* to even have the thought to do it?

I look forward again, desperate for any sign of land. We've sunk low enough that the gale swirling about us rides the waves, lifting up and dropping down between them. A particularly high crest shows a line of darkness in front of us. A spark of hope ignites in my chest as we rush down the other side and slide up the next. It is land, unmistakably.

"We're going to make it!" I shout, restraining myself from pumping my fist. "You've done it!"

He doesn't respond. I risk a glance over my shoulder. He flies behind me, and the symbol on his hand flickers fitfully. He

327

only has to hold out for another few minutes, and then…

Oh. Shit.

"Vengeance!" I shout back at him in sudden panic. His eyelids flicker, but he doesn't respond. "Vengeance! Altos!"

Slowly, laboriously, his eyes open, glassy and unfocused.

"You have to slow us down, Altos! If we keep flying this fast… just slow us down!"

If the image of us skipping across the water had been painful, the thought of plowing into a mountainside at this speed nearly stops my heart itself. I can't tell if he hears me or if he's finally out of power, but our flight dips towards the waves, and we slow with a shudder that rattles my teeth. Air whistles against my face, and I just have time to brace myself before the full force of the wind rips away the bubble we've been traveling in. With the wind roaring in my ears, we start slowing, *fast*…

"No, wait—"

Rather than riding the next wave, we continue to fly level, moving faster than I'd like. I just have time to raise my hands before we plough straight into the water. The impact blasts the breath from my lungs. The undercurrent spins me about. For a second, I can't tell which way is up or down. Opening my burning eyes, glowing light from the sunrise to the east illuminates the way to the surface.

I almost miss the limp body floating a few strokes from mine. Gritting my teeth against the fire in my lungs, I swim over and grab a hold of his collar, driving towards the surface. My sword weighs us down, and no doubt his as well, but I just manage to drag us into the sunlight, lungs heaving in greedy gulps of air.

The waves are large, but gentle. The Vengeance is out cold, or as good as, his lips and eyelids twitching. The bag of provisions he brought for the journey bobs to the surface, still strapped to his back. As we crest the next wave, I have to stifle a groan at the distance to the shore.

"Alright," I mutter, turning my back to the shore and kicking like a frog, arms wrapped carefully around his chest. The sword at my hip tilts us towards the bottom and fouls every third kick, but I can't leave it behind. Not knowing what we're here to do. At least his little bag still floats, lessening *some* of the dead weight I'm carrying. "You got us here, and maybe killed yourself in the process. Least I can do is get us to the beach."

***

The gritty sand is heaven on my salt-stained cheek. The wind takes the water from our clothes and stings the back of my neck with sand. I barely feel it. The sun, hotter by the minute, nears midday before I can force myself up with an involuntary groan. I glance at the Vengeance, who has stopped twitching and seems to have fallen into a more genuine rest.

"I assume you didn't bring anything to set up camp with?" I ask his vacant face. "Didn't think so. Guess I'll have to get you out of the sun before it burns you to a crisp. Just... give me a minute."

Taking several deep breaths, I heave myself to my knees. Trying not to disturb him too much, I shift him until I can pull his bag out from under him. The flap is tied tightly, the knot swelled such that my fumbling, wrinkled fingers can't make any progress. With a guilty glance towards his sleeping face, I draw my sword and saw the cord in half.

"Sorry," I mutter, opening the flap with expectations of seawater and shapeless goop.

To my surprise, the contents of the bag remain dry, if a bit battered. I snatch out the waterskin and take a deep gulp, the cool water filling my chest with life. I break off half of a wedge of yellow cheese and a goodly portion of a thin loaf of bread, alternating bites between them. When my stomach is full, I prop the Vengeance on my lap and dribble some water into his slack mouth. When he swallows, a fear I didn't let myself name falls off my shoulders.

"You know," I say conversationally, soaking some bread in the water to press between his lips. "If someone had told me a year ago that I'd be nursing the Vengeance back to health on a sunny beach in the Khalintars, I'd have told them to stick to realism in their fancy stories. Eternal's shriveled tits, if someone had told me that *yesterday*, I'd have said the same thing."

The Vengeance makes a noise, his mouth moving gently. I lean closer.

"Me... too..."

Chapter 15
Iliana

The Eighty-First Day of Summer
In the year 5223, Council Reckoning

Waking feels like swimming against a current of darkness. It is only with stubborn effort that I manage to pry open my eyes. Flickering firelight off to my right illuminates a smooth stone ceiling, unadorned and featureless. A cot of questionable quality presses to my back.

This is no room I recognize. I shift onto an elbow. Twin rows of the uncomfortable cots fill the room, though only one other is occupied. A man with a ragged brown beard shot through with gray lies on his back two cots down. His face looks haggard in sleep. An eye patch poorly conceals an old injury across his right eye.

Creator's name, where am I?

The man's lone eye springs open, and he rolls to face me. He searches my face, concern and care written in every line of his. After a moment he opens his mouth to speak, then thinks better of it as a concerned frown pulls at his lips. There is an intensity to how he watches me, a tension I can't decipher.

"Good morning," he says slowly, his voice rich and warm and musical. He glances at the stone surrounding us and shakes his head. "At least, I think it's morning."

"Hello," I say, sitting up and swinging my feet over the bed.

"How do you feel?" he asks, mirroring my movements.

"Rested." I raise my arms in a delicious stretch. "I feel like I've been sleeping for days."

"Good. That's good." He lifts his hands towards me, then awkwardly returns them to his lap. I get the feeling that this man is rarely out of his depth, but right now he's swimming in deep waters indeed. "What do you remember?"

"About how I got here? Nothing at all," I say, feeling my cheeks warm. "I'm so sorry if this is rude, and you seem to know *me*, but I can't recall your name."

"It isn't rude in the slightest," he says graciously, though I get the distinct impression I *should* know his name. He stands and takes a slow step towards me. He's going out of his way not to appear threatening, but he needn't worry. Whoever he is, I'm certain he won't hurt me. How, I haven't the slightest. He takes another step around the bed. "My name is Telias."

"A pleasure to meet you, Telias. I'm…" For an embarrassing moment, my name doesn't pass my lips. I shake my head with a smile. "Maybe I got a knock on the head. My name is Iliana, but you can call me Ily."

"Charmed," he says with a grin. Still, there is pain behind that smile, some unnamed sorrow.

"Telias, I'm sorry again, but I get the feeling I *should* know you. Have we met?"

"Once or twice," he says, casting his eyes to the ground. "You've… been through a lot lately. It isn't surprising that you don't remember me."

"I—"

A shout of alarm sounds from outside the room, echoing like we're in a tunnel, the words in a language I recognize dimly as Khalin. A girl answers in a sweet voice filled with laughter. The man grumbles under his breath, just audible over the sound of small feet pattering on stone. A thin, pretty Khalintari girl slides to a stop at the entrance to the room, breaking into a wide grin on seeing me.

"Ily!" she exclaims, laughter in her voice. "I'm so glad you're up!"

332

"Have I... have I been out long?" I ask, scrunching my eyes against a dull headache mounting in my temples.

"Not too long," she says, her grin faltering. She comes to my side, and her small fingers intertwine with mine. "Don't push it. You've been through a lot."

"So I hear," I mutter, pressing a hand to the side of my head to contain the spike of pain. "I keep apologizing, but I just can't seem to remember—"

"Jynn!" the girl says brightly, her smile once again lighting up her face.

A man appears at the door, his dark eyes intense above handsome Khalintari features. A light beard accentuates the line of his jaw and lends him a rakish air. Even as the thought crosses my mind, the corner of his mouth rises into a smirk. He carries two heavy leather bags, one thrown over his shoulder and another in hand at this side, both bulging to bursting with... something.

"Good morning, princess," he says, the smirk disappearing from his face. He glances at the bearded man and gives him a nod. "Masterful acting job, Warmheart. I don't think we'd have pulled it off without you."

"I'm not entirely sure what you've 'pulled off,' to tell the truth," Telias answers, folding his arms across his chest. "And, depending on what you have to tell me right now, I might not have been acting. Did you...?"

"No," he says, rolling his eyes. "I did the opposite."

"What do you mean, the opposite?"

"Kranos managed to marry his power over the body with his power over the mind. His influence was so pervasive because her own body fed the manipulation. He didn't need to be anywhere near her for his suggestion to spread. It was brilliant, really."

"But," Jynn interjects, skipping over and nudging the Khalintari in the ribs. "Bastian, clever boy that he is, didn't remove the connection. He changed it."

"Into what?" Telias asks, tensing.

"She's untouchable," she answers, eyes flicking to me. "We couldn't get back into her mind if it would save our lives. And neither can he."

My head starts to spin. It isn't hard to gather that they're talking about me, but I have no idea what they're hinting at. Manipulation? Something to do with my mind? Who are these people?

"That's... elegant," Telias continues, surprised. "Are you sure?"

"Though I imagine our forgetful friend is a bit confused by all this, we're quite sure," Jynn says, offering me an apologetic smile. "Since I can only *imagine* how she's feeling right now."

"You're speaking like... like you're the Master of Thought," I say slowly.

"Got it in one!" Jynn says happily, raising a hand. A mesmerizing symbol glowing with silver light blooms on the edge of her palm.

"So are you why I can't remember where I am?" I ask, though I think I can divine the answer. I'm not sure if I should feel afraid or violated or both.

"Unfortunately," she says, her adorable face falling. "We don't have time for a real explanation, but I want you to know that you *asked* us to. For... a lot of reasons."

Us?

The Khalintari man—Bastian, apparently—glances off into the middle distance, his eyes going vacant. When he comes to, he tosses a full pack to Telias, handing the other off to Jynn. She moves to me immediately, nimble fingers already pulling open the drawstrings.

"You're right about one thing," he says, refocusing on the present. "We don't have time. Shift change is coming, and they'll notice their comrades' absence. Clothes are in here, old man."

Telias immediately bends to pull several garments out of

334

the bag, stripping out of his shirt without a hint of shame. His body hangs thin and slack on his broad frame. He looks old, worn, yet still strong, like a rock standing proudly against the desert wind. He sorts through the clothing with Bastian's help, hiding his limbs in gossamer-thin white wool. Jynn approaches me with the other bag, already drawing out similar garb for me.

"Wait," I say, my voice hardly above a whisper. She doesn't seem to hear me. "Wait!"

Jynn glances up at me, frowning.

"We don't have time—"

"Then *make* time!" I practically shout, trying desperately to stifle the panic rising in my chest. A flash of emerald light illuminates the room, and dust leaps into the air and dances about in agitation.

"Whoa, okay, uh, Telias?" Jynn says, the silver symbol on her hand pulsing brighter. "I can't... I could use a little help here."

Telias' face softens as he looks my way. He steps towards me, hands spread before him like he's approaching a skittish horse. Even though I can see right through what he's doing, his movements are strangely soothing.

"Iliana—"

"Ily," I correct automatically.

"Ily," he says gently. "I promise that I'll explain everything as soon as we're safe. I'll answer any question you have, any at all. Right now, though, we are *not* safe. There are people here who will try to control you if given the chance. They want your power for their own."

"As the Master of Earth?" I ask, feeling steadied by his voice. He looks relieved that I'm aware of my own power. As if I would forget *that*. "What do they need me to do, move a pile of dirt?"

"Not quite," he says, smiling. "They believe that Bastian made you more, well, pliable to their demands, when instead he gave you freedom."

"Why did I trust them to do this? How did they *both* do it?" I whisper, low enough that only he can hear. I don't give him time to answer. "Telias, why can't I remember anything? I've tried, really tried, and I just can't. I see a few images, a garden maybe, a face without a name. Nothing is connected. Nothing makes sense. Everything else is blank."

He stares at me in sympathy for long enough that Jynn shifts, white clothes in hand.

"I'll tell you," he says, passing a hand before his eyes. "But then we have to leave. For your safety. Fair enough?"

"As long as I believe you," I say reluctantly.

"Your mind was… poisoned, for lack of a better word, ever since you were a child. Jynn and Bastian fought to purge that poison from your mind. Your amnesia is an unfortunate side effect of the cure."

The words make less sense than if he told me rain has decided to fall up.

"Who did the poisoning? How could Jynn *and* Bastian do anything to me? There is only one Master of each element."

"Those are complicated questions, based on a long-standing assumption that has, quite recently, been proven false." Telias takes a deep breath and offers me his hand. "I can't imagine how confusing this has to be for you. Just know that everything we do, and have done, is for you."

I have no reason to trust him. He could be lying, the little girl standing before me blocking my memories even now, using her Creator-given power to influence me to go with them. This could all be some elaborate ruse to get me to… what? My head aches as I try desperately to recall what I should want, or fear. Who was I?

Stone corridors, soldiers in aquamarine armor, a brush through my hair… I was important, respected.

Creator damn it.

I have no reason to trust him, but I do.

I take the white clothing Jynn holds in my direction, shocked by how light it is. Smoother than silk, light as the air, I've never felt anything softer.

Or have I?

Ignoring the twinge of dismay at the impossible question, I turn from the men and, with Jynn's help, don the strange garments. They wrap tightly around my waist and wrists, loosely everywhere else. A pair of narrow but sturdy leather shoes cling to my ankles and, with the long pants tucked in, seal away any exposure to the air. Jynn motions for me to bend down and expertly twists my hair into a tight bun, covering my head with more white wool when it's finished. The cloth is so sheer I almost feel naked.

"Ah," Jynn says, stepping back to review her handiwork. "Perfect."

"I can't deny it's comfortable, in an am-I-really-wearing-anything sort of way, but why exactly am I in this... outfit?" I ask.

"It's what the slaves wear when they head out into the desert," Bastian answers, turning around from where he and Telias politely looked the other way. "Loose enough to keep the sun from your skin, light enough to let in the breeze."

"Desert?" I can't help but ask.

"Not much of a choice, neh?" he says, his handsome smirk returning. "Only enemies in the city."

"I don't even know *what* city I'm in—"

A piercing cry, deep and strange, reverberates through the corridor, its echoes chased by a distant scream. The other three all share knowing, alarmed looks, though I have no idea what animal would, or even could, make that kind of sound. Whatever it is, I don't want to find out. Bastian turns to Jynn immediately.

"Do you know the way out? They've been watching me too closely for casual exploration."

"Follow the corridor east a hundred and twelve paces, go right, then take the second door on your right," Jynn snaps, her girlish cheer instantly replaced with a general's command. "Follow that tunnel straight, ignoring all others. You'll be outside the walls before sunrise. I'll distract them as long as I can."

"Wait, your paces, or mine?" Bastian asks. He grins when Jynn looks affronted. "Thanks. Be careful."

"Bastian?" she calls as he turns to leave. "Hurry."

He gives her a nod and tosses a full pack to Telias. Snatching a torch from its sconce, he shoulders the second bag and steps out of sight. The one-eyed man throws the strap over his shoulder, moving out the door without question. With a shaky sigh, I force myself after them.

The second I leave the room, the sound of violence and combat fills the long stone corridor. Men shout in anger and fear, though a woman's voice, harsh and cold, cuts through the chaos just before another roar drowns out all else.

"At least we're going the other direction," I say to myself, following the two men as they hurry to the east.

"That sounds close," Telias murmurs to Bastian. "How'd they find you?"

"I don't know," he mutters in return. "The general uses combinations of elements that probably haven't been seen since the Creator. For all I know, he's got some mysterious way to track her body even after we've closed off access to her mind."

The sounds of combat fade as we make the turns that Jynn described, ending up in a tunnel with a low ceiling, narrow enough that we have to walk single file. Telias' broad shoulders brush the stone on either side. Bastian glances up appreciatively.

"This is good for us. Even if they break through, they won't be able to follow."

"True," Telias says, still speaking low enough that I have to strain to hear. "They're far too large—"

"Who is too large?" I ask loudly. They glance back at me, Telias smiling and Bastian apologetically. "If we're being hunted, I think I deserve to know what we face."

338

"Our enemy is the Master of Beasts," Telias answers. "Though he can claim more titles than that now. He has used his power to create monsters, warping the bodies of children and the helpless into creatures of mindless rage and towering strength. They have been hunting you ever since you fled with us."

"They've been hunting *me?* Who am I to the Master of Beasts?"

"A tool," Bastian says with a trace of bitterness.

"This may not be the time to get into your history, but Bastian isn't wrong. In brief, you were stolen from your rightful parents, raised the daughter of tyranny, and controlled through indoctrination both magical and literal." Telias glances back, scanning my face. "You have now broken free. The men who enslaved your mind will not allow their greatest asset to slip away easily."

The tunnel twists under my feet, or maybe I'm spinning inside it. Everything they tell me has the ring of truth, yet I have no memory of it. My mind knows the path of recall, the *way* to remember. The waters of memory have worn channels in my consciousness, a riverbed on which remembrance should flow to parade before my mind's eye. When I open those channels, rather than a river, I get a trickle at best.

Of my childhood, I remember a garden, the flow of the earth, the joy of Shaping. I remember... loneliness. A lily, white and alone next to a fence. It feels important, heavy with bittersweet sorrow, but there is no context. Why should a white lily bring me joy and sadness both?

There is less the older I get. My face in an ornate mirror. A book forgotten in my lap as I gaze wistfully out a window. Darting between the crowd of the market in... somewhere.

The memories have no rhyme or reason. It doesn't take long to review them, to lay them next to one another in my mind. We've barely walked a dozen paces before I manage it. Holding them together, comparing them one to the other, I guess the memories I still possess do share one thing: they are all of simple moments. There is nothing impactful or traumatic or joyful or solemn. All of the memories left to me are mundane, free of... complication.

After some minutes walking with only the brush of our feet and the labor of our breath for company, our little train halts. Bastian hands the torch to Telias and works some mechanism on the stone. A doorway levers aside, opening onto an alcove a few paces across. He crosses swiftly and strains at three heavy steel bolts, obstinate with rust and disuse. With a final grunt of effort, he forces the last barrier aside, and a crack opens to allow faint natural light in. The hidden door opens to foliage too thick to see through, the verdant explosion of life stunning after the flat expanse of gray.

"The gardens of Coin are renowned around the world," Bastian says, gesturing grandly to the lush greenery. So that's where we are. "Enjoy the sights, but avoid those who tend them. They are jealous caretakers. If you head southeast, you'll eventually reach the coast. There's money enough in your bags to book passage in Carqos. You'll have the journey to decide where."

"You should come with us," Telias says, squinting towards the rising sun. "I haven't been around her long, but I think I've got the Khal read. She'll never forgive you for this."

"No, she won't," Bastian agrees, glancing back towards the tunnel. "A tempting offer, but I can't leave. He's still here. If I can save him, I must."

"To that I won't argue. Your cause is noble, Bastian. I wish I had a family left to fight for."

"Don't you?" Bastian asks, his eyes sliding to meet mine.

"Too true. Thank you, Bastian Batir," Telias says formally, offering his hand. Bastian takes it with his customary smirk. "For... everything."

"You owe me, old man," he says, laughing. "Don't think I

won't find you to collect someday."

Telias moves into the brush, and Bastian drops the bag he's been carrying to the sand. He steps towards me. His dark eyes burn into mine with a palpable intensity. He bears some weight that I can't understand, some struggle that I no longer remember. If they are to be trusted, then he's saved me from a mental prison of a tyrant's devising. I should probably feel relieved or grateful. I just don't have enough context to evoke either.

"Do you remember what I told you, just before I left?" he asks suddenly, the question so absurd as to be laughable.

"I hardly remember my name," I say honestly, shaking my head. "I don't think—"

"Then remember this. Not the violence, not the death, not the tragedy." He steps closer, his voice resonant and true. As he speaks, I can almost hear the words, an echo somewhere deep in my subconscious. Like the first chord struck of a favorite song, the words thrum through my core and make me... move. My mouth creates the shape of the final words in time with his. "Remember."

"Choose love," I whisper, a nameless sorrow rising like the tide to choke my breath and force tears from my eyes. Yet in that depthless despair, there is a light. A melody.

A hope.

"You are free," he says, his brooding intensity easing. Without it, his face is handsome, his eyes kind. He sighs, relief and weariness and more leaving him in a rush. The smile he offers me is softer, more genuine. "You get to choose to be whoever you want to be. No one will be able to tell you different. Don't let them, neh?"

"They can try," I say, smiling through the blur of tears, tears for a sourceless grief I no longer know.

"And they'll fail. You're too strong for it to be any other way." It looks like it pains him, but Bastian steps away from me.

341

His eyes return to the tunnel, his mind taken once again by whatever awaits him. The person who he can't leave. He glances at me for what I can tell will be the final time. "Goodbye, princess. May the Creator guide you and keep you."

"I hope you find... him," I say, hefting the bag. "And thank you."

He nods, and the gentle smile falls from his face. The weight of somber tension returns to bury his humanity. His shoulders slump slightly, as if he holds them up only with an effort. He disappears into the tunnel without another word, swinging the stone door closed with the dull thud of finality.

Fresh tears prick at my eyes. The source of this sorrow I know keenly. Whatever danger and hardship he faces, I hope he gets to wear that smile again soon. It fits his face so well.

"The way is clear, for now. We should probably hurry though... what is it?" Telias asks in concern.

"Is he a good man?" I ask, staring at the unblemished wall.

"He is trying to be."

"He had such kind eyes," I say, turning to Telias and plastering a smile on my face. "I hope he finds who he's looking for."

"He will," Telias says with a certainty I envy. "Now, are you ready? We're wasting daylight."

Putting my back to the high white walls of Coin, I step into the light of the rising sun.

***

As soon as we skulk past the lush tropical garden surrounding the city, the sun bears down on us with the weight of divine retribution. Heat shimmers along the flat and barren land, while a gentle wind carries loose dust and sand hissing across the ground. I'm imminently grateful for the clothes we've been provided. Though sweat drips down my nose and the long, plodding passage drags at my limbs, the light, flowing material keeps the worst of the sun from reaching my skin. In spite of the heat, it feels more like a summer's jaunt than a soul-sapping trial.

At least, for me. I pause for the third time to allow Telias to catch up. When we set out, he had been talkative, weaving me stories of the world and what little he knew of my life prior to my memory's destruction. After the second hour, he stopped talking, and by the fourth he began to fall behind. I don't mind. It gives me time to think.

I could tell he danced around certain things when he told me of the world and my life, trying to shield me from myself. If this journey will take more than tenday, as he insists, then I'll have the time to pry it out of him. I'll take as much of my history as I can get, tragedies or otherwise. Much of what he describes about the world, I remember, though the source of that knowledge remains in darkness. I can't tell how I learned what I know about the Ways, the peoples, the cultures and languages of the land, but I haven't lost my basic understanding of how things work.

Recent events, though… the war over the Way of the North, the Master of Water's tyranny, and the wave that claimed untold thousands of lives… that I do not remember. I want to believe that he's spinning fiction. I want to demand he tell the truth for once.

But I don't.

Because he is.

After half a minute, he staggers up to me. His proud frame bows under the weight of the pack strapped to his back, and exhaustion has hollowed out its passage in the lines of his face. His breath comes in labored gasps. He slumps to the hard packed earth with a sigh of relief. He looks up at me, his mouth lifting into a weary smile.

"Sorry," he says, pulling the waterskin from his pack and taking a careful sip. "I would have been leading the way, not too long ago. Though maybe not, with the pace you're setting."

"How long has it been since you walked free?" I ask.

"Didn't quite make five seasons," he says drily. "I was looking forward to the sixth, too."

"That does not seem to be so long."

"Over a season of it was spent chained to the bottom of a wagon," he says, sighing. "And before that, my cell was barely wide enough to take a step. I have not gotten the chance to move, let alone walk, in some time."

"Did... did I have something to do with it?" I ask hesitantly.

"No," he says firmly. "You had no idea, and, when you found me, you offered me only kindness."

"Why were you imprisoned?"

"The Sealord and I never saw eye to eye, even before he set out to conquer the world. Thanks to the intervention of a friend, he thought I died on the day of his ascension, but a strange quirk of fate led him to my door nearly twenty years later. He was more than satisfied to give me to his mad dog to break. Kranos was not successful." Telias straightens almost subconsciously at his own words. He turns to me, sudden wariness creeping onto his face. "The only reason I got those twenty years of peace was because of your father."

"You know my father?" I ask, surprised. My memory of him is, predictably, blank.

"Your father and I were like brothers. He is Altos, more commonly known as the Vengeance, the Master of Air and a good and loyal man."

"The Vengeance..."

My skin prickles at the name. Fear, and adrenaline, and... something more. My stomach clenches, and I have to squeeze my eyes closed to contain frustrated tears. These reactions, these disconnected emotions, are playing havoc on my head and heart.

How can you be angry without knowing why? How can you feel sadness without knowing for whom?

The more he speaks, the more I begin to question the

344

wisdom of pursuing any more of my past life.

"Are you rested?" I ask through clenched teeth.

"Well enough," he says, pushing to his feet.

***

The sun is a bloody crimson smear on the western horizon when we decide to make camp. Though the sand retains its heat for the moment, the temperature plummets as soon as night reigns. The cool is a blessed relief after the long trek in the sun. The fine wool Bastian and Jynn provided proves itself once again, warm in the cold despite defending us from the sun. Telias stretches out on the ground the second we stop and closes his lone eye immediately. I'll need to wake him to eat before long, but I can let him rest for now.

Shockingly, I feel fine. Better than fine. I feel as fresh as when we began this morning aside from an ache in my shoulders from the weight of the pack. Whoever I was, whatever I did before all this, my body is in fantastic shape. I fold my arms against the chill and let the night unfurl about me. Even before the last of the light has faded in the west, a multitude of stars wink into being across the sky. The soft glow of infinite starlight turns the sand and earth white. True darkness can never lay claim to this land.

In the silence, I lower myself to my knees. Spreading my fingers, I press my hands to the earth. I've felt it all day, murmuring, whispering, calling. I've ignored its call, trusting in the urgency demanded of us. Now, in this moment of quiet beauty, I will listen.

The flare of emerald light on my shoulder is muted through the diaphanous wool. The symbol of my power, comforting and familiar as nothing else is in this life empty of memory, glows bright and true. The earth, awakened by my touch, longs to stir, to envelop me in its embrace. I offer it no commands. Not yet. For now, I merely feel.

The earth is strong in the desert. I know it, *know* it deeply

345

in my bones. The desert feels the touch of the wind, the brief caress of the beast and the root, but it is owned by the earth. This connection, of spiritual kindred, teases at the dark emptiness of my thoughts, delving, delving, until it uncovers a memory, whole and unbroken. Of a different desert, one of shimmering sand and rolling dunes. Of a different time, when the moon was whole and bright, and a fire burned in the distance…

***

The chill nights in Itskalan surprised me at first. Even in Summer, the caravan builds roaring fires to huddle around like moths to the flame, desperate for warmth. It gives me the chance to slip away. Leaving the Way of the East behind, I walk until the brightness of the moon reclaims the night from the intrusive fires. My feet sink to the ankle in fine sand as I ascend the nearest dune, my legs trembling by the time I reach the top.

I don't care. Not in the slightest. For the moment, at least, I am free.

Creator, to be free. Free of the endless lessons, free of the endless training, free to explore and question and wonder. The air is cold enough to cloud my breath and sear ice into my lungs, yet I breathe it deeply. Slowly, carefully, I open myself to the earth.

Even as cautious as I am, the sense is instantly overwhelming. Grains of sand beyond counting, beyond reckoning, each unique and alone, yet part of the greater whole. I try to narrow my focus, to follow one individual grain under my hand.

We are one. We are many. We are shifted by the wind, transformed by the rain, heated by the sun, pressed under this hand, yet none can truly touch us. Not while we are with our brethren. In this place, where few dare tread, we are powerful. Though we may be separate, we know each other, not just those we touch, but the land entire.

Our perspective widens, racing from one grain of sand to the next, spreading like a wildfire in all directions, floating on the wind, sinking deep below the surface, from one dune to another—

I rip myself away from the feeling before it can tear my mind apart, gasping and laughing both at once. For a moment, I could feel the edges of the whole desert all at once, like the shadow of a leviathan lurking beneath the waves. I have no hope of commanding it, not even close. That task is beyond anyone.

It is as Father spoke of the ocean, grand and beautiful and too great to control…

***

Two mysteries arise from the memory. First, that I am so different now than I was then. The earth surrounds me, stretching as far as the eye can see, no less complex and beautiful as that other desert half a world away. Yet I hold it in my mind, carelessly. Like breathing, my connection with the earth is fundamental and unconscious. Without effort, I can spread my awareness in any direction, racing along that same collective consciousness that nearly broke me before effortlessly, as far as I wish. What strained my mind before barely stretches my imagination. I am so much more than I was.

Has it been so long? By Telias' word, I am not even twenty, but I can hardly recognize myself in the memory.

What have I survived to grow so quickly?

The second mystery is what took me from the memory itself. My eyes find Telias where he rests on the sand. This Father of my memory is not the man Telias described. That man was the Master of Water, which can only mean one thing: the Sealord, the apparent tyrant, was my father. Is my father?

Stolen from your rightful parents.

Or so Telias claims.

The earth stretches to the horizon in all directions. There is nothing out there save my element. There is nothing out there. There is nothing… for me… out there.

A startling, crushing loneliness crashes down on my spirit. Pain lances through my chest such that my fist squeezes at the cloth over my heart.

Creator, I don't know anyone, my friends, my enemies, the people I love and the people I fear. What will I say if someone calls my name? How will I know who to trust? What is my place in this world?

Who am I?

I taste salt. Tears, unbidden and unmarked, wind down my cheeks.

I grit my teeth. I'll not give them sway over me. I'll not allow myself to fall.

Releasing a shuddering breath, I drop again into the earth.

My heart steadies. My soul quiets. We are one, closer kin than any father, closer friend than any stranger. I breathe deeply, and the earth draws close. I breathe out, and the earth sighs away. Like a beacon of flame in an endless blizzard, I huddle close to the earth and know comfort.

When Telias stands some time later, I am not surprised. I already felt when he awoke through the change in the way his steady breathing shifted the dust floating in the air. Even without my eyes, I know his every move. He stretches his hands above his head, fingers clawing towards the sky. Finally, he turns to look at my back where I kneel on the earth. I open my eyes and let my connection to the earth fade.

As far as the eye can see, floating grains of sand and loose earth fill the air. When my will leaves them, they open deaf ears to the call of gravity and fall. A haze of dust too light to succumb remains drifting on the wind. The air glows silver under the tapestry of night, the infinitesimal motes of jagged earth alive with ethereal starlight. Telias curses under his breath as he stares around.

"How far can you reach?" he asks, something like awe in his voice.

"I'm not sure." I stand easily, absent the stiffness I expected after kneeling for so long. "It is hard to measure distance through the earth."

"This is… impressive," he says slowly. "I knew your predecessor well. He lived for nearly three centuries, often honing his craft. Even he…"

"I remembered something," I say when he trails off, avoiding his gaze when he turns sharply towards me. "Traveling in Itskalan. It did not seem so long ago, maybe a few years, but I was different then. Weaker. Significantly so."

"Perhaps… hmm." He combs a finger through his beard, his attention drifting from the present. Eventually, he shakes his head, bending down to rifle through his back. "I'll have to think on it. Hungry?"

"I feel like I should know you, or at least of you." I take the offered strip of salted lamb, though I don't feel like eating. "Tell me of yourself, Telias. Bastian called you 'Warmheart.'"

"A silly moniker," he says. "I was once the Master of Fire, up until the day you were born, in fact."

"Once? What happened?"

"I broke the law." He takes a bite of the tough jerky, chewing as if to give himself a moment to think. "I raised an army of mortal men. I thought that the Vengeance would realize that I would never break the covenant I made with the Council unless I was absolutely certain of my reasons. In the end, our friendship did nothing to change my guilt, only its punishment."

He makes a short, sharp gesture towards his scarred eye. The sight of its ruin makes my skin crawl, but knowing that the hideous injury robbed him of his power, his strength as a Shaper, makes it all the more terrifying. Then his words sink in.

"The Vengeance? My… father?" I ask incredulously. "Didn't you just call him a good man?"

"He is a good man. His actions towards me don't change that. We are complex enough creatures that boiling down our 'goodness' to a single act is an absurdity to be reserved for the simple minded." He sighs, falling to his back to stare up at the stars. "He is a man of duty above all. He took his oaths as seriously as life and death. By the letter of the law, my life should have ended for my crime, but he showed me mercy. By the laws of the Council of Shapers, no Master of any element can lead a military force into battle. I never had the strength to fight Helikos man to man, let alone he and Kranos together. So I raised an army, ostensibly to contest the Sealord, but more as a desperate attempt to wake Altos out of his duty-bound slumber. I failed, and the world as I knew it fell."

"So that was twenty years ago," I say after a brief interlude of quiet contemplation.

"I took another name and set myself up as a historian, scribing for coins and transcribing the history of the world. In reality, I had my ear to the ground to many of the wealthy and powerful families in Donir, and used that position to feed as much information as I could to Altos and Itolas. The Master of Stone," he says helpfully. His smile grows wider, though there is something of pain in it. "I even took in an orphan and helped him find his way. I do hope he's managed without me. When Helikos took me from him, he was just becoming a man worth knowing."

"I'm sorry," I say lamely, lacking a better way to answer his sadness. Better to move on. "Why didn't Altos and his friend take the fight to the Sealord, once they were together?"

"They did. Twice. Early on, before Helikos had a good grip on the surrounding kingdoms, they attempted to overthrow him in truth. Both times, they were betrayed, their forces crushed on the battlefield as traitors fought them from within. They never managed to figure out why, of course. Now that we know that Kranos has stolen Thought, we finally have an answer to that particular mystery.

"Ever since, they've been watching, waiting, not risking the lives of the common man in fruitless conflict. Not only are they outnumbered in manpower and material, they also have, or had, I should say, to contend with three Shapers to their two."

"Me," I say softly, trying, and failing, to suppress a shiver.

"No longer." He must see something in my face, for he leans forward and forces me to meet his gaze. "You are no longer a part of that conflict, not unless you choose to be. I will not ask you to fight. If you want to disappear, to book passage west and leave these lands far behind you, I will walk with you, supporting you, as long as you'll have me."

I don't answer. I don't *have* an answer. Even though there is little left of my life to remember, the pieces of it occupy all of my attention. I haven't, as Bastian pointed out before we left, thought much about where we will go after we reach the coast.

To fight? I don't remember violence. My body, strong and capable even after more than a full day hiking in the blazing heat, may remember differently. It's hard to trust my life to muscle memory that may or may not exist.

Telias returns to eating, so I get the chance to study his profile. A fond smile creeps over my face, a quiet joy kindling in my chest. It is nice, after fighting off waves of crushing solitude, to think of what *we* will do.

With that thought to keep me warm, I have no trouble curling up on the sand, head cradled in my arm, to fall asleep. As I drift towards oblivion, I feel something, like the ghost of a memory. A phantom pressure, a reassuring solidity, as if, for the briefest moment, I am curled around someone strong.

***

We don't sleep long, despite the comfort the earth offers. Before dawn has even begun to spread to the east, we rise wordlessly and press on. There is an urgency infecting my limbs, a need to put more distance between myself and Coin. By his frequent glances backward, Telias must feel the same. Another day passes much the same, plodding east until sundown, camping, communing with the earth, and sleeping.

By the time the sun crests the horizon on the third day, we're miles from our camp. The parched earth soon dances to an invisible melody of sear and scorch. Telias pushes on gamely, but

351

he's not in shape for this kind of odyssey. I do what I can. The earth shifts to meet his feet, turning stumbles into steady steps. Rocks slide aside before they can catch his feet. Cracks that could snarl a toe disappear before he reaches them. The soft sands firm and the hard earth softens. I'm not sure if he notices; judging by the look in his eyes, I'm not sure if he even can. I let my steps slow to a stop.

"Keep… going…" he gasps.

"Drink, Telias," I say gently, offering him my waterskin. He tries to push it away. Exhausted as he is, it isn't hard to evade his feeble attempts. "Drink."

"You need it," he protests, belying his words by taking the skin. "You've hardly had a drop."

"Unlike you, I'm young and healthy and fit, *old man*," I say, trying to hide my concern behind banter. He doesn't crack a smile.

"And more… important," he says.

"I can find us more," I say, opening my hands to encompass the sky. "It may not look like much, but this is my kind of place."

"Prove it," he mutters stubbornly, though his breath is finally coming back under his control. "Show me water, and I'll drink my fill."

"There's a small watering hole there," I point ahead and to the right. "Not too far. Another there, an underground stream flowing below the surface there, and…" I squint ahead, trying to see to the horizon. My eyes fail to pierce the haze of heat, but the earth doesn't lie. "The oasis it feeds should probably be coming into view at any moment now."

"You… you can sense all of that?" He looks forward, following the line of my finger to the horizon. "Isn't it draining?"

"The opposite," I say, shrugging. "The earth lends me strength."

"Remarkable." He holds out the water skin firmly. "But you

haven't proven anything, yet. When you show me water, I'll drink. Until then…"

"Fine, you stubborn ass!" I say, laughing. "We'll just…"

I trail off as a tremor, just at the edge of my awareness, disturbs the earth. I turn back the way we came, though again my eyes can't remotely see what my senses feel. Uneasy foreboding and strange excitement set my heart to racing.

"What do you feel?" Telias asks.

"Hoofbeats."

Chapter 16
Bastian
The Eighty-First Day of Summer
In the year 5223, Council Reckoning

The secret door embedded in the walls of Coin thuds shut at my back. For a moment, I let myself rest against it. I have done all I can for her. She can make her own choices now, and she has Telias to guide her. If I can buy her enough time to disappear, she truly can be free. Even so, I can't shake the feeling that it wasn't enough.

"She'll never forgive you for this."

Don't I fucking know it.

When the Khal finds out that the shiny new Shaper I was supposed to deliver has been spirited from under her nose, she will probably order my death immediately. Telias' offer had been tempting, like a gift of immortality from the Eternal herself. I could almost picture it: making a new life with Iliana, Telias as our teacher, finding lands new and strange at the edges of the map.

But I can't leave Lav.

If I can offer him any comfort, if my presence grants him any solace, then I will give it. When I find him, we'll leave together, and we'll follow. Iliana and Telias are remarkable examples of humanity; it will be hard for them to remain inconspicuous, wherever they go.

I force my thoughts back to the present and my own troubles. In the chaos of the attack, I might be able to feign ignorance, 'aid the search' for Iliana, and push the responsibility for her escape solely on Telias. I shove off the wall and take the long stone tunnel at a jog. I have to get back if I want anything I

354

say to carry any weight.

A chest shaking roar blasts through the corridor as I approach, far sooner than I imagined it would. My jog turns to a sprint, and I quest ahead with my senses for Jynn. She's nowhere to be found, though I feel a dozen other minds in various states of fear and calculation. One stands out above the rest, his thoughts cold and certain.

At a junction with the main corridor, Gabriel crouches in the shadows with a pair of his Hands. He spins, dagger leading, and stops when he recognizes me. His eyes widen, and molten anger spikes in his mind, only to be tamped down immediately. His lip curls, and his attention returns to the crisis at hand, ignoring me. Burying my unease, I force myself to move and crouch next to him.

"What happened?" I whisper, wiping sweat from my forehead. "I got turned around in the tunnels, but the commotion led me back."

"The monsters found us," he says, not bothering to turn. "They are too strong for my people to fight. Your small friend is protecting the Khal in her retreat, and it is my task to lead them away."

"Our task," I say, resisting the urge to clap him on the back. That would probably be too much. "I'm with you."

"As you say." He turns fully to me, his narrow face thoughtful. "Can you aid us? Does your blessing extend to these abominations?"

"It was a struggle at the House, but there were other factors that limited my ability to influence them." Like having a collection of the tortured and insane surrounding me. "So… maybe?"

One of the men at the door looks back and flicks his fingers in our direction in a complicated sign. Gabriel nods once.

"One is coming this way," he whispers, his own hands working to communicate with the others.

355

"Let me try," I whisper back, casting out my senses.

There are other Hands of the Khal at various places throughout the tunnels, hidden watchers passing information from one to the next. Skipping down the chain of consciousness, I make it to a man with eyes on the beast.

Unlike the monster Iliana slew a few nights ago, this creature rides lower to the ground, propelled by no less than six twisted legs, each ending in something that would pass for a human foot. Its torso bloated and thick with rolls of fat, the once-man rolls about in fitful jerks and starts, shockingly fast and agile for its size. The beast darts forward, and the soldier shares my alarm as its bulbous eyes lock onto our presence. Bracing myself, I push towards its mind.

And meet the same blank wall protecting the Empire soldiers known as the Deep.

I claw at the void, but it's like trying to grasp and lift an oiled steel helmet; my fingers slide along its surface and find no purchase. Narrowing my consciousness like a knife, I stab forward, trying to drive through the protection. There is a flash of aggression, hunger, and something for which we *hunt*. The wall holding me back slams closed.

Hunt? They are not mindless monsters. They have a goal, an order to follow. And who could give the order? All of this happened *after* the Master of Beasts left the city, which leaves…

Stabbing at the creature's mind again, I desperately shove an image into its brain before the protection can force me out. I've only seen the man once, a passing look in the flickering darkness at the front of the Hall of the Republic, so I have to fill in some details.

"Stand down, soldier. Return to your room."

The voice is a bare approximation from memory. It will have to serve. Feeling exhaustion eat at the edges of my mind, I return to the soldier watching the creature.

It stops, waving its arms about in confusion. Our fingers—

the Hand's fingers—flick a complicated sign back to the others, its intent some combination of 'wait' and 'ready' and 'question.' The monster opens its mouth and roars. With a speed that shouldn't be possible for its size, it launches a flurry of blows at the empty air. It bellows in frustrated anger, redoubling its efforts on the false image I implanted of the captain in charge of the Deep.

Alright. So it isn't verbal orders, that's for sure. It has to be something else, something related to our power. How, though? Is there an access point, a way in?

After one last furious swipe, the monster stumbles forward. The Hand, confused by the sight and with mounting curiosity, leans out to get a better look. The creature's eyes meet ours. With a roar of unmitigated hate, it darts forward, faster than it should be able to move. A scream builds in our throat where we stand frozen while death comes. Desperate, I throw myself out of his mind.

I open my eyes, my real eyes, just as the terrified scream fills the hall and cuts off sharply.

"Uh, no," I say, already rolling to my feet. "I can't touch them, yet. I need more time, and it's coming this way. Run."

Gabriel motions sharply to his men, and we tear down the corridor, side by side. His men run in near silence, their whispered steps hardly audible over the sound of its pursuit. The monster looses a sharp bellow, almost a hunting cry. It's faster than we are, and its bare feet slap heavily on the stone in a rhythm just close enough to human to make my skin crawl. Even this short sprint sends waves of weariness cascading down my limbs, and I nearly stumble. Driving through the creature's protection took more out of me than I realized.

"Where is the tyrant queen?" Gabriel asks, glancing back at me. "And her handler?"

"No idea," I gasp, trying to focus on running. It is a testament to his discipline and will that he does not seem the slightest bit concerned that a madman's nightmare is bearing

357

down on us. "Did she even wake up yet?"

"Two of my people went to collect them," he says, his jaw clenching. "They died to deliver a message: the tyrant and the Warmheart were gone, their clothes on the ground, their bunks empty."

"Damn," I curse, with feeling. It would have been a sight more convenient if they *hadn't* managed to get that message off. "I nearly... killed myself... for that. What a waste."

The fire igniting in my lungs grows too hot to ignore. At least Gabriel seems satisfied, for now. I couldn't spare the breath to make up any more lies. Despite my best efforts, I start to slow, the strain on my body and soul too great to ignore. Gabriel pulls slightly ahead.

Which is the only reason I see the flick of his fingers indicating a tunnel to our left.

The Khal of Hands drops a shoulder and drives that way without a word. I'm already turning with him, or I would have missed the tunnel and stumbled to a stop, alone in the path of a charging abomination. Even so, I barely make the turn, clipping my shoulder on the hard stone. New agony blazes to life, and I blink madly to keep tears from blurring my vision.

Gabriel glances back, briefly, his eyes flicking over the running men. Do they linger on me? Is that disappointment I detect in his eyes?

Did he just try to get me killed?

I can't afford to divide my attention to find out. We take several more turns at a breakneck tilt. The monster, quick in straight bursts, struggles with the tight turns and falls behind, the grotesque slapping of its feet fading. A frustrated roar disturbs dust from the tunnel ceiling.

Before I can slow in relief, an answering screech, more bird than human, rips into being ahead. Close. Far too close. The discordant scrape of claws digging into stone takes up the pursuit.

Every breath is agony, black and deep, like I'm taking a

rusty saw to my lungs. I've never run this far or this fast in my life. Lost in misery, I almost miss Gabriel twitch his fingers to the right.

Staggering now, I barely survive the turn. My shoulder slams into the opposite wall. I nearly fall. My legs feel like leaden weights. Now that my momentum has been stolen, I don't know if I'll get them to move again. Forcing my head up, I expect to see Gabriel's retreating back fleeing down the corridor. Instead, a sight greets me that floods new life into my legs.

The tunnel opens into a wide room a dozen paces across. Bright natural light illuminates the men waiting their turn at the bottom of a ladder, shining like a beacon of hope sent from the Creator himself. Half of his men have already disappeared up into the embrace of the sun. I groan and force myself forward, willing myself to the light. Gabriel starts up as I stagger to the bottom.

The sound of claws on stone is enough for me to hurl myself after him. Relying on my arms, adrenaline lends me strength. The Khal of Hands disappears above, and I force myself after, sunlight on my face. Every rung, my mind races through images of claws ripping into my legs, stabbing through my chest, plucking me from the ladder and dashing me against the wall.

My hand wraps around the final rung. A shadow blocks the sun. Gabriel, come to help me up and out, to—

His boot slams down on my fingers with an audible crunch. I drown in a sea of suffering. He grinds down, the pressure of his foot the only thing holding my hand to the ladder. I try to reach for his mind, but my power is a distant memory, a mocking ghost dancing out of reach. Slowly, Gabriel lowers his face until he can look into my eyes.

"No one betrays the Khal," he says, his narrow face breaking into a cruel smile. "You should have been more careful. The soldiers you used your power on remembered you approaching, though they don't remember anything after. You were in these tunnels. You helped them escape."

"No, Gabriel, you're wrong, I—"

He leans into my hand, crushing it beyond repair. The agony steals my voice but for screams through clenched teeth.

"I never trusted you, Batir. I told her we should take you out in the desert and leave your body for the vultures. You are a viper, and she hugged you to her chest." A manic light burns in his eyes, zealotry and devoted satisfaction. "It is your nature; it was only a matter of time before you bit."

"Gabriel, please," I whimper, not even sure what I'm begging for. His lip curls in disdain, and he straightens to his full height, balancing easily on the ruin of my hand.

"Die screaming, Batir."

He flicks his boot like he's stepped in something unpleasant. Blood and bone lurch free, and I fall.

I hardly feel the impact. My breath is already gone. If something gives in my chest, it changes nothing, just a new voice singing harmony to the rest of my pain. Something inside my mind begs for me to stand, to climb to my feet and force my broken fingers to grasp the ladder again, to fight for safety until my last breath.

But it hurts.

Creator help me, it *hurts*.

A monstrous snuffling accompanies the click of claw on stone. I don't turn. Whatever it is, I'd rather breathe my last without its appearance to haunt me into darkness. I try to picture something pleasant, a happy field or a laughing face. I can't. There has been too little of that in my life for it to be what accompanies me into death. All I know is pain.

A hand, far too large to be human, wraps claws the length of sabers about my chest. Gently, almost tenderly, the creature lifts me and turns me to face it. I want to close my eyes, but horror holds me rapt.

It is more slender than the others I've seen, a creature of sinew and strength and speed. Spotted feathers the size of palm fronds decorate its arms, though far too few to cover the hideous

360

ruin of its flesh, leathery and mottled like a bat's wing. Its face still bears human features, though its eyes are far too large and colored the pale yellow of birds of prey. It blinks at me, studying me like a child would a fancy bauble.

Its mouth opens. The screech that pours from its throat tears at my sanity, loud and long and grating like shearing metal. I can't take my eyes from it, can't shut this thing away. It lifts me higher, effortlessly, triumphantly. As the echo of its scream dies, it seems almost disappointed. It cocks its head to the side, more bird than man, and shakes its hand. My body rattles in its grasp.

I cry out finally, my ruined hand and broken ribs searing new lines of torture across my mind. It gives a cheerful grunt at the sound. Pulling me close, it stares into my face. My reflection grows in its overgrown eyes, a distorted tableaux of sweat and pain and fear.

Now, Bastian. If you're going to act, it's now. Mustering what energy I can, knowing it is far too little, I throw my will at its mind. There must be a door, a way in. The oily shield around its thoughts defies my waning focus.

Wait. There. Deep in its mind, just like with the princess. My senses find the crack in the wall, plunging through. Its thoughts are savage and cruel, more calculating than I expected. Its face inches from mine, it brings its other hand up.

Shoving aside the distraction, I search frantically. There; a binding thread, a path worn into its thoughts through the endless march of *command.*

Stop, beast! Sto—

With a satisfied twist to its mouth, it plunges its long claws into my stomach.

My lungs constrict. Nothing enters.

Again. Nothing escapes.

Nothing but a choked, wet gurgle.

Sharp and jagged, the claws dig and dig until they meet at my spine. Much of the pain disappears, cut off so suddenly it is relief and terror both. My legs go limp, and the creature twists its face into a smile. With a flick of its wrist, it launches me through the air. My back slams into the stone wall. Something breaks. Me, or the wall, or both.

A breath races into my lungs past the taste of blood flooding my mouth. I regret it. Better to hold it in, anything not to feel…

My swimming vision settles. Another monster has joined the first, larger and more frightening, its hulking form a mass of muscle and brute force. A third crowds in behind, the one from before, its twisted feet pattering on the stone. The other two try to push past, but the third screeches at them, slashing with its claws. They jump back, the largest one rumbling in discontent. As they square off with one another, I am, for the moment, forgotten.

The pain is gone, or mostly gone. Maybe it's just my body giving up. My conscious mind screams not to look, not to see what's been done to me, but my eyes slide down. There is blood, so much blood, gushing from the jagged rents in my stomach. The white of bone juts from my ribs, my back a ruin. Every breath is a trial, like I'm trying to suck in all the air of the world to fill a single mouthful.

The first monster drives the other two back. They hover at the entrance as it turns back to me, cocking its head at the sound of my rattling breath. A cruel smile spreads across its face, and it stalks over to stare down at me.

At whatever is left of me.

The monster shrieks its hideous hunting wail. Its claw comes up to finish breaking the toy it has grown tired of.

Death is not what I thought it would be. I once believed that I would scream and kick and claw to stay in life, that I would refuse to give up this tortured existence no matter the cost. That the emptiness of life would haunt my final moments.

But I can only think of one thing.

"Lav," I whisper, spending the precious breath in my lungs

362

to give his name voice, one last time.

I'm sorry, brother. You deserved better. You deserved more than what I could give. You deserved...

A fist, bigger than the bird thing's head, slams into its jaw. The crunch of fractured bone is loud in the small room. The bigger, hulking monster raises its arms and slams them down on the bird creature, blood and bone spraying.

The third, crying out in rage, leaps upon the second's back, clawing and tearing. Skin rips and gives way, more blood spurting, flesh hanging by threads.

Why are they fighting?

The larger monster reaches back and grabs the creature from its back, ignoring the cuts it takes on its titanic hands. With a single flex of its body, the behemoth launches the six-legged abomination in its hands. The creature slams through the wall, the stone rumbling and collapsing around it.

The behemoth breathes deeply, grunting in satisfaction as the shattered wreckage of its fellows.

As the last stone settles, there is shocking silence. The second monster, bleeding freely from a dozen jagged wounds, slowly turns to me. It growls. Its ponderous footsteps shake the stone.

I am past fear, though I can't help a groan of despair. It was just a dispute among starving wolves to see who would get the pleasure of finishing the kill.

It steps into the light. The monster's hideous features, twisted and broken, are nonetheless familiar. It ambles over, crouching down next to me and moving its face close to mine.

One of my arms still works, as it turns out. For my hand, painted red with blood, comes to rest on its cheek. On *his* cheek.

"Lav," I whisper, and the mountain trembles under my hand, a note of sorrow and satisfaction both. "Brother."

A sound, soft and sweet and joyful, trills from somewhere deep in his chest. His hand, a dozen times too large, sweeps me up to hold me to his chest. My legs dangle limply between his fingers. My ear presses to his chest. Something leaks from me, something vital, something I should want to *keep*. But all I can hear is his heart, here and true, holding strong the tenuous beat of love.

"... see what they've found. Eternal's tits! What managed to kill two of them?"

A voice, harsh, its discord unknown to the harmony of Lav's mighty heart. Fear returns, not for me, but for the man whose protective arms surround me. It is easy enough to tell that I am finished. I can't let them have him.

"Run, Lav." My voice is hardly above a whisper, softer even than the beat of his heart. He shows no sign of having heard. "Please, run."

"See what that one's holding. Hey, ugly, turn around!" A flash of silver light, hardly bright enough to compete with the halo of light still encircling the ladder. The stolen power of Thought, used to command these beasts. Lav shows no sign of having heard that call, either. "I said, turn around."

Lav doesn't answer. He cradles me close, squeezing, suffocating me against his chest. He shifts us to the corner, darkness falling as his bulk blocks the light.

"Show me what you have, beast!" Another flash of silver, brighter this time. "Show me what you have!"

"Looks like it broke, Captain," another voice says, lazy and bored. "Not surprising, really, what they've been through. That one didn't have much to begin with, as I recall."

"Eternal's prison, it's hiding something from me." A sound, soft over the beat of Lav's heart, but unmistakable. A sword clearing a sheath. "Give it to me, beast."

Lav tenses as something scours across his back. His chest jumps against me. One massive arm swings backwards, and he makes contact, for there are shouts of alarm.

The rasp of more swords being drawn is far too loud in the

364

tight space.

Lav flinches and sweeps his arm behind him like he's trying to wave away a biting insect. He catches one man in his grip, crushing the life from him and hurling his body at the others. The next time he reaches back, his hand returns cut and bloody. Mewling like an injured kitten, he jerks as something stabs into his back.

Again, and again, and again.

Blood, too much blood, splashes to the ground.

"No, no, Lav," I whimper, trying to push his impossible strength away. He doesn't listen, doesn't hear, gathering me instead close to his chest with both arms. Without the danger of his warding arm, the sickening sound of swords hacking into flesh fills the room. "Fight, Lav, or run. Leave me, run, run, no, Lav, no, *run please.*"

It takes them minutes. It takes them hours. It takes them an age.

Eventually, his heart, so strong and beautiful, slows, losing its perfect rhythm.

And finally, peacefully, stops.

I did not know pain before today.

Nor did I know silence.

The air is still, his massive bulk shielding me from the murderers who killed him. They speak. I can't understand them. I don't want to.

His giant face settles close to mine. He stares vacantly at the opposite wall, his eyes no longer blank, but empty. He knew me. For the first time since we were children, he *knew me.* Just in time to die.

His massive body shifts aside. After the gloom his silhouette offered, the light burns my eyes. Against my will, my lungs take another tortured breath. Someone grabs me and drags me onto the floor. My broken body screams in agony. I remain silent.

This pain is nothing. Nothing.

Lav...

Creator be damned to oblivion. Just let me fucking die. Please.

The face that comes into focus nearly lifts my labored heart. I can barely make out her face through my tears as Jynn bends close with a concerned frown. Her eyes track over my body, not lingering too long on the parts of me that... it is a mercy that her eyes do not linger. The world grows hazy, dreamlike, silver like the light of my power. I can feel myself drifting.

"Bastian, where is Iliana?" she asks.

"It doesn't matter," I whisper, trying to pierce the fog over my brain. "Gone..."

"No, Bastian, this is important. The Empire sent soldiers after her. They'll kill her if I can't catch them. Which direction did she go?"

"Lav..."

"*Where did she go*, Bastian?"

"East... east..."

Jynn's face wavers and distorts. My vision must be going. No... her image melts and disappears. The silver fog surrounding my thoughts dissipates with her. Pain, unnaturally held at bay, roars back to the fore, bringing with it a startling clarity.

I've just been played. Jynn would never have been here, never been alone...

The captain, Silken, kneels at my side, a satisfied smirk plastered to his face.

No... please, Creator, no...

"Thanks, kid," he says, patting my cheek roughly. "Couldn't have done it without you."

"I'll... kill..." I try to growl, reaching for his leg. My fingers can find no purchase. They don't have the strength to.

"I don't think you'll be killing anyone," he says, standing and turning to the other soldiers. "She went east, probably on

366

foot. We don't have time to waste. I don't need to remind you fuckers of what will happen if we don't bring her back."

They snap salutes and move to the ladder, taking it hand over hand. No, you fucking bastards, *no*. I haven't done much good, maybe *any* good, save for what I did for *her*. This bastard won't undo that. Creator damn it, he *won't*.

Power surges back to my limbs. Silver light ignites, the true symbol of Thought driving back the darkness. Narrowing my focus, shunting aside as much of the sorrow and pain as I can, I reach for his mind. Fuck. He's protected. All of them are.

I can barely do this at my best. Now… doesn't matter. I have to try.

I spit blood. The silver light of my power flickers. I blink, my lips trembling.

They're gone.

I didn't even notice them leave.

Tears join the blood leaking from my body. I can't. I can't let them. I have to… I have to tell her. Gritting my teeth, I force my focus back into the power. Like a ripple in a pond, I pulse my desperation in all directions, trying to ignore the weakness spreading through my limbs. Whatever is happening to my body, it doesn't matter.

Jynn.

She doesn't answer. I choke on the blood welling in my throat.

Jynn!

"*Bastian?*" she asks, her mind's voice distant. She reads my thoughts, confusion melding swiftly with horror. "*What… oh, shit. Bastian, hang on!*"

No, you have to listen. They know. The Empire knows where she went. You have to help…

"*Fuck that, Bastian!*" she screams, emotion I didn't expect, emotion I wasn't ready to face, burning in her thoughts. "*I'm coming for you. Don't you dare die.*"

Promise me. Promise me you'll help her.

"Bastian, please. She's protected; you saw to that. She is still herself. Do you think soldiers, especially soldiers thinking their stolen power will control her, have a chance against Iliana *of all fucking people?"* The sob that comes through our connection is so potent that shouts of terror and anguish echo down from the streets as Jynn's sorrow bleeds into the people of Coin. Her power... when did she get so strong? *"Now stop arguing. Save your strength."*

I don't think... I don't think that's going to matter.

"I... fuck. Creator damn it, Bastian, what happened?"

The memory of Gabriel's sneering face, his boot, the fall. The monster's terrifying strength, its claws... Lav...

"I'll rip his mind to pieces," she snarls, her anger like a volcano. *"His twisted bitch of a master, too. All of them, the Khal, the captain, all..."*

I know you will.

My voice, trapped within this broken body, is placid, calm. She has no answer, surprised into silence. I do not want silence. The silence reminds me of what is coming. Reminds me of a feeling I thought I buried. Here, standing at the threshold, waiting to step over and into the void, the terror comes roaring back to life.

You are worthless. Everything you do, everything you've done, achieved nothing. You leave no mark upon the world. You will not be remembered fondly.

If you are even remembered.

My chest convulses in a sob, the broken parts of me crying out in protest. My focus breaks, the agony too great to ignore. The connection to Jynn wavers.

I force my body to shift, to roll over, to see Lav, his face slack in death. Broken as he is, it is hard to make out his expression. Surely, he is not smiling. That would make no sense. His death was just one more cruel joke the Creator had left to play. On him. On us. No, he can't be smiling.

Jynn does something, some flurry of power I can't follow, and the pain disappears. It leaves me empty, floating, my consciousness set adrift. It is… peaceful.

I couldn't even save him.

"Oh, Bastian, no…"

He… protected me. He died for me. All this time I wanted to save him, and he died for me, Jynn! What kind of fucked up world is this? What kind of bastard is the Creator? If there is something… after… then I'm going to spit in his face.

"You did everything you could."

You know that isn't true. We both do. I never should have left him. I should have stayed at his side, serving him as penance for my sins.

"That isn't what he would have wanted. You had a life to lead, separate from Lav."

After I stole his? No, Jynn. What a waste. What an awful waste of time. In all my life, what have I achieved? Everything I am… everything I've done… meaningless. I failed in the one task that really mattered. All I gave… all I gave to the world was suffering.

Though Jynn cut me off from much of the pain, I still have some dim connection to my body. And it is fast growing cold. Time, which felt so infinite, stretching blindly forward into the distance, suddenly feels very short.

"You're wrong, you realize," she says, the fierceness of her denial reverberating through my mind. "You couldn't be more wrong."

I know who I am, Jynn.

"Yes, you're an arrogant ass. You did a lot of selfish and fucked up things in your life. But you also did so much more. Creator's name, Bastian, you literally gave life a chance on this world. You saved us all."

Bullshit. I've never bought your Seer's claims. Just a mad woman sitting atop a shiny tower…

"They weren't her visions to claim. They were Elitrea's. They

369

were mine." She pauses, though I can sense her doing something in her mind. *"Would you like to see how wrong you are?"*

I don't... I guess I don't have anything better to do.

She huffs out a laugh, silent in our emptiness, yet full of life. Her power surges into my mind, sweeping us both into—

***

"One must be saved."

The boy, Jace, sprints through a hall filled with flowers, chaos around him as the pompous nobility of Donir struggle to catch him. Guards finally shove their way through, lining up crossbows in a lethal volley. One catches him high in the back, and he falls with a grunt. For a second, there is silence broken only by the duke's congratulations on a well-fired shot—

Jace stalks through a dark room, eyes scanning for a painting he knows should be here, ignoring the soft sounds to the side. A woman, surprised rage in her eyes, lurches to her feet, throwing bands of shadow around his arms. He fights against the darkness, refusing to give in until she puts a blade of shadow through his chest. She looks at her companion, opening her mouth to speak—

Jace sits in the dumbwaiter, his hands grasping the ropes securely. He looks across at Iliana, speaking words I know all-too-well. She narrows her eyes suspiciously, honing her focus. Before he can react, shards of glass fly in glittering arcs to slam into his body in three places. Shouting in agony, he releases the ropes and plummets, out of control, falling until he slams into the—

The fire spreads shockingly fast, all the more terrifying because it ignores all laws of nature. It plunges underwater, consuming the fish and sharks and whales and plants as easily as it incinerates dried tinder. It climbs mountains, racing up their slopes faster than the melting snow can fall, tongues of flame snapping forth to consume birds just as the edge of the wall passes on. The flame spreads, one long growing ring of destruction, until it meets on the other side of the world and dies as swiftly as it lived. The bright sparks of life, the creatures fighting for their children, clawing just for the right to breathe for one more moment, the humans and their petty hopes, their worries and their fears.

Nothing but ash.

It begins in Donir...

Nothing moves. Nothing breathes. Clouds of gray and black drift listlessly over mountains melted into smooth and undulating hills, seas smothered in an opaque rain of unmoving gray.

Each of the visions Jynn shows me ends in fire. That boy... that night... we really were *all* at risk?

"With your help, he was saved. With your help, the Worldfire was averted. Thanks to you, we have a chance."

***

"One must be broken."

Iliana stalks across a hall covered in late Spring flowers, her stride determined and steady. It is the same night, the same place. She's just allowed Jace to escape, and she snaps on the young duke who asked it of her.

"I'm glad to know you're loyal to someone. Because you have shown your kingdom no loyalty. You have shown your king no loyalty. And you have shown," she speaks over him as he tries to interject. "No loyalty to me."

"Iliana, that's not true," he says quietly.

"You should have trusted me," she says. Her voice is low and steady. "If you were my friend, as you claim, if you would have been my partner, as you wish, you would have trusted me. Know now you are neither."

"Iliana—"

"Enough." She makes a cutting gesture with her hand. "Enough."

She spins away from him, ignoring the stricken look on his face. She does not look left or right, not even when an Islander woman stumbles through a crowd of vapid nobility. She has a task, a duty; she doesn't have time to worry about the squabbles

371

of her lessers. She passes through the doors, oblivious to the man standing at the other end of the hall, a look of tortured anguish on his face.

So simple a moment, a conversation missed, a friend forgotten…

The possible futures array themselves before me, less like visions and more like images frozen in prescient history. In all of them, every one, Iliana stands at the Sealord's side, her face so cold it could be carved from ice. Her eyes are not the ones I know, so bright and beautifully blue, but are rather the deep, dull gray of the sky in winter. In some she bears scars, in others she is joyful, in many she carries some unknown sadness, but in each one she remains loyal. She continues to believe the lies.

And the Sealord conquers the world. Jynn shows me a dozen possible futures in a moment, and in each, the Sealord stands as Emperor of all, and Iliana, *unbroken* and far from whole, could not shake free of the control.

"It seems so trivial, but without your intervention, she forgets what love is, or could be. She does not care as she hurts, as she kills. She had to know love, and lose it. She had to be broken, so that she may now build herself anew."

***

"One must seek vengeance."

A woman—Kettle, I think her name was—stalks through a garden. A garden I recognize, the same duke's estate in Donir. The party, again. She is wearing the green silk costume from her performance, a look of thinly veiled fear on her face. The pendant of an amulet buzzes on her hip, a constant reminder and distraction. She sneaks towards the high garden wall, silent and swift. The lights are too bright, the guards too aware. There is a shout just as she begins to scale the wall. A crossbow bolt takes her in the ribs, and she screams as the guards surround her…

The vision flickers.

The same moment replays, Kettle's lover stalking at her

side, turning to fight the guards. They cut their way through, driving for the exit, but they take too long. Blades of glass cut through their legs before they can run far, Iliana sweeping towards them like a thundercloud...

The vision flickers.

Kettle cuts her way free, shadow blurring and moving faster than the eye can follow. She leaves the compound, leaves her friends behind to fend for themselves. In the aftermath of the battle, the Empire sends in soldiers, too many to flee or escape, and her family is taken.

The image blurs, racing forward in time, revealing a Kettle both bitter and savage, killing for sport. She finally falls fighting the Sealord himself, water crashing down on her from all directions...

A dozen different futures play before my eyes, some in which she murders the Sealord herself, others in which she stands triumphantly at his side as his personal assassin, but each time her life ends in bitterness and regret.

"But, thanks to you, she survived, and continued to know the love of her family. She has something to fight for, something to avenge. Soon, if all goes well, she will return, and exact the final toll of her vengeance."

***

"And one must choose."

My face, younger, a few less lines. Freshly shaven, the green silk of the Seer clothing fits my form well. The Seer, Min'dei, still alive, regards me solemnly. We are on top of the diamond tower in Isa, the shrine to Light. Her stare is stricken, her peaceful facade broken. I fold my arms across my chest, a look of pure and satisfied spite on my face.

"You won't... help us?" she asks in horrified wonder.

"Piss on you, and the world," my other self says, savage glee in his voice. "You stole my brother from me. I'll steal everything from you."

"I told you, he lives. As soon as this task is complete, we will take you to see him. You can find your brother again, Bastian."

"Don't say my name, bitch. You don't know me." I step forward, pointing a finger in her face. "I know who I left Lav with. He's dead, sure as sunrise, and it's your fault. Remember that, if your delusions are even close to reality. Remember that you sentenced this world to death, not me."

"You would condemn all the future Lavilions, and all the future Bastians who would love them?" Her voice is weak, broken, her surprise total. "You care so little?"

"They aren't my brother, and they aren't me."

A dozen other possibilities flit past, each a mirror to the first. There are—were—futures, many of them, where I chose not to help the Seer and the Ensouled in their mad quest to save three strangers halfway across the world. And, inevitably, the world ends in fire.

"You chose. In all the futures Elitrea foresaw, your involvement meant the possibility of success, and your refusal doomed us to certain failure. You chose, and we all have a chance to live."

A chance against what?

"A storm is coming," Jynn says as the visions fade. She keeps me with her, though, gently holding me to her will. It is mercy, I can tell. She doesn't want me to feel what is happening to my body. *"One that we have little hope of surviving."*

"The Worldfire?"

"No. Most futures end in fire, but that was a calculated risk. If we wish to survive, we will need that fire. There are so few futures in which we survive, a precious handful. Your choices kept those slim hopes alive."

So it's nothing better than that? An unlikely chance?

"Without you, there would be none. Your life was not meaningless, Bastian. You brought suffering to the world, but you also gave it hope. You broke your brother's mind, but you spent the rest of

your life caring for him over yourself. You hurt a lot of people, but you gave Iliana a new life."

There is a pull, subtle, insistent, and growing stronger with each passing second, almost like a voice whispering at the edges of my mind. A voice that is getting harder and harder to ignore.

I hear... something.

"You don't have to listen." Jynn's will holds my soul in a fierce embrace. Yet still I hear the call. *"You can stay, Bastian. You gave me life. I offer you the same. Stay, and live with me here. I'll teach you how to cast your soul into an object, or we will find you a new body. Just stay..."*

No, Jynn. I don't want... that. The voiceless call rises in a crescendo, and I barely hold on. *Is this really what you faced the whole time? How did you resist? How did you not... listen?*

"I have a purpose," she says, soul-weary and slow. *"I didn't listen because I couldn't. I have too much left to do."*

I think... I think I might be done.

"Okay. Okay."

Her voice is fainter the longer we speak. Our connection dims. The grasp of her mind loosens against her considerable will. Her desire is not enough, in the end.

I must want it, too.

I drift back, back to my ruined body, back to the suffering. The pain is a dull ember, a fitful spark that flickers. Flickers.

"Thank you, Bastian."

Jynn's voice, the faintest whisper.

There is gold, suddenly. Golden light. It is warmth, and love, and family, as if he stayed, as if he *waited*—

Chapter 17
Kettle
The Eightieth Day of Summer
In the year 5223, Council Reckoning

There is a moment of impossible stillness.

The mob is struck frozen by the man standing before them. His powerful form is surrounded by a halo of light that has nothing to do with the sun, so bright I have to squint to see him. Even so, there can be no doubt.

Perhaps I've died. Perhaps he died as well, and the Creator is giving us another chance...

"Umbral'te!" he shouts again, the deep bass of his voice crashing like thunder.

I rise to my feet, as my body, long trained to respond to the call, remembers itself. I almost step forward before reason reasserts itself. Sanar's arrival, miraculous and impossible as it is, will achieve little. An entire population seeks my death. No one man, be it the Sealord or the Vengeance himself, could withstand them all. And why is he *glowing*?

"Umbral'te!"

And, unbelievably, they come.

Like a swarm of shadows, they come. Vaulting rooftops and climbing walls, floating on the wind and striding through the crowd, they come. The Umbral Guard, the personal defenders of the Seer herself, come to their captain's call and array themselves before the people of Eshan. A dozen, two, a hundred of the proudest and most capable of the People face the crowd. Though I can only see their backs, I recognize the men and women I trained with, my brothers and sisters.

Hona's demons in the shadows. Haunting my steps, waiting in the night, familiar…

Sanar half glances back at me. A scar, thin and impossibly straight, mars the majesty of his skin. His face is stoic, yet there is an ineffable sorrow in the weight of his gaze, a plea profound and absolute. His face strikes me like a bolt of lightning, setting my nerves afire in fear and hope and…

He turns back as the Amanu steps through the crowd. He says something in his language, a question. Sanar doesn't respond.

"Do you speak the trade tongue of Donir, warrior?" the Amanu asks.

"I do," Sanar rumbles, like an avalanche stirring.

"What is your purpose here?" he calls. If the Amanu is intimidated by the towering warrior and his unnatural glow, he doesn't show it. I, of course, would desperately like to know the answer to that question as well. "It is customary, is it not, for a traveler to announce his presence when entering a foreign land? Especially if you come in such force. Your Isles are far from here. Why have you come?"

"We are the Umbral Guard." It may be my imagination, but it seems that Sanar glows a little brighter at the words. "We have come to serve the rightful queen of these lands. The Eshani, Aea Po'lial, known as Kettle, sister to our Seer and Master of Shadow."

What? By the Depths, *what?* This nightmare has turned to dream, my mind crafting a fanciful view of the world and the place I once called home.

This is impossible. The People hate the Shapers, damn them as cursed and tainted. We—they—believe that the original Shapers *killed* the Creator. And Sanar… Sanar… my fingers press to the scar on my cheek, the place where *he* held the knife and *cut…*

The Amanu's eyes flick back and forth across the line of warriors. He seems to be calculating his odds against the Umbral, and, from the look on his face, he doesn't like his answer. As the silence builds, five figures in the midnight blue of the Ihera weave through the crowd, their silks splashed with a rainbow of color. White, blue, yellow, green, and brown. The Oshei of the Ihera have arrived, and their presence reminds the Amanu of his pride. His arrogance.

"The one known as Kettle is a charlatan who would steal the throne of Eshan," he declares in a ringing voice. "Lay down your arms, and we will let you leave in peace. Surrender, and we will offer you mercy. Resist, and we will treat this as an act of war, by you and, by extension, your precious Seer." He sneers at the last, stepping dangerously close to the tall warrior, closer than I ever would. He looks up into Sanar's eyes and waves him aside. "Move, warrior. This is your final chance."

"No," Sanar says simply.

The Amanu stares at him silently, then spins back to the crowd. He raises his voice, calling out in the *hitaan*, gesturing sharply towards the assembled warriors. The populace hears him, and many shout in enraged agreement, but the balance has shifted. The mob is not so eager to approach the warriors as they were to raid the Baeda. The Umbral's single-edged swords remain at their sides, for now, but a hundred disciplined warriors would cut through the unarmored citizens like butter, and they know it.

"Oshei!" the Amanu calls, and the men and women of his house fall into fighting stances, calling on their power.

A group of six Shapers, however, will break the Umbral much the same. Each brings their elements in pouches at their sides like sheathed swords. Vines form in the hands of Roots, thorns waving deceptively amidst the leaves. Wind's clothes flutter about her, a subtle pressure in the air. Water forms a ball of floating liquid before him, though ice rimes its edges. Earth has a halo of dark soil spinning about his head. And Light...

The Oshei of Light looks confused. His hands extend out before him, an empty space between them. He stares at Sanar, a

378

look of growing comprehension and horror on his face. Sanar opens his arms and bellows from deep within his chest.

"*Umbra'l!*"

A dozen of the Umbral Guard step forward from their line. I blink in surprise. None of them are armed. They drop hands to their hips as if drawing swords from invisible sheathes. As they raise their arms…

The Baeda courtyard floods with light as a dozen shafts of brilliant energy flow into being. Like warriors of fable, they address their assembled foes with a dozen synchronized flourishes from a dozen identical shimmering blades, dropping into ready and threatening stances. The Ihera shield their eyes from the shocking glow. The look of disbelief on the Amanu's face is nothing compared to mine.

What is… this makes no sense. How did they know… who found… how did they change…?

Eternal be damned. There is one answer, and one answer only.

The Seer.

The People have always trusted the Seer. Through a hundred generations, we have trusted whoever took on the mantle. This, though… this is fundamentally opposed to everything the Seers have commanded and stood against over thousands of years. I would be less surprised if the Master of Beasts came to apologize personally for my torture.

There is a shout of command, and the people part for yet another force: soldiers of the Ihera, their long spears sparkling like diamonds in the noontide light. The mob moves aside readily enough before them, happy to let professional warriors deal with the Umbral.

Ebbing and flowing like the waves of a rising tide, the tension in the air spikes higher again. The Amanu snaps several commands, easing behind his Oshei to shield himself from the first attacks. Like the air just before lightning, the taste of violence fills the open street. Any second, the tension will snap, and blood will flow.

Whoever emerges the victor, there will be no winners.

"Sanar," I begin, stepping towards the line of warriors.

"Get back, Aea," he rumbles in the *I'wia*, holding a warding hand my way while continuing to watch the enemy move into position. "We can talk after we deal with this rabble."

"Sanar, stop," I snap, a fearful and tenuous hope lighting in my chest. "Do not fight them."

"We may not have a choice."

"Amanu!" I shout, stepping through the line of the Umbral. I can tell Sanar wants to hold me back, but he doesn't dare touch me. "Tell your men to stand down. There does not need to be bloodshed today. Speak with me, and we can figure out a peace."

"You bring foreign warriors into the heart of my kingdom, and you dare to speak of peace?" The Amanu waves his hand in dismissal, turning and shouting a command. The Ihera soldiers drop the points of their spears, tensing for a charge.

"Wait! Please!" He doesn't listen, doesn't even bother to look my way. He directs his soldiers in his own language, confident in our ignorance. The rest of his people do not speak the language of the west. The violence spirals ever closer. If one act of aggression is made by either side, there will be no retreating from the brink. We have a moment here, a lull the Umbral earned us, if we can just seize it. "By the Depths, will one man's arrogance really start a war?"

"Perhaps not," Sonjur's calm voice says behind me. I glance back at him, and he bows low. "I, too, seek peace."

"Do you have a way to sway him?" I ask, pointing to the Amanu.

"No. And neither do you. But them…" He opens his hand, gesturing to the assembled population of Yohru, their silent faces representing a myriad of emotions from eagerness to fear to unease. "They would listen if you spoke."

380

"They can't understand me even if I did."

"We can help with that," he says, bowing low and lifting something in his hands. A sword. *His* sword. His *keishi*. "She asks that you simply take her hilt, Eshani."

Knowing how close violence lurks, I don't hesitate. Grasping the hilt, the strange buzz of the Ensouled vibrates on my skin, more controlled than the jumping spark of the amulet I stole for Jon Gordyn, gentler than the insistent pressure of Yatan Tecarim in the boots Aurelion wears. Taking a steadying breath, I let the soul waiting at the edge of my palm into my body.

"Thank you for your trust, Eshani," she says softly, no more than a pleasant breeze in the depths of my mind. *"I am Abita Minto, once Master of Metal. Time is short."*

How can you help me?

"There is a technique, one I learned many generations ago from a visiting Oshei of another land. If you let me, I can take the words you wish to speak and translate them."

I don't think we have time for that.

"You misunderstand. When you speak, your intent will be the same, but the words that emerge will be in the hitaan, *not your native tongue. I swear on the honor of all Eshan that I will not attempt to change or guide your words. I will present them faithfully to the people of Yohru, whether they lead to war or peace."*

Wait, you—

"There is no time, Eshani. Choose."

What a cosmic joke. I've spent my entire adult life trying not to be seen, and here I am, seeking a stage. For lack of a better choice, I move to the wall and awkwardly scale to its top, one hand wrapped around the hilt of the Ensouled. Straightening to my full height, I raise my head to face the humanity spread at my feet. The Amanu still shouts, preparing his soldiers to charge, but the people only have eyes for me.

Creator help me, this had better work.

"People of Eshan," I shout, or try to. My tongue twists as it tries to form the words, contorting into strange shapes. I feel like an observer in my own body, like I'm seeing myself from a distance. Trying to let go of the weirdness, I continue. "Honored friends, you know me, or at least believe you do. You hear the words of your Amanu as truth, from a voice you have heard countless times in the past. I do not know what he has told you. I can only offer you the truth as I see it."

My audience stands, frozen with attentive anticipation. The Amanu, shocked into silence by my sudden fluency, watches with the rest of them. At least, I hope that's the case. For all I know, they just can't believe I would stand before them and shout gibberish. Swallowing, I force the words on.

"I am a stranger to you, and have been since I arrived. Let us change that now. I am Kettle, once Aea Po'lial. I was born in the Isles, to the People under the Seer. I trained to become one of the men and women before you, to join the Umbral Guard in defense of my nation. Before my training was complete, I discovered this." The symbol of shadow writes itself across my face in black ink. Sanar's eyes burn into me, but I don't have time for that now. "Driven out by the People, I made a life for myself in the kingdoms to the West. As a thief." A ripple of discontent, a whisper of quiet anger, races through the people. I nod, turning to pace on the wall with the sheathed blade. "Yes, the rumors are true. I was a thief. I did what I needed to survive, and to save the family I forged from those as desperate as I was. I came to your lands as a wanderer, fleeing from a tyrant who would see me dead for crimes both real and imagined. I did not know Eshan, nor its people. I did not know of the legend of the Eshani.

"I have never desired power, people of Eshan. I have never sought to rule over another. When I heard your legends, my first thought was to flee. My coming, celebrated as it might be, could only cause division and conflict.

"Your people would not let me leave. Your prophecy has held me in chains as real as those that support your mighty city. I

382

did not choose to come here. I did not, I *do* not, want the power the Amanu claims I covet.

"I've done what I can to learn of your people, your customs, your honor. I have never had a home, not really. I've been cast out of every land I've lived in. Yet Eshan gives me hope. I see this land and see strangers who uphold their word, even to desperate thieves. I see a people who do not act in haste, but with discernment and intelligence. I see a nation, a proud nation, that will not bow to the will of one man.

"You have no reason to trust me. There are times in my life when I wouldn't have trusted myself. But I offer you this, sincere and true: let me face the test of the Eshani. Let me follow the steps of your Empress. If I fail, allow my people to go in peace, for they have done nothing but defend themselves. If I return, give me the chance to call this beautiful land my home."

The last ringing echo of my words returns to me, foreign and strange. Stillness commands the day. The people of Yohru stare, stone-faced, dark eyes boring into me. I wait with imagined patience.

After what feels like a fragment of forever, a woman in the front rank steps up to the line of Ihera soldiers. Her hands come to rest on their shoulders. The soldiers glance back at the woman, then share a look. They come to silent agreement, stepping crisply to the side and presenting their spears. The woman clears the gap left in the Ihera line, her eyes never leaving me. Like a river of invisible force, the crowd parts in two, leaving a passage wide enough for a single person to walk. The pathway stretches out of sight down the mountain.

I glance at the Amanu, who alternates between glaring at his disobedient soldiers and me. He knows that the moment has gone beyond him. To try to interfere now would show his hand and reveal him the petty tyrant I know him to be. Amanu or no, he is not above this test of the Eshani.

A test I know nothing about. A test that no one, Master of

Shadow or no, has ever walked away from. Sighing, I drop from the wall to the ground. I walk with as much composure as I can muster to Sonjur, bowing low and offering him his sword.

"Well done, Eshani," Abita Minto says in parting, her voice ancient and warm. *"I hope it is you."*

Steeling myself, I turn to Sanar. His face speaks a tale all its own: fear, apprehension, pride, and hope, all wrapped in a stoic facade that hides nothing. His eyes are dark pools of raw emotion. There can be no mistaking that *he* expected this moment, that he knew it would happen. When I look at him, all I can feel is an old ache, dull beneath the numbness of shock.

Gravity has reversed in my world, and I don't know what to make of it. Swords crafted of living light still shine in the hands of a dozen of the Umbral. They must be Ensouled, Masters of Light, found in some long-forgotten vault in the ruins of Isa. That makes sense; of course the Shapers before the Eternal knew how to Ensoul themselves, and would value their preservation.

But this?

The Umbral wielding them?

Sanar coming to *my* rescue?

"I take it the Seer sent you here," I growl, hiding my unsteadiness behind anger. "Meddling, as she always does."

Sanar doesn't respond. Hurt flashes through his eyes, as if he expected a different greeting. What did he think? That I would leap into his arms? That all would be forgiven? I wasn't even sure if he was alive until five minutes ago. The last time I saw him, we gave each other scars, soul deep and indelible.

Blood spurts into the torchlight, shining in ruby contrast to the narrow tendril of darkness that caused the wound. He spins to the ground as the other warriors surge towards me, and the shadow comes to my call...

Not now.

"Who was the Seer is no longer," a man says from the side, tall and strong, his skin a shade lighter than Sanar's. His voice is

384

familiar, strangely so… "Your brother has taken the mantle. We are here on his command."

"Upen?" I gasp, looking closer at the warrior. He ducks his head, a sheepish smile spreading across his face. I remember him as a gangly youth, a bully, always saying I didn't belong. This warrior bears little resemblance to the boy who hated me.

"I am sorry, Aea, for… back then," he says, scratching his head. "I was wrong… we were wrong…"

"That was a long time ago." I glance down the line of the stoic Umbral. More than a few watch me out of the corners of their eyes, even as they keep their attention on the hostile forces of the Ihera. "I do not understand why you are here, where the Seer is not, but I… without your intervention… thank you."

"We are Umbral, sister," one of the women wielding light calls in the *I'wia*, younger than me by a few years. She would have started the training after I left. "We need no thanks."

"Sister?" I echo softly, the word carrying far more weight than its two mere syllables. I glance at Sanar, his eyes burning with pride and more. Pride? In me? My throat thickens, bittersweet sorrow rising—

Not. Now.

"Aurelion!" I call, craning my neck to look between the Umbral. He slides past them, sword still bared in his hand. "Walk with me."

"Oh, no," Corna says, voice short with pain. Arm thrown over Sario's shoulder, she staggers into view. "We started this shit together, we finish it together. Help me, Kraft."

"I don't—"

"You wanna keep breathing?" she cuts in, a dangerous gleam in her eyes.

Aurelion heaves a sigh and takes over from Sario, lifting her so that her broken leg doesn't take any weight.

"Are you sure you do not wish us to go before you, sister?" the same girl asks.

I take in the beaten, exhausted, resolute faces of my family. Corna forces a grin though her eyes are clouded with pain. Aurelion stands tall though his soul is stretched to its limit.

"No, thank you, sister," I answer with a faint smile. "We will be fine."

"Creator be with you, Eshani," Sonjur says, raising his sword in salute.

"Give that, uh, valley? Yeah, give it hell, Kettle!" Hom shouts, his gruff voice filled with emotion.

"Come back to us," Ezil calls, reemerging from the Baeda tower.

I raise a hand in farewell, turning to the silent crowd and the pathway they've made for me. And walk. There is no pretense, no false dignity. I just walk as I would walk, head held high. I don't deign to offer the Amanu even the barest glance.

Corna's pained hiss follows with every step, but she doesn't complain. Though they could hardly outfight Elan in their current state, their presence at my back is more comforting than if an army followed in my steps.

They are my home. My family. My trust. Things I thought lost forever when I fled my people, things rare and wonderful, now freely given.

The crowd, moments ago baying for my blood, stand silent witness to this unnamed trial that looms before me. I keep my eyes straight ahead. If some of them bow their heads in respect, I do not see it. If some of them glare and wish me ill, I do not see it. I focus on my steps, and the path, and the friends who walk it with me.

It does not lead to the lifts, as I expected. We swing to the south, towards the edge of the city, the entire way lined with sentinels draped in silk and silence. Ahead, a set of steps rise to a platform crafted of stone. Delicate carvings of strange symbols and images adorn every inch of it.

The people of Yohru end at the base of the steps. Placing

my feet carefully, I ascend.

At the top of the steps, I gasp. The circular edge drops into an infinity of open air. There is no rail or impediment preventing a long fall to the valley below. I thought I'd grown used to the sight of the world spread out before me in miniature. The landscape, so tiny and distant, takes on a different quality when there is nothing between me and the edge. Heights have never given me pause before, but the edge of the platform feels like it will suck me over the side if given the chance. The stiff breeze at my back doesn't help. Swallowing, I turn back to my friends.

Corna smiles like a predator, fierce, challenging, almost feral, teeth bared. Her serpent's eyes gleam a poisonous green.

"Corna..."

"Whatever this is, you win it," she growls. Aurelion winces as she squeezes him tightly, lightning jumping from her body to the ground. "You own it, whatever it takes. I'll see you on the other side."

"Whatever it takes," I agree, a surge of adrenaline rising in my chest. I'll survive whatever this is. For Timo. For Yelden. For Myn. For Ezil and Hom and Nolan and the rest.

For my children.

My eyes slide to Aurelion, and the concern written on his face. He opens his mouth to speak, but closes it without saying anything. Corna glances up at him and rolls her eyes, then shoves him gently away, balancing on her one good leg.

"Go to her, you big idiot," she mutters.

The moment has stolen his grace, and he nearly stumbles on the first step. I smile at a Tempered struggling to mount basic stairs. He grins in response.

It is the sunrise after a storm.

He stops on the penultimate step, his molten bronze gaze level with mine. He starts to speak, but I hold up a hand.

"I'm sorry," I say softly, reaching out to touch his cheek. "I was... I was afraid. I still am. But I can't let fear rule my mind.

After this, if I make it… through… then we'll talk. About us."

"Talk like last time?" he asks, raising his eyebrows. I laugh nervously, feeling my cheeks burn.

"We'll see."

"Come back to us, Kettle. Come back to *me*."

I nod, not trusting myself to speak. The edge beckons, alluring and terrifying. Far below, far enough that it doesn't seem real, impenetrable darkness cloaks the valley. Yohru was built for this reason, to honor the place where the last Empress of Night passed into legend. And, I guess, to provide a test to the ones who would claim her throne.

A leap of faith.

The shadow clings to my skin under my *dimina*, but I can't reach it. Whatever Kit's Source did to me, there is a barrier now between us I can't cross. If I jump, I will not be able to call on the shadow for help. I will plummet like a stone. The pooled shadow in the valley will have to catch me, and if it doesn't…

At least it will be quick.

Desperate hope for my family has brought me this far. A different kind of hope draws me forward. A face, a *presence*, guiding the shadow.

"Come to me as you are, fledgling. I will welcome you."

Before I can hesitate, before reason can reassert itself, I step off the edge.

***

Wind rushes past my ears and roars my foolishness to the world. By the Depths, I did it. The world takes on a sharp clarity, a crystalline beauty that steals my breath. The distant plains, the rugged mountains, the common people of Eshan camped along the road. They see me, jumping to their feet only to fall to their knees and press their foreheads to the uncaring stone.

A laugh escapes my chest, relief and exhilaration and joy and terror combined in one. Everything I've done has led me here, to this. I have no hand in my fate, merely faith in a voice, in an element that has never before let me down.

The journey is interminable, glorious seconds stretched to marvelous eternities, every breath a miracle, every moment perfection. Too soon, far too soon, the valley approaches, rushing towards my face with startling speed. Eyes open wide, I spread my arms and accept whatever comes. My shadow writhes in response, curling and twisting beneath my clothes.

Light disappears like a snuffed lantern. Darkness, whole and complete, covers the world. The shadow does not flow like the air. Tendrils of darkness caress my face, my legs, my chest, gentle and slow. There is nothing to see, nothing to gauge my speed. I could meet the ground at any moment, too fast and hard to think, to wonder, to fear...

My feet touch down onto bare earth devoid of life. In the tumble through the shadow, it must have righted me, gently guiding me to stand at the base of the valley. Though my connection to shadow is cut off, I can still sense it, surrounding me, holding me, suffusing me. When I breathe, it is not air that fills my lungs.

And then, I can see. Not in the way of sight, but intrinsically, fundamentally, as if the face in the shadow was always, and will always, be here. I don't recognize her, yet she is as familiar to me as the smell of the sea, forgotten until the scent is found again. She sees me without eyes, sees through my skin and to what lies beneath. I feel flensed and embraced at once.

"Welcome, fledgling," she says, in a voice that fills the air and me and all the shadow enshrouding the sky. Her mouth doesn't move. *"I am glad to see you as yourself, free and whole."*

"Nice to see you... too?" I glance around, but there is nothing to see, nothing in all the world but her. "This isn't what I expected."

"And what did you expect? Torture? Pain? Perdition?"

There is something of humor in her words, like she's laughing behind her hand.

"Something like that," I say, smiling in spite of myself. "Is this the test?"

"A test? No. This is something more." She moves closer, circling me in the darkness. She has no form but the shadow, yet the shadow is her form. *"Who are you, fledgling? What is your name?"*

"My name is Kettle." My name feels somehow inadequate, like I've left my answer incomplete. "The, uh, Mother of the Family. And... yours?"

"R'hea, once Empress of Night."

"R'hea!" I shout before I can stop myself. "So the stories... they're true?"

"There are still stories about me?" she asks, the note of amusement returning. *"What do they say?"*

"That you and your comrades killed the Creator and... stole his power."

It isn't until the words leave my lips that I realize *what* I just said. If this is *that* R'hea, then she participated in the murder of a god. She was duped into stealing the power I now wield, Cursed through all of time...

She laughs, so long and loud I imagine she would be crying if she could.

"They say what *about me?"* She continues too quickly for me to respond. *"I figured that I would not be well remembered by history, but murdering the Creator? Who were my comrades?"*

"Yali, Cursed of Earth, Eo, Cursed of Thought, El—"

"I see," she cuts in before I can finish, the laugh in her voice turning bitter. *"I should have known. The Light spread their lies well. Cursed? Eo must have failed to sway them."*

"So you... didn't? Kill the Creator?"

"No, Kettle, I didn't. We didn't. We were simply soldiers on the losing side of a war. Citizens of a kingdom that was destroyed."

"So the Creator isn't...?"

"I don't know. If he still exists, he doesn't speak to me. But the

story is absurd. Humanity slaying a god? Stealing his power? How? In what world would such a thing be possible? How would we even begin?"

"I… see your point," I say, embarrassed. "I never really believed the story, but hearing your name just kind of brought it all back to me. I used to feel as if I knew you. Like we were one and the same, like your spirit really did guide mine."

"In a way, you aren't wrong," she says, giving the impression of a smile. *"I am connected to all of Shadow. I may not be present in every fragment, but it carries my touch wherever it goes. I sent that little shade out in search of the next Master of Shadow. In search of you."*

The shadow beneath my clothes swirls in excited patterns across my skin. I can feel it yearning to join the larger body of darkness, dampened by its closeness to me. A closeness it didn't choose, apparently.

A sudden melancholy overtakes my thoughts. This little bit of shadow wandered the world to find me, leaving this dark ocean of safety behind, dutifully following me in my misadventure. Part of it died at my command, destroyed by living light. I can't reach it, but I give it a mental nudge.

Go. You've done more than could ever be expected of you. You've done your job. I'm here.

It snuggles tighter, ignoring the command. Its embrace lightens my heart. R'hea watches, a faint smile in the darkness. As the moment passes, the feeling of the darkness changes. Anticipation, nervousness, and fear resonate through the valley. The woman in the shadow moves away from me without moving.

"What is it?"

"I like you," she says. Her levity disappears. *"And the shadow trusts you. So I am afraid."*

"Afraid of what?" I ask, heartbeat quickening.

"I told you this is more than a test. I have been waiting for the one who can bring shadow back into the light. There have been many in the millennia since my kingdom fell. None of them had the strength

391

they needed to survive."

"Survive? Survive what?"

"Long ago, the world was in equilibrium, two halves ruled by Sun and Moon. The brightness of Light owned half the world, and Shadow reigned its opposite, two sides of a balanced coin. When the world began to turn, Shadow could not stand before the sun. Without the touch of its Master, Shadow withers and dies in the presence of light."

She falls silent for a time, lost in memories of times so long past they predate written history. The world once didn't turn? There was no day and night? If I wasn't speaking to a woman formed entirely of shadow, I might doubt.

"The only way Shadow can return is if there is a Master strong enough to make it so. I—"

"That is not me," I break in, feeling again the distance between my will and the darkness. "I'm broken. The shadow can't hear my call. I am no more connected to it now than any other person."

"Why?"

"I accepted... power. From the soul you separated from mine. It changed me, in ways I don't understand. I don't feel like I fit inside my body anymore."

"I see," she says, though with an air of thoughtfulness. *"You did not let me finish. The test you now face is one of character first, which your connection to shadow has answered. It would abandon any who did not care for it."* Thanks, buddy. *"Several Masters of Shadow have not walked from this valley because they viewed the darkness as a tool rather than a companion."*

"You said 'first.'"

"Yes. The second test is simple. I have waited for years beyond counting for a vessel strong enough to contain... me."

A chill that has nothing to do with the air races down my spine. There is a pressure at the edge of my awareness, a crackling force I know all-too-well. My soul remembers Tecarim's burning power, his alien will warring with mine for control of my body. It remembers the shocking strength of Kit's power, too great for my body to contain, and the will that guided me to take this shadow for my own.

She isn't pushing, yet, but her soul is the darkness. She is on my skin, in my hair, in my *lungs*...

"Do not be afraid," she whispers, her voice suddenly fragile and open. *"I can tell you have experience with these matters. Perhaps this strangeness with your body and soul is fate personified. You may succeed where all others have failed. I..."* For the first time, she seems uncertain of how to proceed, of what to say. Above all, she seems *tired.* *"I have existed too long, Kettle. Far too long. No soul should endure so many centuries. I have no desire to live again. What I offer is a gift. Of my power, and my wisdom. I offer myself, adding my strength to yours so that you may carve a place for Shadow, open and free."*

There is no deceit in her words. The exhaustion dogging every syllable is matched only by the hope that guides their intent. No part of me doubts her, so why does a tremor of fear ripple through my spirit?

"What aren't you telling me?"

"Every Master of Shadow who has earned this chance has perished."

"Why?"

"Their bodies could not contain my power. They were not strong enough." She pauses, as if afraid to continue. *"They were devoured from the inside out."*

"I... see," I say, trying, and failing, to suppress a shiver. "Do I have a choice?"

"Of course. Yet no Shaper who cares for shadow has ever refused."

The words echo through my soul, ringing true as everything else R'hea has told me. And they are true of me as well. I lived for years believing my sad sliver of shadow was all that the world contained. It has been my constant companion, my most trusted friend. To leave the sea of darkness trapped beneath the earth… it would be like leaving a member of my family behind. I can no more leave it than I could leave Corna trapped with the Master of Beasts.

"Okay." I open my hands at my side. "Do I just let you in? Is there anything else I need to do?"

"Survive."

"Right."

"Whatever happens, Kettle, Mother of the Family, thank you for looking after your shadow. Do what I could not, be what I could not. Bring the Shadow into the Light."

"I'll do my best," I say shakily, trying to control my racing heart. Already I can feel her pressing, pressing, her strength so colossal it beggars belief.

"If these are my final words, I go to oblivion content, knowing it is you."

"You barely know me," I whisper, her words falling on me with such weight I can scarcely breathe.

"Do I?" she says, the hint of laughter returning to her voice. My shadow swirls against my skin. *"Goodbye, Kettle. And good luck."*

It starts as a trickle, like a tendril of lightning curling around my veins.

My fingers twitch. The muscles of my forearm cramp and release too quickly to register the pain.

More. My skin catches fire, my scream contained only by the terror I'll bite off my tongue. The questing lightning reaches my chest, and a storm ignites over my heart.

For a moment, there is peace. Alive with power, every hair stands on end, every part of me brought into incredible focus.

The flow strengthens to a river, then a flood. I do scream now, or I think I do. The barrier between my body and the shadow erodes and disappears beneath a torrent of energy.

I have the time for a hearbeat's relief as my connection to shadow ghosts across my mind before the power rises again. The emptiness hollowed into my body in the last year fills in seconds, the ancient Shaper's power taking its place and spilling over.

More drives into my body, on and on, power too pure to sully, too strong to restrain, a tide of lightning and fire rising to eclipse my sight, to eclipse the world. I feel her, *know* her, as she surrenders and—

A land. Strong and weary, beautiful and broken.

Darkness and starlight, shadowed towers rising to touch the moon—

A face. Strong and weary, beautiful and broken.

Heart and steel, armored against the trials of war and secrecy—

A love. Strong and weary, beautiful and broken.

Eo.

***

The shadow holds me like a child, floating above the floor of the valley in a sea of perfect living darkness. Not because I lack the strength to stand. Not because I am weak or vulnerable.

Because I fear my own strength.

I can feel it. All of it. So much shadow twines itself about the bones of the earth that it may well break the world if I clench too tightly. *So much.* My senses before were little better than the dim awareness of a child in the womb. In my hands, in my soul, lies the fate of the world and all its people. With a simple twist, the shadow would rend and shatter, and all the hopeless might of our nations, all the petty hopes of our people, would end in cataclysm.

She should not have given me this strength. No one should have it.

But I do.

I turn my eyes from the earth and what lies beneath it. Memory floods my surface thoughts, subsuming my terrified wonder under the needs of the present. My family, my friends, trapped with the bared sword of a kingdom resting on their necks. Waiting for me to return.

Take me.

The shadow flows to my whim like an extension of my body. In a stream of darkness, I rise. The black ink of my power writes itself across the sky, for the first time in living memory. Shadow flows from the darkness of the valley into the light in a wave broad enough to drown the world.

The city perched above swims into view. Gentle as a mother's caress, the shadow returns me to the platform I jumped from, what feels like a decade ago. The people remain, their faces frozen in awe. Aurelion and Corna stand where I left them at the bottom of the stairs.

I glance at the sun before it disappears behind a rising tide of darkness. An hour, maybe less. It feels impossible, for the world to change in so little time.

My shadow makes night of day. Like the space between stars given substance, shadow encircles the proud city and offers it its first taste of true darkness. No light, even the light of the sun, can break the curtain of night cast over the city. When it is finished, I take a deep breath and begin to walk.

There is a rustle of movement as a thousand people fall to their knees and press their foreheads to the ground. Whispered prayer and soft weeping barely disturb the stillness that falls over Yohru. My friends start to fall to their knees as well, but a tendril of shadow holds them both aloft before they can manage. Corna winces, and I frown at the memory of her pain.

"Kettle?" she asks tentatively, searching my eyes.

Searching *for* my eyes. They *wouldn't* be able to see, would they… with a thought, I thin the shadow high above, and filtered sunlight paints the world in shades of gray. When she catches sight of me, Corna breaks into the broadest grin her face could contain.

"Yes," I say, smiling softly. "It's still me."

"Thank the fucking Creator," she gasps, tears flooding her eyes. My shadow catches her before she collapses, sobbing. "I thought you were dead, Creator damn it, I thought we *all* were dead."

"Someday," I say, pulling her into a hug. "Not today."

R'hea kept her word, and I am myself. But, as Aurelion's strong arms wrap around us both, I feel something deep in my soul, a faint emotion I could not call mine, even if it echoes mine perfectly. A happy contentment, a quiet joy in the knowledge that, finally, I have the strength to protect the people I love.

And to end anything that may threaten them.

I gently pry myself free of the arms surrounding me. There is work to be done before I can relax.

A threat to deal with.

There are no eyes to see my return journey. Every citizen of Yohru presses their face to the ground in the supernatural gloom. The moment Corna grunts in pain, my shadow lifts her on a throne of living darkness. Her startled curse echoes strangely in the silence of the city.

The Baeda tower comes into view, and a cheer breaks out, joyful and jarring. Hom, Sario, and Ezil stand at the gate and pump their fists over their heads, smiles wide even from a distance. The Umbral slam fist to chest and drop to a knee in unison.

The Ihera all have their foreheads planted on the stone, soldiers, Oshei, and Amanu all. The sight makes my skin cold. Ignoring my smiling family, I walk until my feet are inches from the Amanu's head. He shivers as the sound of my footsteps dies.

"Look at me," I command coldly.

"Eshani, I—"

"Look at me."

He moves slowly, hesitantly, like the weight of his own power holds his head to the earth. He flinches when he sees the mark of power on my face. Tears fill his eyes, terror their companion.

"Eshani, I didn't know, I didn't mean…" He loses momentum before he can gain any, the look on my face grinding his words to a halt.

"Do any of you speak for him?" I ask, casting my gaze over the assembled Ihera. They tremble like leaves in a breeze. None raise their heads. None open their mouths.

A voice, like a distant song, offers me wisdom. It questions. Do we wish to begin our reign with death? Do we wish to rule with fear? The Amanu would be a powerful ally, a unifier of the old power and the new. His strength would be an asset in the time to come, and his guilt would keep him in line better than any threat I could hang over his head. I may well need him.

I just don't care.

"You killed my brother."

"No, I—"

"You killed my sister."

"Please—"

"You tried to kill everyone I love." I raise my voice so that it carries over the assembled citizens. "Any of you can disagree with me. Any of you can raise concerns. Dissent is welcome, and necessary. I will listen with an open ear, and debate with an open mind. Your voices will matter." I turn back to the groveling man at my feet, his handsome face distorted with fear. "But if you threaten me or mine, you have chosen your own fate."

Her voice isn't a voice, but a feeling. There is another way. A way to mend this wound before it can fester.

"Baeda Sonjur," I call, and the Baeda patriarch moves with dignity to stand at my side. He is the first of my new people to meet my eyes.

"What is your command, Eshani?" he says, fighting to keep the smile off his stoic face.

"Bring me a vessel from your tower suitable for a *keishi* to inhabit."

"At once."

"There is one way for you to repair the ruined honor of the Ihera." I look down at the Amanu's frightened eyes. He was young, and arrogant, and stupid. It almost makes me pity him. "Give up your mortal form, and become a *keishi* sworn to my house. Serve me and my mine with honor, and your deeds will be forgiven."

I do not give him a choice. He knows, anyway. It is service, or oblivion.

Sonjur returns and bows, offering a dagger of exquisite craftsmanship. Glossy black like a shard of perfect obsidian, the handle is bone white and pristine. It fits my hand like it was made for me. I look to Sonjur. His Ensouled will know the process, and can guide the Amanu on his journey. With a gesture, I motion Sonjur to place his *keishi* in the young Ihera's hand. At the same time, I flip the dagger and offer it to him, hilt first.

To his credit, the Amanu doesn't hesitate. He meets my gaze one last time with tears in his eyes, then gives me a firm nod. With a slow breath, he grasps the hilts of both weapons. A nova of bronze ignites in the darkness, bright enough to send false shadows dancing through the streets. Loose earth rises from the stone, the sleeves of the crowd's *dimina* flutter, and my feet feel lighter on the street. The city *groans*.

Is he so powerful that...?

The bronze light dims and goes out. My body resettles on the stone as gravity resumes. The city itself seems to breathe a sigh of relief.

And the Amanu slumps to the street.

Sonjur gathers his *keishi,* sheathing her at his side before carefully lifting the dagger. He bows before me, offering me the hilt. I take it, feeling the quiet buzz of the young man's soul at the edge of my awareness. He settles onto my hip without complaint.

Taking a deep breath, I let the shadow fall. Sunlight shines again on the city in full force. The darkness returns to the valley and the caverns below the earth that have been its home for so long. All save for the small cloud of darkness that spins happily about my chest, and the small throne holding Corna aloft.

The shadow has returned, but the valley feels different, as it should. The shadow has awakened from a long slumber.

Let the world take note.

Corna hops down from the throne of shadow with Aurelion's help. She looks out over the sea of downturned faces, then scans the line of Umbral Guard kneeling in salute.

"Well, then," she says, turning to me with a bright grin. "What now?"

"Now?" My eyes turn west, back across the endless plains, back to a room of darkness and crimson light. "Now, we prepare for war."

Chapter 18
Jace

The Eighty-First Day of Summer
In the year 5223, Council Reckoning

The beach remains deserted throughout the day aside
from the occasional crab or seabird. After a rest, I drag the
Vengeance's unconscious body under some scrub and head up
the beach to get the lay of the land. Cresting a loose-packed dune
on shaky legs, I stagger to a halt at the sight of cracked earth and
shimmering heat.

Storybooks always portray the desert as rolling mounds of
golden sand sparkling in the sun. The land before me bears little
resemblance to those tales. A flat, dead scrubland of parched
earth stretches into the distance. There is no movement but for
the hiss of sand on the wind and waver of extraordinary heat.

I don't know the first thing about finding food or water in a
place as inhospitable as this. All I have is the hope that the
Vengeance will awaken soon enough that thirst doesn't become
an issue. As noon approaches, the sun grows hot enough that I
retreat under the scraggly scrub myself, laying down near the
Vengeance and doing my best to keep my mind off the thirst
nagging at the back of my mind.

When my eyes open, the sun soaks the western horizon in
liquid ruby. The soft sand and the sea breeze must have lulled me
to sleep. I glance over and bolt upright. The Vengeance is gone.
Scrambling to my feet, I relax when I see his slender form
silhouetted against the sunset. He doesn't turn as I join him in
looking west.

"Tonight," he rasps softly, the salt of the ocean still caked about his mouth. "We rest tonight, and tonight only."

"Will you be recovered by then?" I ask curiously. I have no idea how these things work. How long does a soul like the Vengeance's require to recover?

"Well enough to fly," he says, squinting at the harsh flat desert like it offends him.

"Well enough to fight?"

"It'll have to be," he mutters, turning and heading down the dune.

"Hey, wait a minute." I suppress a groan as my legs, still sore and heavy from kicking and fighting to keep us alive in the ocean, struggle down the loose sands. "*I* feel like I might collapse at any second. There's no way I'll be fighting fit tomorrow. Do you have some mysterious power of recovery I don't?"

"No," he says flatly, dropping into a meditative pose. "A fight does not wait for you to be healthy and rested and ready. You fight when you have to."

"Which we don't have to," I point out, narrowly avoiding a collapse as I slump next to him. "We can rest up and *then* go looking for trouble."

"We leave in the morning," he snaps, skewering me with a glare. After a moment he softens, running a hand over his face. "Speaking with the wind isn't an exact science. I'm not sure why, or even how, but it's urging me on, demanding that I hurry. If I've learned nothing else in the past two centuries, I've learned to listen when it speaks."

"Alright, then," I say, slowly leaning back onto the sands. "In the morning."

***

Judging by the color of the sky when the Vengeance shakes me awake, we need to discuss his definition of morning. The stars still shine through a dark tapestry, though I could, conceivably, make a claim that the sky over the ocean has lightened. Is lightening. Maybe.

"Up," he says curtly. There's strain in his voice. "You've got until the sun breaks the horizon."

"Alright," I say, levering myself to my feet.

I run through a few of the stretches Reknor taught me in preparation for joining the Shorn. My legs are sore, my skin raw after the exposure to the wind and waves, but the routine wakes up my body and answers the only question worth answering: can I fight?

After a wordless moment, the Vengeance joins me, our movements in perfect sync, feet whispering on the sand.

As soon as we finish, he holds out his arm, and I move so that he can wrap my chest again in a tight hold. Experience doesn't do much to contain my awe as we launch again into the air. The desert stretches below us in a shimmering wave of heat and sparkling sand.

The second we rise high enough to clear any large impediments, we *accelerate* with a crack of ripping air. Pressure builds in my chest, my guts slamming back against my toes. I would scream if I could. Yesterday, I could barely comprehend how fast we were moving. Today, I can barely keep my eyes open against the wind scouring my face. He does nothing to protect us, only pouring on more speed.

There is an urgency to our trip, a desperation that tickles at the back of my mind. Why would he risk our lives crossing the ocean when so little a disruption could kill us? We lost altitude for a few seconds, and we nearly died trying to make it to shore. That margin is thinner than I figured a man like the Vengeance would risk. What drives him now?

The Way of the West comes into view ahead, the wagons and people traveling the perfect expanse of stone smaller than ants. A gleam of metal draws my eyes to the north, where the Way disappears into a sprawling city of white surrounded by a moat of greenery foreign to these parched lands. Golden rooftops shine in the morning light like a diamond buried in the desert sands.

Coin. The Jewel of the West. A mighty river wends its way past the city farther west, flowing south parallel to the Way. Tiny river boats bob along the Vein of the Creator, their white steering sails blending with the froth kicked up from their oars.

A pair of figures stand out in the flat and empty desert surrounding the city, small and silhouetted in the growing light. Whoever they are, they're walking away from the city and towards the flat expanse of desert we just crossed in under an hour. On foot, I don't know how long it would take to cross, but it is not a journey I envy.

Before I can take three breaths, we flash past the city and over the Way, traveling too fast for anyone below to notice until we're long gone. The Vengeance shows no signs of slowing; if anything, he pushes harder, the wind battering my face forcefully enough to bruise. His arm is an iron bar around my chest, and I can't tell if his grip or the blistering speed is stealing my breath.

The ground blurs as miles fly beneath us. Before long, the trackless waste turns to rolling fields dotted with lakes and streams. Herd beasts, absent their shepherds, graze below us, though the startled lowing of cattle can't reach our ears before we've gone.

Without warning, the Vengeance slows and drops us towards the field. I frantically scan for signs of the Lord General, but the fields are empty as far as I can see. The Vengeance drops us none-too-gently to the earth, his arm falling away from my chest as he drops to his knees. He forces himself to kneel, the movement so slow it's like he aged two decades in a morning.

His face is an unhealthy shade of gray, and rings haunt his eyes.

"Two hours," he rasps, but his hands tremble.

"You won't have anything left when we get there," I say, lowering to meet his gaze. "We need to rest."

"Can't."

404

"What's the point of finding Kranos only for him to put you in the ground? You'd be throwing your life away for nothing."

"Not... nothing." He takes several deep, steadying breaths. "He's getting close. We can't let him steal any more."

"Steal?" It hits me like a bolt of lightning. "Another... power?"

Why else would the Master of Beasts risk himself? Why couldn't he bring a whole battalion of soldiers to guard his life?

Because even they would be horrified by what he's attempting.

"Do you know which one it is?" I ask after a moment.

"Something that does not touch air," he says, slumping back to lay on the earth. "So probably an Ethereal."

"I'm sorry?"

"The... oh." He glances at my face, a bitter smile crossing his face. "Forgot they don't educate the youth anymore. The elements are gathered into categories for ease of discussion: the Ethereals, which have no substance, the Ephemerals, which do not last, the Immutables, which do not change, and the Mercurials, which do. Force, Time, and Thought are the Ethereals; Lightning, Fire, Light, and Voices are the Ephemerals; Metal, Stone, and Earth are the Immutables; and Water, Roots, Beasts, and Air are the Mercurials. Then there is the Unknown, which is expected to fill out either the Immutables or the Ethereals, though no one can be certain, aside from the knowledge that its symbol is black."

"Wait, there are two, maybe three sets of four. Doesn't fifteen elements feel... incomplete?"

"The world isn't always symmetrical and satisfying," he says drily.

"So you think he's after... Force, or Thought, or Time?" I ask, slowly.

"Everything else, the air feels," he says, closing his eyes. "Unless the Shaper is being very, very careful."

"So if I used fire… you could feel it?"

"Yes."

"At what range?" I ask incredulously. "Are you feeling him now?"

"It isn't so precise. I know this because I asked the wind to follow Helikos and Kranos and tell me if they ever split from each other." He opens his eyes and raises his head. "It's only as we've gotten closer that I realized what he's after. Now, let me sleep. Two hours."

"Three."

He doesn't answer, his face already slack and vacant.

***

We stop to rest two more times throughout the day, each flight shorter than the last. The Vengeance looks closer to death every time we stop, pushing himself to his limit the second he thinks he has the energy to fly.

The sun bars our way forward with blinding blades of light as it sinks towards a distant mountain range. We've flown over jungle, rolling hills, a small mountain range, and a dozen settlements in our endless race against intangible time. A larger mountain range looms ahead, reaching thick fingers to scour the clouds. We're south of the Creator's Teeth, so this must be some *other* mountain range large enough to bar passage west. Is this… the western edge of the Khalintars?

Impossible… it must be the Teeth. There is no way we've traveled more than three thousand—four thousand?—miles in two days. It just… doesn't…

My face is numb from the endless abuse of the wind. Squinting ahead through the sunset, I can barely make out a village ahead. Mud brick dwellings nestle against the foothills of the mountains, protected by a sharp edge of a cliffside on one side and a mighty escarpment stretching nearly as high as we are on the other.

Though it feels like we should land, Altos slows until we

hover above the ground. I don't break his concentration by looking back at him, but he radiates confusion and wariness.

Narrowing my focus, I study the village. There are no villagers present, which is strange at this hour. Most towns would have their laborers returning home, their people squeezing the last bit of work out of the day before night fell and stole the light. The embers of a fire burn in a pit at the center of the village, so *someone* is definitely here, or was recently. Yet there is no movement. None... at all. Not even smoke from the fire, as if we are looking at a *painting*...

"'Ware!" I shout desperately.

The Vengeance is already moving. A thick branch appears out of nowhere a dozen paces ahead, hurtling straight through the space we just occupied. One second, the air was empty and clear, and the next the twisted, pointed branch tried to skewer us. The wood spins in the air, turning after us like a wolf chasing a rabbit. Like a predator's will guides it.

The Master of Air doesn't hesitate. We drop like stones, headfirst. *Towards* the still image hovering strangely before us. I can't help myself. As we close, I turn my head aside, bracing for an impact.

Like sliding through a soap bubble, we encounter the briefest pressure, then push through.

Carnage. The village, picturesque and still before, is awash in flame, bodies lying where they fell. Their wounds are as gruesome as they are inexplicable. A woman looks to have been cut in half by a massive sword, but the man next to her has wicked slashes across his back, like claws reached into his flesh and severed his spine. Black smoke crawls along the ground in thick clouds.

The Vengeance releases me while we're still moving, and I roll to my feet facing down the street. Facing our enemy.

The Master of Beasts, giant beyond any human proportion, stands ready, hands loosely held at his side, deep brown light glowing from his chest. The jagged branch of wood pursues the Vengeance until he turns and shreds it with a blast of concentrated air. The Lord General of the Empire of the Sea grins when he sees us.

"Altos," he says in a voice like deep music. "I wondered if I'd get the chance to kill you before Helikos did."

"Kranos," the Vengeance returns, drawing his sword. Though he has to be exhausted, his hands are steady. "I can't wait to see your eyes go dim."

"I am more than I was, and you look dead on your feet. And your ally already knows how this will go. You can lay down your arms now, boy," Kranos says, not taking his eyes off the Master of Air. "We both know you don't have the strength to kill me."

"I'll take my chances."

"What chances?" he says, spreading his arms. The massive hilt of his oversized greatsword tilts on his back. "How can you kill a god?"

Light flickers across his chest in a complicated pattern. Green, Brown, Red, Silver, and... Yellow. Yellow? When did he steal Light?

A woman, barely more than a girl, lies at Kranos' feet. Her straight dark hair and tanned skin fit with this area of the world, though her clothes are far finer than the other villagers. She looks unharmed but for the bruising print of a massive hand where it pressed over her shoulder. Inside the mottled flesh is a symbol drawn in black, like a charred remnant burned into wood.

That explains the strange motionless image of the village, quiet and pristine despite the chaos within.

It is the cataclysm of the death of a Master of Light.

Her death.

We were too late.

"I can't imagine why you're here," Kranos continues, shaking his head. "You've left Itolas and your petty rebellion to die. Helikos and all the might of the Tide will soon depart Donir to crush your rebellion." He smiles a wicked smile. "You'll have to thank the Perrea girl for me if she survives. She gave me two priceless gifts in short order: a breakthrough in my research, and the location of your pathetic camp out in the woods."

"I was attacked," I find myself saying, though my throat tries to close when his eyes turn to me. "By two Shapers in the Kinlen Forest. Your work?"

"The first of many," he says, his square jaw dipping in a nod. "What use is there in resisting, Altos? How can any army stand against a dozen Shapers? A hundred? A thousand?"

"We won't have to, after today," Altos says steadily.

"Yes, you're right. There won't be a fight after today. Your friends will be broken with the fall of their mythical leader. After I destroy you, I'll claim your power for my own, and—"

The Vengeance explodes into motion, blurring in my sight. Kranos barely has time to draw his sword before the Master of Air is upon him. In a flicker of steel, three cuts erupt blood on the Kranos' thigh, shoulder, and ribs. His sword comes across so fast it rips through the air, but the Vengeance slides beneath it and cuts him again before he can recover.

Creator help me, the only reason I held the Vengeance at bay is because he *let me.*

Drawing my sword, finally, I move towards the fight, trying to read the Vengeance's patterns. He moves so quickly that it feels like I'm more likely to foul his path than provide any meaningful aid.

I close half the distance, studying the fight, when my instincts scream danger. I spin, edge of my sword leading.

A twisted, monstrous creature looms against the sunset. Like a nightmare's vision of Bota, the creature's apelike fist drives towards my face. My sword takes three fingers from the fist, but agony can't halt the momentum of its charge. Its shoulder clips my chest. Like a child struck by a passing carriage, I slam into the ground, all breath stolen. The monster roars, lifting its fists above its head to break my body beneath them.

Roll.

My body doesn't move, lungs heaving to shift a brick wall.

Roll.

My body finally responds. The monster's fists thunder against the ground an inch from my back. The force of the blow ripples through the earth and throws me bodily into the air. Twisting, I manage to get my feet under me before I fall.

A massive hand hurtles at my chest before I have a chance to set my feet. Slipping to the side, I cut into its forearm. Its muscles resist my blade, closer to wood than flesh. It roars in anger and pain, spittle flying in thick ropes from its broken mouth. I stumble backwards to give myself space.

Over its hulking shoulder, I catch the barest hint of the fight raging down the street. The Master of Beasts is stained red from a dozen cuts, but his sword has lost none of its speed and his feet remain steady. I know from experience that wounds like that won't slow him long. The only way to truly hurt him is to cut off his head, remove his limbs, or break the symbol of his strength.

Despite his speed and skill, the Vengeance hasn't managed any serious damage. But if Kranos manages to land a blow...

The brief lapse in focus nearly kills me. The monstrous ape roars in challenge, thumping a fist against its chest. But its eyes flick over my shoulder.

It wants to hold my attention.

I drop to the ground. Wind rustles my hair as a trio of wicked claws swipe through the empty air. A second monster, scaled like a crocodile, hisses in frustration. I regain my feet between the two abominations. Each is over eight feet tall, outclassing me in reach, strength, speed...

They charge.

The world slows.

My hands move absent my mind's command. My feet fall

410

into steps carved into my bones. In this impossible, infinite moment, my sword is more a part of me than my blood. I am not trapped between two horrific monsters with the strength and speed to break me.

I am between the colored poles, caught in the graceful dance Reknor's shouting voice wrote into my soul.

Pink one.

My sliding crouch ducks beneath the claws of the reptile, sword flicking across its heel as it stumbles past.

Red four.

Leaping above a low sweep, blood blooms on the ape's chest.

Teal seven...

Our dance is as old as time, predator and prey, life and death. My two unwilling partners know their steps. And I know mine.

But all songs come to a close. The steps end. The soundless music fades.

My partners can no longer hold the pace.

The ape is missing an arm, blood spurting in massive gouts as it sways on its feet. The crocodile lies mewling, hands clawing useless at the dirt. The parched earth greedily drinks their bloody offering. At some point, I slipped into the world's fire. Golden light drifts from the two dying crimson fires. My sword, gleaming a bright ochre, is edged in a thin sheen of scarlet flame.

A grunt of pain returns my focus to the other fight. Twin stars clash again and again, one encased in silver and white, the other awash in crimson the color of arterial blood. The Vengeance flits about, his feet skating on solid air, whipping about the Lord General with the grace and speed of zephyrs. Wherever the Vengeance goes, bits of his enemy spray through the white fire of the air. Their blades, a similar color to my own, leave trails of dull light in their wake.

Without the sight, I might think that the fight is going well.

411

More wounds than I can count decorate the crimson bonfire that is the Master of Beasts. Yet he *remains* a bonfire, glowing brightly and steadily. The Vengeance, once a sun in his own right, glows more dimly by the second. As the white fire of his power falters, his movements slow.

The Lord General fights defensively for now, absorbing cut after superficial cut, protecting his chest and neck with steel and strength.

And then, it happens.

The Vengeance's power expires.

Kranos' massive ochre sword whips across and crushes the Vengeance's blade back into his body. He flips through the air and slams into the green light of a mudbrick wall, his sword falling forgotten from his hands. Dim golden light shines from within the dull red fire of his crumpled body.

The Master of Beasts closes the ground in a few quick strides, raising his mighty blade to finish the fight.

He says something, but I don't catch it.

I'll never get there in time. I have to… I *have* to.

My hand comes up, desperate need fueling desperate action. A river of fire, bright enough to outshine the sun, pours from my body into the air. Its color is strange, like a river of molten gold, but it should burn well enough.

My chest tightens immediately, and cold reigns in my veins. Cutting off the flow before the ice can spread, I fall to my knees, hoping it's enough.

The fire flows through the air like a hungry serpent, diving for the Master of Beast's vulnerable back. He doesn't see it coming as the flames wash over him. I clench my fist, a savage joy rising… and falling.

The fire fades. The Master of Beasts remains, uncharred, unburnt, unaffected. He doesn't seem to notice as the golden light disappears.

My sight returns to normal. My heart falls past the soles of my feet. I don't know what I did, or could have done. I didn't even singe the hem of his shirt, and now I can raise my head only with an effort.

The Master of Beasts cuts down. The wall shatters from the impact, and the house collapses in an explosion of dust. I stare dully at the cloud hiding the Vengeance's mangled remains.

My *father's* remains. It doesn't feel real. It doesn't feel possible.

Wind picks up, swirling the dust into a cyclone. I brace myself, pressing to the earth. Even weakened as he was, there is no doubt the Vengeance's death will spark a cataclysm that could well finish the task he failed to complete in life.

And take me with them both.

An explosive thrust of air blasts out of the cyclone and slams into the Master of Beasts. Despite his extraordinary strength, he stumbles back from the blow. A gust of wind gathers the swirling dust and rips it aside. My mouth drops open.

The Vengeance, whole and unharmed, stands in the center of the tornado.

Green light shines to life on Kranos' chest. The pieces of the collapsed house rise and fly towards the Vengeance's back. The whipping air slaps them away without effort. With a gesture, he summons three near-invisible blades of rippling air. They tear into Kranos, one after another.

Wide arcs of blood spray onto the grass, and the Lord General falls to a knee. Silver light blossoms on his chest.

The Vengeance snaps his head to the side, face scrunched in pain, then turns slowly back to glare down at his foe. He raises a hand and spins it over his head. Like a toy flung spinning into the air by a careless child, an invisible hand rips the Master of Beasts from the ground and heaves him to the sky. His form rises so high it nearly disappears among the clouds. Just before he passes out of sight, the Vengeance closes his fist and punches it to the earth.

413

With a scream that echoes through the mountains, the Master of Beasts plummets. Faster than gravity could take him, faster than a diving eagle, he plummets. White light flares from the Vengeance's hand, and his falling body accelerates further just before—

Breaking bone and parting flesh and tearing earth and shattered stone and—

I feel the impact in my chest even from down the street. The force drives a crater into the earth. Exhaustion forgotten, I stumble to my feet. My teeth clench, and my eyes waver.

I had no idea, no idea at all, how powerful he really is.

What world allows for power like this to exist? Who could resist the Vengeance at full strength?

I stagger to the edge of the crater. The gigantic body, once perfect and strong, is a shattered mess. His legs are twisted beneath him, his back separated into three unnatural angles, his bones jutting from his flesh like pale white trees. I barely manage to hold my gorge behind my teeth. The Vengeance steps up next to me, breathing hard, visage locked in a snarl. When he sees the ruin of his enemy, he seems to deflate, an intangible intensity fading from the air.

"How?" I ask in amazement. I gesture at his body, the color in his cheeks, the ease and presence with which he stands. "Just... how?"

"You tell me," he says, meeting my gaze steadily. "I was beaten. I had nothing left. I was sure I was going to die. And then it all disappeared. It was like a fire ignited in my soul, and I gained all my strength back and then some. I still feel it, even now. I'm stronger now than I was this morning."

"I..." I trail off.

The fire. The *golden* fire. Like Juliet's life force and the power I used to save it. Why had I raised my hand? To harm the Master of Beasts? Or to save the Vengeance? It's almost like the fire knew my intent, or the best way to make it happen. What better way to save him than to empower him to save himself?

"Care to explain whatever you just realized?" he says, arching an eyebrow my way.

"I think… I think that my fire might be more than just fire. It could be—"

We snap around at a noise, halfway between a groan and a rasp. The corpse in the crater takes a rattling breath. The wreckage of Kranos' body *moves*. His muscles, once so proud and strong, shift his shattered bones. Even knowing what he is, what he's done, an appalled sympathy mixes with the horror rising in my chest. To live, even for a moment, like *that*…

His fingers twitch, and light flickers on his chest. Red light. The symbol of his strength must be intact.

"Creator save us all, is he trying to put himself back together?" the Vengeance asks incredulously.

"Can he, even?" I ask, my mind struggling to encompass a world where someone can survive, or would *want* to survive, after injuries like these.

"I'm not going to wait to find out if he can," the Master of Air mutters, hefting his sword and jumping into the crater.

The general's massive hand twitches again, accompanied by more red light. Looking at the bloody mess of him, it doesn't seem to be doing anything. If he's trying to fix something, it must be deep in his flesh. The Vengeance takes his time with the uneven footing, though he doesn't have far to go. Kranos has time for one more flicker of power.

The earth crunches behind me. I start to spin.

He wasn't trying to heal himself. He wasn't worried about himself at all. He was—

Agony explodes through my back. The tip of a dirty, jagged claw juts from my stomach, red with blood. At my wheezing cough, the Vengeance doesn't hesitate. He stabs down into the center of the broken mass of the Master of Beasts.

Light shines for a moment, unnatural and strange, emerald

and umber entwined. The earth softens like quicksand. Roots wrap his ruined form and pull. With a grimace that could be a grin, the mangled body of the Lord General disappears into the ground.

The Vengeance roars in anger and blasts the earth with blades of wind, but I can't spare them another thought. Already I can feel my legs weakening as blood pours from the ragged rent in my stomach. I don't have the strength, or the will, to drag my body off the claw holding me upright. Reknor taught me enough about how bodies work to know that I won't be walking away from this.

My sight returns to the worldfire.

Hunger roars to life, hunger like I've never felt or imagined. I gave some of my life to the Vengeance without a whisper of this hunger, but now my body knows only *need*. Frantic, frenzied, my spirit bucks past my weakening will to *consume*.

The dim crimson light lingering in the creature disappears into my body. It isn't enough. Not near enough.

My hand rises of its own accord. A glowing golden symbol burns on my palm, like life and mystery made solid. My fingers open.

And *close*.

Golden fire flashes from my chest and spreads, twisting about the world's flame. The emerald light of the earth, the white fire of the air, the yellow cast of the fading sunlight; my golden light seizes it all, and, like a prismatic river, the world's light *flows* to me. Into me.

Power and life and light explode in my chest. I straighten, the pain a distant memory, the light in my soul bright enough to blind my senses.

There is an itch in my stomach. My flesh is trying to reknit despite the claw buried in my gut. Frowning, I step forward, its ragged edges ripping new pathways through my flesh. The light in

416

my chest dims as it dives to the wound.

There isn't much ambient fire around me anymore. The elements are dead and dark for several steps in each direction. Yet there is more, so much more, just out of reach.

My hand rises again, golden symbol bright.

Open.

Close.

Golden light, hungry light, erupts from my chest, stronger than before, reaching, overcoming, *devouring*. A flood of light in a dozen colors spins towards me like a vortex crafted of chromatic fire. The power floods my soul, life like I've never known, life as it was *meant to be*. The rent in my stomach closes in seconds, smooth and whole as if the claw never struck. The golden symbol on my hand *burns* with power.

How did I live before this?

Joy, ecstasy, perfection, breathing as if I've never drawn breath.

There is a wider area of lifeless ground, out to ten paces at least. The world's fire still flows in all its gorgeous hues in the distance, but the earth and air about me are dark. I squint through the light shining from my chest. No. Not dark. Absent. The fire of the world is gone, taken, consumed to brighten the flame growing in my chest.

A memory tickles at the back of my mind. A sorrow. Two spots of absence, twin silhouettes laid against a backdrop of ice, holes in the perfect tapestry of light...

Distracted, some of the fire drains away from my core, the light of my soul dimming as the power escapes. It's like a fist gripping my chest and squeezing my heart. Terror flows through me. I can't lose this feeling. I can't. I *need* more.

Open.

Close.

Golden fire. A coruscating rainbow flows from every direction. My soul burns brighter again.

417

And within the ambient fire, something else. Something stronger. Like a river of white and gold and silver, so much purer, so much more *potent*. I gasp at its touch, my skin *alive,* my heart *racing*. If the natural fire of the world is water, this is exquisite wine.

More.

The river of white surges. Away from me. Growling, I throw my will against it. A pulse of golden power ripples out, but the white light recedes further.

No. No. *No.*

I can't let it escape. Acting on instinct more than conscious thought, I harness the power coursing in my veins. Like whips, no, like chains, I throw tendrils of golden fire around the glowing light, dragging it back. It bucks against my will, stretching, tearing. My arms and legs go cold, then my chest. The golden fire dims, spent, but I can feel it weakening. Just another few seconds...

With an inaudible crack in the air, the white flame loses the will to fight. It surges towards me, and I *drink*.

Oh, Creator. What power. What life.

There is still a foreign will, somewhere in the white fire, resisting me. It doesn't matter. It will not survive long.

I drink and I drink, my soul growing stronger, my body exploding at the seams with golden power. The light before me dims, my meal nearly consumed. My body feels like it's going to burst at any moment. There is no way I can take any more.

Yet I must. I need more.

Tendrils of white light spread across my face. I ignore them, even tainted with a metallic sheen, instead pulling in another burning pulse of perfect...

The needs of my body roar back to the fore. I can't breathe. My lungs work, yet no air enters. The world's fire flickers, dims, my dull earthly sight returning, focusing...

On a pair of furious, terrified eyes. Blue like mine. Shaped like mine.

Why does he look so afraid?

Even the mundane world fades as darkness falls.

***

I awaken with a gasp. Formless dreams of hunger and despair haunt my sleep, and I shudder involuntarily. The stillness of the late Summer night eases my heart a bit. A fire crackles nearby, though its warmth is hardly necessary. I haven't moved far. The village, pristine again behind the veil of illusion, stands in the near distance.

The heavy weight of the man's gaze across the fire brings me to the present. The white symbol of his power glows brightly on the back of his hand. I figure out why when I try to sit. The air holds me in tight, invisible chains.

"Jace?" he says, his voice more urgent, more concerned than I expect it to be.

"Uh, Vengeance? Where's the big guy?"

"Gone. Are you in control?" he asks sharply.

Memories of fire, of light, of glorious life, and finally of a white flame, resisting my call, chains of golden light...

"Oh," I say. "That... that light... it was you? Did I... did I hurt you?"

"It felt like you stole part of my soul," he says, leaning back so that his face is cast in shadow. "I didn't really believe Itolas, even though he was spooked to the point of terror. I thought you just manifested fire in a different way, a rarer way. But this... what you did yesterday... Jace, you should be dead. That claw ripped through everything that mattered in your guts, but your wounds healed like they never happened. You raised your hand, and the world around you... *died*."

"What? Died?"

"The air stopped, light disappeared, the earth crumbled." He shivers. If I wasn't afraid before, seeing the *Vengeance* unsettled hammers home how haunting this must be. "Everything

419

around you went gray and still. I stepped forward to help you, and I felt it. Like something took a bite of me, leeching away my strength."

"I'm... I'm sorry," I say, knowing the words sound weak but lacking any better. "I've been trying to control it. To harness it. She told me not to use it. She made me promise."

"Perrea?" he asks, though I can tell he already knows. His face darkens. "I knew that welcoming that abomination into my camp was a mistake."

"None of this is her fault." I try to sit up again, forgetting about the chains. All I manage is to flop about a bit. "She didn't ask for that power, and she's only used it to help people. And you *know* she didn't betray us on purpose."

"I know no such thing, regardless of what *you* believe," he snaps. "Especially now that Kranos has all but confirmed it."

"Do I really have to tell you not to trust anything that psychopath says? If anything happens to Juliet, it will aid his cause and harm ours."

"Maybe," he allows, though he doesn't sound convinced. The distant village, falsely preserved in peaceful perfection, looks on as the Vengeance broods across the fire.

"How did you stop me?" I ask after a moment of silence.

"I was fading. I couldn't see what you were doing, but my soul was nearing its limit. With the last of my strength, I prevented the air from entering your lungs. You were panting like a racehorse at full gallop, so it didn't take long from there."

"I felt like... like I wanted to keep going. Like I wanted to consume it all. And I felt like I... *could*. I don't know what would have happened if you didn't stop me."

"I don't, either. And that terrifies me," he says. I notice the grasp of his power hasn't eased an inch.

"She was right," I say, suddenly exhausted. "I should never have used it."

I nearly lost control. I *did* lose control. And, in the

moments when I could feel my power spread, surrounded by the dead earth made ashes in golden fire, I came to understand something fundamental.

The hunger will not be sated. Fire does not stop burning until there is nothing left to burn.

If the Vengeance hadn't been there to stop me, how much would I have burned?

All of it? Everything?

Even knowing how close I came to the brink, my hands tremble at the thought of it. The hunger is a cavernous expanse in my chest, a void demanding to be filled. If I open myself to the fire, I won't be able to stop.

"I can never use it again."

"No," the Vengeance says wearily, waving his hand. The invisible chains wrapped around my body disappear. "You have to learn to control it."

"I can't. Even now, I can feel it, trying to crawl out from under my will and… feed."

"So control it, Blade." He stands to his full height, authority and certainty falling across his shoulders like a cloak. It fits him like he was born to it. "Whatever you are, whatever this power is, it has the potential for great destruction. But it is also the only reason I'm alive, the only reason *either* of us is alive. An untrained swordsman is as likely to cut himself as his enemy. So we'll train."

"But…" The denial dies on my lips. This is the Vengeance talking, the greatest Shaper of a generation, matched only by the Sealord in skill and might. If anyone would be able to train me to master myself, it's him. "I… okay. I'll try. But I am afraid of how this will end."

"For now, sleep," he says, throwing himself onto the ground and folding his arms across his chest. "If Kranos wasn't lying about Helikos and his army, we don't have time to waste, but I can't go on tonight. Just try not to eat my soul until morning."

"I'll do my best," I say, smiling almost against my will.

"And call me Altos," he says without opening his eyes. "'Vengeance' is awkward."

***

Dawn finds me awake, eyes gritty and chest aching. The Vengeance—Altos—rises to his feet as soon as light graces the east. He rifles through the thin bag of food we brought, producing a hard block of cheese and a slightly wrinkled apple. The meager breakfast doesn't do much to quiet the rumble in my stomach, but I don't complain.

The longer we linger, the more the unwavering image of the ruined village claws at my thoughts. The dead within will go undiscovered, trapped behind this illusion of peace, like a painted likeness hung over a gravestone. It will look whole and alive for as long as the light is warped. Based on some of the cataclysms lingering in the world, it may well be forever.

Will someone one day stumble through and pierce the veil? Will the dead remain untouched on the ground, reduced to skeletons, with no one to tell the story of their fall?

When the Vengeance finally stands and offers me his arm, it isn't soon enough.

The flight back east lacks the desperate edge of the sprint west. Kranos' boast looms over us, but I can't help but enjoy the feeling of flight as the Khalintars crawl below us. Villages appear and disappear in their dozens, thin streams of smoke drifting up from their chimneys and cookfires. Most of the people take no notice of us as we fly past high enough to be mistaken for a soaring bird of prey. The tiny figure of a shepherd, lazing among his sheep, leaps to his feet and points frantically at the sky. I can't help it. I give him a little wave. The forward wind lessens as the Vengeance raises the bubble of air to let us speak.

"Hopefully, we've outpaced any word of our arrival," the Vengeance says. "Even with you antagonizing the locals."

"What are you afraid of? There isn't an archer alive that

422

could hit us," I shoot back, breathing deeply. The hunger feels... lessened, with the world spread out before me. "Shame that he escaped."

"More than a shame," Altos says gravely. "A tragedy. I had hoped to remove him from the world before he could break it any further. If I thought we could find him, it would be worth it to stay in the west. But, serpent that he is, he won't peek his head above ground until he's certain he is safe. No, I imagine we'll find him at Helikos' side before long. Like a dog returning to his master."

The problems of the world are far away and insignificant from the perspective of a cloud. Like a living painting, the world is nothing but silent beauty and leisure. The next obstacle looms, yet it feels like we have time before we have to face it.

"Could we just... never come down?" I whisper, reverent wonder overwhelming the emptiness in my chest.

"I've felt that desire more than I care to admit," Altos murmurs, and I push down a flush of embarrassment. I didn't realize he'd hear. "But, if you stay up here long enough, you see things that you *want* to change. It is easy to see the peace of the world and wish it never to end. But what do you do when you see a battle down there? A murder? Could you remain so distant that you would not descend?"

***

The miles crawl by. We rest twice to give Altos' energy a chance to recover, eating the last of our meager rations before the sun reaches its zenith. In the distance, a wavering shimmer appears in the west, which the Vengeance claims is sunlight on the desert sands. By his estimation, we'll reach the Vein of the Creator tonight and camp on its banks. It's a shorter distance than I expected. Apparently, the days were so long because we were chasing the sun west, but now they will be shorter as we head east. What took us two 'days' will take five or more to return.

I don't mind. Neither of us speaks much, yet the silence isn't uncomfortable. I catch him watching me sometimes, a strange light in his eyes. He claimed that he would train me, that we would figure out this hunger together, but his stare reminds me that I nearly killed him when I lost control. If he thinks I'm a danger to him or anyone he cares for, I don't imagine he'll hesitate to eliminate the threat.

We fly higher when we pass Coin in the morning, high enough that the traffic crawling along the Way of the West doesn't notice or care as they move to and from the city. I can see the wisdom in the choice; if their general has returned, they will be on the lookout for us heading back east. It seems unlikely that he would be able to outpace us while tunneling through the earth, especially in the state that he escaped in, but you don't live to your second century by being reckless.

Less than an hour later, a brown stain mars the horizon, resolving quickly into a roiling mass of sand challenging the sky. The sandstorm nearly fills the horizon, though its southern edge is just in sight. As we continue to blithely hurtle towards the bank of drifting earth, I crane my neck towards the Vengeance. There is a frown on his face, his eyes crinkled in confusion. The wind dies ahead of us again so that we can speak.

"What is it?" I ask.

"This storm makes no sense," he answers slowly. "The wind is not right to form something like this, and this land is mostly hard packed earth, not loose sand."

"Could there be another cause?" I ask, eyeing the approaching storm warily. "Shouldn't we... I don't know, avoid it?"

"Yes," he says, and a gust of wind carries us higher.

He's silent for a time, though I can tell his eyes haven't left the swirling sands. The storm roars as we get closer, overwhelming and deafening. As we drift over, something shifts in the back of my mind, like an elusive word dancing on the tip of my tongue. It's almost like there's a pattern, or a *will* behind it. Almost like...

It's a risk. I shouldn't, *really* shouldn't. I just have to know.

I focus on the hunger, on controlling it, on steadiness and control and mastery. When I think I'm ready, silently entreating the Creator for strength, I let my eyes slip into the world's fire.

The entire storm lights up green and white, as expected. The power of the earth and wind are potent this far from any other element. I glance to the south, to the edge of the storm. The emerald light of the desert there is different somehow, pure and perfect. The storm swirls with... intent. I let the fire fade as excitement takes the place of hunger.

"Altos!" I shout over the roar of the storm.

"What is it?" he calls back.

"It's *not* natural. It's Shaped!"

"Shaped? You mean..."

"No way it's anyone else, yeah?" I shout, hoping he understands. "Do you think she... died?"

He's silent for a moment as we drift over the storm, long enough that I open my mouth to shout again.

Without warning, we dive, dropping towards the edge of rushing sand. My mind immediately supplies fearful imaginings of sand lacerating my skin, filling my mouth, blinding my eyes...

I just manage to close my mouth before we hit.

Chapter 19
Iliana

The Eighty-Third Day of Summer
In the year 5223, Council Reckoning

Telias shades his hand to stare back west. The horses on our trail won't be in sight for some minutes yet, but the drum of their hoofbeats grows more distinct with every passing second. There are ten, no, eleven distinct sets spread out in a wide wedge.

"Are you sure they're coming this way?" he asks after a moment.

"Very," I say, folding my arms over my chest. "And they're spread out like they're trying to find something. Us, I'd guess."

"Damn." Telias holds his hand out, and I give him the waterskin he just refused. Downing half of it in a moment, he wipes his mouth and scowls. "What can you tell me about them?"

"It isn't like I've got eyes on them," I say, shrugging.

"True. Who it is will matter greatly about how we should approach this encounter. If it's the Empire, they'll probably try to kill or capture me, but treat you with honor and respect. If it's the Khal's people, it's harder to guess which way the wind will blow."

"*Should* we wait? I can kick up some dust and obscure our passage if you think we should."

I know my answer. I'd much rather figure out who is pursuing me and listen to what they have to say. I don't want to risk Telias, though.

"No. Better to know your enemy."

I can't hide the satisfied smile that spreads on my face as he echoes my thoughts.

A cloud of dust, the first sign of our pursuers, appears on

the horizon. The glint of metal soon follows as bits of armor wink in the desert sun. The soldiers astride the horses waver into view shortly thereafter. Dressed in a motley assortment of leather and armor, they look more like mercenaries than official soldiers, but their pale skin and flashes of piecemeal turquoise armor show their loyalty. They're approaching a dead gallop, whipping their horses on. If they've been pushing this hard, the beasts can't have much left.

"Empire, I take it?" I murmur to Telias over the growing thunder of their hooves.

"Yes. And I recognize two of them." He glances at me, worried yet hopeful. "We're about to put Bastian's claims about your mind to the test."

Despite the growing heat, my blood runs cold at his words. None of the approaching soldiers stands out from the others, and something tells me the Master of Beasts would stand out, but if these soldiers can invade our thoughts, I hope Bastian and Jynn are right about my mind.

The soldiers drop to a canter, then a walk as they realize we aren't running. Ten of them come to a halt at respectful distance, but their leader continues until he towers over Telias and I. Balding and unathletic, the pieces of seafoam armor strapped to his body fit him about as well as they would a child. His eyes linger for a moment on me. There is nothing I would call human in their depths. I have to suppress a shiver as he finally turns lazily to Telias.

The man throws a leg over his horse and dismounts clumsily. The animal trembles, chest heaving, white spittle clinging to its mouth. Blood streams down its flanks where his crop cut its skin. If I knew nothing else, his disregard for his mount is enough. His eyes slide back to me, and I tense. Shockingly, he drops to a knee, lowering his head to the parched earth.

"My queen," he says, his voice dry and slow. "Thank the

Creator we found you."

"Crawl back into your master's shadow, Silken," Telias commands. "You have no power here. Iliana is fr—"

There is no signal, no order given. Yet the ten soldiers raise their hands in unison. Silver light burns into being, and Telias cuts off like his vocal cords were severed. He falls to his knees, moaning, fists pressed to his temples. I crouch at his side and throw an arm around his broad shoulders, but he doesn't seem to notice.

"Stop it," I shout, shocked to see tears dripping down his craggy face from his one good eye. "Stop hurting him."

"We can't, my lady," Silken says, raising his dead stare to me. "He lies better than any man alive. He will ensnare you and confuse you if we let him speak. Clearly, he already has. I don't know what he's done to you, but he can't be trusted."

"I know my..." A tremor of fear ripples through my spirit. I was about to say 'I know my own mind.' But do I? "Let him go."

"He is a dangerous criminal, my lady," Silken continues patiently. "He plans sedition against your father, the rightful emperor of all the lands 'tween Coin and Donir. If he had his way, he'd kill all that love you and yours."

"But..."

Telias groans at my side, grinding his knees into the dirt. The silver light glowing from the soldiers brightens, and he cries out in pain. His remaining eye looks permanently closed against the agony. Still, impossibly, he lifts one leg and plants his foot firmly on the ground.

"My queen, step away from him," one of the soldiers calls, her voice shaking. "We can't hold him much longer, Captain."

"Please, my lady," Silken says, holding out his hand. "We've come to save you from his deceit. I can tell by the look in your eyes that you don't know me, but I'm a loyal servant of your father and the Lord General Kranos. I could never forgive myself if you were stolen or killed on my watch. Please."

428

"I…"

The sun burns brightly. Too brightly. I feel a chasm opening beneath my feet, like I'm teetering on the edge of a fathomless drop with my eyes closed. The abyss is a step away, hungry for my fall, but which way lies safety?

These soldiers came for me across long miles of desert, killing their mounts to catch up. They call me queen, and the title feels *right*. Like I deserve such respect. They bow and scrape and kneel to me. They speak of powerful men, emperors and generals, who care desperately for me.

Yet they come with violence, and I do not see life in their captain's eyes. His words smack of truth, but his eyes do not speak.

If I take that step, I go to a world of plenty and power, a world where my word sets nations to trembling. There is… joy, savage yet real, in that thought. The path seems so right, so true, but my foot trembles. If I step forward, am I throwing myself into the chasm? Will I once again become a thrall, as Telias claims?

To step the other way is to step into darkness and uncertainty. I awoke in an underground complex, greeted by strangers. Strangers who freely admitted that they did something to my mind, much as Silken intimates. Strangers with a wild story of stolen lives and false parentage and magical enslavement. If I had even a sliver of my memory, and if they weren't so earnest about it, I'd discard their claims as outlandish and absurd.

But I trust Telias. When I comb through what little memory I have, I trust Bastian, too. They risked their lives to smuggle me out of the city. They were honest when they had no reason to be. If they had told me Silken was the perpetrator of my destroyed memory, I'd have believed them, especially after meeting the man.

Yet what am I choosing?

A life on the run. A life spent looking over my shoulder, struggling to make ends meet, when I could be wearing a crown.

429

"Your… master… can't break me, Silken," Telias growls from the earth, voice growing stronger with each word. "Neither can you."

Telias shoves himself to his feet. He steps, slowly, agonizingly, towards Silken. The captain glances at him with a kind of disdainful pity. A symbol pulses to life on Silken's neck, and Telias groans and drops to the ground. His fingers carve lines of pain in the hard ground, grasping at sand and weathered dirt as if they will offer him succor from his torment. Silken flicks his hand towards one of his subordinates. She drops from the saddle and approaches, drawing a knife as she comes.

"Wait, don't—"

"He is too dangerous to be kept alive," Silken interrupts, his voice strained. Keeping Telias down must be harder than he makes it look. "Come. Quickly."

The soldier reaches Telias and bends down, her knife sharp and shining.

"Stay your hand."

I raise my chin, trying to inject as much authority as I can into the command. The soldier turns, not to me, but to Silken. My stomach drops as the captain nods. Glancing at me warily, she bends to Telias where he groans on the ground. Taking a hold of his hair, she raises his face to expose his throat.

Is this what it means to be queen? Ignored by my own soldiers?

I don't have time. I don't have *time*. I have to choose. Which way to jump? Which way lies the abyss?

The earth erupts under the soldier with the force of a charging bull. She flips through the air over the heads of her fellows and rolls to a crumpled stop past the line of their horses. My arm is still raised, hand clenched into a shaking fist. I can do nothing but stare at my traitorous hand.

I didn't make a conscious choice. Yet my soul, and the earth, have chosen for me.

430

There is a frozen moment. The soldiers stare at me in shock. None look to their motionless companion. That is enough to reassure me of my choice. For his part, Silken looks furious and terrified at once.

"My queen, don't let delusion—"

"Enough," I snap, a cold anger dousing my uncertainty like a torch in water. "You come before me with false humility, claiming to be a faithful servant, yet every word I speak is ignored. You hurt an unarmed man merely because he speaks harshly towards you, and order his murder against the wishes of your 'queen.' I do not trust you, and I won't be coming with you. I'll give you this singular chance to dismount from your exhausted horses and walk them back to Coin. Turn. And walk."

The others, just like the would-be executioner, look not to me, but to Silken for their cue, like wolves following the leader of the pack. Like starving, desperate wolves who believe they've cornered prey.

They are fools if they do not realize that they've found something else entirely.

The symbol on Silken's neck pulses brighter as his dead eyes focus on me. A touch, featherlight, slips across the surface of my mind. It is a command, to kneel, to follow, no louder than a distant whisper. His face contorts in hideous anger, and he growls like an animal. Without warning, he rips his sword from its sheath and storms towards me.

"You're coming with me one way or another, you sniveling bitch. Now, get..."

I tune him out. His Shaping can find no purchase in my thoughts. By Bastian's word, it never will. But, just like they warned me, he *tried*.

And that I can't forgive.

I call, and the earth *answers*. The sand and dry dust rise. Impenetrable walls of earth shroud the horizon, then the sky and the sun, until nothing but a dim and diffuse light dances on the mercurial ground.

The soldiers cower in terror in the sudden gloom, fighting to keep their horses calm. Silken stares, slack jawed, his sword forgotten in his hand. Telias, free from their assault, levers himself to his feet, staring about in equal awe.

I don't need to look at the storm of earth. I can feel it. I have eyes only for my enemy. Silken seems to sense my regard, turning slowly to look me in the face. His sword drops from nerveless fingers.

"Alright," he says, his voice hoarse and cracking. "We'll go. We meant no harm."

"What? You *meant no harm?*" I ask, tilting my head. "I thought I made myself clear. You got one chance."

"Iliana…" Telias begins, but my raised hand cuts him off before he can speak.

"No, please," Silken whines, dropping to his knees. Several of his soldiers turn their horses and gallop into the swirling sands, while others mouth prayers or drop from their horses to press their faces to the earth. "We was just following orders."

"You should have followed *mine.*"

The earth flows to my command, dancing to my will. It is like breathing, so natural my soul sings its harmony. It knows my intent even as I know it, so there is no delay as the storm gathers at my back.

Gathers, and swarms.

A cloud of serrated sand rushes to my enemies. And cuts. Lines of blood, thinner than pressed parchment, shallow as a Summer stream, appear on every inch of their exposed skin. Their first screams cut off instantly as their tongues drown in mouthfuls of blood and sand. They twitch and fall, writhing beneath the sting of countless cuts, until finally they lie still.

Telias flinches at my side as small pops of silver light herald their deaths. They must be weak, or their deaths would have affected him more. To me, it is no more than a Spring

432

breeze.

Silken never gets the chance to move. What is left of him remains on its knees, the hollow bone of his cheeks and scalp showing white through the mass of crimson blood where strands of flesh still stubbornly cling together.

I spare the horses, of course. They've suffered enough cruelty from man.

"Iliana..." Telias says like he's speaking through a stab wound.

"Ily."

"Why did you kill them?"

"They were enemies," I say, watching as a horse walks sedately by. Without its rider, it doesn't seem to care about the dust storm raging around us. There are a few splatters of blood on its flanks, but otherwise it's unharmed. I turn to Telias. "They would have killed you and taken me if I let them."

"They wanted to leave. You could have let them go."

"They wanted to leave *after* they threatened us both," I say, offering him a look of frank disbelief. "I told them they had one chance. One. I don't know if I'm different than I was before, but *this* me believes that when I say a thing I mean it."

He opens his mouth as if to respond, then pauses, seems to think better of it, and finally frowns. He turns slowly in place, taking in the bloody corpses and exhausted horses, the swirling sands and still earth. Slowly, almost regretfully, he gives me a slow nod.

"It isn't weakness to show mercy," he says, choosing his words carefully.

"No," I agree, shrugging. "But I didn't think it made sense in this case. Would you rather be bleeding out on the ground right now?"

"Of course not, I just... I worry."

"Well, don't. I may not be who you *want* me to be, but—"

I pause. Something strange is happening in the storm. Now

that it's begun, it would be more effort to reign it in than to let it run wild. But something is disrupting it, calming it, easing the wind and settling the air.

At the same time, something pushes the earth aside, like a bubble of emptiness tracing a path through the air at extraordinary speed. There is nothing, subconscious or otherwise, that makes sense about what I'm feeling.

"What is it?" Telias asks, glancing around at the dying storm.

"Something... something's happening." Air brushes across my skin, and the emptiness turns and accelerates. Towards us. "Something's coming."

Telias follows my gaze up and to the west. Whatever it is, it's *fast*. The storm boils in sudden agitation as it blazes our way.

Should I resist its approach? The sand, even the smallest drifting dust, is pushed aside before an invisible wave of power. None of the earth can get close enough for me to sense whatever it is. As fast as it moves, I might not be able to react if I wait to know.

And I don't have time to deliberate.

Before it can appear, I gather my focus. The earth erupts into the air like the Creator's own fist, wide and hard enough to break whatever comes for us. Impossibly, the emptiness reacts, slipping aside and skating along the edge of the rushing sand.

With a growl, I raise my hands, and two thick hands of earth rise on either side of it. I clap, and the earth slams together.

White light pulses bright enough to shine through the churning storm. The emptiness accelerates even faster, darting between the crashing earth like a mosquito dodging a crushing hand. I don't have time to prepare another attack, but desperately I begin a call to the earth when Telias grabs my arm. I shrug him off, reaching deep.

"Ily, stop!" he shouts. "That's..."

And the emptiness appears. A man, no, two men, skim

along in a sphere of air. The white light of the Master of Air glows so that I have to squint to look at them straight on. Wait, the Master of Air... my...

The Shaper drops his cargo, and the man he's carrying falls. Creator, he's going way too fast. The hard ground will break his bones and rip his skin to shreds. Yet the falling man doesn't seem concerned. He tucks into an agile roll as his feet touch down. Once, twice, then a third time, he rolls to bleed momentum, then pops up in a run before sliding to a halt in front of us.

He glances at me with eyes of deep blue, his skin a match for mine, his hair nearly the same shade. He looks strong, capable, ready to explode into motion at a moment's notice. Even if I hadn't just seen him take a fall that would have killed a lesser man, I would know to be wary of this one. He dismisses me almost instantly, eyes locking on Telias with startling intensity. He freezes in place, stricken.

Are those... tears?

The stranger surges forward so quickly I flinch back. He and Telias slam together in a fierce hug. The fiercest *I* can remember.

The errant thought is half hilarious and half melancholy. I'm happy for Telias, at least. So long as those are joyful tears. The flying Master of Air settles down a safe distance away from me. Blonde hair and a trimmed beard, piercing blue eyes... if he is my father, as Telias claims, then I must take after my mother. Maybe in the shape of our eyes, the line of our jaw...

His face is flat and stoic, but his eyes are a hurricane.

"Uh, hello," I say after a moment of silence. "You... I've heard we might be... related."

He nods, short and stiff. Fragile.

"So I don't remember much," I continue when he doesn't say anything. "I'm somewhat rediscovering... well, everything. I guess we weren't close?"

435

"The last time I saw you, you tried to kill me," he says, voice as dull as the look on his face.

"Oh," I say, not really sure if I should apologize or not. "I don't feel like killing you now, if that's any consolation."

"Strangely, it is," he says, a small, astonished smile growing on his face.

"And Telias only says good things about you," I continue, remembering their history. "So that's a win, I'd say."

"Very much so," he agrees, smile fading. "It's more than I deserve."

"Telias doesn't seem like the type to be wrong about people."

"No, he doesn't."

"Right, well, if we aren't going to kill each other this time, why don't we start fresh? Does that sound good?"

"I'd like that," he says too quickly, unconsciously stepping forward. "Please."

"Ily," I say, offering him my hand. "Daughter."

"Altos," he says, shaking it with a bewildered smile. "Father."

He glances around at the storm still raging all about us. I've kept my attention on it loosely so that no other strange relatives might decide to drop in, but there's been nothing else out of the ordinary. If feeling the motion of a miles-wide sandstorm is ordinary.

"Is this you?" the young man asks, Telias and he having apparently finished their tearful reunion. Telias keeps his hand on the stranger's shoulder, as if afraid he'll disappear. His blue eyes dart about the bloody corpses slowly being covered by drifting sand. "All of it?"

"Maybe I went a bit overboard," I offer, shrugging.

"We thought you died," he says, shaking his head. "How are you holding this much power?"

"I'm getting the feeling it isn't normal, but this isn't hard." I

436

meet his eyes, feeling a strange sense of familiarity steal over me. A surreal recognition that feels like it goes beyond my amnesia. "I'm sorry, but have we met before?"

"You said the exact same thing when you saw me before," he says, grinning.

"Damn," I say, rubbing my face.

I feel suddenly *weary*, though I can't tell the source. Either the Shaping is taking more out of me than I thought, or the constant reminder of my missing memories is exhausting. Or both. With a thought, I loosen my grip on the storm. Immediately, the sand falls, and dust drifts on natural wind.

"Do we know each other well?" I ask, peeking between my fingers.

"No, not at all," he says, suddenly frowning. "The last time I saw you, you tried—"

"—to kill you," I finish, groaning. I shoot Telias a glare. "I seem to have been more murderous than you made me out to be."

"These are specific cases," he says carefully, glancing between the three of us appraisingly. "Creator, now that you're all together, the family resemblance is remarkable. No wonder Helikos took such an interest in you after the ball."

"Wait, you're saying…"

"Apparently, I'm your, uh, twin," the stranger says, rubbing the back of his neck self-consciously. For such a capable-looking fellow, he certainly manages to look awkward. "According to rumor, I guess."

"No, Telias is right," Altos says, folding his arms across his chest and glancing between us. "Definitely related."

"You guys aren't working some elaborate deceit, are you?" I ask, scowling at Telias.

The three men stare back at me steadily.

I sigh and offer him my hand.

"Ily. Sister."

"Jace. Brother."

The sun manages to burn through the fading storm as we speak, and the temperature immediately spikes. Telias and I are fine in our white wool, but the other two glance warily at the burning sun.

"So what do we do now?" I ask, opening my arms to encompass the desert.

"Would you like to come with me... us?" Altos asks me, though he glances at Telias out of the corner of his eyes.

"Ily?" Telias asks. At the expression on my face, he steps close and lowers his voice. "Everything I promised remains before you. If you want to head west and leave all this behind, I'm with you every step. If you want to make a new life, I'll help you however I can. If you want to go with them, I will follow. You have a second chance at life. I'll not try to sway you one way or the other."

I turn and step away from the three of them, turning my eyes west to the shimmering horizon. Lands uncounted lie that way, lands that don't know my name or my past. A chance at a fresh start, a new life. A chance to make friends or fall in love, without the threat of a history I can't remember rearing its seemingly ugly head. With my strength and Telias' wisdom, we could carve a life for ourselves wherever we go.

And, maybe someday, Bastian and his brother will find us, as he promised, and grace me once more with the regard of his kind and gentle eyes.

Yet the way west is decorated with the dead. I've been gone for two days, and already the long reach of my enemies has caught up to me. I frown and shiver. I didn't know what to believe half an hour ago, but already I think of them as enemies. Even trying for it, pushing for it, I can't bring myself to mistrust Bastian or Telias. Their words resonate with truth, and their sacrifices speak louder than any words.

If I leave this family behind, this father I've never known, this brother I've just discovered, I abandon this new life as well.

There will be conflict, of that I am certain. By Telias' word, and by the actions of their soldiers, there are powerful tyrants who will seek our heads. If I leave now, I will always look over my shoulder, waiting for the moment that they appear to enslave me once again.

"Alright," I say softly. I turn back to face them, these three men who could be—will be—my family. "We'll go. Together."

***

The ocean is a tapestry of sparkling sapphire from this high up. A town of white buildings and sprawling streets, Carqos doesn't look real in the setting sun. It is an artist's perfection, a dream made tangible. Only the salt in the air lends the picturesque scene a sense of reality it would otherwise lack. Before we can be spotted by its inhabitants, Altos angles us towards an out-of-the-way spot behind a hill a few miles from the small city.

As it turns out, flying is harder the more people Altos carries. After he claimed that, due to how draining flying is, we would make better time on horses in the long run, we discussed options. He and Jace had, apparently, flown across the center of the Great Sea on the way over, but four is too many for Altos to manage the same feat. Taking the Way of the North seems like asking for capture and death, so we ruled that out.

In the end, we agreed to our original plan to take ship east. By ship, the passage normally takes half a season, but Altos assured us that, with a friendly wind, we'll be there much sooner.

Getting into the city is easier than I imagined it would be. There is supposed to be a garrison of the Wave at Carqos, but local militia greet us at the gate. When Telias asks, they say that the Wave disappeared almost ten days ago. Deserted, if rumor is to believe. Something about not having been paid in nearly a season.

Altos hustles us to the docks even though the sun is

dropping in the west. He has a graceful gait, but he looks uncomfortable on the ground, like a bird restraining itself from bursting into flight. We get a few strange looks as we pass through the streets, though I don't get the sense anyone recognizes us.

When we reach the harbor, Altos and Telias scan the ships, murmuring to one another about drafts and speed and other esoteric nautical nonsense. Jace leans against the wall of a tavern nearby, eyes tracking Telias like a loyal hound its master.

"So you must be the orphan he took in," I say, leaning back against the wall next to him. Like a sun-warmed stone on the shore of a creek, the heat of it seeps into my bones and eases a dull ache in my back. "How did you guys meet?"

"I tried to rob him," Jace says casually. "Best day of my life. How did you meet him?"

"Originally? No idea. I woke up three days ago remembering nothing, but his was the first face I saw."

"You really don't remember anything?"

"Flashes here or there." I think for a moment. "We met before, right? Tell me the story."

"Now?" I stare at him flatly. "Okay, sure. Once a year, the King, or I guess the Emperor now, invites the wealthy and powerful to a ball…"

He regales me with a story of glittering jewelry and swirling dresses, of kings and generals, and of a princess both sad and welcoming. He continues the tale as we follow Telias and Altos down into the harbor. I try to see myself in that girl as he speaks, to remember the shape of her, but I can't. It is a world foreign and strange, from a life I no longer possess.

"So what happened to this Torlas fellow?" I ask after he finishes.

"I'm not sure," he says, frowning. "He was still in Donir under the Sealord's thumb when I saw him last. But he's a powerful duke in the kingdom, so I'm sure he's fine."

440

"Strange," I say. The lone white lily inexplicably rises to the forefront of my memory. "When I think of him, I feel... sad. I don't even know his face, but it's like my soul mourns a loss."

"I'm sure he's fine," Jace says hurriedly, levering himself up to join the conversation between the two men. Feeling like I've said something wrong, I sigh and follow.

"It's the only ship that can make the passage quickly," Telias is saying to Altos.

"They'll kill me if they get the chance," Altos protests evenly, shaking his head. "And the kids as well. Creator knows, they might even take a shot at *you*, considering what you once were."

"So we'll be subtle. It's not like they'll have any idea why the wind blows perfectly. Keep your hands in your pockets, and that shiny white symbol out of sight, and they'll never be the wiser—"

"Unless," a strange, amused voice says, lightly accented with the spice of the far south. "They hear you discussing your Curse out loud in the street."

A woman, dark of skin and hair, stands in the center of the street as if she owns it. Leather crosses her chest in a dozen concealing straps beneath a pair of finely toned arms crossed over her chest. A smug smirk adorns her face as she takes in the surprised look on the men's faces.

"You aren't the first Cursed to try to sneak aboard my ship," she continues, flicking her gaze between us all. "But you're definitely the most obvious. No one comes in from the desert with so little in the way of supplies."

"You saw us enter?" Telias asks, raising the eyebrow over his good eye.

"Had the gate watched for four days now. On the fifth, I was to leave with the dawn," she says, rolling her shoulders and turning to go. "Took you long enough."

"What do you... you were waiting for us?"

441

"I go where the Seer wills," she calls over her shoulder. "But *Mason's Fall* won't wait forever."

***

Dawn finds us lifting up and down with rolling waves as we make our way north along the coast. Wind fills our sails to their very limit, but not beyond. The ship practically skips across the water under Captain Te'ial's skilled direction. The beach, just in sight to the west, races past faster than a horse's gallop. It is speed that would have astonished prior to our short flight from the wastes of the Khalintar of the Shield to Carqos yesterday. After seeing the miles devoured through Altos' power, though, it feels pedestrian at best.

The rolling of the deck does some strange things to my stomach in the first few hours, but the feeling fades by midmorning. Altos stands at the prow, a lonely figure balanced easily on the skipping edge of the ship. Jace and Telias huddle together near the main mast, exchanging stories like old friends.

Around noon, the captain shouts a command in her native language. A woman steps up to replace her at the wheel, and Te'ial saunters over to where I trail my arm over the railing to feel the spray kicked up by the massive ship cutting through the water.

"Your people don't seem to trust us," I say by way of greeting, trying to ignore the subtle glares of the crew as they go about their business.

"Consider yourself lucky. Last Spring, we would have fled you or fought you at the first sign of a Curse," she says, shrugging languidly. "The People have always feared and hated the Cursed, for your sin is unforgivable." She pauses, eyes on Altos' back as he continues to stare north. And the white symbol glowing on his hand. "The Seer has told us that the legends of our people are a lie, and now we are to embrace the Cursed as *th'ris'ka*. As Blessed. Not all of the People have taken to this new truth."

"You say the Seer's name with such anger. Do you dispute

the Seer's declaration? His leadership?"

"No," she says, sighing. "I love him."

"And that makes you angry?" I ask, bemused.

"He has rocked the boat and stirred the waters more than any Seer in living memory," she says, scowling. "*I* trust him. I know he is following the dreams of the future. But there are those who doubt him because his sister was Cursed as well. Blessed. Ugh." She spits over the side like she's trying to get a bitter taste out of her mouth. "The oldest ways are the hardest to drown, even for me."

"What a strange life," I say, though I have to pause and stifle a laugh. Me? Calling someone else's life strange? "Let me get this straight. The Seer, a man you love, tells you to go to a city halfway around the world and wait for your ancestral enemies in order to take them wherever they want to go?"

"If the Creator was alive, he would be laughing," Te'ial agrees grimly. "After this, I don't care what Talan says. My ship's course is my own to plot."

Altos turns from his place at the front and calls out to the others. Jace jumps to his feet, grinning, and runs belowdecks for a moment, returning with their swords. He tosses a bare blade to the Vengeance like he's tossing him a spare blanket, but Altos catches the hilt smoothly and falls into a ready stance opposite Jace. The crew look like they want to gather immediately to observe the fight, though their mistrust and wariness keep them back.

When the two men come together, their feet in perfect harmony, their blades little more than narrow streams of liquid silver in the high noontide sun, the whole world seems to pause to watch. They did not look like father and son before now, but there is little mistaking their kinship with the blade. No step out of place, every cut perfect, they move like dancers who've practiced their steps a thousand times.

They finish in a sudden crescendo, Altos taking advantage

of the swell of a passing wave to press Jace towards the rail. I don't see the blow that ends the fight, but both stop as if they planned it, lungs heaving from exertion. And laughter.

"Perhaps it is we who are the lucky ones," Te'ial mutters, eyes narrowed after the display.

***

The journey passes in a pleasant, lazy blur. As soon as we cross the Way of the North, the ocean calms and the ship's passage is smoother than silk. The days are spent on deck, sparring and joking and learning from one another. Te'ial and some of her crewmates eventually lose their reluctance and take part as well, dancing about the deck with a grace that only comes from vast experience on the sea. They aren't quite up to the level of Jace and Altos, but they're quick and deadly fighters.

Te'ial lends me one of her long daggers so that I can take part. They have to go easy on me to start, but my body remembers even if I do not. Before long, I'm pushing Telias and holding my own against Jace and Altos. Something feels like it's missing from my style, some way to incorporate the earth. I don't press for it. I've got plenty to handle with the unfamiliar blade, and it's not like Altos is leaning on his Shaping to fight.

The nights are spent swapping stories. I begin by listening, but the others don't let me take a passive role. They all seem eager to hear about what pieces I remember and how it feels to know so little. The best storyteller is, of course, Telias, as he weaves voices and characters into the telling. Jace has a flair for the dramatic, shamelessly embellishing stories to such hyperbolic levels it feels like every moment is an adventure. Altos, having lived longer than all of us put together, shocks us all with a steady style that slowly wraps his listeners in its web.

For all the mock violence on deck, the ship is peaceful in a way that separates us from the rest of the world. Though we have none of the bonds of family that we might have had, there are glimpses of what could have been, had we the luxury of a normal

444

life.

The dream passes all too quickly. With the Master of Air to fill the sails, the *Mason's Fall* crosses the sea in days. By the dawn of the fourth day, with the Way of the North on our right, land appears ahead.

"Where do you wish to be let off?" Captain Te'ial calls from the wheel.

"That won't be necessary," Altos says in a normal voice, though, with a flash of white, the sound carries to everyone on the ship. "I'd rather *not* be seen doing something so mundane as walking off a ship. Have to maintain my air of deadly mystery, after all."

"Mundane! We just crossed the Great Sea in three days, Vengeance!" Te'ial shouts gleefully, and he turns to regard her. She waves her arm towards the sails straining against the perfect wind. "Blessed or Cursed, if you ever want to ride the waves, you've a place on my crew."

I expect him to laugh or throw the idea aside, but Altos doesn't speak for a while, like he's actually contemplating the proposition.

"You know, when this is all over... if this ever really ends... I'll think about it."

Te'ial gives him a fierce grin and slaps her hand against the wheel.

"We'll be the fastest ship on the seas," she cackles. "The money we'll make, Cursed! Can you imagine?"

"Ah yes. The money," he says, offering her a smile. "Until then, Captain, be safe."

We don't need any more prompting to say our goodbyes and gather at the bow where Altos stands. Every second brings more of the shore into sharp detail. If he wants to leave without being seen, he'll need to hurry. He glances between us, his face turning solemn.

"Kranos claimed that Helikos and the entire might of the

445

Tide will march on my people in the Kinlen Forest. Even if he isn't fully trustworthy, he had no reason to lie. I know him; he believed he was going to win that fight. So there's a good chance we'll be heading right into the thick of it from here," he says, eyes locking onto me. "This is the last chance to walk away. I... I almost hope you will."

"This is my second chance, right?" I meet each of their eyes in turn, finally ending on Altos with a smile. "I get to choose who I want to be. And I won't be the girl who left her family to fight alone."

"We're disembarking so far north for a reason, yes?" Telias asks, continuing before Altos can answer. "You want to cross Donir, don't you? To determine if Kranos' claims are accurate?"

"I've flown over these lands a thousand times. I'd like to think I would notice if he emptied the lands of the Tide."

"How many times will we rest?" Jace asks.

"I can make it," Altos says, but already Jace is shaking his head.

"If we are going to battle against an army, we can't have you trembling like a newborn foal again. You're carrying four this time, and you're lucky to be alive as it is."

"Fine." The Master of Air speaks like he's got a knife in his gut. "Once."

Altos offers his hands to Jace and Telias, who then link hands with me to complete the circle. I glance over my shoulder at the wheel, where the captain watches us dubiously.

"Thank you for the lift, Captain!" I call cheerfully. "Don't let the Seer push you around!"

"Good luck, *chela*," she says, smiling. "And be safe."

The wind in the sails dies, and the ship rolls as it loses momentum. Te'ial, cursing, shouts orders to her crew. As pressure builds and the winds begin to rotate around us, I offer the *Mason's Fall* a silent prayer. Of safety, and speed. Let them return and be granted the freedom they deserve. Let Te'ial travel

446

where she may, love at her side.

With a sudden rushing roar, our feet lift off from the deck, and we leave the ship bobbing in the waves.

***

Altos takes us high enough that the clouds periodically drench us in icy mist. The Way of the North stretches out of sight east and west, a line so straight it cannot be natural. Paralleling its course, we drift silently past a dozen towns and hamlets crafted to take advantage of the commerce flowing along the ancient road. A land of wide green spaces interspersed with copses of trees and quaint cottages, it trades the primal beauty of the desert and the ocean for the quiet solidity of ancient trees and manicured fields.

This is, apparently, my home. After the first hour, I stop searching for something I recognize. I felt more kinship with the desert we left behind than this idyllic kingdom. I keep waiting for something, some touchstone perhaps, to ground me, to connect my formless present to my formless past. I don't think I'll find it in the lands crawling past below.

The end of the Way comes into sight around midmorning as sprawling Donir's mighty walls swallow both the North and the East. As soon as it appears on the horizon, Altos takes us down into a little stand of pine away from any sign of human habitation. Telias shares out provisions Te'ial allowed us to take from the ship, and we spread out in the trees and eat in silence. An unspoken strain stretches taut between us.

We are now deep in the lands of our enemy. Anyone who sees us could be a blind loyalist who would sell us to the Sealord for a bellyful of bread. Any soldier may take a stab at becoming a legend by bringing down the Vengeance. We have no idea what we're flying into. The Master of Beasts claimed that an army marches on our destination. The Master of Stone defends them, which should be a ray of light piercing the clouds, but Altos doesn't seem reassured.

Kranos claimed the Sealord was coming to personally end

the fight.

After a few hours, we resume our flight east. Many times larger than any city we've seen since Coin, Donir crawls past over the course of an hour. Gray and brown and cramped near the walls, buildings grow farther apart and taller the closer they are to the center. A castle stands at the highest point, girded in a skirt of trees and gardens.

My home. Once upon a time.

Just another castle, cold and foreign.

We climb into the mountains as the sun races the opposite direction. Time feels like it's flowing faster, daylight like sand hissing through a sieve. Jace, floating a few paces to my left, begins to scan the trees, no doubt searching for signs of our enemy. There's every chance we might miss an army even with our perfect perspective. The Kinlen Forest is large enough to swallow all the cultivated lands of the kingdom, its overarching canopy dense enough to obscure any sight of the ground. Regardless, I join him in the search.

It all looks the same. Different, in the uniqueness of the trees, their height, the ever-ascending slope, yet the same. Green trees, gray rock, green trees, gray rock, flash of the brown pine needles carpeting the forest floor, green trees, more trees... my attention begins to wane after ten minutes. It's like combing a beach for a particular grain of sand.

But this is supposed to be an army. Thousands of soldiers. Shouldn't there be some sign? Smoke from a fire? Sunlight flashing on metal? There is no way the Sealord himself is sleeping on cold ground. Yet there is no sign of a camp anywhere.

Perhaps the Master of Beasts was lying after all.

We hardly have to descend by the time we reach the highest mountains. The trees grow sparser the higher we climb, and soon most of earth gives way to stone and snow. Angling between two silent gray sentinels of rock, I can't see any sign of our alleged allies.

A shout pierces the evening air as we near the pass, though its origin remains a mystery. The Vengeance drops us gently in a clearing surrounded by a dozen low boulders half-buried in the ground.

And people appear like magic.

A dozen, two dozen, each walking with the surety of trained fighters. A bald man with a trim blonde beard steps up to the Vengeance and greets him with an easy familiarity. If there is an army approaching, these people do not show it. A man with unnaturally twisted legs bounds over and embraces Jace before bowing to Telias. A beautiful blonde woman jumps into his arms.

Yet I register these details only distantly. A pair of eyes, emerald and beautiful, lock on to me from the crowd. Her face is strong, and soft, and startling. Like the flame her hair embodies, it is captivating and perfect, crooked nose and all.

And somehow, I *know* her.

Not her name or her past, not her face or her body, but innately. Intrinsically.

She moves like a ghost, drifting between bodies in a crowd we've both forgotten. She pauses only when she stands before me. Her mouth moves, its shape forming my name as it was meant to be said.

"Ily…"

And then, she's in my arms. Strong as tempered steel, she trembles. Warm, smelling of earth and whetstone oil, her embrace is all the fierceness and love and hope I've searched for in the dark ruin of my mind.

I don't know her name, yet I'll never let her go.

For in her arms, I am home.

Chapter 20
Jynn
The Eighty-First Day of Summer
In the year 5223, Council Reckoning

So.

That's what tears taste like.

I'd forgotten.

There hasn't been much to mourn in the short time I've spent breathing once again. Nothing worth tears, at least. I've watched the life leave the eyes of a thousand men, dying by my hand. I've watched every person I ever loved die as their city collapsed on their heads. I've watched the end of the world, the end of *all life*, a thousand times. I thought my heart was beyond death's mournful reach.

Pleasant, in a way, to be wrong again.

The safe house we've retreated to feels like any of a dozen throughout Coin that the Khal of Nothing keeps for her personal use. This one is better appointed than most, complete with expensive wooden chairs, a goose feather sofa, ornamental rugs from the west, and a complete kitchen. I can't picture the Khal cooking, nor any of her streetwise followers.

"What is it? What happened?"

The Khal's good at hiding her thoughts. Even now, *knowing* she must have given the order, I can't detect any deceit. Her face is a smooth porcelain mask, unreadable and unknowable. Masterful, really. I'd be impressed if she hadn't just murdered my only friend in the world.

No loyal dog bites without its master's command.

I force my hands, my frail child's hands, to release their

white-knuckled hold on the back of the ashen wood chair. I force my face, my innocent child's face, to resume the sunny smile I've worn every day since I claimed it for my own. I force my heart, my ancient child's heart, to resume beating slowly and steadily despite the agony.

There will be time to mourn later. He is past worry. I am not.

"Nothing," I say brightly. "I think the danger has past. Soldiers are recapturing the beasts, and their leaders have taken horse heading east out of the city. Seems like Iliana was the target, after all."

"And you said she's safe?" the Khal asks.

"Safer than we are," I assure her.

"What about the others? Did we lose anyone? Bastian? Gabriel?"

I make a show of concentrating, flaring the silver symbol on my hand. I *do* have to concentrate, but to not rip her mind to pieces. How *dare* she mention his name. In the Creator's name, in *Elitrea's* name, I'll break her so wholly they'll be looking for the pieces for—

No, no. That's not me. That's the child's body talking for me, running rampant with my emotions. I forgot what it feels like to feel the blood pulse through your veins, to feel your vision go hot and deadly, to feel your eyes *ache* you're so angry—

Nope. Cold. Calculated. You knew this was a possibility. You saw it, even if you didn't *want* it to come true.

New minds enter the web of my awareness, a dozen at least, led by the very devil of which she speaks.

"Gabriel will let you know himself, here in a minute," I say aloud, my skin tingling with anticipation.

I may not have been able to save you, Bastian.

But I can sure as hell avenge you.

After a complicated series of knocks, a dozen of the Khal of Hands' soldiers crowd into the room, followed by the man

451

himself. Gabriel strolls in, his expression clear. It'd be a convincing lie, if I wasn't the oldest and most capable Shaper of Thought the world has ever seen. He deliberately refuses to look my direction as he comes to attention before his Khal. Good thing. I might not be able to restrain myself.

"What were our losses?" the Khal asks, her voice devoid of emotion.

"Three Hands, and another who will be out of commission indefinitely. Broken spine. And..." he trails off, looking troubled. And he is. Because he has no idea how I'll react.

"Spit it out," the Khal snaps impatiently.

"The Shaper," Gabriel says, doing a passable job of appearing sorrowful.

"What?" she asks woodenly, her eyes unfocusing. She stumbles back and slumps onto the couch. After a moment, her eyes clear, and she glares at him. "Wouldn't we have felt his death? What happened?"

His death didn't leave a cataclysm because he spent every ounce of his power before he died. To talk to me.

"Yes, Gabriel," I urge aloud, voice high and childlike. He flinches like a puppy before a raised fist. Good boy. "Tell her what happened."

"What did you do?" she asks quietly. Far too quietly.

"The beasts were after us, so close our only chance was to flee the sewers. When he was climbing the ladder, I kicked him down. I had to. If I let him live, he would continue to poison our thoughts and use us for his own ends. I told you he couldn't be trusted—"

He falls silent the instant Saran holds up her hand. She stands in one powerful, abrupt movement. She steps close to Gabriel, and he hunches so that she doesn't have to look up at his face.

"Why?"

"He betrayed us," he says, words tripping over each other

452

to rush out of his mouth. "He let the tyrant queen and the Warmheart free, injuring my men in the process. When the beasts struck, we were defenseless because he and that little monster silenced our sentries. We would have known and evacuated faster without their betrayal. My Hands would still be alive."

"Monster, am I?" I ask, giving him a smile with too many teeth. "Let me show you how monstrous I can be."

"You see, my Khal? She cannot be trusted. She——"

The Khal raises her hand again. She turns to me. I don't have to read her thoughts to know she's furious. Because I *can* read her thoughts, I know she feels the sting of betrayal.

"Is this true, Jynn?" she asks, voice barely restrained.

"Well, yes," I say, shrugging. "We didn't know the monsters would attack."

"You harmed my people, stole the Shaper, and released the Warmheart?"

"They should have woken up with a hole in their memory and a minor headache." I keep my hands in the slender pockets I had specifically tailored into my skirts. I step forward, and the men around me tense, blades appearing in a glittering ring. I barely restrain the urge to scoff at them. As if I need to be close to hurt someone. I look up steadily into Saran's dark eyes. "You say 'stole.' What right do you have to possess anyone, let alone an abused girl who just escaped her previous captors? You're a pragmatic leader. She wasn't yours to be stolen, so chalk it up as an opportunity lost and move on."

"I see," she says. Steady. Cold. She isn't used to being challenged, and she finds that she doesn't like it. "You should have spoken to me about your concerns. It may not look like it, but I listen to my people."

"Respect and all that, but bullshit," I say, offering her a regretful smile. If I could freeze the apoplectic look on Gabriel's face forever, I would. "I know you, Saran of the Weligo. Your desire for power comes from a righteous source, but still it controls you. You would never have let Iliana walk."

"A pity," she says, stepping back. The bared blades lower to point at me in a threatening ring. "I trusted you, Jynn. I let you into my confidence, a privilege few have ever been granted. I am sorry about Bastian. But I can't let you live."

I glance around at the grim men surrounding me. Each is a devoted member of the Khal's organization, willing to fight and die for her. They don't even need a reason past her command.

Idiots. Thoughtless, brainless, no more useful than a hammer or knife. I let my contempt show, curling my lip in disdain. Sensing danger, Saran takes another step back, putting two of her men between us. How little she understands.

"You're wise and capable, great Khal. Let that wisdom speak to you before you... ah. I see you've made up your mind."

"Kill her," the Khal says coldly.

Gabriel, particularly eager to remove what he views as a cancer rotting next to the heart of his beloved Khal, steps forward, lifting his dagger, victory dancing in his eyes.

And freezes in place, muscles straining against invisible chains.

Her men don't move to help him. They can't.

"I think, *great* Khal, that you've forgotten who I am," I say conversationally, stepping between the frozen men. "It's the face, isn't it? Too cute to be taken seriously."

"Fight her!" Saran shouts, stepping further away. "Gabriel!"

"Come now," I chide, clicking my tongue in disappointment. "Who am I, Saran?"

She lunges to a rope and rings an alarm bell. A dozen more Hands, hidden beneath and throughout the house, dart out of hiding, desperately throwing themselves at me to protect their Khal. They freeze as well, their momentum dropping them to the soft carpets. One slams face first into the stone counter, and I wince.

"That had to hurt."

I step towards Saran again, and she flinches back. She produces a hidden blade, short and curved, her hand steady. A pulse of power, and her fingers forget their task. The dagger falls to the floor. She tries to run, and her legs forget how. She manages to regain enough control to stagger to the sofa because I let her.

She stares up at me, fear finally registering in those dark eyes.

"Who am I, Saran?" I ask her again, offering her my customary bright smile.

"You're Jynn Dioran," she says, trying to steady the quaver in her voice and failing.

"That's my name," I agree, nodding helpfully. "But *who am I?*"

I raise my hand, and the Hands all stand, raising their swords and knives and pointing them at their own throats. A few shake and resist for a few bare seconds, but another pulse of power crushes what remains of their will. Saran looks around at all of her loyal followers, ready to cut at the wave of my hand, and returns her gaze to me.

And finally, finally, she *sees*.

"You're... you're the Mind Razor."

"There it is."

I snap my fingers. All of the Hands collapse in boneless heaps. All save their leader.

"I should have listened to Gabriel," Saran says slowly. "He told me that welcoming you would be like—"

"Hugging a viper to your chest, yes," I finish. "Wrong. Stupid. Short-sighted."

"I had... I had no idea you could..." She stares at the bodies of all her soldiers, slowly moving her head half an inch to the left, then to the right, over and over again, an unconscious denial she would suppress if she were aware of it. "But, I never... Bastian...?"

"Bastian, Creator spare him, was a powerful Shaper." I lean forward, and she leans back, again unconsciously, until her head bumps against the wall. "He was also a buffoon wielding a sledgehammer. I am the world's greatest duelist, and my sword is sharp indeed."

"Get it over with, then," she says, distant eyes finally refocusing on me.

"Oh, I'm not going to kill you," I say, turning away from her and stepping carefully over the collapsed Hands.

"So you would enslave me. You are no better than me, Jynn Dioran, if you would do to me the same as I would have done to the tyrant queen."

"I'm not going to do that, either." I pick my way to stand before Gabriel, who remains standing, frozen, bared knife pressed to his throat. "You didn't give the order."

"You can't leave me alive. If you know me as you claim to, you know I'll never forgive your broken trust. I'll never forgive you for all of the loyal men and women you've killed today. Today you have made a mortal enemy."

"They aren't dead," I say, waving my hand. A collective groan rises from the fallen Hands as they twist about on the ground. With another pulse of power, they drop back into oblivion. "As I said before, you're a pragmatic leader. You see what I am capable of. I could burn away their minds with less effort than it takes to spare them." I glance over at her. "You can be useful to me, if you allow your wisdom to regain control instead of this childish petulance."

I let the smile the words bring out in me spread across my face. It shocks me almost as much as my audience to hear my words delivered in the high, childlike voice of a twelve-year-old.

"Useful?" she asks in a brittle voice. "You are one person, alone, no matter your power. I have thousands of loyal followers, any of whom would die for me. If you let me walk, we will find a chance to kill you, no matter how long it takes."

"Creator's name, do you *want* to die?" I ask incredulously. "How did you rise this high spouting nonsense like that?"

"By following through on my promises," she says evenly.

"Don't be a child," I say. A child. A giggle escapes me before I can hold it back, but I force my face sober as quickly as I can. "And I'm not alone."

The doors opens as if on cue. Which of course it is. I led them here with visions sent directly to their minds, but then I asked them to wait.

For dramatic effect.

Tana walks into the room looking resplendent in a flowing black dress in the Khalintari style. Behind her comes Commander Ghali, every inch the terrifying and competent warrior. And behind them... an elderly woman whose shoulders refuse to bow, and a drab little woman wearing spectacles. The newcomers take in the scene with a remarkable dispassion. These women have seen far worse.

"Commander Ghali needs no introduction, nor does our lovely and capable friend Tana, but you may not recognize our new friends," I say, glancing at the Khal.

"I know them," she says, mind churning through the depths of my betrayal. To have contacted *them*...

"Well, then," I say aloud, smiling. "Ministers, meet the Khal of Nothing."

The two women say nothing, merely offering the Khal a steady glare.

"I thought we were coming here to parlay," the Minister of Swords, Yamina Jazhri, grunts.

"And we are," I say, opening my hands. "Would you be so kind as to tell the Khal of our preparations?"

"Is that wise?" Tahana Zhayet, the Minister of Bulls, says, glasses flashing as she turns to me.

"There's nothing to worry about," I assure her. "If she doesn't see the wisdom of our partnership, she won't be walking

457

out of here."

"Let's get on with it," Jazhri mutters.

"We were approached by Lentana Tenkal on behalf of the Master of Thought to arrange a formal strike against the Empire forces plaguing our lands," Zhayet says promptly, like she's reading off a report. From the rumors about her attention to detail and her love of transcription, she might very well be. "I agreed to offer financial support and provisions for the rebel army, should one coalesce. Which is when I received a letter from my colleague the Minister of Swords. Yamina?"

"When they wanted to invade the Kingdom, they asked me for every able body that could swing a sword," she says, her wrinkled face contorting into something that could passably be called a scowl, but is actually her famed grin. Opponents used to be terrified when they saw Yasmina Jazhri smile in combat. Though time has weathered her like a well-worn rock, her eyes are sharp and her arm strong. "I gave them everyone of age. Just not the elderly or the young." Her grin widens. "They left me my veterans and my prodigies. I've brought close to three hundred old swords, and half again as many youths with more capability than any Empire pig sticker."

"And I've gathered a thousand spears, more or less," Ghali puts in.

"Steed managed to offer us another thousand horse to throw into the fray, stabled near the gates throughout the city," the Minister of Bulls continues. "Do we know how many swords the Empire can bring to bear?"

"Khal?" I ask, turning to Saran. She glares at me from her seat on the couch.

"I'll make no deals with conquerors," she spits, rage trembling through the words.

"Ladies, give me a moment with her," I say, gesturing towards the kitchen. "There is a rose wine the Khal favors beneath the counter. Quite expensive, I'm led to believe."

"Never going to get used to this," Jazhri says, shaking her head as she looks at me. And my innocent face. "A child, offering me wine."

"May as well," Zhayet says, stepping carefully over the supine bodies of the Khal's Hands. As she ducks around Gabriel's frozen form standing in the middle of the room, she doesn't voice the rest of her statement, but I catch it all the same. *"And I could use one, seeing this."*

I move to the Khal and bend close, lowering my voice so that only we can hear. Tana looks like she wants to approach, but I silently ward her off. Talented as she is, she's still a bit nice for moments like this.

Saran's face twists with rage, and she opens her mouth to growl some inane threat my way. A ripple of invisible power steals her voice. At least, her memory of how to speak. The look of terror on her face as she lifts her hands to her throat wrests some sympathy from whatever is left of my heart, but I don't show it.

"You're listening right now, Saran. Not speaking. Do you understand?" She hesitates, then nods, frustrated tears glistening in her eyes. "You are a strong, capable woman. But for a single mistake, you would have remade the Republic to benefit you and your people, and may have even made it strong enough to withstand the Sealord for some time. By doing so, you would have cost the Khalintars millions of lives. Before you doubt, remember that I served the Eternal for three decades, and spent much of that time following her into the possible futures. I have *seen* this, do you understand?"

Another nod.

"Now, you're feeling betrayed right now. Bastian and I were your shining stars, your Shapers that lent you credibility you'd never managed without us. Know this. Bastian never betrayed you before Iliana. Not once. He had the opportunity to crush your mind and escape more times than I can count, and he

459

stayed, because he believed you, *in* you. He trusted that you would do your best by the Republic."

"And I do," she answers quietly, glancing down in surprise as she regains her voice.

"I know. Otherwise, we wouldn't be having this conversation." I lean back and sigh, feeling the weight of millennia pressing down on my shoulders. "Listen, I had nothing to betray. I never swore myself to you. But I like you, Saran. And, to put it frankly, I need you. Your strength, your vision, and your numbers."

"You have a strange way of showing it," she says, gesturing towards her comatose warriors.

"This can go one of two ways. You can join us in throwing the usurpers out of your lands and take your rightful place as a legitimate force in governing the nation that will follow."

"Or?"

"You don't, and we fight you *and* them. Khalintari blood will flow in the streets as your people fight mine, all while the Sealord laughs and prepares a second army to crush our pathetic rebellion before it has a chance to grow."

"How about I offer a third?" she says, a measure of her old confidence returning. "You let me go, and I vow to continue to work for the good of the Khalintars, as I have always done."

"This isn't a negotiation," I say wearily. "Look, I'm not threatening you. I swear on the Creator's forgotten name I'm not. But remember this, Khal. I know every agent you have in the city, down to name, alias, and capabilities. I know every asset you've squirreled away, every stack of coins you've hidden under every floorboard." So that part might be a lie. But it sounds true, which is the same as being true right now. "You've let me stand at your side for long enough that I know *everything*. Your people will die, your wealth will vanish, and everything you've ever built will crumble." I stand, debating the wisdom of asking for a glass of wine, but think better of it. The Minister of Swords might try to spank me before she remembers who I am. "Oh, and don't try to deceive me. That would be the height of stupidity, and we've already established that you are anything but stupid."

I leave her and run to hug Tana, squeezing her tight. She hugs me back and jokingly ruffles my hair.

"Great job, Tana! To convince the Bull *and* the Sword?"

"With your word backing me," she says, humble as always. She looks around at the frozen chaos of the room. "What is all this?"

"Oh." The sorrow surges in my chest, deeper and stronger than before. For a moment, wrapped up in all the excitement, I almost forgot. "We saved the princess. Smuggled her out of the city. Gabriel caught wind of it and... Bastian, he..."

"Stop jesting," she says stiffly. "Where is he?"

"Tana, I'm so sorry," I say, biting my lip to hold back a sob. I've got to be strong for a bit longer.

Her eyes waver and wander, lost. The conversation reminds me of something I still have to do. I give Gabriel control of his eyes so that he can watch me walk until I stand before him. The feeling gives him hope, like my control might be wavering. The grim smile I offer him steals what little remains.

"No, Saran," I say before the Khal can speak. "I know what you're thinking. You'll bargain Gabriel's life for our alliance. Join us or don't, you won't be speaking to him again."

"Who made you the judge and executioner?" she asks woodenly.

"I did," I answer.

"He has been at my side, reliable and faithful, for longer than anyone else. I need him."

"You'll make do. You did not order Bastian's death, yet he took it upon himself to murder one of the greatest assets you've ever possessed. What good is a rabid dog?"

She doesn't respond, but I can feel my words working through her thoughts, and I know the exact moment she accepts

461

reality. I stand on my toes so that I can get closer to his wide and panicked eyes. I could insert my words into his mind; they're only for him.

But words carry different weight when spoken.

"You killed my only friend in the entire world," I whisper. "And you didn't even have the decency or bravery to do it yourself. You left him for monsters to tear apart. It would be wise to be merciful, but I can't and won't let you draw breath after you stole his. Well, let me clarify. I'll *let* you draw breath. You'll just *wish* you could stop."

The nightmare I give him is personal. Only a few seconds long, it loops, endlessly, a refrain of despair and pain. His screams begin the moment I let his mind resume control of his body, piercing and long. He falls to his knees, sightlessly staring ahead, shrieking all the while.

There are tears in my eyes as I turn away, but not for him. They're for the memory I gave him to relive. Bastian's final moments, from ladder to claw. Ladder to claw. Ladder to claw. All the pain, fear, horror *he* felt is now Gabriel's. Over and over again.

Forever.

His screams go hoarse and silent after a moment as the other women look on. Yet still he screams. I offer them all my widest smile.

"I think the Khal is ready to join us," I say brightly. "Shall we get to work?"

***

Against the backdrop of a blood red sun three days later, a figure wavers into sight out of the desert to the west. He's farther away than he appears, big as he is. He walks slowly, methodically, carefully placing each step even on the flat ground. I let loose a shaky breath, feeling the weight of the moment now that it's upon us.

Hidden from view, I reach for my power.

He stiffens as if he senses my touch. After a moment, he continues forward, his plodding steps weary. The soldiers on watch, resplendent in shining azure armor, salute the Master of Beasts as he staggers under the arch of the mighty gates. His body, once as perfect as he could make it, looks closer to falling apart than staying together. His chest is a ruin of broken bone and torn muscle, his mighty legs trembling beneath a weight beyond any normal man.

He is vulnerable, away from his army. He knows now that the Vengeance and his lost son have been reunited, and they are beyond him. He and Helikos will have to fight together if they are to conquer their enemies. For now, he needs to rest, to recuperate. He has spent far too much of his soul moving unseen, burrowing through the earth with the aid of roots and subterranean denizens of the desert. He didn't risk exposure to the open air until he came within sight of the city walls.

It isn't until he moves back into the sunlight that his exhausted mind recognizes the trap closing about his neck.

Behind the broad white parapet of Coin's walls, two dozen Spearsisters and half as many Edge swordsmen rise from hiding and silently close on his back. The soldiers standing watch throw off their confining helmets and reveal Khalintari faces that draw Khalintari swords. More fighters appear from the barracks near the gate, enough to challenge him even at his best.

And he is not at his best.

He roars, spinning and lunging for the gate. He knows that his only chance at escape is to disappear into the earth again and slink his careful way back to his master. But the streets of Coin are crafted of the finest stone, an element he still lacks.

More eager than the rest, the first swordsman to reach him is young, hardly past puberty, but she's been raised on the sword. She spins into a graceful pirouette, thin blade flashing in the setting sun. Against any other opponent, it would be a killing strike. The Master of Beasts accepts the blow on his chest, then reaches forward to break her skull between his mighty fists. He rips her sword from his flesh and throws himself into the fray.

His body shifts and morphs as spears and swords cut at him from every angle. His soul may not bear the strength of the Sealord's or the Vengeance's, but he has mastered skills they can scarcely imagine. Pristine skin moves away from unavoidable strikes, and ruined flesh moves to accept further punishment. Muscle contorts to remain usable as surgical strikes fall on uncaring meat rather than anything vital. His organs and blood remain within him as a dozen weapons pierce his flesh. For each blow that falls, he takes another life. He is a master of his element, greater than perhaps any since the time of the Eternal.

Yet he is a virtuoso playing a symphony on a broken instrument. No matter the musician, there is only so much that can be done with snapped strings and cracked wood.

He kills a dozen, then two, but there are more than enough talented warriors to take their place. He staggers as a lung fails to move aside from a thrusting spear. He roars and falls to a knee as the great muscle of his thigh parts beneath a keen sword. He chokes as Ghali's spear finally rips his heart in two.

Even then, he refuses to die. As he slumps to the stone, as he gasps his last, as his body fails, he does not *die*. He waits, a trickle of power circulating through his organs, preserving and maintaining only the most critical functions. He understands the human body better than anyone since the Creator himself. There is only so much that can't be rebuilt or recovered. We can survive extraordinary trials if given the proper care.

I walk forward finally, threading my way through the gasping, bloody Khalintari who survived, stepping over those who perished. His giant's body rests in a growing pool of blood, torn and slashed in too many places to count. His eyes are open and staring, his mouth gaping vacantly.

"*A nice touch,*" I send into his thoughts. "*You can fool them, Kranos, but you can't fool me.*"

"Cut him apart," I say aloud.

With a last grating roar, spitting blood, Kranos lunges upwards. Ghali steps aside and pins him to the stone on the end of her spear. The others fall on him, blades flashing, as the sun finally drops below the horizon, and darkness falls.

***

Kranos blinks, the white walls of Coin appearing once again before his sight as the vision I offered him fades. He gasps, the agony of his imagined death so very real. He looks up at his soldiers on the wall, sharpening his gaze to study them closer. Are they his? Was he offered a glimpse of the future? He scans the wall for the hidden assassins waiting for his entrance, but he sees no sign.

Until I climb up on the parapet and wave my hand, glowing silver even from the distance between us.

"It's real," I pulse into his mind. *"Every bit of it."*

"Who are you?"

"Jynn Dioran. The Mind Razor, by legend."

No need to dance around it. Not with this man.

"I see." A pause. *"I can assume you won't tell me how you're still living?"*

"You can work that out for yourself, if you make the right choice today."

He stops and thinks, contemplating, turning over the possibilities in his mind. He accepts the fact of my existence as a matter of course. It is natural, I guess. He has broken every natural law that was once held sacred, so it is typical that he accepts others will do the same. To think of others wielding the holy power, not granted by the Creator but created by man... to see the abominations this man has created, both physical and spiritual... I try to remain cool and collected, but he feels the heat of my anger, and its source.

"Who are you to judge me?" he says after a moment, his voice resonating between us. *"No matter the method, I imagine there*

are those who would call your survival unnatural."

"I have no desire to justify myself to you."

"Because I am mad?" he asks, a challenge as much as anything.

"No, Kranos. Though many would name you insane, I know better. I know what motivates you. I know your why, *Master of Beasts, for I helped give it to you."*

A reaction, finally. His mind snarls and spits at my claim, surging against its chains before he can wrestle his emotions back under control. I wait for his anger to drain like a wave receding.

"Do not speak as if you know me. Do not pretend to understand. I am singular."

"Sure, sure, whatever you say." I smile slightly as the bellow of his anger reaches my real ears. *"Regardless, you need to turn around and go, tail between your legs, or you won't be breathing by the time the sun touches the horizon."*

"Why should I trust you? Why should I run scared? You've ripped the fangs from your own maw by revealing your hand."

"There are a thousand horse circling opposite the city, waiting to fall upon you should you run. Your soldiers are all dead or captured. Your puppet queen is deposed. You are alone in a city of millions of angry citizens, any of whom would happily slit your throat." I pause to let the words marinate. *"Even if you don't believe me, your soul is at an ebb, your body ruined, and your only safe harbor thousands of miles east. I knew which way you would come, when you would arrive, and my thoughts can reach farther than you imagined this power could. Would you rather retreat today at little risk if I'm lying, or hazard your life to call my bluff?"*

He is silent for a time, his thoughts churning low enough they're hard to follow. It's intentional; he knows something of my power, after all.

"Why?" he asks finally.

"It is not your time to die."

"Should I be thanking you?"

466

"No."

Without another word, he glows briefly green and sinks beneath the earth. In seconds he passes beyond my range, and his thoughts disappear. I sigh in relief and collapse. Tana catches me before I can pitch over the edge of the wall. She easily cradles my small frame in her arms.

"What did you say to make him leave?" she asks loudly, fighting to be heard over the din of the pitched battle echoing in the courtyard behind us.

I let my head loll so I can see how it's going. The hundred best swordsmen of the Edge hold the gate against twice their number of Empire soldiers led by a vanguard of Tide. The Empire has the advantage of numbers and armor in a pitched battle like this, but any of the Edge are the match of two or three typical Wave soldiers. The Tide carries the fight to the Edge and the morale of their fellow soldiers both. If they were to fall...

"No time," I mutter, forcing my weary body upright. In my past life, I would have been able to finish the conversation with the Master of Beasts and then turn to wipe the enemy's minds away with a single gesture, but I've been too long Ensouled, too long a parasite. My power has weakened to the point that even the most trivial tasks are exhausting. I glance up at Tana. "Listen. You see that brute of a man? The one with the dented shield? He's the lynchpin. If you can kill him, they'll fall apart."

She turns to the surging warriors and scans their ranks. Noticing the man, his face red with roaring and his sword wet with blood, her mouth firms and she rises to her feet. The warrior spirit inside of her wants to obey, but she doesn't put me down. The sorrow of Bastian's death is too fresh, too raw. Fear creeps into her thoughts, fear of leaving me here, too weak to defend myself, easy pickings for any soldier with murder on his mind...

"What about you?" she asks, eyes remaining locked on the leader of the Tide. "Exhausted as you are, you really are no better than a twelve-year-old."

467

"I'll be fine. No one's worried about the wall. Now go poke him with that stick Ghali's been training you on and end this before anyone else has to die."

She lowers me carefully to the stone, and she's gone an instant later. Her feet take the stairs down three at a time, sure and steady. She disappears into the surging crowd, her spear held low and at the ready.

I close my eyes and try to get comfortable on the stone. At least it's been worn smooth under the feet of countless soldiers marching on watch over centuries. I quash the tremor of fear for Tana before it can grow. She'll survive. Probably. I shouldn't care. She isn't important enough to the future for her life to matter.

Though it matters to me.

I sigh, briefly and vainly wishing for my old strength back. Then, I wouldn't have to fear for those I care for. I could protect them. I sigh again when I think about Tana's question. What did I say to the Master of Beasts to keep him away?

The truth. Every single word.

Or what *could* have been the truth.

My masters always said I was skilled in deception. Having seen a dozen of the myriad ways this day could have played out, I merely had to *believe* one of the dead paths was true, as it *could have been*. It's a strange trick that gives me a headache, but I'll take a headache to save the lives of thousands.

The vision of Kranos' death would have been accurate... if Bastian survived. The thought leaves me feeling sick and hollow. So many are dying because of Gabriel's cruelty. The young men and women bleeding their last on the stone of the courtyard would have lived, and the larger battle rampaging across the Plaza of Stars would never have occurred. I'm too weak to end this without him.

I can't muster the energy to sigh again as my thoughts turn to the darkness I just unleashed. Even if Bastian survived, even if the ambush *would* have ended the Master of Beasts, certain as

468

sunset, I would have scared him away.

For he is not mad. The words he was given drive him to a greater purpose.

"It is not your time to die."

The truest words I offered him. If only they didn't sentence millions to suffering and death.

When Elitrea cried on her throne, eyes staring sightlessly into the future, I never understood. Not really. Their lives did not touch me. Any cost for the future. Yet now that it is here, the decision made… now that their deaths are *my fault*…

So slowly I hardly realize I've done it, I curl into a ball, here on the stones of the mighty walls of Coin.

And weep.

***

Tana finds me in the same position when the battle finally ends. I look up at her through puffy, swollen eyes. Though a cut high on her arm bleeds freely, relief fills her eyes when she sees me. I don't bother to get up. I don't have the energy. Looking suddenly weary herself, she slumps down, back against the parapet.

"We won," she says slowly. "Here and in the Plaza of Stars. Coin is free again."

"I know."

"It's just as you said. Once the Tide fell, the rest surrendered in short order."

"Saran's intelligence held true," I say, finally forcing myself to rise and sit next to her. "These soldiers haven't been paid in far too long. Only the zealots in the Tide keep them in line, and fear of their masters, who are suddenly absent. What would you do? Fighting a desperate fight in the streets, terrified that the populace will rise against you? And where are your leaders? Where are the mighty Shapers who carry the standard of the Empire? There is no Sealord here. The queen has vanished. The Master of Beasts did not appear. Patriotism extends only so far in the face of death."

"What did you do to make him leave?"

"Told him the truth. Or at least, the truth as it could have been." I shrug against the white stone. "There's no doubt this would have gone very differently had he come into the city."

The sun finishes setting as we rest against the wall. The rising moon, full and bright, swiftly takes its place. Its pure white light places a veil over the stars for a bit longer as the sky darkens to a deep violet. If it weren't for the cries of the wounded and the stench of death on the air, it would have the beginnings of a lovely night.

"You should get that stitched before it festers," I offer after a minute.

"I'll live."

The words hang between us in silent judgment. For we both remember who does not get to utter those words ever again. When my eyes blur again, I don't bother to force the tears down. Now that the city is safe, there is time to mourn.

"Was it... was it bad?" Tana asks in a broken voice.

"A lot of it." I bite my lip. "But not the end. He was ready. He passed thinking only of love."

"Why is it so sad?" she asks after another long pause. "He complained all the time, and he did so many horrible things. He wasn't even a good person."

"You don't know the half of it," I say, a laugh escaping my chest in place of a sob. "You know that, every time he had a halfway decent thought, he asked if it came from me?"

"Didn't it?" Tana asks, laughing through her tears.

"Sometimes," I admit guiltily. "But he was changing. Slowly. It's hard to have any care for others when you know their every thought. How many unpleasant things do we never speak aloud? How many hurtful and hateful urges do we keep inside? We need good people around to keep us grounded. Friends. Bastian was alone so long he didn't understand what it was like to be human. You reminded him, and Te'ial reminded him, and I reminded him, and Lav reminded him."

"He told me once, when he was exhausted and nearly asleep on that terrible ride through the wastes, that he was terrified of dying." Though Tana's smile has faded, the laugh a distant memory, there are no more tears. "That he feared he would leave no mark on the world, and that it would just keep going without him, and everything he ever did would serve no purpose."

"He was wrong."

"He was wrong," she agrees, leaning her head back to watch as the stars begin to peek through the darkness.

The city, like a held breath expelled, comes to life with the night. Joyful shouts and cheerful celebration echo through the streets, though there is an edge to it. The people know that the yoke of the enemy has been thrown only temporarily. The Sealord will not allow our little rebellion to go unanswered. But there is joy nonetheless. Afraid they may be, but the people are happy to draw even a single free breath.

The lights are bright at the House of the Republic. The Ministers will be burning the midnight oil for many days as they try to piece their nation back together.

After true darkness falls, a lantern winds its way up the steps of the walls. The Khal of Nothing walks, alone, and sits carelessly across from us. She stares at an empty bit of parapet between us, face stoic as always.

"Jynn. Tana. I can't tell whether to thank you or curse you. You've given me legitimacy, and all the bureaucratic burdens that come with it." She glances between us, a ghost of a smile briefly twisting her lips. "Definitely more of a curse, I think."

"You can end it, if it would make you feel better," I say, closing my eyes to slits.

"I didn't..." she trails off, then shakes her head. She was thinking of Gabriel. And his screams. "Thank you."

"He deserves it, though."

"Thank you anyway."

That she left Gabriel to rave and tear at his face this long in the darkness is testament to how much she fears me. Yet despite her fear, she chose to seek us out. Without Bastian and Gabriel, I imagine we're the only ones she has left.

"What do we do now?" Tana asks after a moment, letting her gaze fall to me.

"We show the Sealord, and all the world, what we're capable of." I stand, turning my gaze east. "That even from the depths of ruin, we will rise."

Epilogue
The Vengeance
Mourningtide, the First Day of Autumn
In the year 5223, Council Reckoning

The waves crash far below him, the raucous cacophony of water's defiant roar. Much of the sound comes from the Maelstrom, barely in sight to the north. It, and all its mystery, is not his goal today.

No, Altos is here to answer a question that has burned in him for more than a century. A question of how a young Master of Water became the Sealord. A question of what changed him, so far beneath the waves. The Vengeance discovered the location after nearly eighty years of searching, but other concerns have taken his attention before now.

Not anymore. Not after whatever the boy did out in the desert.

He is here looking for more than one answer.

Altos calls to the wind like an old friend. It wraps him in ever-tightening layers until an invisible sphere of dense air whirls about him with the force of ten hurricanes. Anything trapped in the screaming wind would be torn apart in an instant.

Tilting forward, he drops towards the ocean's rocky surface. He falls fast, gaining speed with every second. The wind drives him on, drives him down, until he is a blur ripping through the space the air has left behind.

He doesn't flinch as he slams into the surface of the Great Sea. Into, and through. Instantly, all sound disappears but for the rippling gurgle of water displaced. The shield of air keeps the ocean at bay, and the momentum of his hurtling fall drives him deep. Past air, past light, he falls until the world is alien and strange, lit only through the paltry glow of his pure white power, feeble before the strength of the mighty ocean.

For the first time in many a year, Altos feels small.

Finally, his momentum runs out, and he takes a moment to reorient. Already the invisible currents of the Maelstrom, strong even a hundred miles north, have dragged him off course. With a pulse of focused power, he sets off, deeper and to the south.

The search for this place partly took so long because Helikos was jealous of his secrets. While the Sealord still pretended friendship with the council, Altos had managed to sneak his journals from their hiding place in his quarters. He had been clever, hiding them behind a constantly moving seal of water, but air can go places no other element expects.

The larger problem lay in that the notes were incomplete. The last few years were destroyed, what remained in a code so foreign it was never meant to be read by any other soul. Still, the hole at the center of the puzzle became clear after a few decades of worrying the problem: somewhere north of the ruins of the Eternal's kingdom, somewhere on the *bottom of the ocean*, Helikos had found something.

Someone.

For forty years, Altos had searched. But how could a Master of Air seek something so foreign to his element? How could he comb the bottom of the Great Sea?

He couldn't. So, foolishly, he abandoned the search thirty years ago. Still, the problem stuck in his mind. And luck, fortuitous and kind, had gifted him the answer.

A season before the Sealord's betrayal, a particularly unfavorable storm had blown him off course on his way from the Republic to Itskalan. He had been forced to stretch his senses to their limit to calm the raging storm. And, reaching so far, he had felt it. Air, but not above or around him. Below him, at the barest edge of his awareness. A pocket of air, somewhere deep beneath the waves.

The deep water, and its denizens, do not wait for his remembrance. A hideous creature crafted of nightmare and evil swirls past, twice the length of a man and bristling with fangs and rugged flesh. As soon as it breaks the circle of light, it flinches away and out of sight. Altos pays it no mind, his attention occupied by the growing pressure squeezing at the shrinking ball of air that keeps him safe.

If he lets the shield lapse, the weight of the ocean will crush him so quickly he won't have time to fear.

Gritting his teeth, he pushes on. It is not far, now. Another man might feel panic, but the Vengeance knows his limits precisely. He'll make it.

The shape of it is regular, a collection of straight lines, unnatural in this unclaimed place. The first broken pillar of worked stone, still pristine, looms out of the darkness. Like jagged teeth, a dozen more poke this way and that from the silt at the bottom of the sea.

Ahead, a block of stone stretches towards the light forgotten so far above. White light reveals high windows containing glass of various colors, depicting shapes almost familiar. An arched doorway stands open, and only darkness waits beyond.

Air fills the open doorway and refuses the water entry into the towering edifice.

Here, faced with an impossibility, even the Vengeance has to steady himself before he can continue.

He steps through the invisible barrier without a hint of resistance, leaving the ink-dark ocean behind. Bracing himself even though it won't save him, he lets the hurricane shield fall.

The first breath nearly makes him gag: rot and decay and ancient, stagnant seawater. Steeling his resolve, he steps forward, holding his glowing hand aloft to illuminate the way.

He's in an antechamber of some kind, plain but for another

set of double doors, twice the height of a man, leading onwards. Closed, their embossed golden faces would complete a circle filled with runes of power, no doubt representations of the elements of the Creator.

But the left-hand door has been pushed just wide enough to admit a man. A thick layer of dust coats the floor, scuffed where someone braced themselves to shove the heavy door aside. Judging by the marks, it could have happened yesterday. Whoever did this could still be here. Altos starts to draw the blade at his back, but halfway through he pauses, mind stunned by a realization.

These are the marks of Helikos' journey, preserved more than a century. This is the place that changed him. And the Vengeance is struck, faced with this ornate door at the bottom of the sea, with sudden doubt.

Why is he here? Does he not risk following Helikos into madness?

For his suspicion has turned to certainty. He knows, in his heart of hearts, that if he speaks with what lies beyond this door, he will never be the same. Even so, he doesn't hesitate long.

He has to know.

The room beyond the doors stretches into cavernous darkness, eerily silent. The timeworn stone should creak, or the moving water should roar, or the sea creatures should lament the intrusive light. Yet the stillness is total. A throne stands at the far end between a row of mighty pillars. Pure white, Altos knows almost instinctively that the throne is not stone, but something more.

Before the throne, a motionless man rests on his back, hands arranged in a funereal pose. He looks young, his hair a vibrant brown in Altos' light.

Behind him, so pale and slight she barely stands out from the throne behind her, sits a woman. Her shadow is more distinct that her body, offering an outline of a figure far too thin to be real.

Or human.

"I wondered if you would come," she says suddenly.

The words are simple and softly delivered, yet they resonate to fill the entirety of the empty space like invisible waves rising to drown the world. He gasps, his breath coming short, his lungs constricting. It is like nothing and everything he's ever heard. As the echo of her voice fades, he staggers as if struck.

"Sorry," she says in a quieter voice, and there is no doubt she means it. It feels impossible that she should lie.

He wanders closer, wary of further words. She does not squint against the light. She does not focus at all. She may have been beautiful, once. Her raven hair hangs ragged and matted from her skull, and her high cheekbones seem ready to cut through the paper-thin skin of her face.

Empty and blind, still her eyes follow him as he approaches.

"Do not pity me," she whispers. Her lips crease into a gentle smile. It is filled with pain. "I might die from the irony."

"Did you wonder if I would come? Or did you know?" he asks finally.

"Your choices are yours, whatever I see."

"Do you know why I'm here?"

"Now that you *are*, there is no doubt," she says, smile broadening. "Ask, and I will answer."

"How…" he trails off, realizing he has forgotten his reason for coming. Seeing her, seeing this place… she answers his unspoken question regardless.

"The key to immortality is not Time. No, you've seen the power that sustained us." She pauses. Though there is no physical sign, she looks suddenly weaker, fragile, like a stiff wind would blow her away. "Sustained me."

"But… *why?* This existence… I don't know what I expected, but this…"

"A long time ago, I saw something. I was always gifted in

my ability to read the future, which is, of course, how I created an empire. But I was not satisfied. I didn't want a mighty *legacy*. I wanted to rule. Forever. So I continued to search, selfishly, the infinite realm of possibility, until I saw something that changed me forever."

"What?"

"An end. Inexorable and irrevocable. There was no doubt that this world, and all that lives upon it, would die."

"Was?" he asks, noticing the discrepancy.

"I set out to change the unchangeable. To avert the disaster I saw coming. I did not expect that I would trade one for another."

"The boy," Altos says, horror dawning. "What I felt... what he can do..."

"Yes," she says. "If he loses control, he will consume the world. That we are here now is only due to your quick thinking. Had he finished taking your soul, there would have been nothing to stop him. In nearly all the futures I have seen, his fire consumes us all."

"Then I'll end it." Altos turns to go, the blade, forgotten in his hands, returning to life. "Now, before—"

"Sit, Vengeance," she says. There is no command in her voice, only a tired fear, rehearsed so many times it has lost its bite. He pauses, trembling. "The world will end in fire, someday. Almost certainly. But it will *absolutely* end should you kill him."

"If I wait until he's exhausted, his death can't cause—"

"So you would pass this power on to another?" she asks, gently raising her eyebrows. There is no crease of age on her forehead, only the smoothness of youth. "Another who will need to be guided, watched, trained, and protected. One not raised by Telias Warmheart to join the Shorn, nor one who will find a father in Altos Orivian, Vengeance of the Council. I chose your son among endless options. You would give this power to a stranger?"

"He nearly lost control already."

478

"And if he does, neither of us will have time to regret it."

"Then all is lost?" Altos asks in despair.

"No. For he is a blade with two edges. Our doom, and our only hope." She settles back against the throne, seeming to find comfort in its hard surface. "We are not ready for what comes. Even if we were, we will need him to have even the faintest chance. And no, before you ask, I can't tell you. I risk too much as it is. The longer I have endeavored to meddle with the future, the less control I seem to have."

"Can you tell me anything? When? Who?"

"You won't live to see it," she says, with an unassailable certainty. "Nor will I."

"You will die?"

She lets the words fall unremarked.

"What did you tell Helikos?" Altos asks after a moment's pause.

"That he would unite the world."

"Will he?"

"That depends." She turns sightless eyes towards the sound of his voice, sending a shiver down his spine. "On you and your friends, and he and his allies. Whoever the victor, the world must unite."

"Do you care who wins?"

"No."

The word doesn't echo. No sound does in this forgotten place. The burden she lays on him is heavy, though he is used to such weight. There must be a victor for the future to exist. If he wishes it to be the future he wants, the future he would have crafted for his children had destiny given him the chance, he must fight, and win. It changes nothing.

She pushes herself to her feet with an effort. He is faintly surprised; after five thousand years, or eight, or ten, or however long the Eternal has existed, he almost expected her to be rendered immobile. How can a human body endure such time?

479

"If you win," she says, reaching to the throne. A piece of it shifts aside at her touch to reveal a tiny recess. She draws a scroll no longer than her hand, tightly rolled and perfectly preserved. She pulls the scroll back when he reaches for it. "*If* you win, you will face a decision. A question not easily answered. This scroll will help you decide."

"I should not open it until then?" he asks, taking the thin parchment from her offered hand.

"Do what you like," she says, lowering herself slowly back to the floor. "I'll not tell you anything more. Be careful with that, though. It isn't often that parchment survives the passage of seven thousand years."

Carefully, almost reverently, he tucks the scroll into his shirt near his heart. There is a sense of finality and dismissal to her words, so he turns to leave. Before he does, he glances down at the dead man at her feet. It seems impossible he should be older than thirty, yet it is impossible that he should be younger. There are no steps other than his own and the Sealord's outside this chamber. Unless the Eternal can pluck people directly from time…

He shivers, the thought not worth pursuing. He takes a step away, then another, when a sound brings him up short. He glances back at the Eternal. She sits in the same position, with the same posture. But tears shine in her sightless eyes.

"Altos?" she asks, her voice suddenly shaky. "This is… you are the last person I'll ever speak to. Will you… sit with me? Even for a moment?"

He fears some trick; that, in delaying him here, she is crafting his unmaking. But his decision has already been made in coming. If she wishes him ill, her words have already worked calamity into being.

Above all, he believes her. Any resonance and majesty her voice once held has disappeared, and she sounds nothing more than a lost and lonely girl. A girl who has been trapped here,

480

alone, for a very long time.

So he sits.

THE ETERNAL DREAM
WILL CONTINUE...

If you enjoyed this adventure and wish for more, the best way you can support me is to tell every human you've ever met about this book and leave a detailed review so that others can share in the experience!

Follow me for more updates at theeternaldream.com

Acknowledgments

I'd first like to acknowledge you, the reader, for your eyes are the reason these words exist. For making it this far, thank you. Hopefully it wasn't too painful to get here. There will be more.

The two people who helped most in the creation of this book would require a novel unto themselves, so I'll keep their acknowledgement short. Pop, thanks for listening to a hundred thousand ideas, some of which are related to plot points that won't be relevant for ten flipping books, and doing your best to understand and follow along. Your love and pride has always inspired me to keep fighting. Ellen, thank you for your endless support and love. Your belief in me allowed me to believe in myself. Thank you for reminding me that love exists. And for kicking me in the ass when I needed it.

To my beta readers: Mom, Dad, Wells, Mark, Evan, Meagan (if I forgot someone, I will accept your everlasting anger). Your contributions allowed me to see where my wayward brain was, well, wayward. Thank you for taking the time to make this monster so much better.

Thanks especially to Evan Chabot and Emma Kenemer, without whom the lovely map and cover art for this story would not exist. Your talents constantly amaze. Again. Seriously. Someone hire these people and pay them more money.

Thanks to all my students, who told me that they would love to read this book before it ever existed. Hopefully, the product lives up to the hype.

Finally, thank you to the fantastic teachers who, perhaps unwittingly, nudged me along this path. The most potent is Mr. Ahern, who took my Legend of Zelda fanfiction in 3rd grade, stained it with tea, burned the edges with flame, and gave me the first belief that my writing could do something magical. What a wonderful thing to do for a child. Thank you to all my fellow teachers, especially those who encourage little nerds that their stories are worth hearing.

Made in the USA
Middletown, DE
22 May 2023

31218302R00295